# XPD

**"HIS BEST THRILLER IN YEARS, VINTAGE DEIGHTON, SENSATIONAL... AND RICH."**

*John Barkham Reviews*

# XPD

**"SUPERIOR FARE, TOLD WITH A REAL FLAIR FOR SUSPENSE AND EMOTION AND A PROFOUND UNDERSTANDING OF CHARACTER."**

*Penthouse*

# XPD

**"A THRILLER OF THE FIRST RANK!"**

*St. Louis Post-Dispatch*

# XPD

**"DEIGHTON'S MOST AMBITIOUS SPY NOVEL TO DATE... ENGROSSING!"**

*The Associated Press*

# XPD

Also by Len Deighton
*Published by Ballantine Books:*

THE IPCRESS FILE

SS•GB

FIGHTER

# XPD

Len Deighton

BALLANTINE BOOKS • NEW YORK

Originally published in Great Britain by Hutchinson & Co. (Publishers) Ltd.  Published in the United States by Ballantine Books, a division of Random House, Inc., New York.

Library of Congress Catalog Card Number: 80-7629

ISBN 0-345-29906-X

This edition published by arrangement with Alfred A. Knopf, Inc.

Manufactured in the United States of America

First Ballantine Books Edition: May 1982

"The Second World War produced, in the end, one victor, the United States, one hero, Great Britain, one villain, Germany . . ."

*Hitler*, by N. Stone

# 1

In May 1979, only days after Britain's new Conservative government came to power, the yellow box that contains the daily report from MI6 to the Prime Minister was delivered to her by a deputy secretary in the Cabinet Office. He was the PM's liaison with the intelligence services.

Although the contents of the yellow box are never graded into secret, top secret and so on—because all MI6 documents are in the ultra secret category—one rather hastily handwritten report was "flagged." The PM noted with some surprise that it was the handwriting of Sir Sydney Ryden, the director general of MI6, and selected that document for immediate attention. Attached to the corner of it there was an advertisement, clipped from a film journal published in California the previous week.

A film producer, unlisted in any of the department's reference books, announced that he was preparing what the advert described as "A major motion picture with a budget of fifteen million plus!" It was a Second World War story about plundering German gold in the final days of the fighting. The cutting bore the rubber stamp of DESK 32 RESEARCH and was signed by the clerk who had found it. WHAT IS THE FINAL SECRET OF THE KAISERODA MINE? asked the advertisement. Kaiseroda had been underlined in red pencil to show the word which had alerted the Secret Intelligence Service clerk to the advert's possible importance.

Normally the space the blue rubber-stamp mark provided for reference would have been filled with a file number but, to his considerable surprise, the research clerk had been referred to no file under the Kaiseroda reference. Instead the Kaiseroda card was marked, "To director general only. IMMEDIATE."

The Prime Minister read carefully through Sir Sydney Ryden's note, baffled more than once by the handwriting. Then she picked up a telephone and changed her day's appointments to make a time to see him.

The elderly police constable on duty that afternoon inside the entrance lobby of 10 Downing Street recognized that the man accompanying Sir Sydney was the senior archivist from the Foreign Office documents centre. He was puzzled that he should be here at a time when the PM was so busy settling in but he soon forgot about it. During the installation of a newly elected government there are many such surprises.

The Foreign Office archivist did not attend the meeting between the PM and Sir Sydney, but remained downstairs in the waiting room in case he was required. In the event, he was not.

This was the new Prime Minister's first official meeting with the chief of the espionage service. She found him uncommonly difficult to talk to: he was distant in manner and overpowering in appearance, a tall man with overlong hair and bushy eyebrows. At the end of the briefing she stood up to indicate that the meeting must end, but Sir Sydney seemed in no hurry to depart. "I'm quite certain that there is no truth in these terrible allegations, Prime Minister," he said.

He wondered if "madam" would be a more suitable form of address or perhaps "ma'am," as one called the Queen. She looked at him hard and he shifted uncomfortably. Sir Sydney was not an addicted smoker, in the way that his predecessor had been, but now he found the new Prime Minister's strictures about smoking something of a strain, and longed for a cigarette. In the old days, with Callaghan and before him Wilson, these rooms had seldom been without clouds of tobacco smoke.

"We'll discover that," said the Prime Minister curtly.

"I'll get one of my people out to California within twenty-four hours."

"You'll not inform the Americans?"

"It would not be wise, Prime Minister." He pressed a hand against his ear and flicked back errant strands of his long hair.

"I quite agree," she said. She picked up the newspaper cutting again. "For the time being all we need is a straight, simple answer from this film producer man."

"That might be rather a difficult task, if my experience of Hollywood film producers is anything to go by."

The PM looked up from the cutting to see if Sir Sydney was making a joke to which she should respond. She decided not to smile. Sir Sydney did not appear to be a man much given to jesting.

## 2

The exact details of the way in which the Soviet Union's intelligence services were alerted to the activities which had so troubled Britain's Prime Minister are more difficult to piece together. Soviet involvement had begun many weeks earlier and certainly it was the reason behind a long two-part radio message beamed in the early evening of Easter Sunday, April 15, 1979, to the Soviet embassy main building on the east side of 16th Street, Washington, D.C. This unexpected radio transmission required the services of the senior Russian cipher clerk who was enjoying an Easter dinner with Russian friends in a private room at the Pier 7 restaurant on the Maine Avenue waterfront near the Capital Yacht Club. He was collected from there by an embassy car.

Intercepted by the National Security Agency and decoded by its ATLAS computer at Fort George Meade, Maryland, that Sunday evening's radio traffic provided the first recorded use of the code name that Moscow had given this operation—Task Pogoni. The written instructions issued in 1962 by the GRU, and later given to the KGB and armed forces, order that the choice of such code names must be such that they do not reveal either the assignment or the government's intention or attitude, and adds a supplementary warning that the code names must not be trivial or of such grandeur that they would attract ridicule should the operation go wrong. And yet, as the NSA translators pointed out in their "pink flimsy" supplementary, Moscow's choice of code word was revealing.

Literally, *pogoni* means epaulette, but for a citizen of the U.S.S.R. its implications go deeper than that. Not only can it be used to mean a senior personage or "top brass"; it is a symbol of the hated reactionary. *"Smert zolotopogonnikam!"* cried the revolutionaries, "Death to the men who wear gold epaulettes!" And yet the possible overtones in this choice of the KGB code name can be taken further than that; for nowadays the senior Russian military men who control one of the U.S.S.R.'s rival intelligence organizations (the GRU) again wear gold epaulettes.

How Yuriy Grechko interpreted the code name assigned to this new operation is not recorded. Grechko—a senior KGB officer—was at the time the U.S.S.R.'s "legal resident." Under diplomatic cover, it was his job to keep himself, and Moscow, informed on all Soviet espionage activities in the U.S.A. In seniority Grechko ranked a close second to the ambassador himself, and he was there solely to keep all the covert operations and "dirty tricks" entirely separated from official diplomatic business. This made it easier for the ambassador to deny all knowledge of such activities when they were detected by the U.S. authorities.

Grechko was shown in the diplomatic listings as a naval captain third rank, working in the capacity of assistant naval attaché. He was a short man with dry curly hair, blue shiny eyes and a large mouth. His only memorable feature was a gold front tooth which was revealed whenever he smiled. But Grechko did not smile frequently enough for this to compromise his clandestine operations. Grechko was a man who exemplified the Russians' infinite capacity for melancholy.

It was difficult to reconcile Grechko's diplomatic listing with his appearance and life-style. His expensive hand-made suits, his gold watch, pearl tie-pin, the roll of paper money in his hip pocket, the availability of sports cars and his casual working day all suggested to those men in Washington who are employed to study such details that Grechko was a KGB man, but at this date it was not realized that he was the "legal"—the senior espionage administrator in the embassy.

Since Grechko's movements were restricted, he summoned his senior secret agent to Washington. It was contrary to the normal procedures, but his radioed instructions had stressed the urgency of his task. Grechko therefore took a trip that morning to the Botanic Gardens on the other side of the Anacostia River. He took his time and made quite sure that he was not being followed when he returned downtown to keep his appointment at the prestigious Hay-Adams Hotel which commands a view across Lafayette Square to the White House.

Mr. and Mrs. Edward Parker met Grechko at the 16th Street entrance to the hotel where Grechko had booked a table in the name of Green. Edward Parker was a thick-set, bear-like man, with Slavic features: a squarish jaw, wavy grey hair fast becoming white, and bushy eyebrows. He towered over his Japanese wife and Grechko, whose hand he shook with smiling determination. Parker, prepared for Chicago weather, was wearing a heavy tweed overcoat, although Washington that day had temperatures in the high fifties with some sunshine.

Grechko gave Fusako Parker a perfunctory kiss on the cheek and smiled briefly. She was in her middle thirties, a beautiful woman who made the most of her flawless complexion and her doll-like oriental features. She wore a coat dress of beige-coloured wool, with a large gold brooch in the shape of a chrysanthemum pinned high at the collar. To a casual observer, the three luncheon companions looked typical of the rather conservatively dressed embassy people who crowd into Washington's best restaurants.

Parker was an importer of components for cheap transistor radios. These were mostly manufactured and partly assembled in Taiwan, Korea and Singapore, where the labour forces were adroit enough to do the work but not yet adroit enough to demand the high wages of the U.S.A. and Europe. In this role Parker travelled freely both in the U.S.A. and abroad. It was perfect cover for the U.S.S.R. "illegal resident." Parker was the secret spymaster for the Russian oper-rations in America, with the exception of certain special tasks controlled from the Washington embassy and the extensive "Interbloc" network centred on the United Nations in New York City.

It was 2:20 by the time Grechko finished his cheesecake. When they ordered coffee and brandy, Mrs. Parker asked leave to depart to do some shopping before returning to Chicago. Grechko and Parker agreed to this, then the two men began their business discussion.

Parker had been planted in North America for nearly twelve years. His English was more or less faultless and he had easily assumed the bluff and amiable manner of the successful American man of business. Yet Parker had been born a citizen of the U.S.S.R. and had served for three years with the KGB First Main Directorate's Scientific and Technical Section before his U.S. assignment. Now he listened with care and attention as Grechko talked rapidly in soft Russian, telling him of the priority that had been given to Task Pogoni. Parker was empowered to assign any of his sleepers to active duty. Such freedom of decision had only five times before been given to the American resident during Parker's tour of duty. Similar powers had now been provided to the residents in Bonn, Paris and London.

Furthermore, Grechko confided, the First Main Directorate had assigned control to "Section 13." Both men knew what that meant. Although since 1969 it had been renamed the Executive Action Department, what old-timers still call Section 13 of the KGB First Main Directorate handles "wet business" *(mokrie dela),* which is anything from blackmail through torture to murder. The section was at that time headed by the legendary Stanislav Shumuk, a man highly regarded by the Communist Party's Administrative Organs Department, from which the KGB is actually controlled. Shumuk reputedly would go to any extreme to provide results.

Parker did not reply. Grechko sipped his black coffee. It was unnecessary to point out that failure could result in unpleasant consequences for both men. After that they resumed conversation in English. It mostly concerned the mechanical problems that Parker had experienced with his wife's car, which was still under warranty. Parker noticed, not for the first time, that Grechko was a miserable sort of man. It contradicted the stories he had heard about him, and Parker wondered why Grechko should become so despondent only with him.

Mr. and Mrs. Parker flew back to Chicago on the evening flight. Yuriy Grechko kept an appointment with his girlfriend, a Russian citizen employed by the Trade Delegation. In the early hours of the following morning he was heard arguing loudly with her in a motel where they spent the night just across the state line in Virginia. Grechko had been drinking heavily.

## 3

In spite of his smooth assurances to his Prime Minister, the director general of MI6 did not immediately dispatch an agent to California. The reason for this delay arose out of a conversation that the DG had with his daughter Jennifer. She had a candidate for a task on the far side of the world: her husband.

"Boyd is being quite beastly," she told her father. "Not all our friends know we are separated and I have a horror of finding him sitting opposite me at a dinner party. I wish you'd send him to do some job on the far side of the world." She gave her father a hug. "Just until the divorce is over."

The DG nodded. He should never have agreed to her marrying a man from his own department, especially such a rootless disrespectful young man. It would have been better to have let the love affair run its course; instead Sir Sydney had pressed them to marry with all the regrettable consequences.

"He's on the reassignment list, Daddy," she coaxed.

Boyd Stuart, a thirty-eight-year-old field agent, had just completed the mandatory one year of "administrative duties" that gave him a small rise in salary before returning him overseas. Such field agents, put behind an office desk in London for twelve months, seldom endear themselves to the permanent staff there. They are often hasty, simplistic and careless with the detail and the paperwork. To this list of deficiencies, Boyd Stuart had added the sin of arrogance. Twelve years as a field agent had made him impatient with the priorities displayed by the staff in London.

"There is something he could do for us in California," said the DG.

"Oh, Daddy. You don't know how wonderful that would be. Not just for me," she added hastily. "But for Boyd too. You know how much he hates it in the office."

The DG knew exactly how much Boyd Stuart hated it in the office. His son-in-law had frequently used dinner invitations to acquaint him with his preference for a reassignment overseas. The DG had done nothing about it, deciding that it would look very bad if he interceded for a close relative.

"It's quite urgent too," said the DG. "We'd have to get him away by the weekend at the latest."

Jennifer kissed her father. "You are a darling," she said. "Boyd knows California. He did an exchange year at UCLA."

Boyd Stuart was a handsome, dark-complexioned man whose appearance—like his excellent German and Polish and fluent Hungarian—enabled him to pass himself off as an inhabitant of anywhere in that region vaguely referred to as central Europe. Stuart had been born of a Scottish father and Polish mother in a wartime internment camp for civilians in the Rhineland. After the war, Stuart had attended schools in Germany, Scotland and Switzerland by the time he went to Cambridge. It was there that his high marks and his athletic and linguistic talents brought him under the scrutiny of the British intelligence recruiters.

"You say there is no file, Sir Sydney?" Stuart had not had a personal encounter with his father-in-law since that unforgettable night when he had the dreadful quarrel with Jennifer. Sir Sydney Ryden had arrived at four o'clock in the morning and taken her back to live with her parents again.

Stuart was wearing rather baggy, grey-flannel trousers and a blue blazer with one brass button missing. It was not exactly what he would have chosen to wear for this encounter but there was nothing he could do now about that. He realized that the DG was similarly unenthusiastic about the casual clothes, and found himself tugging at the cotton strands remaining from his lost button.

"That is a matter of deliberate policy," said the DG. "I cannot overemphasize how delicate this business is." The DG gave one of his mirthless smiles. This mannerism—mere baring of the teeth—was some atavistic warning not to tread further into sacred territory. The DG stared down into his whisky and then suddenly finished it. He was given to these abrupt movements and long periods of stillness. Ryden was well over six feet tall and preferred to wear black suits which, with his lined, pale face and luxuriant, flowing hair, made him look like a poet from some Victorian romance. He would need little more than a long black cloak to go on stage as Count Dracula, thought Stuart, and wondered if the DG deliberately contrived this forbidding appearance.

Without preamble, the DG told Stuart the story again, shortening it this time to the essential elements. "On 8 April 1945 elements of the 90th Division of the United States Third Army under General Patton were deep into Germany. When they got to the little town of Merkers, in western Thuringia, they sent infantry into the Kaiseroda salt mine. Those soldiers searched through some thirty miles of galleries in the mine. They found a newly installed steel door. When they broke through it they discovered gold; four-fifths of the Nazi gold reserves were stored there. So were two million or more of the rarest of rare books from the Berlin libraries, the complete Goethe collection from Weimar, and paintings and prints from all over Europe. It would take half an hour or more to read through the list of material. I'll let you have a copy."

Stuart nodded but didn't speak. It was late afternoon and sunlight made patterns on the carpet, moving across the room until the bright bars slimmed to fine rods and one by one disappeared. The DG went across to the bookcases to switch on the large table lamps. On the panelled walls there were paintings of horses which had won famous races a long time ago, but now the paintings had grown so dark under ageing varnish that the strutting horses seemed to be plodding home through a veil of fog.

"Just how much gold *was* four-fifths of the German gold reserves?" Stuart asked.

The DG sniffed and ran a finger across his ear, pushing away an errant lock of hair. "About three hundred million dollars worth of gold is one estimate. Over eight thousand bars of gold." The DG paused. "But that was just the bullion. In addition there were three thousand four hundred and thirty-six bags of gold coins, many of which were rarities—coins worth many times their weight in gold because of their value to collectors."

Stuart looked up and, realizing that some response was expected, said, "Yes, amazing, sir." He sipped some more of the whisky. It was always the best of malts up here in the DG's office at the top of "the Ziggurat," the curious, truncated, pyramidal building that looked across the River Thames to the Palace of Westminster. The room's panelling, paintings and antique furniture were all part of an attempt to recapture the elegance that the Secret Intelligence Service had enjoyed in the beautiful old houses in St. James's. But this building was steel and concrete, cheap and practical, with rust stains dribbling on the façade and cracks in the basement. The service itself could be similarly described.

"The American officers reported their find through the usual channels," said the DG, suddenly resuming his story. "Patton and Eisenhower went to see it on April 12. The army moved it all to Frankfurt. They took jeeps and trailers down the mine and brought it out. Ingenious people, the Americans, Stuart." He smiled and held the smile while looking Stuart full into the eyes.

"Yes, sir."

"It took about forty-eight hours of continuous work to load the valuables. There were thirty crates of German patent-office records—worth a king's ransom—and two thousand boxes of prints, drawings and engravings, as well as one hundred and forty rolls of oriental carpets. You see the difficulties, Stuart?"

"Indeed I do, sir." He swirled the last of his drink round his glass before swallowing it. The DG gave no sign of noticing that his glass was empty.

"They were ordered to begin loading the lorries just two days after Eisenhower's visit. The only way to do that was simply by listing whatever was on the original German inventory tags. It was a system that had grave shortcomings."

"If things were stolen, there was no way to be sure that the German inventory had been correct in the first place?"

The DG nodded. "Can you imagine the chaos that Germany was in by that stage of the war?"

"No, sir."

"Quite so, Stuart. You can *not* imagine it. God knows what difficulties the Germans had moving all their valuables in those days of collapse. But I assure you that the temptation for individual Germans to risk all in order to put some items in their pockets could never have been higher. Perhaps only the Germans could have moved such material intact in those circumstances. As a nation they have a self-discipline that one can only admire."

"Yes, sir."

"As soon as the Americans captured the mine, its contents went by road to Frankfurt, and were stored in the Reichsbank building. A special team from the State Department were given commissions overnight, put into uniform and flown from Washington to Frankfurt. They sifted that material to find sensitive papers or secret diplomatic exchanges that would be valuable to the U.S. government, or embarrassing to them if made public. After that, it was all turned over to the Inter-Allied Reparations Agency."

"And was there such secret material?"

"Let me get you another drink, Stuart. You like this malt, don't you? With water this time?"

"Straight please, sir."

The DG gave another of his ferocious grins.

"Of *course* there was secret material. The exchanges between the German ambassador in London and his masters in Berlin during the nineteen-thirties would have caused a few red faces in Whitehall, to say nothing of red faces in the Palace of Westminster. Enough indiscretions there to have put a few of our politicians behind bars in nineteen-forty . . . members of Parliament telling German embassy people what a splendid fellow Adolf Hitler was."

The DG poured drinks for them both. He used fresh cut-glass tumblers. "Something wrong with that door, Stuart?"

"No, it's beautiful," said Stuart, admiring the antique panelling. "And the octagonal oak table must be early seventeenth century."

The DG groaned silently. It was not the sort of remark expected of the right sort of chap. Ryden had been brought up to believe that a gentleman did not make specific references to another man's possessions. He had always suspected that Boyd Stuart might be "artistic"—a word the DG used to describe a wide variety of individuals that he blackballed at his club and shunned socially. "No ice? No soda? Nothing at all in it?" asked the DG again, but he marred the solicitude by descending into his seat as he said it.

Stuart shook his head and raised the heavy tumbler to his lips.

"No," agreed the DG. "With a fine Scots name such as Boyd Stuart a man must not be seen watering a Highland malt."

"Not in front of a Sassenach," said Stuart.

"What's that? Oh yes, I see," said the DG raising a hand to his hair. Stuart realized that his father-in-law wore his hair long to hide the hearing aid. It was a surprising vanity in such a composed figure; Stuart noted it with interest. "Oxford, Stuart?"

Stuart looked at him for a moment before answering. A man who could commit to memory all the details of the Kaiseroda mine discoveries was not likely to forget where his son-in-law went to university. "Cambridge, sir. Trinity. I read mathematics."

The DG closed his eyes. It was quite alarming the sort of people the department had recruited. They would be taking sociologists next. He was reminded of a joke he had heard at his club at lunch. A civil service candidate made an official complaint: he had missed promotion because at the civil service selection board he had admitted to being a socialist. The commissioner had apologized profoundly—or so the story went—he had thought the candidate had admitted to being a sociologist.

Boyd Stuart sipped his whisky. He did not strongly dislike his father-in-law—he was a decent enough old buffer in his way. If Ryden idolized his daughter so much that he could not see her faults, that was a very human failing.

"Was it Jennifer's idea?" Stuart asked him. "Sending me to California, was that her idea?"

"We wanted someone who knew something about the film trade," said Sir Sydney. "You came to mind immediately. . . ."

"You mean, had it been banking, backgammon or the Brigade of Guards," said Stuart, "I might have been trampled in the rush."

The DG smiled to acknowledge the joke. "I remembered that you studied at the UCLA."

"But it was Jennifer's idea?"

The DG hesitated rather than tell a deliberate untruth. "Jennifer feels it would be better . . . in the circumstances."

Stuart smiled. He could recognize the machinations of his wife.

"Little thought you'd find yourself in this business when you were at Trinity, eh Stuart?" said the DG, determined to change the subject.

"To tell you the absolute truth, sir, I was hoping to be a tennis professional."

The DG almost spluttered. He had a terrible feeling that this operation was going to be his Waterloo. He would hate to retire with a notable failure on his hands. His wife had set her mind on his getting a peerage. She had even been exploring some titles; Lord and Lady Rockhampton was her current favourite. It was the town in Australia in which her father had been born. Sir Sydney had promised to find out if this title was already taken by someone. He rather hoped it was.

"Yes, a fascinating game, tennis," said the DG. My

God. And this was the man who would have to be told about the Hitler Minutes, the most dangerous secret of the war. This was the fellow who would be guarding Winston Churchill's reputation.

"The convoy of lorries left Merkers to drive to Frankfurt on 15 April 1945," said the DG, continuing his story. "We think three, or even four, lorries disappeared en route to Frankfurt. None of the valuables and the secret documents on them were ever recovered. The U.S. Army never officially admitted the loss of the lorries but unofficially they said three."

"And you think that this film company in California now has possession of the documents?"

The DG went to the window, looking at the cactus plants that were lined up to get the maximum benefit from the light. He picked one pot up to examine it closely. "I can assure you quite categorically, Stuart, that we are talking about forgeries. We are talking about mythology." He sat down, still holding the plant pot and touching the soil carefully.

"It's something that would embarrass the government?"

The DG sniffed. He wondered how long it would take to get his message across. "Yes, Stuart, it is." He put the cactus on the coffee table and picked up his drink.

"Are we going to try to prevent this company from making a film about the Kaiseroda mine and its treasures?" Stuart asked.

"I don't give a tinker's curse about the film," said the DG. He patted his hair nervously. "I want to know what documentation the film people have." He drank some of his whisky and glanced at the skeleton clock on the mantlepiece. He had another meeting after this and he was running short of time.

"I'm not sure I know exactly what I'm looking for," Stuart said.

The DG stood up. It was Stuart's cue to depart. In the half-light, his lined face underlit by the table lamp, and his huge dark-suited figure silhouetted against the dying sun, Ryden looked satanic. "You'll know it when you see it. We'll keep in contact with you through our controllers in California. Good luck, my boy."

"Thank you, sir." Stuart rose too.

"You've seen Operations? Got all the procedures settled? You understand about the money—it's being wired to the First Los Angeles Bank in Century City." The DG smiled. "Jennifer tells me you are giving her lunch tomorrow."

"There are some things she wants from the flat," explained Stuart.

"Get to California as soon as possible, Stuart."

"There are just a few personal matters to settle," said Stuart. "Cancel my holiday arrangements and stop the milk."

The DG looked at the clock again. "We have people in the department who will attend to the details, Stuart. We can't have operations delayed because of a few bottles of milk."

# 4

"We have people in the department who will attend to the details, Stuart," said Boyd Stuart in a comical imitation of the DG's voice.

Kitty King, Boyd Stuart's current girlfriend, giggled and held him closer. "So what did *you* say, darling?"

"Not this gorgeous little detail they won't, I told him. Some things must remain sacred." He patted her bottom.

"You fool! What did you really say?"

"I opened my mouth and poured his whisky into it. By the time I'd finished it, he'd disappeared through the floor, like the demon king in the pantomime." He kissed her again. "I'm going to Los Angeles."

She wriggled loose from his grasp. "I know all about that," she said. "Who do you think typed your orders this afternoon?" She was the secretary to the deputy chief of Operations (Region Three).

"Will you be faithful to me while I'm away?" said Stuart, only half in fun.

"I'll wash my hair every night, and go early to bed with Keats and hot cocoa."

It was an unlikely promise. Kitty was a young busty blonde who attracted men, young and old, as surely as picnics bring wasps. She looked up, saw the look on Stuart's face and gave him a kiss on the end of his nose. "I'm a child of the sexual revolution, Boyd darling. You must have read about it in *Playboy?"*

"I never read *Playboy;* I just look at the pictures. Let's go to bed."

"I've made you that roasted eggplant dip you like." Kitty King was a staunch vegetarian; worse, she was an evangelistic one. Amazing, someone at the office had remarked after seeing her in a bikini, to think that it's all fruit and nuts. "You like that, don't you?"

"Let's go to bed," said Stuart.

"I must turn off the oven first, or my chickpea casserole will dry up completely."

She backed away from him slowly. In spite of the disparity in their ages, she found him disconcertingly attractive. Until now her experiences with men had been entirely under her control, but Boyd Stuart, in spite of all his anxious remarks, kept her in her place. She was surprised and annoyed to discover that she rather liked the new sort of relationship.

She looked at him and he smiled. He was a handsome man: the wide, lined face and the mouth that turned down at one side could suddenly be transformed by a devastating smile, and his laugh was infectious.

"Your chickpea casserole!" said Boyd Stuart. "We don't want *that* to dry up, darling." He laughed a loud, booming laugh and she could not resist joining in. He put out his hand to her. She noticed that the back of it was covered with small scars and the thumb joint was twisted. She had asked him about it once but he had made some joke in reply. There was always a barrier; these men who had worked in the field were all the same in this respect. There was no way in which to get to know them completely. There was always a "no entry" sign. Always some part of their brain was on guard and awake. And Kitty King was enough of a woman to want her man to be completely hers.

Boyd Stuart pushed open the door of the bedroom. It was the best room in the apartment in many ways: large and light, like so many of these rambling Victorian houses near the river on the unfashionable side of Victoria Station. That was why he had a writing desk in a window space of his bedroom, a corner which Kitty King liked to refer to grandiosely as "the study."

"Kitty!" he called.

She came into the bedroom, leaned back against the door and smiled as the latch clicked.

"Kitty. The lock of my desk is broken." He opened the inlaid walnut front of the antique bureau. The lock had been torn away from the wood and there were deep scratches in the polished surface. "You didn't break into it, did you, Kitty?"

"Of course not, Boyd. I'm not interested in your old love letters."

"It's not funny, Kitty. I have classified material in here." Already he was sifting through the drawers and pigeonholes. He found the airline ticket, his passport, the letter to the bank, a couple of contact addresses and an old photo of a man named Bernard Lustig cut from a film trade magazine. There was also a newspaper cutting that he had been given by the department.

**An all-expenses-paid trip to the movie capital of the world and the luxury of the exclusive Beverly Hills Hotel**

Veterans of the US Third Army and attached units who were concerned with the movement of material from the Kaiseroda salt mine, Merkers, Thuringia, Germany, in the final days of the Second World War are urgently sought by B. Lustig Productions Inc. The corporation is preparing a major motion picture about this historical episode. Veterans should send full details, care of this newspaper, to Box 2188. Photos and documents will be treated with utmost care and returned to sender by registered post.

Kitty King watched him search through the items.

"Nothing seems to have been taken," said Stuart. "Did you leave the door open when you went down to the dustbins?"

"There was no one on the stairs," she said.

"Waiting upstairs," said Stuart. "The same kid who did the burglaries in the other flats, I'll bet."

"Are you going to phone the department?"

"Nothing's missing. And the front door has no signs of forced entry."

"The papers for your trip were there, weren't they?"

He nodded.

"Then you must have known about going last Sunday—when you put the tickets and things in there." There was a note of resentment in her voice.

"I still wasn't sure until I saw the DG late this afternoon."

"I wish you'd discussed it with me, Boyd." He looked up sharply. This was a new side of Kitty King. She had always described their relationship as no more than a temporary "shack-up." She was a career woman, she had always maintained, with a good degree in political science from the London School of Economics, and the aim of becoming a Permanent Secretary, the top of the Administrative Class grades.

Stuart said, "If I phone the night duty officer, they'll be all over us. You know what a fuss they'll make. We'll be up all night writing reports."

"You know best, sweetheart."

"A kid probably, looking for cash. When he found only this sort of thing he got out quickly, before you came back upstairs again."

"Does your wife still have her key to this place?" Kitty asked.

"She wouldn't break open my desk."

"That's not what I asked you."

"It was just some kid looking for cash. Nothing is missing. Stop worrying about it."

"She'd like to get you back, Boyd. You realize that, don't you?"

Boyd put his arms round her tightly and kissed her for a long time.

# 5

The Steins—father and son—lived in a large house in Hollywood. Cresta Ridge Drive provides a sudden and welcome relief from the exhaust fumes and noise of Franklin Avenue. It is one of a tangle of steep winding roads that lead into the Hollywood hills and end at Griffith Park and Lake Hollywood. Its elevation gives the house a view across the city, and on smoggy days when the pale tide of pollution engulfs the city, the sky here remains blue.

By Californian standards these houses are old, discreetly sited behind mature horse-chestnut trees now grown up to the roofs. In the thirties some of them, their gardens blazing with hibiscus and bougainvillea as they were this day, had been owned by film stars. Even today long-lost but strangely familiar faces can be glimpsed at the check-outs of the Safeway or self-serving gasoline at Wilbur's. But most of Stein's neighbours were corporate lawyers, ambitious dentists and refugees from the nearby aerospace communities.

On this afternoon a rainstorm deluged the city. It was as if nature was having one last fling before the summer.

Outside the Steins' house there was a white Imperial Le Baron two-door hardtop, one of the biggest cars in the Chrysler range. The paintwork shone in the hard, unnatural light that comes with a storm, and the heavy rain glazed the paintwork and the dark tinted windows. Sitting—head well down—in the back seat was a man. He appeared to be asleep but he was not even dozing.

The car's owner—Miles MacIver—was inside the Stein home. Stein senior was not at home, and now his son Billy was regretting the courtesy he had shown in inviting MacIver into the house.

MacIver was a well-preserved man in his late fifties. His white hair emphasized the blue eyes with which he fixed Billy as he talked. He smiled lazily and used his large hands to emphasize his words as he strode restlessly about the lounge. Sometimes he stroked his white moustache, or ran a finger along an eyebrow. They were the gestures of a man to whom appearance was important: an actor, a womanizer or a salesman. MacIver possessed attributes of all three.

It was a large room, comfortably furnished with good-quality furniture and expensive carpets. MacIver's restless prowling was proprietorial. He went to the Bechstein grand piano, its top crowded with framed photographs. From the photos of friends and relatives, MacIver selected a picture of Charles Stein, the man he had come to visit, taken at the training battalion at Camp Edwards, Massachusetts, sometime in the early nineteen-forties. Stein was dressed in the uncomfortable, ill-fitting coveralls which, like the improvised vehicle behind him, were a part of America's hurried preparations for war. Stein leaned close to one side of the frame, his arm seemingly raised as if to embrace it.

"Your dad cut your Uncle Aram out of this picture, did he?"

"I guess so," said Billy Stein.

MacIver put the photo back on the piano and went to look out of the window. Billy had not looked up from where he was reading *Air Progress* on the sofa. MacIver studied the view from the window with the same dispassionate interest with which he had examined the photo. It was a glimpse of his own reflection that made him smooth the floral-patterned silk tie and rebutton his tartan jacket.

"Too bad about you and Natalie," he said without turning from the window. His voice was low and carefully modulated—the voice of a man self-conscious about the impression he made.

The warm air from the Pacific Ocean was heavy, saturated with water vapour. It built up towering storm clouds, dragging them up to the mountains, where the air condensed, dumping solid sheets of tropical rain across the Los Angeles basin. Close to the house, a tall palm tree bent under a cruel gust of wind that tried to snap it in two. Suddenly released, the palm straightened with a force that made the fronds dance and whip the air loudly enough to make MacIver flinch and move from the window.

"It lasted three months," said Billy. He guessed his father had discussed the failure of his marriage and was annoyed.

"Three months is par for the course these days, Billy," said MacIver. He turned round, fixed him with his wide-open eyes and smiled. In spite of himself, Billy smiled too. He was twenty-four years old, slim, with lots of dark wavy hair and a deep tan that continued all the way to where a gold medallion dangled inside his unbuttoned shirt. Billy wore thin, wire-rimmed, yellow spectacles that he had bought during his skiing holiday in Aspen and had been wearing ever since. Now he took them off.

"Dad told you, did he?" He threw the anti-glare spectacles on to the coffee table.

"Come on, Billy. I was here two years ago when you were building the new staircase to make a separate apartment for the two of you."

"I remember," said Billy, mollified by this explanation. "Natalie was not ready for marriage. She was into the feminist movement in a big way."

"Well, your dad's a man's man, Billy. We both know that." MacIver took out his cigarettes and lit one.

"It was nothing to do with Dad," Billy said. "She met this damned poet on a TV talk show she was on. They took off to live in British Columbia. . . . She *liked* Dad."

MacIver smiled the same lazy smile and nodded. He did not believe that. "We both know your dad, Billy. He's a wonderful guy. They broke the mould when they made Charlie Stein. When we were in the army he ran that damned battalion. Don't let anyone tell you different. Corporal Stein ran that battalion. And I'll tell you this"—he gestured with his large hands so that the fraternity ring shone in the dull light—"I heard the colonel say the same thing at one of the battalion reunions. Charlie Stein ran the battalion. Everyone knew it. But he's not always easy to get along with. Right, Billy?"

"You were an officer, were you?"

"Captain. Just for the last weeks of my service. But I finally made captain. Captain MacIver. I had it painted on the door of my office. The goddamned sergeant from the paint shop came over and wanted to argue about it. But I told him that I'd waited too goddamned long for that promotion to pass up the right to have it on my office door. I made the sign-writer put it on there, just for that final month of my army service." He gestured again, using the cigarette so that it left smoke patterns in the still air.

Billy Stein nodded and pushed his magazine aside to give his full attention to the visitor. "Is it true you pitched for Babe Ruth?"

"Your dad tell you, did he?" MacIver smiled.

"That was when you were at Harvard, was it, Mr. MacIver?" There was something in Billy Stein's voice that warned the visitor against answering. He hesitated. The only sound was the rain; it hammered on the windows and rushed along the gutterings and gurgled in the rainpipes. Billy stared at him but MacIver was giving all his attention to his cigarette.

Billy waited a long time, then he said, "You were never at Harvard, Mr. MacIver; I checked it. And I checked your credit rating too. You don't own any house in Palm Springs, nor that apartment you talked about. You're a phoney, Mr. MacIver." Billy Stein's voice was quiet and matter of fact, as if they were discussing some person who was not present. "Even that car outside is not yours—the payments are made in the name of your ex-wife."

"The money comes from me," snapped MacIver, relieved to find at least one accusation that he could refute. Then he recovered himself and reassumed the easy, relaxed smile. "Seems like you out-guessed me there, Billy." Effortlessly he retrenched and tried to salvage some measure of advantage from the confrontation. The only sign of his unease was the way in which he was now twisting the end of his moustache instead of stroking it.

"I guessed you were a phoney," said Billy Stein. There was no satisfaction in his voice. "I didn't run any check on your credit rating; I just guessed you were a phoney." He was angry with himself for not mentioning the money that MacIver had had from his father. He had come across his father's cheque book in the bureau and found the list of six entries on the memo pages at the back. More than six thousand dollars had been paid to MacIver between December 10, 1978, and April 4, 1979, and every cheque was made out to cash payment. It was that that had encouraged Billy's suspicion.

"I ran into a tough period last fall; suppliers needed fast repayment and I couldn't meet the deadlines."

"The diamonds that you bought here in town and sent to your contact man in Seoul?" said Billy scornfully. "Was it five thousand per cent on every dollar?"

"You've got a good memory, Billy." He smoothed his tie. "You'd be a tough guy to do business with. I wish I had a partner like you. I listen to these hard-luck stories from guys who owe me money and I melt."

"I bet," said Billy. Fierce gusts pounded the windows and made the rain in the gutters slop over and stream down the glass. There was a crackle of static like brittle paper being crushed, and a faint flicker of lightning lit the room. The sound silenced the two men.

Billy Stein stared at MacIver. There was no malevolence in his eyes, no violence nor desire for argument. But there was no compassion there either. His private income and affluent lifestyle had made Billy Stein intolerant of the compromises to which less fortunate men were forced. The exaggerations of the old, the half-truths of the poor and the misdemeanours of the desperate found no mitigation in Billy Stein's judgement. And so now Miles MacIver knew no way to counter the young man's calm judicial gaze.

"I know what you're thinking, Billy . . . the money I owe your father. I'm going to pay every penny of it back to him. And I mean within the next six weeks or so. That's what I wanted to see him about."

"What happens in six weeks?"

Miles MacIver had always been a careful man, keeping a careful separation between the vague confident announcements of present or future prosperity —which were invariably a part of his demeanour—

and the more stringent financial and commercial realities. But, faced with Billy Stein's calm, patronizing inquiry, MacIver was persuaded to tell him the truth. It was a decision that was to change the lives of many people, and end the lives of several.

"I'll *tell* you what happens in six weeks, Billy," said MacIver, hitching his trousers at the knees and seating himself on the armchair facing the young man. "I get the money for the movie rights of my war memoirs. That's what happens in six weeks." He smiled and reached across to the big china ashtray marked CAFÉ DE LA PAIX—Billy's father had brought it back from Paris in 1945. He dragged the ashtray close to his hand and flicked into it a long section of ash.

"Movie rights?" said Billy Stein, and MacIver was gratified to have provoked him at last into a reaction. "Your war memoirs?"

"Twenty-five thousand dollars," said MacIver. He flicked his cigarette again, even though there was no ash on it. "They have got a professional writer working on my story right now."

"What did you do in the war?" said Billy. "What did you do that they'll make it into a movie?"

"I was a military cop," said MacIver proudly. "I was with Georgie Patton's Third Army when they opened up this Kraut salt mine and found the Nazi gold reserves there. Billions of dollars in gold, as well as archives, diaries, town records and paintings. . . . You'd never believe the stuff that was there."

"What did you do?"

"I was assigned to MFA&A, G-5 Section—the Monuments, Fine Arts and Archives branch of the Government Affairs Group—we guarded it while it was classified into Category A for the bullion and rare coins and Category B for the gold and silver dishes, jewellery, ornaments and stuff. I wish you could have seen it, Billy."

"Just you guarding it?"

MacIver laughed. "There were five infantry platoons guarding the lorries that moved it to Frankfurt. There were two machinegun platoons as back-up, and Piper Cub airplanes in radio contact with the escort column. No, not just me, Billy." MacIver scratched his chin. "Your dad never tell you about all that? And about the trucks that never got to the other end?"

"What are you getting at, Mr. MacIver?"

MacIver raised a flattened hand. "Now, don't get me wrong, Billy. No one's saying your dad had anything to do with the hijack."

"One of Dad's relatives in Europe died during the war. He left Dad some land and stuff over there; that's how Dad made his money."

"Sure it is, Billy. No one's saying any different."

"I don't go much for all that war stuff," said Billy.

"Well, this guy Bernie Lustig, with the office on Melrose . . . he goes for it."

"A movie?"

MacIver reached into his tartan jacket and produced an envelope. From it he took a rectangle of cheap newsprint. It was the client's proof of a quarter-page advert in a film trade magazine. WHAT IS THE FINAL SECRET OF THE KAISERODA MINE? said the headline. He passed the flimsy paper to Billy Stein. "That will be in the trade magazines next month. Meanwhile Bernie is talking up a storm. He knows everyone: the big movie stars, the directors, the agents, the writers, everyone."

"The movie business kind of interests me," admitted Billy.

MacIver was pleased. "You want to meet Bernie?"

"Could you fix that for me?"

"No problem," said MacIver, taking the advert back and replacing it in his pocket. "And I get a piece of the action too. Two per cent of the producer's profit; that could be a bundle, Billy."

"I couldn't handle the technical stuff," said Billy. "I'm no good with a camera, and I can't write worth a damn, but I'd make myself useful on the production side." He reached for his antiglare spectacles and toyed with them. "If he'll have me, that is."

MacIver beamed. "If he'll have you! . . . The son of my best friend! Jesusss! He'll have you in that production office, Billy, or I'll pull out and take my story somewhere else."

"Gee, thanks, Mr. MacIver."

"I call you Billy; you call me Miles. OK?" He dug

his hands deep into his trouser pockets and gave that slow smile that was infectious.

"OK, Miles." Billy snapped his spectacles on.

"Rain's stopping," said MacIver. "There are a few calls I have to make. . . ." MacIver had never lost his sense of timing. "I must go. Nice talking to you, Billy. Give my respects to your dad. Tell him he'll be hearing from me real soon. Meanwhile, I'll talk to Bernie and have him call you and fix a lunch. OK?"

"Thanks, Mr. MacIver."

"Miles." He dumped his cigarette into the ashtray.

"Thanks, Miles."

"Forget it, kid."

When Miles MacIver got into the driver's seat of the Chrysler Imperial parked outside the Stein home, he sighed with relief. The man in the back seat did not move. "Did you fix it?"

"Stein wasn't there. I spoke with his son. He knows nothing."

"You didn't mention the Kaiseroda mine business to the son, I hope?"

MacIver laughed and started the engine. "I'm not that kind of fool, Mr. Kleiber. You said don't mention it to anyone except the old man. I know how to keep my mouth shut."

The man in the back seat grunted as if unconvinced.

Billy Stein was elated. After MacIver had departed he made a phone call and cancelled a date to go to a party in Malibu with a girl he had recently met at Pirate's Cove, the nude bathing section of the state beach at Point Dume. She had an all-over golden tan, a new Honda motorcycle and a father who had made a fortune speculating in cocoa futures. It was a measure of Billy Stein's excitement at the prospect of a job in the movie industry that he chose to sit alone and think about it rather than be with this girl.

At first Billy Stein spent some time searching through old movie magazines in case he could find a reference to Bernie Lustig or, better still, a photo of him. His search was unrewarded. At 7:30 the housekeeper, who had looked after the two men since Billy

Stein's mother died some five years before, brought him a supper tray. A tall, thin woman, she had lost her nursing licence in some eastern state hospital for selling whisky to the patients. Perhaps this ending to her nursing career had changed her personality, for she was taciturn, devoid of curiosity and devoid too of that warm, maternal manner so often associated with nursing. She worked hard for the Steins but she never attempted to replace that other woman who had once closed these same curtains, plumped up the cushions and switched on the table lamps. She hurriedly picked up the petals that had fallen from the roses, crushed them tightly in her hand and then dropped them into a large ashtray on top of MacIver's cigarette butt. She sniffed; she hated cigarettes. She picked up the ashtray holding it at a distance, as a nurse holds a bedpan.

"Anything else, Mr. Billy?" Her almost colourless hair was drawn tightly back, and fixed into position with brass-coloured hair clips.

Billy looked at the supper tray she had put before him on the coffee table. "You get along, Mrs. Svenson. You'll miss the beginning of 'Celebrity Sweepstakes.' "

She looked at the clock and back to Billy Stein, not quite sure whether this concern was genuine or sarcastic. She never admitted her obsession for the TV game shows but she had planned to be upstairs in her self-contained apartment by then.

"If Mr. Stein wants anything to eat when he gets home, there is some cold chicken wrapped in foil on the top shelf of the refrigerator."

"Yes, okay. Good night, Mrs. Svenson."

She sniffed again and moved the framed photo of Charles Stein which MacIver had put back slightly out of position amongst the photos crowding the piano top. "Good night, Mr. Billy."

Billy munched his way through the bowl of beef chili and beans, and drank his beer. Then he went to the bookcase and ran a fingertip along the video cassettes to find an old movie that he had taped. He selected *Psycho* and sat back to watch how Hitchcock had set up his shots and assembled them into a whole.

He had done this with an earlier Hitchcock film for a college course on film appreciation.

The time passed quickly, and when the taped film ended Billy was even more excited at the prospect of becoming a part of the entertainment world. He found show-biz stylish and hard-edged—"stylish" and "hard-edged" being compliments that were at that time being rather overworked by Billy Stein's friends and contemporaries. He rewound the tape and settled back to see *Psycho* once more.

Charles Stein, Billy's father, usually spent Wednesday evenings at a club out in the east valley. They still called it the Roscoe Sports and Bridge Club, even though some smart real-estate man had got Roscoe renamed Sun Valley, and few of the members played anything but poker.

Stein's three regular cronies were there, including Jim Sampson, an elderly lawyer who had served with Stein in the army. They ate the Wednesday night special together—corned beef hash with onion rings—shared a few bottles of California Gewürztraminer and some opinions of the government, then retired to the bar to watch the eleven o'clock news followed by the sports round-up. It was always the same; Charles Stein was a man of regular habits. A little after midnight, Jim Sampson dropped him off at the door—Stein disliked driving—and was invited in for a nightcap. It was a ritual that both men knew, a way of saying thank you for the ride. Jim Sampson never came in.

"Thought you had a heavy date tonight, Billy?" Charles Stein weighed nearly three hundred pounds. The real crocodile-leather belt that bit into his girth and bundled up his expensive English wool suit and his pure cotton shirt was supplied to special order by Sunny Jim's Big Men's Wear. Stein's sparse white hair was ruffled, so that the light behind him made an untidy halo round his pink head as he lowered himself carefully into his favourite armchair.

Billy, who never discussed his girlfriends with his father, said, "Stayed home. Your friend MacIver dropped in. He thinks he can get me a job in movies."

"Get you a job in movies?" said his father. "Get

you a job in movies? Miles MacIver?" He searched into his pocket to find his cigars, and put one in his mouth and lit it.

"They're making a movie of his war memoirs. Some story! Finding the Nazi gold. Could be a great movie, Dad."

"Hold the phone," said his father wearily. He was sitting on the edge of the armchair now, leaning well forward, his head bent very low as he prepared to light his cigar. "MacIver was *here?*" He said it to the carpet.

"What's wrong?" said Billy Stein.

"*When* was MacIver here?"

"You said never interrupt your poker game."

"When?" He struck a match and lit his cigar.

"Five o'clock, maybe six o'clock."

"You watching TV tonight?"

"It's just quiz shows and crap. I've been running video."

"MacIver is dead." Charles Stein drew on the cigar and blew smoke down at the carpet.

"Dead?"

"It was on Channel Two, the news. Some kid blew off the top of his head with a sawed-off shotgun. Left the weapon there. It happened in one of those little bars on Western Avenue near Beverly Boulevard. TV news got a crew there real quick . . . cars, flashing lights, a deputy chief waving the murder weapon at the camera."

"A street gang, was it?"

"Who then threw away a two-hundred-dollar shotgun, all carefully sawed off so it fits under your jacket?"

"Then who?"

Charles Stein blew smoke. "Who knows?" he said angrily, although his anger was not directed at anyone in particular. "MacIver the Mouth, they called him. Owes money all over town. Could be some creditor blew him away." He drew on the cigar again. The smoke tasted sour.

"Well, he sold his war memoirs. He showed me the advertisement. Some movie producer he met. He's selling him a story about Nazi gold in Germany in the war."

Charles Stein grunted. "So that's it, eh? I wondered why that bastard had been going around talking to all the guys from the outfit. Sure, I saw a lot of him in the army but he wasn't even with the battalion. He was with some lousy military police detail."

"He's been getting the story from you?"

"From me he got nothing. We were under the direct order of General Patton at Third Army HQ for that job, and we're still not released from the secrecy order." He ran his fingers back through his wispy hair and held his hand on the top of his head for a moment, lost in thought. "MacIver has been writing all this stuff down, you say, and passing it to some movie guy?"

"Bernie Lustig. MacIver was going to introduce me to him," said Billy. "Poor guy. Was it a stick-up?"

"He won't be doing much in the line of introductions, Billy. By now he's in the morgue with a label on his toe. Lustig—where's he have his office?"

"Melrose—he hasn't yet made it to Beverly Hills or even to Sunset. That's what made me think it was true . . . If MacIver had been inventing this guy, he would have chosen somewhere flashier than Melrose."

"Go to the top of the class, Billy." He eased off his white leather shoes and kicked them carelessly under the table.

"What was he like, this MacIver guy?" MacIver had now achieved a posthumous interest, not to say glamour. "What was he really like, Dad?"

"He was a liar and a cheat. He sponged on his friends to buy drinks for his enemies. . . . MacIver was desperate to make people like him. He'd do anything to win them over. . . ." Stein was about to add that MacIver's promise to get Billy a job in the movie industry was a good example of this desperate need, but he decided not to disappoint his son until more facts were available. He smoked his cigar and then studied the ash on it.

"Did you know him in New York, before you went into the army?"

"He was from Chicago. He was on the force there,

working the South Side—a tough neighbourhood. He leaned heavily on the 'golden-hearted cop' bit. He joined the army after Pearl Harbor and gave them all that baloney about being at Harvard. There was no time to check on it, I suppose. . . ."

"It *was* baloney. He as good as admitted it."

"They wouldn't let MacIver into Harvard to haul the ashes. Sure it was baloney, but it got him a commission in the military police. And he used that to pull every trick in the book. He was always asking for use of one of our trucks. A packing case delivered here; a small parcel collected here. He got together with the transport section and the rumours said they even sold one of our two-and-a-half-tonners to a Belgian civilian and went on leave in Paris to spend the proceeds." Suddenly Stein felt sad and very tired. He wiped a hand across his face, as a swimmer might after emerging from the water.

"What are you going to do now, Dad?"

"I lost five hundred and thirty bucks tonight, Billy, and I've put away more white wine than is good for my digestion. . . ." He coughed, and looked for his ashtray without finding it. In spite of all his reservations about MacIver, he was shocked by the news of his murder. MacIver was a con-man, always ready with glib promises and the unconvincing excuses that inevitably followed them. And yet there were good memories too, for MacIver was capable of flamboyant generosity and subtle kindness, and anyway, thought Charles Stein, they had shared a lifetime together. It was enough to make him sad, no matter what kind of bastard MacIver had been.

"You going to find this Bernie Lustig character?" said Billy.

"Is that the name of the movie producer?"

"I *told* you, Dad. On Melrose."

"I guess so."

"You don't think this Lustig cat had anything to do with the killing, do you?"

"I'm going to bed now, Billy." Again he looked for the ashtray. It was always on the table next to the flower vase.

"If he owed MacIver twenty-five thousand dollars . . ."

"We'll talk about it in the morning, Billy. Where's my ashtray?"

"I'll catch the TV news," said Billy. "Think they'll still be running the clip?"

"This is a rough town, Billy. One killing don't make news for long." He reached across the table and stubbed his cigar into the remains of Billy's beans.

## 6

The man behind the desk could have been mistaken for an Oriental, especially when he smiled politely. His face was pale and even the sunshine of Southern California made his skin go no darker than antique ivory. His hair was jet black and brushed tight against his domed skull. "Max Breslow," he said, offering a hand which Charles Stein shook energetically.

"I was expecting to meet Mr. Bernie Lustig," said Stein. He had selected one of his most expensive cream-coloured linen suits but already it was rumpled, and the knot of his white silk tie had twisted under his collar. He lowered his massive body into the black leather Charles Eames armchair, which creaked under his weight.

"Mr. Lustig is in Europe," said Max Breslow. "There is work to do there for our next production."

" 'The Final Secret of the Kaiseroda Mine'?" said Stein, waving his large hand in the air and displaying a heavy gold Rolex watch and diamond rings on hands that were regularly manicured. When Breslow did not react to this question, Stein said. "Mr. Miles MacIver is an old friend of mine. He promised to get my son a job with your film." Breslow nodded. Stein corrected himself. "MacIver *was* a close friend of mine."

"You were in the army with him?" He had a faint German accent.

"I didn't say that," said Stein. He stroked his sideburns. They were long and bushy, curling over his ears.

Breslow picked up a stainless-steel letter-opener, toyed with it for a moment and looked at Stein. "It was a sad business with Mr. MacIver," said Breslow. He said it with the same sort of clinical indifference with which an airline clerk comforts a passenger who has lost his baggage.

Stein remembered MacIver with a sudden disconcerting pang of grief. He recalled the night in 1945 when MacIver had crawled into the wreckage of a German *Weinstube*. They were in some small town on the other side of Mainz. The artillery had long since pounded it flat, the tanks had bypassed its difficult obstacles, the infantry had forgotten it existed, the engineers had threaded their tapes all thorugh the streets, and left DANGER BOOBY TRAPS signs in the rubble. Stein remembered how MacIver had climbed down from their two-and-a-half-ton winch truck saying that the god-damned engineers always put those signs on the booze joints so they could come back and plunder it in their own sweet time. Stein had held his breath while MacIver climbed over the rubble and across the wrecked front parlour of the wine bar. For a moment he had been out of sight but soon he reappeared, flush-faced and grinning in triumph, fingers cut on broken glass and sleeve dark and wet with spilled red wine that shone like fresh blood. He was struggling under the weight of a whole case of German champagne.

MacIver had eased a cork and it had hit the roof of the cab with a noise like a gunshot. They poured it into mess tins and drank the fiercely bubbling golden champagne without talking. When they had finished it, MacIver tossed the empty bottle out into the dark night. "It's a long time between drinks, pal."

"For an officer, and a flatfoot, you're a scorer," said Stein.

It was a hell of a thing for an officer to do. "A long time between drinks": he could never hear that said without thinking of MacIver.

"I beg your pardon," said Max Breslow politely.

His head was cocked as if listening to some faint sound. Stein realized that he'd spoken out loud.

"It's a long time between drinks," said Stein. "It's an American saying. Or at least it used to be when I was young."

"I see," said Breslow, noting this interesting fact. "Would you *like* a drink?"

"OK," said Stein. "Rum and Coke if you've got it."

Breslow rolled his swivel chair back towards the wall so that he could open the small refrigerator concealed in his walnut desk.

"It's darned hot in here," said Stein. "Is the air-conditioner working?" His weight made him suffer in the humidity and now his hand-stitched suit showed small dark patches of sweat.

Breslow set up paper napkins and glasses on his desk top and put ice into one of them before adding the rum and Coke. He did it fastidiously, using metal tongs, one cube at a time. For himself he poured a small measure of cognac, without ice.

Stein had been nursing a floppy straw hat. As he eased himself slowly from the low armchair to get his drink from the desk, he tossed his hat onto a side table where film trade magazines had been arranged in fan patterns.

He didn't get his drink immediately; going to the window he looked out. Melrose came close to the freeway here in one of the older districts of the city. This office was an apartment in a two-storey block repainted bright pink. Across the street brick apartment buildings and dilapidated little offices were defaced with obscene Spanish graffiti and speared with drunken TV antennae, and the whole thing was bird-caged with overhead wires. The freeway traffic was moving very slowly so that the Hollywood hills beyond wobbled in a grey veil of diesel fumes. Stein pulled his sunglasses from his face and pushed them into the top pocket of his jacket. He blinked in the bright light and dabbed his face with a silk handkerchief. "Damned hot." The sun was blood red and its light came through the slats of the Venetian blind to make a pattern across Stein's wrinkled face. It was always like this the day after a bad storm.

"I've spoken to the janitor," explained Breslow. "The repairmen are working on the air-conditioning. Yesterday's heavy rain got into the mechanism."

"MacIver owed me money," said Stein, "a lot of money. He gave me a part of his interest in your movie as surety."

"I hope you took the precaution of having him put that in writing," said Breslow.

"Right," said Stein. He did not enlarge upon it; it was best to keep such untruths as brief as possible.

"We are not even in the pre-production stage at present," said Breslow. He put the cognac to his mouth but it did no more than moisten his lips. "It is possible still that we will decide not to make the film. Unless we make it, there will be no money."

"All MacIver's war experiences, was it?"

"Together with some anecdotes he gathered from his comrades, some guesses about what went on in high places, and some creative writing concerning MacIver's intrepid contribution to the Allied victory."

Stein took his drink from the desk and tasted it before adding another measure of Coke. Then he looked at Breslow, who was still enjoying his own description of MacIver's manuscript.

"The movie-going public is always interested in such stories," explained Breslow. "A little gang of rear-echelon soldiers stealing everything they could lay their hands on." His eyes were still on Stein and he smiled again. "Crooks in uniform: it's an amusing formula."

Stein's hands went out with a speed that was surprising in such an overweight physique. His huge fingers and thumb grasped Breslow's shirt collar with enough force to rip the button loose. He shook Breslow very gently to mark his words. "Don't ever act disrespectful to me or to MacIver or any of our friends, Breslow. We don't let strangers discuss what we did back in 1945. We left a lot of good buddies out there in the sand and the shit and the offal. I buried my kid brother on the battlefield. We stumbled on a little good fortune . . . that's the way it goes. The spoils of war . . . we were entitled. You just remember that from now on." He released his grip and let Breslow straighten up and adjust his collar and tie.

"I'm sorry to have offended you," said Breslow, with no trace of regret. "I understood you to say that you were *not* one of Mr. MacIver's comrades."

Stein realized that he had been deliberately provoked into revealing more than he'd intended. "The spoils of war," said Stein. "That's what it was."

"No offence intended," said Breslow, with a humourless smile. "You can call it anything you want; it's quite all right with me."

Disarrayed by his exertions, Stein hitched up his trousers and tucked in his shirt with a practised gesture. "Were you in the war, Mr. Breslow?"

"I was too young," said Breslow regretfully. "I spent the war years in Canada working for my father."

"Breslow," said Stein. "That name comes from Breslau, the German town, right? Were your folks German?"

"What do I know about towns in Germany!" said Breslow in a sudden burst of irritation. "I am a U.S. citizen. I live here in California. I pay my taxes and stand at attention when they play the national anthem. . . . What do I have to do? Change my name to Washington, D.C.?"

"That's a good joke," said Stein, as if admiring an expensive watch. He took the Coca-Cola can and shook the last few drops into his glass before draining it.

"You'll get your money, Mr. Stein," said Breslow. "Providing, of course, that you furnish the necessary agreement signed by Mr. MacIver. We'll not wait for probate, if that's what's worrying you." Breslow sipped a little of his cognac. "There is a lot of money available to buy the documents Mr. MacIver spoke of."

"What documents?"

"Secret documents . . . about Hitler. Surely you've heard of them."

"I might have heard rumours," admitted Stein.

"A great deal of money," said Breslow.

"And the job for my son?"

Breslow looked again at the biographical résumé that Stein had put on his desk. "Well, he has no experience in movie making, and of course no labour-union membership." He pursed his lips. "Still, it might be possible to make a place for him. Especially if he's inherited his father's forcefulness."

Breslow tucked the résumé under the leather corner of his large blotting pad. Then he took the Coke tin and the glasses, wiped away a few spilled drops and threw the paper napkins into the waste basket. It was a fussy gesture and Stein watched him with contempt. "I'll get my secretary to fix an appointment for me to meet your son," said Breslow. He smiled and moved towards the door. Stein did not move. "Unless you have any questions . . ." said Breslow to spur his departure.

"One question, Mr. Breslow," said Stein. "Why are you carrying a gun?"

"Me?"

"Don't kid around with me, Breslow. It's in a holster in your belt. I saw it just now."

"Oh, the tiny pistol."

"Yeah, the tiny pistol. What's a nice respectable movie producer like you doing with a Saturday night special in your waistband?"

"Sometimes," said Breslow, "I have to carry a lot of cash."

"I knew there had to be a reason," said Stein. He reached for the broad-brimmed, floppy hat and plonked it on his head.

Max Breslow watched the street through the slatted blind. He saw Charles Stein go to the Buick Riviera with the vinyl top which he'd left in the empty dirt lot behind the liquor store, and waited until he saw the car bump its way over the pavement edge and join the eastbound traffic. Only then did Breslow unlock and go through a door into the adjoining room.

It was as bleak and impersonal as its neighbour: plastic woven to look like carpet, plastic coloured to look like metal, and plastic veneered with wafers of richly coloured woods.

Sitting at a side table, in front of a small sophisticated cassette recorder and a pair of discarded headphones, a broad-shouldered man was waiting patiently. Willi Kleiber had close-cropped hair and a blunt moustache of the sort that British army officers used to favour, but no one would have mistaken Willi Kleiber for such. He had the wide head and high cheekbones that are so often the characteristics of Germanic people from the far side of the River Vistula. His nose was large, like the cutting edge of a broken hatchet, and his body was heavy and, in spite of his age, muscular. He had taken off his khaki golfing jacket and loosened his tie. His legs were stretched out so that his shiny, black high boots could be seen below his trousers.

"What do you think, Willi?" Max Breslow asked him.

Willi Kleiber pulled a face. "You did all right, Max," he said grudgingly.

"What will happen next?"

Kleiber held the headphones together and wound the wires round them carefully as he considered his reply. "We've got rid of Lustig. You've let Stein know we can pay a lot of money for the documents, and soon he will discover that he's lost a great deal of money. Then he will come back to us."

"How did you get Stein's money?"

"Not me; the Trust. When you have the active assistance of some of the most successful bankers in Germany, such swindles are easy to arrange."

"What did you mean . . . 'We've got rid of Lustig'? You said you'd given him money for a vacation in Europe."

Kleiber grinned. "You leave that side of things to me, Max. Don't give Bernard Lustig another thought; the less you know about him, the better." He zipped up the front of his jacket to make a sudden noise.

"I wish I'd never got into this," said Breslow. He could not muster the enthusiasm and energy that Kleiber brought to these crazy adventures, and wished he'd been able to stay out of this madness. Listening to Kleiber talking of such antics over coffee and cognac was amusing; but now he was involved, and he was frightened.

"The Trust needed you," said Kleiber.

Breslow looked at him and nodded. Kleiber was simplistic, if not to say simple. Orders were orders and obeying them was an honoured role. Breslow had not changed since the nineteen forties, when he was a young man. All that wonderful idealism, and the sense of purpose that is known only to the young, all squandered to the whims of Hitler and his fellow gangsters. What a tragic waste.

"You were a Nazi, Max. Don't ever forget it. And don't count on anyone else forgetting it."

"That was a lifetime ago, Willi," said Breslow wearily.

Kleiber closed the lid of the tape recorder with a sound that was intentionally loud. "Remember last year, when the old woman recognized you in that coffee shop in Boston? She shouted 'SS murderer' at you, didn't she. She won't forget, Max. You need the Trust. They're not Nazis either, Max, but they will help."

"That old woman in the coffee shop was mad," said Breslow.

"You left your breakfast and rushed into the street, Max. You told me so yourself."

Billy Stein was waiting in the shiny new Buick Riviera parked alongside the liquor store. He leaned across the passenger seat to open the door for his father, and had the engine started by the time his father climbed into the car. The warning buzzer sounded. "Can't you do something about that buzzer? I hate these darned seat belts." Finally Stein senior got the safety belt round his enormous frame. "Let's go," he said. He moved a canvas overnight bag onto the back seat.

The car bumped out of the car park and into the traffic. "Not exactly like Metro, is it? I guess he works out of that apartment to evade the city business tax." They drove past the liquor store with rusty bars on the windows and a new wire cage on the doors. "Melrose sounds like a good enough address for a movie company," said Billy, "until you see which end of it they're located."

"Right," said his father. Charles Stein opened the

glove compartment and found some cigars. He ripped the metal cap off one of them, and used the dashboard lighter to get it going. He puffed on it energetically before he spoke. "Seems like our Mr. Bernie Lustig is not around anymore." He worked his lips to get a fragment of tobacco leaf out of his mouth. "Seems like he's gone to Europe for an unspecified duration."

"So who did you talk with?"

"A gent who calls himself Max Breslow."

"German?"

"Canadian," said Stein sarcastically. "It must be one of those Red Indian names."

"You don't like him?" said Billy.

"He's a Nazi, Billy. I can always recognize them."

Billy nodded. He was used to such pronouncements about anyone with a German name who was not immediately identifiable as Jewish. "He says he was too young to be in the war."

"But you don't believe him?"

"He's got very black hair," said Stein. "And when a guy's hair suddenly goes black overnight, he's old."

Billy Stein laughed and his father chuckled too.

"And he has a gun," added Charles Stein, realizing that his verdict on Max Breslow was not carrying much weight with his son.

"Half the people I know in this town have a gun," said Billy. He shrugged. "At home we've got that damned great souvenir gun you brought home from the war."

"But I don't go around with it stuck in my waistband," said Stein. Billy smiled. It would be hard to imagine such a large piece of ordnance anywhere but on the wall of Charles Stein's study.

"So you want to go straight to the airport?"

"With just one stop at Jim Sampson's law office. La Cienega, in the big Savings and Loan Building—he's expecting me. Then take me to the airport. We'll go south to La Tijera. It's a fast way. Right?"

If Billy had hoped that the meeting with his old army friend Jim Sampson would get his father into a better state of mind, his hopes were dashed by the sight of Charles Stein emerging from the Savings and

Loan Building on La Cienega. His father slumped into the passenger seat. "The airport." He searched in the glove compartment and found an airline timetable. "I knew I would have to go to Switzerland, Billy. I'm going to have to go right now."

"I don't like to see you worried, Dad. Is there anything I can do?"

"There's a direct flight. . . . I don't like what's going on here, Billy. Colonel Pitman is going to have to hear about it, and I never like putting this kind of thing in writing." He pulled his nose. "And it's risky talking on the phone these days."

"It will be good for you," said Billy. "A change of scene."

While Billy picked his way through the heavy airport traffic his father made sure that he had enough cash and his credit cards for the trip. At last his son swung the car into the parking lot with an arrogant skill he had developed as a car park attendant during his college days.

"Looking forward to seeing the colonel again? You like him, I know. Stay through the weekend, Dad. Have a good time."

"I always get a real kick out of seeing him," said Stein. "He's an old man. He's running out of time, you know. A great man, Billy. Make no mistake about that." He puffed on the cigar.

Billy switched off the engine and looked at his watch to see how long there was before his father's plane departed. "Say, Dad, if this colonel of yours was such a gung-ho hero, how come that when he got out of West Point they didn't send him to the Rangers, or the Airborne, or the Green Berets or something?" He flinched as he recognized a sudden anger in his father's face. But his attempt to modify this implied criticism only made matters worse. "What I mean is, Dad, why did the colonel end up running some little quartermaster trucking battalion?"

Charles Stein took his son's arm in a grip that caused him pain. "Don't ever let me hear you say anything like that again. Not ever. Do you understand?" Stein spoke in a soft and carefully measured voice. "Do you think you'd have had your fancy

Princeton education and your T-bird and your Cessna and your yacht if it wasn't for the colonel and what we risked our necks for back in 1945?"

"Jesus, Dad. I'm sorry. I didn't mean anything."

In a moment the anger had passed. "It's time I told you all about it, Billy. I'm not getting any younger and the colonel has been a lot on my mind lately. Last night I dreamed about the night we stole those trucks." And Stein told his son about the fateful night when he went to the colonel suggesting the ways in which the paper work could be fixed so that the trucks carrying the bullion and treasures would be documented as if they were taking rations to an artillery company right near the Swiss border. Billy listened with amazement.

"Was it your idea, Dad? You never told me that."

"I never told you half of it, Billy. Maybe I should have told you a long time ago. Yes, Colonel Pitman was in town when our secret orders arrived from Third Army. Pitman was a major then, I was the orderly room corporal. A motorcycle messenger brought an envelope marked with the rubber stamp of Army HQ and plastered with SECRET marks. The guy on the motorbike wanted his receipt signed by Pitman. I couldn't tell him that Pitman was in town with a bottle of scotch I'd got for him and planning to screw a young fraulein he'd met that morning in the mayor's office. It was war-time. The battalion was on alert and ready to move. For being off base and fraternizing with a German civilian he would have been court-martialled."

"You forged his signature?"

"That's what orderly room corporals are for."

"You saved his career, Dad."

"And he saved my ass a few times too, Billy. We made a good team."

"And what were those secret orders?"

Stein laughed. "Secret orders from Army HQ. The war in Europe was in its final few hours. I was convinced it contained orders shipping us stateside and I wanted to be the first one to know." He leaned closer to his son. "I figured I might be able to get a couple of bets on before the official announcement was made." He laughed again. "So I was mighty disappointed when I read we were to supply transport for an escort detail. Just a milk run from Merkers to Frankfurt, I remember thinking at the time. Little did I realize that I was holding in my hand a piece of paper that would net me several million dollars."

The two men sat silent in the car for several minutes, then Stein said, "Just look at the time. We'd better get moving or I'll miss the flight to Geneva and find myself changing planes in Paris or London or something."

"Take care of yourself, Dad."

"You bet your ass I will, Billy," said Charles Stein.

It was Friday, May 25, 1979.

# 7

On that same Friday in London, Boyd Stuart and Jennifer had lunch at Les Arcades, a small brasserie in Belgravia. There was an auction at Sotheby's across the street and the tables were crowded. Jennifer Ryden—as she now preferred to be known—wore a pale fur coat. Her eyes were bright, her lipstick perfect and her skin glowing with health. She was the same bright, beautiful girl that Boyd Stuart had fallen so madly in love with, but now he could see her with clearer vision.

"Daddy has been quite wonderful!"

"Sending me to California, you mean?"

"Isn't that supposed to be secret?" she said. There was no mistaking the rebuke. She stabbed a small section of dry lettuce and put it into her tiny mouth. She never ate food that might dribble down her chin or drip onto her clothes. That was how she always managed to look so groomed and clean.

"I have no secrets from you, Jennifer," said Boyd Stuart.

She looked up from her plate and smiled to acknowledge that her ex-husband had won the exchange. "You haven't come across that inlaid snuff box, I suppose?"

"I'm sure it's not in the flat, Jenny."

"Nor the gold watch?"

"No," said Stuart.

"It's inscribed 'to Elliot' . . . an old watch, a gold hunter."

"You've asked me a dozen times, Jenny. I've searched high and low for it." In response to Stuart's signal the waiter served coffee.

"I've brought a list," she said. She reached into her Hermès bag for a small leather pad and gold pencil. He had always dreaded those little lists which she presented to him. There were shopping lists and reading lists, appointment lists and, only too often, lists of jobs that others had to complete for her. "I found the photo of Mummy in the silver frame," she said, carefully deleting that from the list of possessions before passing it to him. "Jennifer Ryden" was engraved at the top of the sheet of watermarked paper and the handwriting was neat and orderly without errors. "It's the gold watch that is most important," she added. "That detective story book is from the London Library; if we can't find it, I shall simply have to pay them. . . . Did you look in the tiny drawer in the dressing table, the one that sticks?"

"I've told you, Jennifer, if you don't believe I'm capable of finding these odds and ends, you can look around yourself. You still have your key."

She gave a theatrical shiver. "Seeing all the furniture and things would bring all the horrors back to me."

"You've taken most of the furniture," said Boyd Stuart, "and the bedroom and the hall have been redecorated."

"It was Daddy's watch. He's so attached to it. I do wish you would have a proper look." She tipped her head to one side and gave him her most winsome smile.

"Are you meeting someone?"

She swung round to see out of the window. There was a spindly young fellow waiting outside. He looked like the sort of young man Jennifer had always had to carry parcels, hail taxis and hold umbrellas over her. His checked cap was pulled low over his eyebrows and he wore a regimental tie and a well-cut suit. He saw Jennifer getting to her feet and waved to her. She didn't wave back. "Now don't just *say* you'll look for them," she said, touching the sheet of paper, "and please arrange for someone to forward my mail."

"Jennifer darling," said Boyd Stuart, "divorcing you is going to make me the happiest man in the world."

"That's loutish," said Jennifer Ryden, using one of her favourite terms of disapproval.

"I am a lout," said Boyd Stuart. "I've always been a lout."

"Well, don't be a lout about Daddy's gold watch," she said.

"I'll search for it," said Boyd Stuart.

She looked at him as she drew the fur over her shoulders, and felt bound to offer an explanation. "It has sentimental value. Mummy and Daddy are furious with me for losing it."

"Jennifer, you didn't let yourself into the flat and force open that antique desk of mine, did you?"

"Boyd! How could you suggest such a thing?"

She glanced at herself in the mirror and touched her hair in a gesture which reminded Stuart of her father. She kissed him goodbye but, heedful of her lipstick, she did not allow their lips to touch. Boyd Stuart watched her as she walked out, saw the effect she had upon the eager young man awaiting her and recognized something of himself. He was still thinking of her when the waiter brought him the bill for lunch.

## 8

Geneva was cloudy and cool when the jumbo jet brought Stein there on the afternoon of Saturday, May 26, 1979. Erich Loden, Colonel Pitman's chauffeur, had been permitted to go through the customs and the underground tunnel to wait for Stein at the gate.

"Your son phoned to say you were coming, Mr. Stein. The colonel was resting but I was sure he'd want me to come out and meet you as I usually do. . . . Two pieces of luggage, Mr. Stein?"

"Shiny aluminum," Stein handed him the baggage receipts. "I'll step across to change some money at the bank counter, Erich. I'll see you at the customs—green door. Where's the car?"

"Immediately outside—arrivals level."

Stein nodded. He laid ten hundred-dollar notes on the counter and received in return a disappointingly small number of Swiss francs. Stein liked large-denomination money—it simplified his calculations and kept his silk-lined, crocodile-leather wallet from bulging too much.

He followed the driver past the immigration desk and through the crush of people waiting outside the customs hall. There was the white Rolls-Royce, with Swiss registration plates, parked exactly outside the glass doors. The driver was holding the door for him.

"A new one, Erich?"

"We just had delivery, sir. The colonel has a new Rolls every five years. Always white, always the same tan upholstery, tinted windows, stereo hi-fi, FM radio and telephone. He still has the Jaguar, of course. He prefers that when he's driving himself." Stein tapped the roof before getting in. "When is he going to change over to a Mercedes, Erich?"

"The colonel would never buy a German car. You know that, Mr. Stein. He sent the colour TV back to the shop when he discovered that parts of it were manufactured in Germany."

Stein laughed. He liked Erich Loden, who had been the colonel's driver, servant and general factotum for over twenty years and remained devoted to him.

Stein got into the back seat of the Rolls and twiddled with the knobs of the radio, but reception was blocked by the steel-framed airport buildings. He pulled a cassette from the box and plugged it into the player. The music of Django Reinhardt filled the car. He turned the volume down.

The driver slid behind the wheel and started the engine. "Any calls downtown, Mr. Stein? You want me to go past the cake shop?"

"Well," said Stein as if considering the suggestion

for the first time, "why don't I just stop by for a cup of coffee at Madame Mauring's."

"Yes, sir," said the driver. It was a joke that both men understood. Stein rarely took the trip from the airport to Colonel Pitman's house without stopping at the well-known Mauring's Tea Room & Confiserie near the cathedral.

The decision made, Stein leant back and watched the world go by. The modern factories gave way to expensive apartment blocks and tidy lawns, then came the shopping streets, displays of carefully arranged cheeses and sausages, and the scaly glitter of wrist-watches, swimming through the windows in endless shoals.

Madame Mauring was an elderly woman with tight, permanently waved grey hair and a ruddy complexion. She made many of the cream cakes herself, as well as some marzipan slices of which Stein was especially fond.

"I've brought you a present," said Stein, producing from his flight bag some perfume he had bought on the plane. "For my favourite girlfriend. 'Infini.' "

"You are a nice man, Mr. Stein," she said and gave him a swift decorous peck on the cheek. Stein smiled with pleasure. "And now I bring for you the new almond cake. It's still warm but never mind, I will cut it." This was a considerable concession. Madame Mauring did not approve of any of her creations being sliced before they were quite cold.

Stein sat down in the little tea room and looked round the bright wallpaper and the old-fashioned cast-iron tables with something of a personal pride. Charles Stein had financed Madame Mauring's little business venture after tasting the cakes she supplied to a large restaurant on the Rue du Rhône. That was eighteen years ago, and last year he had allowed Madame Mauring to buy him out.

"Next year, or the year after, I am giving the tea room to my daughter. Her husband works at a good restaurant in Zurich. They will both come back here to live."

"That will be nice for you, Madame Mauring. But

I can't imagine this place without you. What about all your regular customers?"

"I will keep my apartment upstairs," she said. "And your room, too—that will be untouched."

"Thank you, Madame Mauring. This is where we began, you know."

"Yes," she said. She had heard many times the story of how the Americans had started their merchant bank in these rooms above a jewellery shop in the narrow street which wound uphill to the cathedral. Prosperous trading in the immediate post-war period had enabled them to move the bank to more appropriate premises facing the lake on the Quai des Bergues. Every nook and cranny of this place brought back memories to Stein. He had been back and forth across the Atlantic frequently in those days, learning quickly how deals were made in Switzerland, giving the colonel courage enough to fight the competition and calming down irate clients when things went wrong. Madame Mauring had always insisted that one room upstairs was his but Stein had almost forgotten the last time he had used it.

"Take the rest of the almond cake with you," she said. "I have a box all ready." Stein did not resist the idea. He found it very reassuring to have some food with him, even in such a well-organized house as that of Colonel Pitman.

"She's a good woman," he told the driver as he settled back into the leather seat of the Rolls and brushed from his lips the last crumbs.

"The colonel never goes there now," said the driver. "He says that the cakes and coffee are not good for his digestion. The 'nut house' he calls it, did you know that?"

Stein grunted. The truth was that Colonel Pitman was not interested in food. One look at him would tell you that: thin, finickety and abstemious. Most of the West Point officers seemed to be the same. The colonel was always boasting of how he could still fit into his wartime uniform. It was not an achievement by which Stein set large store.

"There will be a traffic jam downtown. It's rush

hour and with the bottlenecks at the bridges there is just no way to avoid it."

The car was halted by traffic when the driver spoke again. "I wouldn't want to step out of line, Mr. Stein . . ." he began hesitantly.

"What is it?"

"I thought you should know that the colonel takes a rest every afternoon. That's why he didn't come out to the airport. You may not see him until you go down for drinks."

"How long has this been?"

"Some three weeks," said the driver. "The doctor brought a heart specialist from Lausanne and gave him a check-up last month. He told him he's got to slow down."

"I see."

"That didn't go over well with the colonel—you can probably imagine what he said—but he took the advice just the same."

"He's quite a man, the colonel," said Stein.

"You've known him a long time, Mr. Stein. It's just wonderful the way all you men from the same battalion kept up your friendships and put together enough money to finance a business together. It was some idea, Mr. Stein! A little private bank, here in Geneva. How did you think of it?"

"I don't know," said Stein. "One of the boys suggested it in fun, and then we considered it seriously."

Stein remembered that night when they realized how much gold they had stolen. There were all sorts of crackpot ideas about what to do with it. Burying it in the ground was the most popular suggestion, as he recalled. Only Stein came up with anything sophisticated: start a private bank. It was the one kind of business where the gross overprovision of capital would not be too conspicuous. Stein had little trouble getting the colonel to agree. Ever since that day when Lieutenant Pitman had arrived at battalion headquarters he had always looked to Stein for advice. But it was Colonel John Elroy Pitman the Third who had turned on enough charm to get a retired U.S. army general and an impoverished English knight to take seats on the bank's board. Thus equipped with names on the letterhead, the rest was relatively easy. The Swiss authorities had been very cooperative with British and U.S. nationals in those days: they'd even opened up Swiss banks to Anglo-American teams searching for Nazi loot.

"How long have you known the colonel, Mr. Stein? If you don't mind my asking."

"I first met the colonel in 1943," said Stein. "He was only a lieutenant in those days but he was the toughest son of a bitch in the regiment, I tell you. He took the regimental boxing championship in middleweight three times in a row. For a middleweight he was heavy, see. He was one hundred and fifty pounds and having trouble staying under the prescribed one hundred sixty, on account of all the drinking he was doing in the officers' club. Yes, quite a man."

"We never see any of his family over here," said the driver. He moved in his seat to see Charles Stein in the mirror and hesitated before saying, "It's a shame the colonel never got married. He loves children, you know. He should have had a family of his own."

"The battalion was his family," said Stein. "He loved those men, Erich. For some of those dogfaces he was the only father they ever knew. Don't get me wrong, now, there was nothing unnatural about it; the colonel just has a heart bigger than any man I ever knew."

The guitar music came to an end and Stein pushed the cassette back to repeat it. "How long since the colonel was stateside?" Stein said.

"Not since he got out of the army."

"That would be about 1948," said Stein. "It's a long time." He watched the scenery. The Alps loomed large above them by now, and lost in the mist and cloud there were the Juras on the far side of the lake. It was cold near the water without the sunshine. Such a place would not suit Charles Stein; he found the surrounding mountains oppressive and the inhabitants cold and formal. They were near to the French frontier here but there could be no mistaking the Swiss orderliness as they passed through villages where the dogs were securely chained and the logs sorted by size before being stacked outside the houses.

The Rolls turned in as soon as the gates swung open. The gravel crunched under the tyres and the Rolls moved slowly past the well-tended lawns and the summer house where Colonel Pitman sometimes took afternoon tea. The gravel drive ended in a circle round an ornate fountain. It provided an appropriate setting for the grand mansion that faced rolling lawns and shrubs as far as the trees that lined the lake shore. It was a sinister old place, thought Stein. The sort of large property that unscrupulous Geneva property salesmen are likely to say belonged once to Charlie Chaplin, Noël Coward or the ex-Shah of Iran. On the steps there was a servant in a green baize apron ready to help the driver with the guest's baggage.

The house was a cheerless assembly of turrets and towers, looking like a scaled-down version of some neo-Gothic town hall. Inside, Stein's footsteps clattered on the decorative stone. Even now, in late May, it was chilly. The furniture was massive—shiny red mahogany sideboards and tall, glass-fronted cupboards filled with forgotten crockery. Four suits of armour were guarding the hallway, only the shine of their metal distinguishable in the gloom. On the hall table, under a large bowl of fresh flowers, were the day's newspapers and some magazines and letters, all unopened and unexamined.

A servant showed Stein up to a bedroom on the first floor. Alongside a big mahogany bed with a cream silk *duvet* cover, there was an antique table with fresh fruit in a bowl and a coffee-table book on vintage cars. Over the bed hung a painting by some Dutch eighteenth-century artist: sepia sailing barges, sepia water, sepia sky. The servant opened the windows to reveal a wrought-iron balcony just large enough to permit the window shutters to fold back fully and provide a view of the garden and the lake colourless in the grey afternoon light.

"Would you like me to unpack now, sir?"

"No, I'm going to climb into a hot tub and get some of that travel dust out of my wrinkles."

"Very good, sir. You'll find everything you need, I

think." The servant opened the cabinet alongside the window. There were tumblers and wine glasses with some bottles of claret in a rack and an unopened bottle of Jack Daniel's bourbon.

"And in the ice box there'll be branch water," said Stein delightedly. "The colonel never forgets a thing."

"That's right, sir," said the servant. He paused respectfully and then said, "Dinner will be served at seven-thirty, sir. The colonel will have a drink in the study about seven. He would like you to join him there."

"I sure will," said Stein.

"The bell is by the door should you require tea or coffee or anything to eat." He always said the same thing, but Stein did not interrupt, knowing that he preferred it this way: he was Swiss.

"No, I'm just fine. I'll see the colonel at seven, in the study."

With a short bow, the servant departed. Stein opened the bottle of Jack Daniel's and poured some down the sink. He had long since lost his taste for bourbon, but there was no point in hurting anyone's feelings. After flushing some bottled water after it, Stein held the whisky to his nose. That sweet smell brought the memories flooding back upon him. He marvelled at the silence and stood for a moment or two in the sunless light, holding the whisky and looking out across the mauve rippling surface of the lake. From the hall below there came the soft chimes of the colonel's favourite clock. He remembered his mother quoting the old Polish proverb, "In a house of gold, the hours are lead."

There were other guests for dinner. Stein's arrival at such short notice made it impossible to change the arrangements. They were all casual acquaintances, people whom Pitman had met by way of business. A commodity broker from Paris on vacation with his wife and teenage daughter, and a French couple who owned a car-leasing agency in Zurich. The conversation was confined to polite banalities. So although Stein was able to outline the MacIver episode before the guests arrived, it was not until dinner was finished that Stein and Pitman were alone.

"You're looking well, Stein."

"You too, Colonel."

"What about a nightcap? Shall we see what we have in the cellar?"

It was always the same ritual. They went downstairs into the neatly arranged basement, passing the coal storage and the gleaming racks of logs to enter the long corridor where the wine was stored. "Claret or burgundy?" the colonel asked.

"The wine we drank at dinner was delicious."

"We might be able to do better than that," promised the colonel, searching carefully through the ranks of dusty bottles. "For an old army buddy we serve only the best."

Behind the wine there was a storage area where old suitcases were piled. There were some stags' heads and other hunting trophies there too, tusks and antlers grimy and cobwebbed. Stein remembered when they were the colonel's pride and joy, but some of the boys from the battalion had made jokes about them at a party back in the late sixties, and the colonel had changed his mind about them. Colonel Pitman set great store by the opinion of his men. Perhaps sometimes he overdid this tendency.

"Hermitage!" said the colonel. "You'll enjoy this one, I'm sure. It has the real flavour of the north Rhône and will make an interesting comparison with that Châteauneuf-du-Pape we had at dinner." The decision made, Pitman led the way upstairs to his study, negotiating the cellar steps with a care that made Stein concerned for him. "I get a little giddy sometimes," he explained.

"Let me take that bottle, Colonel."

Colonel Pitman held tight to the rail and picked his way up the steep steps. "I've never fallen," he explained, "but the light here is deceptive."

"All these wine cellars are the same," said Stein. "The steps wobble as you go out. You'll have to cut back on the Evian water, Colonel."

The colonel chuckled softly, appreciating Stein's attempt to relieve his embarrassment.

They went to Pitman's study. It was a small room, decorated like a businessman's office. There was an oak desk arranged between the windows, two comfortable leather armchairs with a battered foot rest and brass ashtray near them. The walls were filled with photos and certificates and souvenirs of the colonel's army days and his hunting expeditions. On the shelf near the door were some silver motor-racing trophies.

The light was better in here and Stein was shocked to see how much Colonel Pitman had changed since his last visit just a few short weeks ago. Age seemed to be shrinking him.

Pitman sat down and began to remove the cork from the wine bottle. "We're all getting older, Corporal, there's no denying that. I had some ghastly news the other day—you'd better prepare yourself for a shock. One of our number is gone."

"That's bad news, Colonel."

"Master Sergeant Vanelli. Can you believe it, a fine strong man like that?"

"Yes, sir, you told me about Vanelli," said Stein. In fact the colonel had told him on his last two visits to the house.

"Reach me two of those stem glasses from the case behind you. Yes, Vanelli left a wife and two daughters. The best senior NCO in the battalion, I would have said. Don't you agree?" He took a tissue and carefully wiped any trace of sediment from inside the neck of the bottle, then poured wine into the two glasses Stein had set up on the desk. "They got the usual cash settlement, of course. We sent it within fourteen days, as we always do. It came to a lot of money, but only because the U. S. dollar is not what it used to be in the old days. It's not so long ago that we were getting over four Swiss francs to a dollar; now I'm lucky to get one-seventy. You'd be appalled to hear what it's costing me to run this house. And, with a lot of money tied up in long-term U.S. fixed-interest investments, we've taken quite a beating over the last few years. I think I've shown you the figures, haven't I?"

"Yes, Colonel, you have. It was something no one

could have foreseen." Stein walked over to the window. The sky had cleared. It was a fine summer's night, still bright enough to keep a few birds fidgeting in the purple sky before settling down. Pitman came across to the window as if to discover what Stein was looking at. "No one could have foreseen what would happen to the money markets," said Stein.

Clumps of young beech trees and some willows made a pattern upon the oily-looking lake. It was just possible to see the movements of motorcar lights crawling along the road that skirted the far shore. It was Saturday evening and the road was busy. Colonel Pitman was holding two glasses of wine. "Taste that, Corporal," he said handing it to him.

"Thank you, Colonel," said Stein with a courtesy appropriate between master and man. In deference to both colonel and climate, Stein had changed into a sober, dark, woollen suit.

The two men drank and then Pitman said, "MacIver you say his name was?"

"Military police platoon. He was the lieutenant with them." So the colonel had been thinking about Stein's news all through dinner.

"I just can't seem to place him somehow," said Pitman. "And you went along to the film company and talked?"

"Like I told you, Colonel. They said that Lustig—the man MacIver had talked about—was away in Europe. I spoke with a guy who calls himself Max Breslow. He says he's probably going to make the film."

"What kind of man is he?"

"Not the kind of guy I'd want to share a seat with on a hang-glider. I have a feeling they know something. I have a feeling they're going to give us a lot of trouble."

"We already have a lot of trouble," said Pitman gravely. "I've been personally checking things at the bank, and we are facing a disaster."

"Disaster?"

"The bank is in trouble. We're in conflict with the Creditanstalt. Unless we can get them to change their attitude, it looks as if we stand to lose one hundred million dollars."

"One hundred million dollars." Stein smiled. "You're kidding, Colonel. Come on now."

"I wish I was kidding," said Pitman. "But I'm afraid we have been the victim of a monumental swindle."

"One hundred million dollars," said Stein breathlessly. So it was the colonel who had the most surprising news after all. Stein had put his drink down by now and his arms were thrashing about as he drowned in an ocean of dismay. "We've got a highly trained and highly paid Swiss and German banking staff downtown. How in hell could we be gypped out of one hundred million?"

"The Creditanstalt is the biggest bank in Austria and it's state-owned. They gave a man named Peter Friedman—and that's probably a fake name anyway—letters of credit for one hundred million dollars for ten big consignments of pharmaceuticals which were in the Zurich airport free zone. The documents say that Friedman was exporting these drugs from Holland to Yugoslavia, where the deal was to be handled by Interimpex, which is the Yugoslavian international trade corporation. Friedman can't transfer the Austrian bank's letters of credit—because they are not transferable—but he can't be prevented from getting money by assigning the benefit to someone."

"How did we get into the act?"

"Our bank gave Friedman the money, in exchange for that assignment of the benefits of the sale of the pharmaceuticals. A perfectly ordinary trading sequence; and it can be very profitable, as it has been in the past."

"OK, Colonel, never mind the commercial. What happened next?"

"Friedman vanished. We checked the cases in the Zurich airport free zone. . . ."

"Aspirin?"

"Not quite, but nowhere near as described in the shipping documents. Maybe worth two million dollars."

"Can't we still cash the letters of credit with Creditanstalt?"

"I wish we could, but letters of credit are not negotiable—so we can't handle it—and become void if any part of an import/export transaction is illegal, or even misdescribed. This was misdescribed: the cases contain the wrong drugs. And today we hear from the Yugoslavs that these pharmaceuticals are not even destined for Yugoslavia. Interimpex are only acting as agents in a deal for someone else."

"Shit!"

"We are the victims of a carefully planned swindle," said Pitman. "I'm not a banker—never have been, never will be—but I've learned a thing or two in over thirty years of watching those experts we employ to run our bank. One thing I'm sure about: old Mr. Krug is even more upset than you are. And the young cashiers are worrying in case word of it gets around and affects their careers in banking. It's not an inside job."

"Did they check it with you, Colonel? Before they paid out the money, did they check it with you? You're in the bank almost every day, Erich told me so."

"They check everything with me," said Pitman. "They all run in and out of my office clucking like old hens. I've even seen Krug holding banknotes up to the light, to check out the watermarks before cashing fifty dollars for a tourist. But this seemed like a gilt-edged investment . . . with no risk at all."

"What about references?"

"Friedman gave us wonderful references. My manager suspected that the drugs were not destined for Yugoslavia, because one hundred million dollars seemed far too much for a poor country like that to spend on one type of pharmaceutical. But that made it look better, rather than worse. Such things have happened before, and the bank has made a lot of money from such deals."

"Why didn't those crazy bastards check the references out?"

"Easy, Corporal. There's nothing to be gained by getting excited. My manager did exactly that. We got a glowing reference from one of the best banks in West Germany. It said Friedman had been doing business with them regularly over the last eight years and they gave him a first-class rating."

"I don't get it," said Stein.

"I've been on the phone to the president of that bank in person, a Dr. Böttger. He says that they have no record of such a letter ever having been sent. Furthermore, he says that it is their policy never to give such recommendations."

"And the letter. . . . No, don't tell me."

"It's missing from our files."

"Jesus!" Stein hit himself on the face in anger. "One hundred million dollars. Can we stand that kind of a loss? What happens now?"

"I've been reluctant to let news of our trouble leak out, but I'll have to turn to other banks to help us. We tried one of the big ones yesterday and they turned us down flat. But that's not significant. We'll ride out the storm, Corporal, I'm convinced of it."

"Why our bank? Are we the most stupid?"

"By no means. But we were suited to this kind of swindle. There's no doubt that the people concerned studied our methods carefully and maybe got someone inside to steal the reference from the files. But references are not normally guarded very carefully. A cleaner could have stolen it. There was no reason to think it would be something a thief would want. Furthermore, they knew enough about our banking methods to guess that we would say yes to the Peter Friedman deal. It was rather like deals we've made before and made money from. And they perhaps guessed that we'd finance it alone, rather than syndicating it with other banks."

"And who is this Dr. Böttger? What do we know about him?"

"He's the president of a very successful German bank," said Pitman.

"Shit," said Stein again, banging a hand on the chair in a purposeless display of energy.

"There is nothing we can do about it right now," said Pitman. "Better that we talk about the documents. You saw Lieutenant Sampson?"

"Yes," said Stein.

"A good young officer," said the colonel. "An excellent transport officer, always kept his paperwork in order, I remember."

"Well, he's not an officer and he's certainly not young anymore," said Stein. "I play poker with him every week. He's got a big law practice with offices in L.A., San Francisco and Santa Barbara. Two partners do nearly all the work nowadays. Jim Sampson is in semi-retirement."

"Time flies," said the colonel.

"OK," said Stein. "Well, I went to see him and told him that we've got people talking about making the Kaiseroda mine business into a movie."

"And he gave you a legal opinion?"

"He went bananas!" said Stein. "He sat down heavily and went a pale shade of white. But he kinda got used to the idea after a while. I pointed out to him that doing a movie about the Kaiseroda mine doesn't have to mean showing us stealing any trucks. Maybe they just want to do a story about the treasure."

"And if they *don't* just do a story about the treasure?"

"Sampson says that the MFA&A and the Allied Reparations Agency issued statements in 1945 that there was nothing missing. Jim Sampson says that, to prosecute us, the U.S. government would have to admit that they were lying through their teeth. He thinks it's unlikely."

"I can see why his partners put Jim into semi-retirement," said Colonel Pitman testily. "You didn't tell me he was senile. Doesn't he read the papers? Doesn't he know that all the world's governments tell lies all day every day, and show no sign of contrition even when they are caught out in such untruths?" Colonel Pitman reached for the wine bottle and poured more for both of them. "Goddamned idiot, Sampson. I knew he'd never make captain."

Stein tried to placate him. "Jim says it's unlikely the U.S. government will act. They'll just say they know nothing about it."

"Very cool, calm and collected, was he?" said Colonel Pitman sarcastically. "Do you remember Jim Sampson on the day I offered to cut him into our caper?"

"Lieutenant Sampson was in charge of the maintenance platoon," said Stein. "We had to have him with us so that he could verify to the military police that we'd got a mechanical failure and had to stay halted at the roadside while the rest of the convoy continued."

"Never mind the details," said Pitman. "Can you remember all that stuff Jimmy Sampson gave us about having a sick mother who would suffer hardship if he went to Leavenworth?" The colonel gave a cruel little laugh as he remembered the scene. He put down his drink and walked across the room to the humidor next to the drinks tray. He opened it with the key that released the pressure on the air-tight lid. "Want one?"

He didn't wait for an answer, nor did Stein reply. He had never been known to decline a good cigar, and certainly not one of the cigars that Colonel Pitman had delivered from Davidoff, the best cigar merchant in Geneva.

The colonel selected a large cigar with considerable care. "I'm not allowed cigars nowadays," he explained. "But I'll enjoy watching you smoke one." He cut the tip from it, presented it and lit it for Stein. "What are we going to do, Corporal?" he said at last.

"Losing one hundred million will wipe us out," said Stein.

"Word of it will get around," said Colonel Pitman. "Maybe the bank could sustain the loss, but lost confidence will make it very difficult for us to continue trading, unless we find someone who will buy us out. There are the government guarantees and so on. So far, I haven't taken advice about the legal implications because I don't want to go spreading the story all round town."

"Say two million dollars from the cases of drugs in Zurich airport free zone," said Stein. "What else have we got in fixed-interest stocks and gold and stuff that we could sell?"

"Maybe three-quarters of a million U.S. dollars," said the colonel sadly. "I've been all through our assets time and time again. We've taken a terrible beating with the decline in value of the U.S. dollar. We should have diversified much more. If I sold this house, maybe I could put another million into the pot."

"Forget it," said Stein. "None of the boys would want to put you on the street, or even in some lousy little apartment block downtown. By the time we'd shared it out, it wouldn't be so much. We all shared in the benefits and we all have to share in the losses." He rubbed his nose. "I guess this is the end of the bank."

"My fault," said Colonel Pitman. "I take a nice fat salary for looking after everyone's money. I can't go on living in luxury after letting you down."

"Then maybe we should sell the documents to Breslow, or to the highest bidder," said Stein.

"Let's not jump out of the frying pan into the fire," said Colonel Pitman. "At present we are only short of money—and, let's face it, none of the boys are paupers. If we put those old documents on the market, we might find ourselves facing fifteen years in Leavenworth. I'd want to get a lot of legal opinion before we let anyone know what we've got."

"Maybe you are right," said Stein.

"You read all that stuff years and years ago," said Colonel Pitman. "I can remember you sitting upstairs, buried under it all. What's in them?"

"All kinds of junk," said Stein evasively. "My dad spoke fluent German. He always wanted me to learn, but you know how kids are. I have difficulty reading it, and that stuff we have is all written in the sort of bureaucratic double-talk that make our own official documents just as baffling."

"I remember you showed me one lot of documents," said the colonel. "It was the minutes of the meeting. You were very excited by it at the time, you almost missed your lunch." The colonel grinned. "The pages were annotated and signed 'Paul Schmidt' in pencil. You told me that he was Hitler's interpreter."

"Schmidt was head of the secretariat and chief interpreter for Hitler and the Foreign Office in Berlin." He tasted the cigar, letting the smoke come gently through his nostrils. The last remaining shreds of light caught it, so that it glowed bright blue like some supernatural manifestation.

"I remember it," said Pitman. He was speaking as if the effort of conversation was almost too much for him. "FÜHRERKOPIE was rubber-stamped on each sheet. You said it was the minutes of some top-secret meeting."

"That's right," said Stein softly. Outside in the hall the old long-case clock struck midnight; the chimes went on interminably and sounded much louder than they did in the daytime. "What did you do with those documents?" said Colonel Pitman.

"It's better you don't know," said Stein in the edgy voice of Corporal Stein, the orderly room clerk who never got anything wrong.

"Perhaps it is," agreed Pitman. He went across to switch on extra lights, as if hoping that they would illuminate the conversation too. He looked at the Persian carpet that was hanging on the wall. It was a Shiraz—all that now remained of the treasures from the Kaiseroda mine. The carpet had been thrown from the truck when they first began to unload, a dirty stain on the canvas wrapping into which it had been sewn. The colonel still recalled the markings: ISLAMISCHES ABTEILUNG, part of the Prussian State Museum's treasures, put into the salt mine to keep them safe from Allied bombs and Red Army artillery. In the hysterical atmosphere of that night, Jerry Delaney, who had driven the first truck right behind the colonel's jeep, had shouted, "A present for the colonel," and the soldiers had cheered. They were good boys. Colonel Pitman felt a tear welling in his eye as he remembered them. Now he touched the surface of the carpet to feel the tiny knotted pile and the tassels. They were fine men; he had been proud to lead them.

"What must we do?" said Colonel Pitman.

"We'll have to know more about these film people, Colonel. They could be very dangerous, but"—he fluttered his hand—"but maybe they can be handled. Let's see what they're after."

Pitman turned to look at him and nodded.

"I'm going to take a few other documents back to California with me," said Stein. "I'll feed them some odds and ends to see how they react. Meanwhile you follow up this trouble we've got with the bank. Talk to the other banks, see if they'll support us. Maybe it's someone connected to this Breslow guy."

"You know best, Corporal, you always have done," said Pitman.

# 9

All cops who regularly ride the cars have an eating spot. Doughnut shops are a favoured choice. Such places always have good coffee ready to drink and, if a radio call comes in during the break, a doughnut can be snatched up and taken along. Also, doughnut shops are usually situated near busy intersections and have conveniently large parking places for their customers. All in all, a doughnut shop is a good place to start looking for a cop.

The cars outside the Big O Do-nut Shop, where the Santa Monica Freeway passes over La Brea, were parked nose to the wall, except for the "black-and-white." That was parked nose out, the way all police drivers leave their vehicles while taking a refreshment break. The two uniformed police officers could be seen inside the brightly lit windows. It was 11:34 p.m. on Saturday, June 2, when a local resident, an eighteen-year-old auto mechanic named William Dawson, went up to the table occupied by the police officers and said he wanted to report a crime. This public-spirited action was prompted by some difficulties Dawson was having at the time with the county Probation Department.

Dawson, whose interest in motor cars extended all the way from repairing them to stealing them and driving them while under the influence of drugs, had become curious about the presence on La Brea of a dented green Cadillac. It was a 1970 Fleetwood Eldorado, featuring the 8.2-litre engine—the biggest production car engine in the world. In his written statement, Dawson said that he was looking closely at the car with a view to finding its owner and purchasing it. He said he wanted to fit the engine into a hot rod he was building, although more than one officer in the detectives' room expressed the opinion that Dawson was about to steal the car.

Accompanying Dawson to the parked Cadillac, the two officers were shown blood marks on the road surface under the car. Forcing open the capacious luggage space, they discovered the bound body of a man. His age was difficult to determine, for his head had been removed from his torso and was not anywhere in the vicinity. The smell—which had first prompted Dawson to go to the police—was enough to indicate that the victim had been dead for a week or so. One of the police officers vomited. For his assistance to the police, Dawson was given a letter stating the facts for the Los Angeles County superior court, to which he was responsible for the probation order.

That the murderer, or murderers, had been interrupted or disturbed during the commission of the crime became apparent to the investigating officer within a few hours. It seemed likely that the criminal, or criminals, had intended to eliminate both the Cadillac and the corpse by running the car into the Pacific Ocean. The police computer revealed that the car was registered in the name of Bernard Lustig, who lived in a large house in Portuguese Bend in the Palos Verdes peninsula, a plush suburb known locally as "The Hill."

The door of the Lustig ranch-style home was opened by a Spanish-speaking maid when the detectives called the following morning, Sunday, June 3. Mr. Bernard Lustig was not at home. He had left the house at about nine o'clock in the evening, on Wednesday, May 23, together with two guests with whom he had sat drinking and talking for about an hour. The maid, whose comprehension of the English language was limited, thought that the three men had been talking about movies. That was, she explained, her employer's principal interest. In fact, she added, since his separation from his wife fourteen months earlier, movie making had been Mr. Lustig's only interest.

Detective Lieutenant Harry Ramirez looked the girl up and down. She was young and attractive.

"Could I see your papers?" said Ramirez. "Do you have a resident alien's card?"

"Everything is with my aunt at her house in San Diego," said the girl.

"California driving licence?" The girl shook her head. Ramirez changed to Spanish. "Half the inhabitants of Los Angeles County have left their papers with that aunt of yours in San Diego," he told her bitterly.

"I can get them," said the girl impassively. They both knew it was a game. The girl had come across the border without permission to work. But Ramirez knew that, even in the old days, illegal immigrants he had deported were back at work within seven days. Now, since Mexico had discovered oil, the U.S. immigration officials could seldom be persuaded even to start the paperwork. Ramirez snorted and called the girl a bad name. When he remembered the way in which his father had conscientiously gone through the process of getting his papers, so that Harry and his brothers and sisters could grow up as citizens, it made him angry that the authorities turned a blind eye to this generation of wet-backs.

"You share his bed," said Ramirez. "Don't tell me no, I say you share his bed—*puta!*"

The girl began to cry. Whether that was at the shame of being called a whore or at the prospect of being deported, no one could be sure, not even the girl.

"He's dead," shouted Ramirez. "They cut off his head and we still haven't found it. Maybe it's here."

The girl's eyes opened wide in terror.

"Now, tell me about the men," said Ramirez.

The girl nodded and sat down wearily. "It is true," she said sadly. "Once I go to bed with him. Just once. It was after his father died. He was crying. He was so sad—" Even with the girl's full cooperation the description of the two men was sketchy.

The first lucky break the homicide officers got on the Lustig killing was a direct result of the killers' haste. In order to prevent identification, they had removed the head and started to remove the hands. The forensic laboratory technicians stripped the lining from the luggage compartment of the Cadillac and discovered, down under the tank, a very thin gold calendar wristwatch. A fresh cut in the leather strap confirmed that it had been worn by the victim (and the watch was identified as Lustig's property by his housemaid). On the assumption that the dismemberment of the body would have taken place soon after the killing, the watch provided an indication of the probable time and date of the murder. The watch had stopped at 2:23 a.m. on May 24, following the visit the two men made to the house.

The second lucky break came several days later. Marilyn Meyer was one of the meter maids who patrolled the streets of downtown Los Angeles in specially built single-seat vehicles, from which they pounced to affix parking tickets upon cars parked in violation of local by-laws. Like so many pretty girls in Los Angeles, she had come to the city in search of a career in the movie industry and stayed to enjoy the climate.

It was this meter maid who remembered the black Porsche sports car parked outside Bernard Lustig's office on the afternoon of Wednesday, May 23, and again on the following morning. She remembered that the ticket she had affixed to the car the previous day was still in position and she added a new one. It was not a tow-away zone so she took no further action, but the Porsche parked carelessly on the pavement stayed in her mind. She noted the Illinois licence plates and regretted that out-of-state scoff-laws could get away with such traffic violations. She even told a friend that the city should find some way of collecting out-of-state fines.

Detective Ramirez passed a formal identification request to the traffic authorities in the state capital of Illinois, Springfield, where the computer revealed that the registered owner of a black Porsche 928 with that licence number was an Edward Parker. Further inquiries revealed that Edward Parker and his Japanese-born wife had lived in Chicago for nine years; previous to that he had lived for more than three years in Toronto, Canada, and before that he had resided overseas. These inquiries also extracted from the computer the triple-digit code that indicated that all police inquiries concerning Edward Parker must first be cleared with the Federal Bureau of Investigation (Identification Department) in Washington, D.C.

The bungled murder of Bernard Lustig, instead of resulting in a simple disappearance, had started a homicide investigation. In early June details of this became known to KGB's Moscow Centre. To what extent the reckless way in which Parker had risked becoming entangled in the investigation was also known to the Centre is unrevealed. Certainly by this time more than one meeting had taken place between officers of the First Directorate's Illegals Section, who directly controlled Edward Parker, and specialists of the Communications Division, who would, if the worst came to the worst, arrange his escape route and temporarily close down his most vital networks.

Subsequent to these meetings in Moscow, one of the KGB's most senior and experienced officers flew to Mexico City, where on Monday, June 11, there was a meeting at the Soviet embassy. This curious turreted building, looking like the sort of Gothic folly in which wealthy nineteenth-century industrialists installed their mistresses, crouches behind some tall, straggly trees and a high fence. It was a hot day and the unending traffic on the Calzada de Tacubaya could be heard through the double glass of the ambassador's private study, in spite of the noise of the air-conditioning. His Excellency was not present; he had been asked to vacate the room, since it was the one most recently tested for electronic devices.

The short notice at which Moscow had arranged this meeting in Mexico City is evidenced by the documents the Technical Operations Directorate—which provides KGB documentation, both real and forged—gave to Moscow Centre's representative. Described on his diplomatic passport as a consular clerk grade three, he was a KGB general.

He was a tall, grey-faced man, gaunt to the extent that the bones and ligaments of his face and hands were clearly discernible, like those of an anatomical model. General Stanislav Shumuk, a Ukrainian born in Kiev, was recognized by the American agents who photographed him entering the embassy in that day in June.

Shumuk had made his reputation in the late 1960s when, using a computer, he had compiled details of thousands of Canadian residents who had relatives living in Poland, the German Democratic Republic or the U.S.S.R. A large proportion of such people were Ukrainians. Systematically, Shumuk enrolled many such Canadians into the service of the KGB by threatening reprisals against their relatives. Described as a masterly operation in the KGB Secretariat's 1969 secret report to the Central Committee, it was used to justify the cost of the enormous computer which was provided for the KGB in April 1972. This was the largest computer—measured by information storage—in use in the U.S.S.R.

Stanislav Shumuk consulted the steel pocket-watch he kept in his waistcoat pocket. He was dressed in a grey-flannel suit, its Moscow-style tailoring baggy compared with Edward Parker's beautifully fitted, hand-stitched suit. Parker had arrived thirty minutes early for the meeting, having flown in the previous evening from a convention in Kingston, Jamaica.

Shumuk put his watch away. "What time was Grechko expected?"

"Downstairs they said he was booked on the Braniff non-stop flight that arrives at two o'clock."

"For a meeting arranged for two-thirty," said Shumuk, "I regard that as inconsiderate."

Parker nodded. He knew it was no use suggesting that they begin talking without Grechko. Shumuk had a reputation for keeping to the rule book.

It was Edward Parker's first sight of the renowned general, whose mouth was turned down in a permanent sneer and whose face registered disdain for everything from the fine old engraving of Karl Marx to the jungle of potted plants which filled the sundrenched windows. The only thing that won Shumuk's approval was the tiny cups of strong black coffee that the Mexican kitchen maid brought to them every fifteen minutes or so.

It was after three o'clock when Yuriy Grechko arrived. Anticipating the mood of his superior, he was agitated and nervous. Mounting the stairs two at a time was rash: Mexico City's altitude forbids such exertions and Grechko came into the room gasping and red-faced. When Parker shook hands with him he noted the damp palm that Grechko offered, and there was no doubt that Shumuk noted it too.

Stanislav Shumuk opened his briefcase and began to sort through his papers. The other two men watched him. There was only a few years' difference in age between Edward Parker and Shumuk but they represented two different generations. "Stash" Shumuk had been a combat soldier with the Soviet army—or the Red Army, as it was still called then. He was one of the young officers who had taken NKVD detachments forward during the first big German attack in the summer of 1941. They had had to stiffen Red Army resistance, and they had done it by means of the firing squad. Colonels, generals, even political commissars had fallen to his bullets during those grim days when the Germans advanced as far as Moscow's suburbs.

The reputation Shumuk's execution squads had gained for him then had done his career no harm. After the war he had applied the same single-minded determination to his studies at Moscow University before returning to become deputy chief of the Training Section and later to chair the First Main Directorate's Purchasing Committee for a year. Shumuk had changed very little from that tall, young NKVD lieutenant in the badgeless uniform, his shoulder bruised blue from rifle recoil and his face impassive. He had the same toneless voice in which he had read the death sentences, the same unseeing pale grey eyes, the same shaved skull, and the same trim waistline that came from a daily routine of strenuous exercises.

Shumuk looked up and studied his two colleagues. and there was no admiration in his gaze. He decided that they were mentally, morally and physically inferior to him. Yuriy Grechko, with his expensive Western clothes, curly hair and soft mouth, was decadent, if not depraved. He had been corrupted by Western living and the sheltered life of the diplomatic service, and he should never have been appointed to the vital position of legal resident in the U.S.A. He was too young, too inexperienced and too lacking in stamina. Shumuk decided to say so in the report. Edward Parker was little better: he had spent the years between 1941 and 1945 not in resisting the Fascist hordes but in guarding some remote Red Army supply depot from a Japanese invasion that never came. Now, while his wife and grown-up daughter worked as booking clerks for Aeroflot and struggled to make a living in one of the less salubrious suburbs of Sverdlovsk, Parker was sharing his bed with some Japanese woman and living in a vast house in Chicago. The woman was a long-term Party member, of course, and the whole arrangement had been approved if not instigated by Moscow Centre, but Shumuk was old-fashioned enough to find it distasteful.

He lit a cigarette. He was old-fashioned about cigarettes too; he preferred this coarse Makhora tobacco. Waving the smoke away impatiently with thin bony fingers, he noticed Edward Parker's nose twitch. He must have detected the aroma of the tobacco; did it remind him of his youth, as it did Shumuk?

Little wonder then that the meeting was bitter and recriminatory. Shumuk started by announcing that he had already decided to pull Parker out, and proposed giving him until the end of June to get his networks prepared for regrouping. Parker would report in person to Moscow Centre on Monday, July 2.

There was a moment's hushed silence before Yuriy Grechko attacked this plan. It was obvious to everyone present that there was little chance that Grechko would survive such a drastic reshuffle as would surely follow the change in illegal resident. The arguments continued for over two hours. Grechko and Shumuk had clashed before, in the Dzerzhinsky Square building, and this time the discussion degenerated into what was little more than a shouting match. It was Edward Parker who decided the matter. He explained that he had gone to Los Angeles simply because his agent needed him there. As resident, such a decision was rightfully his to take. Furthermore, he told them, he was using an agent who might refuse to work with any new resident that Moscow assigned to the job. It had taken him years to build relationships with some of his top men. It was pointless to discuss the advisability of having him back in Moscow unless the KGB was prepared to start building up what would be badly damaged networks.

It was a power-play of course. Shumuk knew that; so did Grechko. Grechko was sweating; Shumuk's grey face twitched as it used to when he was running his agents through the German lines in the last few months of the war, trying to make contact with the remnants of the Communist Party in Hungary and Czechoslovakia. Not many of those agents survived but the work had been done. Hungary and Czechoslovakia were now workers' democracies, their stability a tribute to the secret political police that Shumuk had helped install there. He was proud of that, as he was of the Order of Alexander Nevsky which his wartime contribution had earned for him.

The harsh words and shouting died suddenly; as if by common consent, the contest was finished. Grechko wrung his hands and Parker sat down in a heavy oak armchair which was placed in the window amongst the luxuriant plants.

It was all right for the other two, thought Parker. Shumuk was concerned only with the paperwork on his desk in Moscow, and as for Grechko, if it all went wrong, Grechko need fear little more than being declared PNG, persona non grata. Only Parker faced the prospect of twenty years in a federal penitentiary, the sort of sentence which would ensure that he died in prison.

"In the Ukraine," said Shumuk primly, "we have a saying: there are some nightmares from which the only escape is to awaken."

The other two men looked at him but did not reply. Their hostility was unmistakable. Shumuk said, "I'll grant you another month." He brandished his papers again. He had not referred to the papers from his case, noted Parker, never quoted them or read them. He used them simply to toy with; the Soviet Union was overprovided with men who liked shuffling official papers. "It's against my better judgement," added

Shumuk. "We'll leave it another month, but it's against my better judgement." He put the papers into his case and locked it using the combination lock. Then he glanced scornfully at the two men and went strutting from the room like a dowager duchess.

*"Apparatchik!"* said Grechko bitterly, although he was not a man much given to criticizing the bureaucratic tendencies of his superiors.

Parker, who had spent twelve years absorbing the mores and manners of North America, said, "He's a horse's ass, Grechko, and you know it."

Grechko smiled nervously. "Tell me about this man Kleiber in Los Angeles," he said hurriedly. "Is he reliable? Do you know anything about him? Will he continue to work with us?"

Parker shrugged, drank the dregs of his cold coffee and shrugged again.

Grechko waited for some further reaction but none came. The shrug could mean that Kleiber was reliable or that he was not. It could mean that Parker did not know, or that he did not intend to discuss the matter.

# 10

The job in California did not prove to be the sun-drenched poolside sinecure that Boyd Stuart's girlfriend Kitty had predicted. By that same Monday, June 11, he was sitting in a grimy office on Venice Boulevard in Los Angeles, talking to an earnest young Englishman.

This near to the freeway, the boulevard is a six-lane highway strung with overhead wires, littered with palms and generously provided with gas stations and religious meeting halls. The buildings are low and hastily finished. In June they are hot and the noise of the heavy traffic loud and unceasing.

The Secret Intelligence Service in London had made contact with Lustig Productions' new man, Max Breslow. They had found a young commercial attaché in the British embassy in Washington who had once had dealings with Breslow about a previous film production. Now he had been urgently sent to Los Angeles in order to bump "accidentally" into his old acquaintance in the Polo Lounge of the Beverly Hills Hotel.

Stuart's visitor was wearing a dark-blue flannel blazer with regimental buttons and a motoring-club badge on the pocket. His hair was long and straight and so was his nose. Even without the accent and the clothes, there would be no mistaking him for anything other than what Jennifer called "Eton and Harrods."

"There would in fact be considerable advantages if this fellow actually made the film in England," said the visitor. He looked round the dingy little office which the department had provided for this meeting. It was his first experience of Her Majesty's Secret Intelligence Service.

"Spare me all that sales talk," said Boyd Stuart wearily. "Just tell me about Max Breslow." From somewhere at the back of the building there came the sound of someone practising scales on an out-of-tune piano.

"Not just the government allowances that all films can get, but special tax deals can be arranged if he uses British crews and British studios."

This was the right man to send, noted Stuart approvingly. No one could doubt this lad's pitch was anything but sincere. He wondered how much they had confided in him before sending him. "How old is Breslow? What's he know about the film industry?"

"He's old enough to set up a film," said the young man with a smile. He poured himself some more tea from the teapot on the desk. "He's a businessman. He's put together a couple of small productions in New York using front money from Germany and then sold them to television on the strength of the rough assembly. He's got good contacts in Germany."

"Television?"

"Television here in America, but cut into a feature film for Europe and Asia. It's done quite a lot nowadays."

"Only two films?"

"Only two here but he's produced a dozen or more cheapies in Europe, mostly in German studios. He works with an executive producer who stays with the movie while Breslow goes after the money boys." He drank some tea and then said, "Breslow isn't an old-time movie mogul. He's not a Goldwyn or a Cohn. You won't meet any stars sipping champagne round his pool. He doesn't live in Beverly Hills or Bel Air. He has a modest little condominium somewhere out near Thousand Oaks on the way to Ventura and shares his pool with a few neighbours. No, Breslow is not a movie man. You only have to talk to him for five minutes to discover that. He couldn't distinguish a zoom lens from a Coke bottle, and he's perfectly willing to admit it." The young man stretched his feet out and propped his teacup and saucer on his chest. Doubtless it was a mannerism copied from some elderly tutor, a rich uncle or an ambassador, thought Stuart. "You can see if you agree. I've fixed an invitation to dinner for you chez Breslow tomorrow. He thinks you represent a firm with money to invest in films." The piano exercises paused for a mercifully long time, then started from the beginning once more.

"Breslow's in his fifties . . . a well-preserved sixty perhaps. I'm not trained for the cloak-and-dagger stuff." The visitor smiled but, getting no response to his smile, continued, "Quite tall, lots of hair, no sign of going grey. Good firm handshake, if that's anything to go by, and very friendly."

"Has anyone put him on the computer?"

The visitor drank his tea and looked at Stuart. In Washington they had hinted that he was going to meet one of the SIS's best agents but the young man found Boyd Stuart older, wearier and far less polished than he had expected. "Ah well," he said, "that's something I'm not supposed to know about, but I'd say it's rather unlikely."

"Why unlikely?"

"My briefing was rather circumspect, old chap, but I gathered that nothing is so far being communicated to our American friends. And we both know that anything that goes through the Bonn computer will be known in Washington within twenty-four hours."

Stuart nodded and concluded that his visitor was less idiotic than his manner would indicate. "Have some more tea," he said, "and tell me what else you got out of him."

"You brought this with you, I suppose," said the visitor, watching the tea being poured. "It's a damned funny thing, I buy the self-same brand of English tea in my supermarket in Washington and it never tastes the same."

"You think he's going to make the film?"

"He didn't seem to be in a great hurry."

"I heard he has a script."

"It's still not right, he says."

"Where is the front money coming from?"

"He says it's all his own." The visitor scratched his chin. "I think he's fronting for someone. I don't know what you're up to with this fellow but I'd advise caution."

"What do you mean?"

"That your Porsche outside?" It was a casual question. Too casual.

Stuart laughed. "What a hope! Back in London I spend most of my spare time on my back under a 1963 Aston Martin."

The young man came to life. "A DB4! You lucky dog. In Washington, I've picked up a Sunbeam Tiger fitted with an American V8 engine but one of the bearings is giving me trouble. It's all in pieces at the moment. . . . That's one of the reasons I cursed the orders that brought me here to the coast. You should see my garage—bits of the engine all over the place. If my wife goes in there and trips over one of those bowls in which I'm soaking the valves. . . ." He pulled a face to indicate the pain it would cause him. "Not yours, eh, that Porsche?"

"Which bloody Porsche?"

"I saw it at the airport when I arrived. It was parked in the hotel car park. Then yesterday I saw it cruising slowly down Sunset Boulevard when I was talking with our pal Breslow."

Boyd Stuart got up and walked to the window. "Where is it now?"

"In a lot across the road, alongside the Pioneer Chicken."

Stuart looked through the dark tinted glass which

was advertised as a way of cutting air-conditioning costs. It gave the office privacy from passersby. Across the street he could just see the back of a black Porsche tucked behind a Chevrolet pick-up. Sitting inside the Porsche was Willi Kleiber, and behind the wheel Rocky Paz, a local strong-arm man turned car dealer. But even had Stuart seen their faces it would have meant nothing to him; he had never met either of them. "A Porsche," he said doubtfully. "Not exactly inconspicuous, is it?"

"In this town it is. Look for yourself; the streets are full of them, especially black Porsches."

"In that case perhaps you're overreacting," said Stuart. "How can you be certain that this was the same car you saw? Did you get the licence?"

"It's an Illinois licence. And he's got a hand-operated spotlight mounted behind the windscreen slightly off centre—it's a 1978 Porsche 928. It's the same car all right."

"At the airport, you say?"

"When I got off the plane from Washington. It was a million to one that I should notice him, but I notice cars like that."

"Always the same man driving?"

"Couldn't see who was inside, I'm afraid. I thought it was one of your people, to tell you the truth."

"You've got the green Datsun at the kerb?"

"Hertz; from the airport."

"Give me three or four minutes to get my car ready to go. Then get in your Datsun and take a ride around Palos Verdes Drive. You know where I mean? Let's take a look at him. Would you do that for me?"

"You bet I would! Do you really mean it?"

"And keep going until we find a nice lonely stretch of road, without any filling stations or McDonald's. We'll shake an explanation out of him."

"Depend on me," said the young man, galvanized by new-found enthusiasm.

"And pull this door locked when you leave."

Boyd Stuart opened the door of the battered cupboard that held two brooms and some telephone directories and rattled around the wire coat-hangers to get his jacket. He put it on and said, "Wait a minute, though. Let's do it another way. Why don't you take my car? It's a white BMW with dark tinted glass."

"No rainbow-paint job or flashing light on top?" said the young man sarcastically.

"And I'll take your Datsun. OK?"

The visitor got the car keys from his pocket and gave them to him. "It's a rented car, remember. Don't bend it."

"Good," said Stuart, handing over the keys of his BMW. By this time Stuart had begun to have second thoughts about the chase but it was no longer socially possible to voice such thoughts.

"If you lose me, phone me at the apartment tonight." He looked at his watch. "Let's say about ten-thirty."

"I won't lose *you,*" said the visitor. "I've done enough rally driving to hang onto a Datsun with a BMW. But I can't guarantee to keep the Porsche in sight if he tumbles to what's going on."

The temperature touched 100° Fahrenheit in Los Angeles that day. The hot Santa Ana wind brought the sour smell of the desert and made the city unbearable. Overhead the sky was white and baleful. Stuart hurriedly fitted the keys into the Datsun and started it up. He watched the BMW come into view and glanced in the mirror in time to see the driver of the black Porsche toss the remains of his chicken into the trash bucket, together with a shower of fried potatoes and a dollop of coleslaw. The tinted window closed with a purr and the car shivered in a blue haze as the engine came to life with a deep roar. By the time Stuart had the Datsun moving, the Porsche came bumping its way out of the Pioneer Chicken parking lot. He followed both cars onto Venice Boulevard.

The San Diego Freeway traffic was thin and fast on the southbound side of the elevated highway. He matched his speed to the other cars and trucks, and found the black Porsche and his own BMW in the number one lane. He pulled ahead of them and positioned himself so that he could see them in the mirror. Then the Porsche accelerated suddenly and the youngster from the embassy gave chase. It was a foolish thing to do.

Somewhere in the complex crossover of the Marina Freeway intersection Stuart lost sight of the other two cars. One moment they were clearly visible behind a huge Vons delivery truck. Then the great articulated vehicle changed lanes to find the westbound loop that would bring it to the Marina del Rey. It closed out the rearward view like the curtains closing upon the last act of a play. As the truck passed across the mirror, the highway reappeared but this time empty. Damn! They'd left the freeway. It was about half a mile before the next exit sign appeared. It seemed like a hundred miles. Stuart slammed his car into the slow lane and roared down the ramp at Centinela Boulevard. One way the road dead-ends. Stuart swung down into the street and on to the pavement as he squeezed past an angry lady in a Buick to make an illegal U-turn at the lights, almost hitting the large sign which says such turns are forbidden here. He came back under the freeway, his engine roaring at its concrete confines. Only then did he realize that there was no entrance to the freeway here and he changed lanes to make a left turn. Coming through the amber he caused a panel truck to flash its lights as he narrowly missed hitting a motorcyclist. Stuart swore again. To get to the northbound side of the freeway he had to drive a block to find the next ramp.

This side of the freeway was crowded with commuters making an early start back to their families in the valley. Stuart weaved through the heavy traffic that now and again slowed to a crawl. There was no sign of the other two cars, and eventually he turned off the freeway and returned to the Marina del Rey. His department had arranged for him to live on the *Hare Krishna II,* a thirty-five-foot cabin cruiser moored near the California Yacht Club building and using the power, telephone and TV antenna hook-ups.

He put the air-conditioning to its coldest, took off all his clothes, poured himself a big malt whisky and drank some before stepping under the shower. It had been a frustrating day and he was continually hampered by having to work in a city with which he was only superficially acquainted and where he was almost totally devoid of the sort of contacts he needed.

He wrapped himself in a big bathrobe and looked at the time. It would be the middle of the night in England; he abandoned the idea of phoning Kitty. He switched on the television and went rapidly through some quiz games, "Bugs Bunny" and a black-and-white film about the French Revolution. He made himself a toasted ham sandwich, opened a tin of mixed nuts and settled down in front of a situation comedy. The boat moved lazily as a big ketch slid out from its mooring.

It was 9:30 when the telephone rang. A polite voice inquired if he was Mr. Boyd Stuart.

"Rampart Division, Los Angeles Police Department. Sergeant Hernandez. Traffic accident investigation."

"What's wrong?"

"You rent a white BMW from Citisenta Rentcar?"

"That's right? Where is it?"

"Right now it's being shovelled into the back of a dump truck, Mr. Stuart. When did you miss it?"

His mind raced ahead, trying to decide whether to confirm that his car had been stolen.

"Are you still there, Mr. Stuart?" the police sergeant asked.

"Was the thief hurt?"

"He sure was, sir. The gas tank exploded and made a fireball that scorched three lanes of the Harbor Freeway. Nothing left of him to identify, I'm afraid."

"No other car involved?"

"No sir. We figured it was stolen. The car rental company knows about the accident already—that's how we got your number—but you'll have to come down to the station tomorrow and do some paperwork with me. Ask for AI Follow-up. Would noon be OK?"

"I'll see you at noon, Sergeant Hernandez."

Stuart fetched the notebook from his jacket pocket. There was a phone number scribbled in the margin of the page of addresses. They had told him to use it only in an emergency. This was an emergency. He dialled the number and heard an answering machine telling him that Dr. Curtiss was not available at this time but, if the caller would leave a name and address and telephone number, he would call back. If the caller was in pain, the recorded voice added, an osteopath on emergency call would be sent immediately.

"I'm in pain," said Stuart and gave the South Pasadena address that London had told him to give in such a situation.

He sat with the lights off and the curtains drawn back. He could see the harbour lights reflected in the water and the dark outlines of countless boats. An osteopath was a good cover for a case officer, he thought. Not too difficult to get a licence, and it would account for him going anywhere at any time of day or night.

The osteopath arrived at midnight. Stuart heard him clatter down the gang plank. This was the man whom London had assigned to control him. Some agents in the field could operate for years and never meet their controller and Stuart studied him with interest. This man was a swarthy forty-year-old, with short hair and tired eyes which he rubbed sometimes with the back of his fist. He was wearing light-blue cotton trousers, an open-neck shirt and a dark-blue cashmere cardigan. He carried a black leather case which he put down just inside the front door.

"We'll close the curtains if you don't mind," said the man. He walked across the cabin and closed them without waiting for a reply.

"The pain . . ." said Stuart.

"Never mind all that crap that London told you to say," said the man. "Just pour me a scotch and water and tell me why I had to be dragged away from my chess game."

Stuart gave him the whisky and watched him pour a lot of water into it. Then the man switched on the TV and tuned it to the Japanese channel. "Sit close and talk softly," said the man.

"Didn't you check this boat for bugs?" said Stuart.

"Sure we did, but why take chances?" He sipped his drink. "Are you a chess player?"

"Not seriously," said Stuart.

"We play for money, and I was on a winning streak tonight. . . ." He pulled a face. "No matter, tell me the story."

Stuart went carefully through the whole business. At the end of it, the man did not react for a long time. He stared at the small screen of the TV set as if enjoying the Japanese singing contest. "Centinela Boulevard exit from the freeway," he said finally. "Just about the only one I can think of, in the whole city, where there's no entrance ramp on the other side."

"That's why I lost them," said Stuart.

"Could be they chose it for that very reason. It would be a good way to do it. Stick in the fast lane all the way to the changeover . . . cut suddenly across the lanes to the exit, and leave you ahead with no alternative but to take the Centinela ramp and find yourself in a tangle of street traffic. . . . Too bad you didn't get a better look at the man in the Porsche."

"It was a deliberate killing you mean?"

The case officer did not answer him. He said, "The accident investigation cops have a routine they call AI Follow-up. I don't want you getting tangled into it. You make sure you're Mr. Clean when this Sergeant Hernandez talks with you tomorrow."

"OK."

"Give me the keys of that kid's Datsun; I'll handle that. I'll give you another car and put the keys into your mailbox well before noon. Just forget you ever saw this British kid from the Washington embassy. Tell the cops you left your car in the marina car park with the key in the ignition. Plenty of people do that; the cops won't be arguing about it. No other keys on the ring, were there?" he said, suddenly anxious. The Japanese vocalists were becoming noisy.

"I'll switch that TV to some other station."

"Leave it," said the case officer. "Were there any other keys?"

"Just the hire-car keys."

"Are you sure?"

"Yes, I'm sure," said Stuart forcibly.

"Well, at least you did something right," said the case officer with a sigh. Stuart let it go. A man dragged away from a game he had been winning deserved some indulgence. "Go through with your dinner with Breslow tomorrow. Don't mention losing your car unless he brings it up. Play the innocent. Say the embassy guy phoned you to put you in touch."

"It could be Breslow had a hand in the killing," said Stuart, irritated by the man's casual manner.

"So you're not just a pretty face," said the case officer with mock admiration. He reached for his black leather medical case and opened it to reveal a thick wedge of documents and a cardboard box. He opened the box before giving it to Stuart. "I brought this for you," he said. It was a brand-new, blue-finish .38 revolver still in the special preservative wax-paper wrapping. "You know how to use it, I suppose?"

"Point it and pull the trigger?"

He shook his head and reached into his pocket for ammunition. "No. You have to load it first." He took the gun, broke it and spun the chamber. "You'll get the hang of it. I'm going back to my game." He got to his feet and swigged the remainder of his drink.

"Good luck," said Stuart.

The case officer smiled for the first time. "The same for you, feller," he said. "You realize that the guys who zapped that white BMW probably figured you were inside it?"

"I'm not just a pretty face," said Stuart.

"Don't buy a holster for that piece. Tuck it in your trousers. It's difficult to get rid of a holster in a hurry, and I might not be around to help you out."

"Can I switch off the Japanese singing now?" said Stuart.

"Can you manage that on your own?" said the case officer as he went back up the gangway.

Stuart remembered the keen young man with the dismantled sports car which would never be put together again, and only with some difficulty resisted the temptation to get very drunk. Involving an outsider in an operational role was considered an unpardonable sin; and this youngster had been "diplomatic." Stuart knew it would go into his personal file in letters of fire.

## 11

On the Ventura side of the county line, tucked between the mountains and the freeway, Westlake is a "planned community" landscaped tastefully round a man-made lake. It is replete with countless pools and Jacuzzis, tennis courts and stables, and there is a country club where, from the large picture windows of the restaurant, members fresh from the whirlpool baths can look across the tops of their cocktails and anticipate with satisfaction the completion of the second eighteen-hole golf course.

Max Breslow turned off the Ventura Freeway at the Westlake intersection. He turned into the shopping mall's huge parking lot, passed the realtors, Swensen's ice cream, Joe's Photo and the hairdressers. He noted his wife's yellow Chevette with the "Small is beautiful" bumper sticker outside the supermarket and parked his Mercedes 450 SEL outside Wally's Delicatessen.

"Good evening, Mr. Breslow," said the manager.

"Good evening, Wally," he replied, accepting the common fiction that the manager was the proprietor.

"Your order is just about ready to go. Can I fix you a drink while it's packed?"

"The usual, Wally."

"A bloody mary with all the fixings coming up, sir."

Max Breslow noted with approval that the manager must have had a cold can of tomato juice ready and waiting for him, for the drink arrived almost as soon as he had ordered it. He sipped it while the manager waited for his reaction.

"Excellent," said Breslow. The manager smiled and moved away to get the pickled herring and Westphalian ham which had been ordered by phone. Breslow realized that he had been manipulated into having a drink. The food was probably not even prepared yet, but he didn't mind that at all. He was always happy that men—and women too—should find him easy to manipulate, for in that way he was able to read their motives more easily and retain for himself the final control over any situation. That was the relationship he had contrived with Charles Stein. If that fat fellow thought that he was exploiting Max Breslow, well and good. Max would not wish to deprive Stein of that satisfaction. Even years later, long after this delicate business was settled, Max Breslow would allow Stein to brag and bluster about the Hitler Minutes, should he wish to do so. Max would be happy to go to his grave with his share of the secrets. But Kleiber was different. Breslow had the uncomfortable feeling that nowadays Kleiber had gained control.

"Hello, darling."

Max looked up and smiled. His wife had changed her hair style and he knew it was important that he comment upon it. "You look wonderful, my dear," he said. The Italian silk jacket and the matching skirt were cut in a design exported only to the U.S.A. Her afternoon at the beauty salon, the faint tint in her hair, the professionally applied rouge and eye shadow, the bright scarf at her neck, all provided her with that healthy outdoor look which made Californian women so attractive to him, and made her look so much younger than her true age.

And Marie-Louise had adapted to this part of the world with a zeal that still surprised her husband; she went to classes in Japanese flower arrangement and low-calorie Mexican cooking, and even played sitar music on the quadrophonic hi-fi. And yet, despite all her time in America, Marie-Louise had not been able to eliminate from her speech the traces of her Berlin upbringing. Max Breslow dismissed it from his mind and gave his wife a decorous kiss that did not smudge her make-up. She would, he thought resignedly, say "darlink" for the rest of his life, and for the rest of her own life too, probably.

"You haven't forgotten that we have visitors for dinner?" she reminded him.

"I haven't forgotten," he said. He had been thinking of this man Boyd Stuart while driving home through the canyon. Willi Kleiber, who knew much more about such things, guessed that Stuart must be an agent of the British Secret Intelligence Service. It would be an interesting evening, thought Breslow. Stuart's organization was one which Max Breslow held in high esteem.

Marie sat down beside her husband but would not have a drink. She was still trying to lose another five pounds. It was absurd that she should wait for him, since they would both have to go home in their separate cars, but she preferred to do so. The manager brought the ham and herring wrapped in heavy moistureproof paper bearing the name "Wally's Deli" and a card that said, "We are sorry you cannot join us but please call again soon—Wally."

Max toyed with the parcels. He was pleased that his wife had asked him to get these items. He had worried lest once again the meal was going to be vichyssoise followed by quenelles, purèed vegetables and a Bavarian cream. And his wife was not the only one obsessed with these new food-processing machines. Nearly every dinner party they went to nowadays served machine-mashed baby food. Max detested it.

"Will you write the name cards, Max darling? I always get the spellings wrong."

"And what line of business are you in, Mr. Stuart?"

Boyd Stuart was sitting next to his hostess but Max Breslow interrupted a conversation about the gasoline shortage to answer down the length of the table, "Mr. Stuart is considering putting some of his company's money into a film I'm making."

There was a silence and then Marie Breslow offered second helpings of her lemon mousse round the table. Max Breslow's response was a fixed smile of displeasure. Sometimes he wondered whether his wife enjoyed provoking him.

"Mr. Stein was actually *there,*" announced Max Breslow suddenly in the silence. He nodded to where Charles Stein was upending a large cut-glass bowl of mousse and scraping the last of it on to his plate.

"Actually where?" said the bearded man sitting opposite Stuart. He was a psychiatrist who lived—together with his wife, who taught the art of relaxing to

East Los Angeles delinquents—in a split-level town house almost next door to the Breslows.

"Merkers, Thuringia . . . a place in Germany. I'm making a film about it."

"Oh, that place," said the bearded man. "Would you think me rude if I poured myself a little more of that German wine? You must be the last people in Westlake holding out against the Californian whites."

Max Breslow smiled but made no comment.

Stuart said, "I'm interested to hear that you were at Merkers, Mr. Stein. Did you go into the mine itself?"

"The place where the treasure was found," explained Mrs. Breslow to the psychiatrist's wife.

"Can't say I did," said Stein. "More's the pity. I would have liked to get my hands on some of that stuff they found in there."

Charles Stein was too large for the delicate little dining chairs, too large in fact for the dining room with its frail antique dresser and tiny side tables. He sat with his belly resting against the table edge, having finished a large second portion of lemon mousse after emptying the final dregs of the cream jug on to it. Now he had turned his attention to the basket of dark breads and biscuits which accompanied the cheese platter. He selected a slice of pumpernickel and spread it with butter before biting a corner from it.

"Mr. Stein was a friend of the man who first wrote the story," explained Max Breslow. "He's going to be a wonderful help to the scriptwriter."

"Chuck," said Stein. "Everyone calls me Chuck." He rocked back on the rear legs of the antique dining-room chair. Mrs. Breslow watched in open-mouthed horror.

"You were there?" persisted Stuart.

"I was with a quartermaster trucking battalion," said Stein. Leaning forward with his knife poised, he chopped off a segment of Camembert cheese and popped it into his mouth. "Our people moved some of the stuff out of the mine." His words were distorted by the cheese in his mouth.

"Have you been able to contact many people who were there?" Stuart asked Max Breslow.

"There are not so many of them left," said Breslow.

"It's a long time ago and men have died, are sick, have forgotten or wish to forget."

"Is it so long?" said Stuart.

"Most of the soldiers involved were rear-echelon personnel," said Stein, struggling to cut through the rind of the Stilton. "The fighting troops were youngsters and in peak physical condition, but the average age of the men in the support units was much higher, and we got the physical rejects too."

"From what I heard," said Stuart, "there was not only gold in the mine. There were paintings, rare books and secret documents too."

Stein pushed the rest of the cheese and pumpernickel into his mouth so that he could reach forward with both hands to move the vase of carefully arranged flowers. Now Stuart had a clear view of the fat man. He had the sort of figure with which no tailor could cope. Already his white linen suit had become rumpled and creased, and there were gravy stains on his lapel.

"Rare books," said Stein. He nodded. "Rare German army material, secret government archives . . . Nazi stuff and personal documents concerning Hitler himself."

"How do you know?"

"I handled some of it and I saw the inventory sheets. I was an orderly room clerk. They used our mimeograph machine to duplicate the records. One of the sergeants—a man named Vanelli—made an extra copy and kept it as a souvenir."

"That sounds interesting," said Stuart. "Have you kept in touch with Vanelli?"

"I know where he is," said Stein looking Stuart straight in the eyes.

"I'd like to meet him," said Stuart.

"I doubt that it could be arranged."

"Enough film talk," said Mrs. Breslow bringing in a large pot of coffee. "Let's all sit on the soft seats, shall we?" Again she watched Stein tilt back on one of her fragile dining chairs.

"I'll tell you this," said Stein, not taking his eyes off Stuart, "there was stuff in that mine that would destroy Winston Churchill's reputation overnight." His voice was strident and seemed unnaturally loud in the small room.

The bearded psychiatrist turned so that his good ear, rather than his slightly deaf one, was towards Stein and cupped it so that he could hear better. "What was that about Winston Churchill?" he said with mild interest.

"Rumours, Charles. Rumours," Max Breslow told Stein with studied calm. He handed Stein a large glass and took the stopper from a brandy decanter. Stein watched while the brandy poured.

"Rumours perhaps," agreed Stein, slowly and grudgingly like a peevish child.

"Come and sit in the lounge," Max Breslow urged in a warm voice that expressed his pleasure at Stein's reply.

Everyone at the table got to their feet. The psychiatrist's wife was the first one into the large lounge that overlooked the man-made lake. At the dock of each house a small boat was tied, humming quietly as it recharged its batteries at the power line. No internal combustion engines were permitted to pollute the water. On the far side of the lake, the residents and guests of other houses gestured and reacted inside the yellowlit, plate-glass boxes, a dozen doll's house dramas reflected in the dark water.

The psychiatrist's wife spread her arms wide apart and whirled around fast enough to make her long Pucci silk dress float. "That was a divine meal, Marie-Louise." She was one of the very few people, apart from Max, who called her Marie-Louise. "Have you ever tasted such delicious poulet au champagne, Mr. Stein?"

"No," said Stein, "I never have."

"You are so kind," said Mrs. Breslow. To what extent her neighbour was trying to demonstrate her psychological skills she could not tell, but she was grateful for her help in smoothing over what could have become an embarrassing scene between Mr. Stein and the young Englishman. Mrs. Breslow began pouring the coffee into tiny Limoges cups. "Try some of the chocolates too," she urged Stein with that tone which diet breakers conspire. "Hand-coated brandy cherries from a tiny shop in Munich. Max used to buy them for me before we were married."

Stein popped one into his mouth, crushed it between his teeth, tasted the sweet alcohol filling and reached for another before he swallowed.

"Where do you buy them?"

"Max has his business partner bring them over from Munich," said Mrs. Breslow.

"He didn't tell me about his business partner in Munich," said Stein. He smiled at her. "But the chocolate-coated cherries are dandy, Mrs. Breslow. Really dandy." He lifted the lid of the box high above his head so that he had to twist his neck to read the label. "Yes, sir." He helped himself to another as he replaced the box on the table.

"You heard the story about them finding Hitler in São Paulo?" said Stein suddenly, his mouth filled with chocolate and cherry. Everyone turned to look at him. "They ask him to come back and run Germany. No, he says, he won't go. So they keep trying to persuade him. They bring in the public relations guys, and the ad agency men. They offer him money and anything he wants." Stein looked round to see if everyone was listening. They all were. "Hitler says he likes it in São Paulo. He's got his mortgage almost paid, and a grown-up son and a married daughter by a second wife. He don't want any part of going back to Germany. But finally he gives in. But before he goes back to be dictator of Germany again he insists on one thing . . . right!" Stein waved a finger in the air in imitation of Hitler, and hoarsely yelled, *"No more Mr. Nice Guy!"* Stein laughed to show it was the punch line of the joke.

Stuart had heard the joke before but still he laughed. Somehow Stein had managed to imbue this thin story with all the pathos of his Jewish soul. When he told this joke it was outrageous and funny. He laughed loudly and Stuart joined in. But no one else laughed.

"I got a million stories like that," said Stein.

The party broke up about eleven o'clock: the psychiatrist had an early patient and his wife had booked the tennis coach for 7:30 a.m. "Everybody wants him," she explained.

Boyd Stuart was getting up to go when he felt the heavy hand of Charles Stein on his shoulder. "Stay for another cup of coffee and a glass of something more," said Breslow. "We have some business to talk over, my dear," he explained to his wife.

"I shall only yawn or say something silly," she told Stuart. "If you'll excuse me, I'll go right to bed."

"Of course, Mrs. Breslow. Thank you for a wonderful meal, and a truly delightful evening."

"Switch the dishwasher on before you come to bed, darling," she told her husband.

Max Breslow gave his wife a perfunctory kiss before opening a door in the antique sideboard to get his best brandy. "Charles has something he wants to show us," he said over his shoulder. Stein went to the coat closet by the front door and came back straining under the weight of a rectangular carton. He undid the string with elaborate precision and drew out of the cardboard container a very old metal box. Such fire-resistant filing boxes had been used by the German army for documentation carried by regimental staffs or at battle-group level. This one was worn shiny at the corners but in the ancient green paintwork a six-figure letter-and-number combination and instructions about closing the fireproof lid could just be discerned. The traces of large letters which might have been BBO remained on the outside and there was a large shiny patch which looked as if something had been deliberately obliterated.

"Can you read German, Mr. Stuart?"

"Well enough," said Stuart. Breslow nodded and exchanged a significant glance with Stein. The British would not be so foolish as to send a man who could not read German fluently.

"Have you ever heard of Dr. Morell?" said Stein. "Dr. Theodor Morell?"

"Hitler's personal physician?"

"Good," said Stein as a school teacher might approve the unusually bright answer of a backward pupil. He began removing from the metal box cardboard covers containing varying numbers of documents.

"Not only Hitler's personal physician but a man upon whom Hitler totally depended, who went everywhere with him and had even more influence on him than Martin Bormann. Hitler told everyone that Dr. Morell had saved his life over and over again." Stein tapped the pile of papers. "These are Dr. Morell's medical files on his patient Adolf Hitler!"

Boyd Stuart picked up the top folder. The papers smelt musty and stale. They were not in chronological order. This file was dated January 1943. At the top corner someone, perhaps Morell himself, had scribbled in pencil, "The great disaster at Stalingrad." There was a log of medical prescriptions and injections, beginning with anti-depressants and sedatives. There is a note about the first use of prostacrinum—manufactured from seminal vesicles and prostate glands—and an extra page, added at some later date, said that from this time onward the patient was given this drug every other day until the end of his life. There was a carbon copy of a long letter from Dr. Morell to Hitler's tailor, explaining that the Führer could not any longer endure bright light. Notes and a drawing, fixed to the page by means of a paperclip which had rusted and eaten deep into the paper, showed how the peaks of the Führer's caps must henceforward be made larger.

Stein watched Boyd Stuart's face as he flipped quickly through the medical file. "You find it interesting, eh?" Nervously Stein reached for another of the chocolate-coated, brandied cherries and popped it into his mouth.

"Where does it all start?" said Stuart, turning the heavy dossiers over on the low coffee table at which the three men sat.

"Here," said Max Breslow. He moved coffee cups and an ashtray to make more space. "But Hitler only comes in at the end of it."

The file he had selected was a slimmer one, and quite different from the Chancellery file covers. Once red in colour, it was now faded to pink. It bore Dr. Morell's name and fashionable Berlin address on the cover in elegant script printing. The contents too were different: heavyweight stationery with engraved head-ings. Even the file cards were printed with Morell's name and Kurfürstendamm address, although some of the patients were indicated only by initials. It was a precaution particularly important in a medical practice that specialized in treating venereal diseases and catered to some of Germany's most wealthy and famous personalities. Here were Berlin's nobility and industrialists and stars of the Berlin stage, film and theatre.

"Hoffmann," said Stein, pointing to a sheet. "Hitler's personal photographer and a close friend." He picked up an ancient manila envelope and took from it a desk diary. It had been used as a physician's appointments book. It was dated 1936. "This is how Dr. Morell first met Hitler," Stein said. "Hoffmann was sick—H.H. are Hoffmann's initials, M.F. is *'Mein Führer'*—look at that!"

Morell had written, "Met M.F. at Hoffmann's home, Munich." Then a page or so later, "M.F. provided his personal aircraft for professional visit to H.H. in his Munich home."

Again Stein turned a page of the diary. "Now we come to Morell's first professional opinion of Hitler," he said. He turned the diary so that Stuart could read it more easily. "Saw M.F. First impression of him shocking. Complains of headaches, stomach pains. Also ringing in the ears. Neurotic."

Max Breslow went into the kitchen to make more coffee. Boyd Stuart turned the sheets to find Dr. Morell's first physical examination of Hitler. The report was dated January 3, 1937, and the medical took place at the Berghof, Hitler's mountain retreat near Berchtesgaden. The doctor noted that, according to the patient, he had not submitted himself to a physical examination since he left the army in 1918. The record showed that Hitler—now referred to as "patient A"—weighed 67.04 kilos and stood 175.26 cm tall. Blood group A. The examination showed no abnormalities: pupillary reflexes were normal, good coordination, normal sensitivity to heat and cold and to sharp and blunt touch. His hair was dark and thinning slightly, and his tonsils had been removed when he was a child. A scarred leg was the result of shrapnel during the First World War. A badly mended fracture of the left shoulder blade—resulting from a fall when the police fired upon the Nazis during the 1923 putsch—had left patient A with a stiff shoulder so that he could neither rotate nor abduct his upper arm.

Curious, thought Stuart, that, had his right shoulder been affected instead, there could have been no Nazi salute. He turned the page.

The patient complained of severe stomach cramps and Morell found a swelling at the place where the stomach joins the duodenum, as well as at the left lobe of the liver. When he touched the region of the kidney, the patient complained of slight pain. Patient A was also suffering from severe eczema on the left leg and was having difficulty wearing high boots. "Necessary for parades and rallies," Morell had noted in fountain-pen ink which had faded to a very pale shake of blue.

Now the file was given over to letters concerning Hitler's diet. His other physicians—Professor Bergmann of the Charité Hospital, Berlin, and Himmler's SS medical officer in chief, Ernst Grawitz—had cut patient A's eating down to dry wholemeal bread and herbal tea, while treating him with lotions and ointments. Morell changed this to a more varied vegetarian regime.

The next letter was on the headed notepaper of the Bacteriological Research Institute at Freiburg and was signed by Professor A. Nissle, its director. It reported dysbacterial flora in the specimen of excreta sent there by Morell, who had not named the patient. Nissle advised that the patient should be given "Mutaflor" to replace coli bacilli. Morell adds a note about a preparation of vitamins, heart and liver for the patient. To be put into unmarked containers. "Vegetarian patient," Morell wrote on his instructions to the pharmacist. "Make no mention of the animal origins of this prescription." All Morell's notes at this time were on notepaper of the Berghof. Clearly Morell had taken up residence there.

"Can't tear you away from it, can we?" said Stein. He chuckled with satisfaction.

"I want to know the end of the story," said Stuart.

"Did the handsome young doctor cure his famous patient? I'm a sucker for the nurse romance."

"Dr. Morell was fat and ugly," said Max Breslow. "Hitler said that if Morell could cure his eczema and make him better within a year, he'd be given a fine house."

"What happened?"

Breslow said, "Morell pumped Hitler full of a medicine he'd invented himself. 'Vitamultin' he called it: every kind of vitamin together with calcium, ascorbic acid and caffeine and so on . . . you'll find the formula in his papers there. He marketed some of his compounds later, and made a fortune, they say."

"And Hitler got better?"

"Dextrose and hormones and lots of sulphonamide drugs kept Hitler feeling very well. For years he didn't even have a virus infection. Whenever he was going to make a speech, Morell gave him an extra dose of glucose and stuff to pep him up. Hitler was pleased. You'll find the carbon of a letter that Morell sent to say thank you for the house on the island of Schwanenwerder. Hitler kept his promise."

"And this documentation continues right through the war?" said Stuart. "It's priceless stuff."

"Hitler seldom let Morell out of his sight. And Hitler confided in this man. From time to time the stomach cramps returned. Morell makes a note of the fact that Hitler dated his trouble from the summer of 1934. A cryptic pencil annotation, in Morell's writing, records that this was the time when Hitler had his best friend Röhm executed. Morell gave Hitler more and more powerful medicaments, like intramuscular injections for the gastric wall, and combined these with medicine that would make some of the vegetarian stuff he ate easier to digest."

"But why is all this sort of material in the medical file?" said Stuart. "Why keep a carbon of a letter about the house he got from Hitler?"

The coffee machine in the kitchen hissed steam and switched off. Breslow fetched the fresh jug of coffee before answering. "Perhaps Morell had literary ambitions."

"A biography of Hitler by his private physician?" said Stuart.

"Churchill's physician published such a book," said Breslow. "It was a bestseller, as I remember."

"And no historian has ever seen this material?" said Stuart.

"No one knows it exists," said Stein.*

"It was taken to the Kaiseroda mine?" said Stuart.

"This is what makes it so interesting," said Max Breslow. "Our film, I mean," he added hurriedly.

"Yes, of course, the film," said Stuart. "You mean you have access to other material like this?"

Stein nodded and rummaged around the wrappers in the almost empty box of chocolate-coated cherries until he found one. He chewed into it and smiled as he saw Boyd Stuart's look of consternation.

"I'm afraid he's quite right, Mr. Stuart," said Max Breslow. "For better or for worse, reputations are going to be turned upside down."

"Hitler and Churchill, you mean?" Stuart asked.

"Drink your coffee and have one of those delicious chocolates," Max Breslow told Stuart. "We have done enough for one night."

Stuart had a feeling that there were no chocolates left, and that Max Breslow already knew that.

## 12

The Marina del Rey provides a luxurious and convenient base for yacht owners who have business in Los Angeles, says one of the brochures. It is crammed tight with magnificent boats and surrounded by modern apartment buildings, as well as restaurants and discos, and has the swanky yacht club as a centrepiece. A Marina address is all you need to attract a lot of wisecracks about the swinging bachelor life. Cer-

* The documents were an interesting addition to the available material. The National Archives in Washington, D.C., have Morell's records filed under reference NA Microcopy T 253 but there is nothing about Adolf Hitler. The Bundesarchiv at Koblenz and at Freiburg have virtually nothing.

tainly the Marina del Rey is a place where the number of people dressed in yachting attire greatly exceeds the capacity of the yachts. But Boyd Stuart liked living on the boat. It was near Culver City, Century City and Beverly Hills and conveniently close to Highway 1, which would take him to Malibu, to Santa Barbara, and beyond.

He swung off the San Diego Freeway at the Marina del Rey sign and tried to stop thinking about the documents he had seen that night. And yet he could not forget the smell of them and the way the brittle paper had crackled in his hands. "Outside of this room," Stein had told him, "it's possible that there is no person still alive who has seen these documents." The short stretch of the Marina Freeway ended and Stuart began to count the apartment blocks. He still found it possible to get lost in this enormous city.

He left his newly rented car in the open parking lot. There had been muggings in the underground garage, and two o'clock in the morning was not the best time to be blundering round down there, worrying if the elevator was still working. He switched off the ignition and sat still for a moment. There was a full moon and he could have counted a thousand stars if he had had the time or the inclination.

Suddenly he noticed a cigarette lighter flare inside a car in one of the parking places near the yacht basin. Boyd felt a moment of panic, and cursed his foolishness in not bringing with him the pistol he had been given. Two men got out of the car but then, at a signal from the driver, the second man got back inside again. The man had walked halfway across the parking lot before Boyd Stuart was quite certain that it was his case officer.

"Have a nice evening, Stuart?" he asked as Boyd opened the window to greet him.

"Have you been waiting here for me all night?"

"No," said the CO. He walked round the car and got in alongside Stuart. "We took the liberty of putting a small device into your cassette player. It tells us where you are, give or take half a mile or so."

"Am I supposed to say thank you?" Stuart said irritably.

"It could prove a benefit to you some day," said the case officer. "Tell me what you talked about. This ex-Corporal Stein was there, wasn't he?"

"You are well informed," said Stuart.

"But not quickly enough informed," said the case officer.

Boyd Stuart explained what had happened in considerable detail. The controller listened all the way through without interruptions or comment. "I don't like the sound of it," he said finally.

"You should have seen that stuff. It's chilling to think what else those two might have tucked away."

"Are they after money?"

"A film would focus attention upon the two of them. Stein and Breslow could spin this stuff out for years. The possibilities are endless: bestselling books to follow the film, radio and TV appearances, video cassettes—God knows what else they might have in mind. It's not just the commercial possibilities . . . think of what world-famous personalities Stein and Breslow would become. Can you imagine them in London on BBC TV, with the Foreign Office sending a spokesman to discuss the implications?"

"I'll buy it until something better comes along. Partners then, you think?"

"Stein seems to call the shots."

"I wish like hell London would let us risk putting these two on the Washington computer. We know little or nothing about them. One glimpse of their tax returns might tell us the whole story." He searched his jacket pocket and then said, "Give me a cigarette, will you? How I hate this lousy town."

"I'm trying to give them up," said Stuart.

The man cursed. "No matter," he said. Now that the air-conditioning was not going, the car's interior was becoming stuffy. He fingered the window switch but thought better of it. "I dare say London will replace me very soon. It will be good to get back to Europe again."

"I thought you were Mexican," admitted Stuart.

"You make a great secret agent, Stuart," said the CO mockingly. "I'm Hungarian. Ever hear of Györ? No. Why the hell would you have heard of a dump like that? When I lived there, I'd never even heard of Los Angeles."

"You got out in 1956? In the revolution?"

"Is that what it was? My appointments diary said 'fiasco.'"

"There are cigarettes on the boat."

"Screw the cigarettes. I'm a forty-a-day man already. Do you know, Stuart, there are days when I wish I'd never left home."

It was said half in jest but the other half was suspended in the air between them. Some employees of the department would have thought it necessary to report such a remark, and both men knew it. For a moment they sat in silence. Then Stuart said, "Is that one of your people with you in your car?"

The CO seemed not to have heard him. "My father told me to get my mother and my sister across the border, and never mind him. He stayed there; my mother died six months later, in a transit camp in Vienna; my sister was so miserable that she went back to look after my father." He toyed with the seat-belt catch, clicking the belt, fastening it into place and releasing it. "1956," he said, "who can forget it? *My Fair Lady* got the New York Drama Critics Award, and Elvis sang 'Hound Dog'. Everyone in America was reading *Peyton Place* and Yul Brynner shaved his head and got an Oscar for playing the King of Siam in a musical movie."

"London is going to replace you?"

"London is getting very excited about this caper," said the CO in a voice which suggested that he did not share their excitement. "The guy in my car is section head for the whole west region. Being a goddamned desk man, he's read all the manuals and so he is sitting over there in order not to see your face. He came in person to brief me about a highly unlikely information source that London Operations have found. He wants you to fly to London tomorrow and go to East Anglia to talk to some geriatric German who says he helped load this junk on board a train when they were putting it *into* the Kaiseroda mine."

"Is that what you've come out here in the middle of the night to tell me?"

The CO reached into his pocket for an airline ticket and gave it to him. "I'm afraid so," he said. "This little bastard didn't come out here to consult me, he made it an order. Why the hell he didn't just put it on the telex, I still don't understand."

"Southern California can be very pleasant at this time of year," said Stuart.

"That's about the size of it," he said. "A jaunt for the top brass—and it keeps us field men on our toes." He slapped his leg and reached for the door catch. Then he stopped. "The cops found Mr. Lustig," he said. He paused.

"And?"

"Someone had hacked his head off. Another few minutes and they would have had his hands off, and they wouldn't have got fingerprint identification from his alien's registration."

"When?"

"We're not sure. The cops have been keeping it very quiet. Death on May 24 according to my source. Body found about a week later."

"What do you mean, keeping it very quiet?"

"We're trying to find out, but it's not so easy. There's been a lot of coming and going, with FBI and Justice Department lawyers in and out of police headquarters . . . CIA people too, we think. It could be connected with the Lustig killing."

"An official news blackout, you mean?"

"It's a good time for you to go to London," said the CO. "It could get hot here. Another few days will tell us what's going to happen."

"I doubt it," said Stuart.

"So do I," he confided, "but that's the way this jerk from London likes to see it. Anyway, have a good time. The contact's name is with your airline ticket and I've put some English money in there too: not much I'm afraid, but it will buy you the chance to use the headphones on the plane. I know you like music. Nothing covert about this one; use your own passport and credit cards and so on. I'll keep an eye open this end. Report to London in the usual way."

He gave Stuart the brown envelope. "And stop worrying about that boy from Washington. It wasn't your fault." Stuart didn't answer. He knew only too well that it was his fault and that all the reports and reviews would say so.

The man got out. Stuart watched him walk across the park to his own car. It was a hot night and the case officer took his time. There was a moment or two before the headlights were switched on and another delay before they drove away. Stuart supposed that the section head from London was taking off his false beard.

# 13

East Anglia is the lost continent of Great Britain. Windy and rainy, it is not a part of the industrialized north nor of the more prosperous south. This is fenland, some of it below sea level, drained by elaborate dykes and ditches built by Dutchmen whose names can still be found in every local telephone directory. No great motorway networks serve this part of England, and grass grows through the train tracks. Here are endless fields of potatoes and peas, ducks and turkeys—all the bounty of the freezer—with rain-swept holiday trailers huddled together as if sheltering from the elements. Its horizons are little changed since medieval times, the blunt towers of its flint churches buttressing the turbulent clouds. And yet a short walk off the roadway in almost any direction will bring you to derelict control towers, ruined operations blocks and cracked hardstands. For long, long ago, this was "Little America." From here the great bomber fleets went out to attack Hitler's Germany, and young men from Tacoma to Tallahassee called these East Anglian villages home.

Boyd Stuart saw the spire long before he found the road sign for Little Ashfield. He turned off the Thetford road and went through the villages of Elmstone and Great Wickmondgate. He felt happier in his own car; better an ancient dented Aston, he reasoned, than a factory-fresh Datsun. The village he sought was no more than a dozen small box-framed houses with a flint rubble church. The sky above it was slate grey and there was a trace of rain in the air.

"I'm looking for Franz Wever's house," Boyd called to an old woman in a floral-patterned pinafore. She was hanging over her garden gate watching her small mongrel puppy gnaw a bone.

"He'll be in the church," she said. "What do you want him for?"

"In the church?"

She laughed. It was a shrill laugh. "The church. Polishing, not praying," she said. "Every week, regular as clockwork, old Mr. Wever is in the church, polishing the pews and sweeping the floor. He's a dark horse, that one!"

"Thanks," said Stuart, and drove to the end of the village street and parked by the lych gate. It was a fine old church, its great roof a maze of king posts, hammer beams and rafters. Wever was there: a small bespectacled man with a bony pointed nose and thinning fair hair which had still not gone completely white. His eyes were bright blue and his skin untanned but leathery—it was the face of a man who had spent his life outdoors.

"Mr. Wever?"

"Is it the eggs for the Rendezvous des Gourmets?"

"Is it what?"

Wever resumed sweeping the floor. "I thought you were from the new restaurant on the main road. I had trouble starting my van this morning."

"I'm from London, Mr. Wever. I was told that you could help me with an inquiry we have about a wartime movement of German archives."

Wever raised his eyes quickly, his movement frozen. "So *they* sent you," he said wearily. "Is there no end to their questions?"

"I have no idea what you are talking about," said Stuart.

"1945 again. That's it, isn't it?"

"Yes."

"I've told you all I know, over and over again." Wever picked up the dustpan and his jacket. "Will it take long?"

"I can't tell at this stage."

Wever sighed. Stuart followed him through a vestry door and along a corridor to a broom closet. He watched him collect together his polishing rags and dusters and pack them away. "I came here as a prisoner of war in 1945," said Wever. "I have been here ever since. Always a prisoner, in a manner of speaking."

"You regret it now, do you?" Stuart asked. "Prefer the old country?"

Wever looked at him contemptuously. "I've never been back there, Mr. . . .?" The German accent was easier to hear now that he was angry.

"Stuart. Boyd Stuart."

"Mr. Stuart." Wever washed his hands at a small washbasin, dried them carefully and put on an old green tweed jacket and a soft cap.

"I imagine you have a car, Mr. Stuart? My wife is using our vehicle. Friday is a busy day for her. The restaurants, hotels and boarding houses all want our chickens and eggs before the weekend business."

Wever followed Stuart out to the elderly sports car. He made no comment until the engine started. "It has a roar like a tank. Is that what you like?"

"Yes," said Stuart. "Which way do we go?"

"We have twenty-three acres on the back road to Elmstone. Follow this road and turn right after the Red Fox."

"Chickens?"

"Rhode Islands. We get fine brown eggs from them. People prefer them to white ones but there is no difference really." Wever seemed talkative, as if he could keep 1945 at bay by discussing the present day. "Nearly lost the whole lot when we began." Wever sat silent for a moment. "They peck each other to death, you know. We had to chip the beaks off."

"Right at the Red Fox, you said?"

Wever did not answer him. "We've got them in proper batteries now. Factory farming they call it; over two thousand of them, that's nearly five thousand eggs a week. Then we've got a bit of barley. It's hardly worth the price we get, but it's insurance. You can be ruined overnight by one of these diseases that the hens get."

Stuart turned off after the Red Fox, a dilapidated

old pub with a broken billboard depicting girls in swimsuits drinking Martinis. The countryside was more rolling now: a promise of the sort of landscape that Constable and Cotman found here.

"A hard life," said Stuart after another long silence. He wanted to keep him talking.

"We have milk from a cow and vegetables from the garden, while a pig provides us with the only meat we get." Wever's English, although imperfect, was precise and sometimes pedantic.

"He goes to the butcher?"

Wever snorted. "Why should I share my meat with a butcher? I kill them myself. I kill all the pigs hereabouts. With four children and only a few acres from which to scratch a living, you cannot be squeamish about killing pigs, mister."

The Wevers lived in an isolated timber-frame house separated from the road by a quarter of a mile of muddy cart track. The bottom half of the building was of flint rubble construction; the upstairs part was covered in stained and broken weatherboarding. At the back some new brickwork showed where two extra rooms had been added but the toilet was an outdoor shack; there was no mains sewer.

Boyd Stuart parked his car on a gravel patch just off the lane, and they walked up the muddy path between some stunted apple trees and a line of freshly erected beanpoles. Chicken wire was nailed to the front wall so that sweet peas could climb it; their bright pinks and reds made the only colour in the drab landscape. Just outside the front door, there was a collection of rubber boots and a large toy tractor with its front wheels missing. A dog barked at the sound of their footsteps. Wever shouted to it but the barking continued.

Mrs. Wever was already at home. She was a muscular woman; ruddy cheeked and bucolic, she was about ten years younger than her husband. Her dark hair was drawn tightly back into a bun, and her eyes were quick and clear. She was making pastry on the kitchen table, measuring flour and chopping butter with the speed that comes with boredom and impatience.

"This is Mr. Stuart," said Wever. "He's come down from London to talk to me." The grey, overcast sky and the tiny windows made it dark inside the kitchen. Wever pulled up a chair for Stuart and it screeched on the lino. The woman reached for the kettle. It made a loud roaring noise as she filled it from the brass tap. She placed it on the solid-fuel cooking range, lifting the stove lid so that the hot coals let a red glow strike the ceiling. She set three mugs down on the fresh newspaper which covered the big table, and plunked down an almost empty bag of sugar alongside.

"Take off your coat and sit down, Mr. Stuart," said Wever. His voice was soft, as if he were embarrassed at the silent hostility which filled the room. The only other sound was the tick-tock of an old long-case clock.

"Where are your children then?" said Stuart. It was an attempt to be friendly. He took off his blue anorak and put it over the back of the chair.

"The eldest is the second engineer on a super-tanker," said Wever. "Two daughters are married and live locally. Only the youngest is still here with us."

"He must have seen young Johnny's tractor," said the woman, as if the visitor were not present. Her voice was hard and marked with a strong local accent.

"My grandson," explained Wever. "He spends the day with us sometimes." In another voice, "You delivered the eggs to the Rendezvous des Gourmets, did you?"

"They want to pay by the month. I said they would have to talk to you about it." She smiled. "They'll never make a go of that place. They'll be the third owners it's had in three years. Trying to make it fancy," she said spitefully. "Trying to call it French names and serve wine. They'll run up a bill with us and leave us without a penny if we're not careful, Franz."

"They paid you?" Wever leaned forward, loosened the laces in his heavy boots and then twisted each foot to make more space for his toes.

"I said I'd take the eggs back if they didn't." She smiled. "They knew I meant it. And the chickens too."

She opened the purse which was on the table in front of her and selected some pound notes. She folded them into a tight packet and put them on the dresser. "That will be for the last payment on the rototiller," she said.

The kettle began to sing. She put water into the brown teapot, cradled it to feel its warmth and then tossed the water into the sink. The tea was measured into the pot: three people, three level spoons of tea. The boiling water sizzled as it passed over the hot metal of the kettle spout. She put a knitted cover on the teapot and reached for a jug of milk from the pantry. "Would you like a piece of toast, Mr. Stuart?" she said. The anticipation of the tea seemed to put her in a better mood. "We don't have biscuits or any fancy cake in this house."

"Just tea," said Stuart.

The woman tipped some water into the bowl of flour and fat, and pummelled it fiercely. Then she sprinkled flour over the clean newspaper and tipped the soft pastry onto it with a loud plop. She reached for a rolling pin and began rolling the pastry. Her movements were energetic and determined, like someone completing physical exercises that she didn't enjoy. She pursed her lips and stared down at the ever-expanding sheet of cream-coloured pastry.

"I never heard a shot fired in anger," said Franz Wever suddenly. "I wore a uniform and saluted my superiors and drew my rations, but most of the work I did in the army could have been done by a civilian."

"And what was that?"

"I am a Berliner," said Wever. "I left school when I was fifteen. I learned shorthand and typing and worked in the Berlin office of the Hamburg-Amerika shipping line until I was drafted into the army. After basic training I went to the army signals school in Halle and became a teleprinter operator with Army Group 6 HQ in Hanover. I worked in that communications room for about a year. I was the only professional operator in the place—most of those kids had never even seen a teleprinter until they went to the signals school; they had to use me for anything important. Naturally I wanted to be near my parents and eventually I got a posting to the signals company of Wehrkreis III (Berlin-Brandenburg). Then I went to Zossen. . . ." He raised his eyes quizzically, to see if Stuart had heard of Zossen.

"The general staff headquarters. Its communications room handled every order the German army ever got."

Wever nodded. "It was a boring job. Everything was in code . . . meaningless jumbles of letters and numbers. Even working for the Hamburg-Amerika line was more interesting than that." Wever spooned three large spoons of sugar into his empty cup. "Pour out the tea, Lucy. It's brewed."

The woman finished rolling out the pastry. Briskly she rubbed the flour from her red-knuckled hands. Then she slapped the pastry onto a dish of cooked rhubarb, cutting the overhanging edges away with deft movement of the knife. "Why can't you men pour out your own tea?" she muttered, but she did it for them. Stuart realized that what he had at first thought was hostility to him was really her response to their talk of war. It was a part of her husband she could never share—like the happy moments of some previous marriage.

"I'll do the milking," said the woman accusingly. She put the teapot back onto the warm stove. "Someone will have to do it before it gets dark, and you'll be talking about the war." Wever did not reply. The woman climbed into a battered sheepskin coat, her movements jerky and violent as if to demonstrate her anger. She turned up her collar before facing the bad weather, and banged the door after her.

"Sugar?" said Wever.

"I'm trying to lose weight," said Stuart.

The bag was almost empty. Wever tore it open in order to release the final few grains of sugar from its folds. He tipped them into his cup with care. "My wife loves that clock," he said.

"It's a fine piece," said Stuart. It was probably the only valuable item in the entire kitchen; virtually everything else seemed improvised, plastic or broken.

"Obsessed with it," explained Wever. "Wouldn't hear of selling it, not even when we needed money to buy seed a couple of years ago. It belonged to her father. She nursed him through those last few months." There was a silence in which the tick of the clock seemed to be louder than ever. "Nothing is too good for that clock," said Wever with a brief and bitter laugh. "No tractor oil for that mechanism; special oil from a shop in Norwich. Only yesterday she had someone come and replace one of the chimes. It had been on order for over two months." He drank some of his tea but could not take his eyes off the clock. "I can't stand the sound of that ticking," he confided. "And the damned thing is always slow."

He brought out a large linen handkerchief and blew his nose with studied care. Then he drank some tea and resumed his story. "From Zossen I was selected for duty with the signals detachment at the Wolfsschanze. Only the very best operators were sent there," said Wever. Even over such a long passage of time his pride was still evident. "That was the Führer's headquarters in the Görlitz forest. It was a great honour. . . ." Wever wiped his nose again. "But I wasn't too pleased at the time—no more weekly visits to my parents, no more cinemas, dances and all the pleasures of Berlin. The Wolfsschanze was in the middle of nowhere. The Görlitz forest is in a swampy area, sweltering hot in summer and plagued with mosquitoes; in winter it's buried in deep snow, and in between times you get the rain and fog. My parents were pleased about it; I was made an officer soon after that, in charge of the Fernschreiberkompanien. And they were pleased because all of us permanent personnel knew we would never be sent to the Russian front."

"Why?"

"It was a special order of the Führer. He was frightened that the Russians might capture one of us and obtain information about him and the day-to-day life at the headquarters."

"You were close to Hitler?"

"Sometimes I would see him every day. It was in February that the signals officer of Hitler's private train—the Führersonderzug—went into hospital and I was assigned to it. Of course, there were drawbacks to the job. Every uniform had to be well pressed and spotless. No swearing, no smoking, and my communications staff were overworked."

"And whose job was it to look after the records?"

"One man could not have handled the paperwork," said Wever wearily. "It's difficult to explain it to you." He folded his handkerchief and pushed it back into his pocket. "The Führersonderzug was like a travelling circus. The train always carried a dozen aides and adjutants, two or three secretaries and two physicians, as well as a surgeon. Then there would be the press men, Hoffmann, Hitler's photographer, two or three people from the Foreign Office, and Hitler's personal staff—three valets and two drivers—a dozen or more railway employees, and just as many catering staff, five railway policemen and three officials of the post office. There were two girls who did nothing other than keep the silver clean and polished and counted! And all that is without his military bodyguard or his SS bodyguard, or the aeroplanes and dozens of motor cars that followed the train to be ready in case Der Chef wanted them en route. Then there was the endless paperwork of the army personnel, flak-gun crews, field kitchen, military police. . . . Can you imagine how much paper was being filed away?"

"I want to know about Hitler's personal documents," said Stuart. "I'm trying to discover where they went in the last days of the war. My people say you know about this."

Wever gave no sign of having heard him. Dabs of rain hit the window. It was growing darker in the kitchen, but electric light—like remnants of pastry and the last traces of sugar—was carefully husbanded in this household. Franz Wever's head settled deeper into his hunched shoulders and he almost disappeared into the gloom.

"I was with Hitler almost until the end." Wever drank some tea. "On December 10, 1944, at seventeen hundred hours, we took the Führer's special train out of Berlin to a place near Giessen where a convoy of cars took him to Adlerhorst, his headquarters. I was asked to take the place of the signals officer of the FBB—the army escort battalion. He'd been on leave in Berlin on the night of December 9 and was killed in an air raid."

Wever was still, his eyes closed. In the wretched little kitchen, the daylight fading, he seemed to be asleep. When he spoke again it was enough to make Stuart start in surprise. "The train returned to Berlin on January 16, 1945. The Führer was bent and seemed unwell. We arrived about ten o'clock in the morning. The fleet of black three-axle Mercedes cars was waiting in the forecourt of the railway station. A small crowd had gathered but the police were keeping them moving. There were growing fears about another attempt on his life. Now that the Third Reich was nearly finished, there was anti-Nazi talk in the bars and Berliners had invented some bitter jokes about the Nazi leaders taking gold to South America. There had always been anti-Nazi jokes in Berlin—it was renowned for them—but the jokes were different now. . . .

"Once we were back in Berlin, Der Chef spent more and more time down in the underground bunker where he eventually died. The American bombers would arrive just before lunch and the RAF about midnight.

"For a few days the Führer kept his apartment in the small Old Chancellery building and continued to hold his military conferences in the big new Chancellery which Speer had designed. It had suffered several direct hits but the Führer's study and dining room were intact. On Wednesday, March 21, when the news was coming in that Patton's infantry were entering Ludwigshafen, Der Chef sent for me. By that time the tapestries and valuable paintings had been removed for safekeeping and we had to detour through side passages because of the damage. Many of the windows were broken and had been crudely closed off with heavy cardboard which rattled noisily with the wind from the garden. It was depressing for anyone who remembered it as it had once been.

"I arrived at the entrance together with Colonel General Guderian and his adjutant. They had to go through exactly the same security checks that I was subjected to, and there were armed sentries every ten paces. The whole Zitadelle—the part of Berlin where all the government buildings were—was teeming with troops. A company of the Führer Begleit Bataillon was moved out of the Lichterfelde barracks at short notice and put into the Chancellery with the SS Begleit Kommando. It was chaos because the Leibstandarte Adolf Hitler Wache Reichskanzlei was still there with no room to spare.

"At the end of every corridor my papers were checked against a log book entry. When we got to the ante-room I took my pistol from its holster and gave it to the Waffen SS guards. There was a table filled with them, each gun tagged with the name of the owner. Even Guderian and his adjutant had to hand over their briefcases for the guards to examine inside and out. There were no body checks but I don't think anyone with a lumpy uniform would have got into the ante-room." Wever smiled.

"Once inside the ante-room I saw all the big brass waiting for the daily conference. There was Keitel, Dönitz, Jodl, some of Himmler's RSHA people and, sprawled in the armchair looking miserable, I saw Göring himself. I sat down on one of the embroidered gilt chairs feeling out of place, then the study doors opened and Günsche came into the ante-room."

"Günsche was Hitler's adjutant," said Stuart to display his newly acquired knowledge. "His SS adjutant."

"Hitler had dozens of SS adjutants," said Wever, showing no admiration for this interjection. "Four SS *persönliche Adjutanten*—it was bureaucracy running wild. . . ." He brushed aside the interruption with a movement of the hand and sipped some more tea. "But SS Sturmbannführer Günsche was one of them and combat commandant too. At the end it was Günsche who soaked Hitler's body in petrol and set it afire. He beckoned to me, and told the others—including Göring—that the Führer would receive them in five minutes. They looked at me as I was ushered into the study to see what it was that made me so important. I was trying to guess. As always in this sort of situation, it is guilty fears that predominate. I wondered if I was going to be executed for telling some anti-Hitler joke or complaining about the dehydrated cabbage. Everyone had heard me complain about that cabbage.

"Günsche took me through the enormous study, with Hitler's gigantic desk and the painting of Bismarck, to a side room where they stored documents of the sort the Führer might require at short notice during his daily conferences. It was a small room and Hitler stood in the middle of it. As I came closer to him I could smell the medicated sweets he used whenever he had a sore throat. He had a pathological fear of contracting a disease of the throat.

"He was a shocking sight. You must remember that I had seen him often. On the train I would sometimes be giving him teleprinter messages by the dozen. When things were going well, the Führer would exchange a few words. He remembered the names of my parents and my mother's birthplace—Linz in Austria. Now I could hardly recognize him. His face seemed to have aged forty years, his eye sockets were deeply sunken and the skin of his cheeks dark, as if bruised. He was stooped and seemed to have lost the use of his left arm, which trembled constantly. His voice was very low and hoarse and almost unrecognizable to anyone who had heard his speeches of earlier years—and which of us had not! When he spoke he leaned forward and used his right hand to grasp his throat, as if to help his vocal chords.

"Der Chef was wearing his usual plain grey, army-style jacket. But this day I noticed that there were stains on the lapel. You can't imagine how amazing it was to see him in anything except carefully pressed. spotlessly clean clothes. I looked at his plain black trousers and civilian shoes but these were not up to his usual standard either.

"The Führer was standing against a small table and I noticed that he put his weight against it, as if to steady himself. This confirmed the rumours I'd heard of a loss of balance and dizzy spells. Under his direction, Günsche was sorting the papers and documents into separate heaps. Against the wall there were half a dozen metal filing boxes painted dark green. FHQU was stencilled on each box, together with the word PERSÖNLICH and a six-figure letter-number combination."

Stuart almost shouted with excitement. What had looked like BBO on the box of Dr. Morell's papers was actually FHQU—Führerhauptquartier—and the shiny patch next to it was the place from which the word "personal" had been removed.

"The Führer smiled. I'm afraid my face must have registered my horror at his appearance. I stood transfixed, giving the *Heil Hitler,* arm upraised. But he did not respond to my salute.

" 'Captain Wever,' he said. Even in those last days he hadn't lost his trick of remembering names. But he lowered his eyes, and that surprised me, for he usually fixed his visitors with an unyielding stare that was almost hypnotic. I lowered my arm. He motioned his head impatiently, to indicate that I should not stand at attention. 'I have an important task for you, Captain Wever.' He looked up and stared me straight in the eyes again. 'A very important task.' I knew him well enough to understand that I was not expected to reply until asked a direct question. I said nothing. 'The enemy is now using his heaviest weapons against me in Berlin.' I noticed particularly that he said 'against me' as if it were a personal vendetta. 'There are certain personal documents that I have decided should not be risked. And, in the interests of history, must not be destroyed. I have therefore decided that these documents—which I have personally selected for this purpose'—Hitler indicated some piles of papers which were separated from the others—'should be put into safekeeping for future generations. It is a great trust that I place into your hands, Captain Wever.'

" 'Yes, my Führer.'

" 'Günsche will provide you with all the necessary paperwork that will ensure you cooperation from the Reichspost, the Reichsbahn, the armed forces and my SS. You will leave Berlin tonight, using my train.'

" 'The Führersonderzug, my Führer?'

"Hitler nodded. 'To Frankfurt am Main. There will be cars and an armed escort there to take you onwards. Your exact orders and subsequent destination will be given to you later; you will unseal them on the train. You will use the train's communications to keep me informed of progress—the necessary codes and ciphers will be included in your orders—and if the train is stopped or delayed by enemy action you can call upon whatever resources you require from the appropriate authority. Is that clear, Captain Wever?'

" 'Yes, my Führer."

"And there it was," said Wever with a self-deprecatory smile. "That was my grand meeting with the twentieth-century Napoleon, and what had I contributed: 'Yes, my Führer,' repeated over and over again. It was like that with all the people who met him: generals, admirals, inventors, U-boat captains, kings and presidents. He had you in the palm of his hand, and yet you came out of that study thinking that you'd just persuaded a highly intelligent man to do something you'd been planning all your life. That's how it was with those damned papers."

"So you went back to the train as its sole passenger?" Stuart asked.

"You don't understand the devious nature of the higher command," said Wever. "Hitler had instructed Günsche to prepare my movement orders and documentation. The SS Sturmbannführer did it in consultation with Kaltenbrunner, head of the RSHA, who ran the Gestapo, the Kripo and Sicherheitsdienst: one of the most powerful people in the Third Reich. Not the sort of man who would let an army captain take personal charge of top-secret papers, just because the Führer had decided that the mission required a highly experienced communications expert."

"He flouted Hitler's orders?"

"Not at all. He provided an SS officer to accompany me. The orders instructed the Reichsbahn and the Reichspost officials—'in the name of the Führer' rather than the more usual 'in the name of the Reich' —to provide the SS officer with facilities required, so that Captain Wever and his 'special baggage' could be transported. The wording of those orders ensured that my role was little more than a baggage porter. It was the SS that would call the tune."

"Who was the SS officer who went with you?"

"Oh don't misunderstand me," said Wever. "This Leibstandarte officer was an old friend of mine. It wasn't the rank and file who were wasting valuable games; we knew the end was near. . . . He was only a junior rank—Obersturmführer, like a first lieutenant—but he was an old-time regular. He'd been through the peacetime SS Junkerschule at Bad Tölz, and that was no picnic. I'd known Breslow since childhood, he was a decent man." Wever smiled at another recollection. "You can imagine that I wanted to visit my parents before we journeyed south. The way things were going, with the Allies and the Russians so close, I had the feeling that I might never see the old people again. My home was near Tietz department store; I could be there in five minutes. I got out, using my day pass, but ran into the guard commander when I returned. He was a pig. He kept me in the guard room and phoned the military police. Luckily, Max Breslow came to my aid. He got one of the SS adjutants to straighten it out . . . but it was a narrow squeak for me, and I owe my thanks to Breslow. I could have been shot." Wever drummed his fingers on the table. "Did you ever try to give up smoking, Mr. Stuart?"

"Frequently."

Wever pushed his hands deep into his pockets as if to punish them for drumming on the table. "Breslow was practical. When we departed he had brought two pistols—he knew I didn't have one—and was wearing an MP 40 over his shoulder. He was right, of course—how could we have undertaken that sort of responsibility without guns? He had put a Führerhauptquartier cuff-band on his sleeve too. I was surprised—almost everyone had ceased wearing them long before—but Breslow said it would impress the country yokels. You see," Wever added, "Breslow was a Berliner." His tone of voice suggested that this accolade explained everything. Stuart had known many Berliners, and liked the distinctive sort of roguish wit—*Schalkheit*—that the city seemed to beget. But Berliners were not renowned for modesty or simplicity. How much of Wever's story was window dressing, designed to hide something else? "The family lived in a big house in Pankow, his father was Georg Breslow, the actor, a famous man in Germany. He was the one who anglicized the family name. Breslow's mother had been a soprano with the Berlin State Opera." Wever reached into his pocket for a tin, tapped it on the table and then put it back into his pocket again.

"Yes," said Wever. "Breslow was wearing his Führerhauptquartier cuff-band. I was wearing a reversible winter camouflage jacket. It was a combat soldier's garment. I'd never been anywhere near the front line, and that bothered me, so I wanted to wear that jacket and look like a fighting man. Even so, Breslow, in his battered leather overcoat, and an old peaked mountain cap crushed on his head, looked more like a fighting man than I ever could."

"Breslow had been a combat soldier?"

"He was wounded at Kharkov in the winter of 1943. The Leibstandarte was part of the SS Panzer corps. Breslow was badly shot up and lost some toes with frost-bite. When he came out of hospital he was permanently assigned to the Chancellery guard. Breslow had a chestful of awards: Iron Cross First Class, assault badge, wound badge and so on. Nothing grand, but he was a man who could take his overcoat off—as we said in the army about men who had awards on their jackets." Wever smiled. "So it's Breslow you are interested in?"

"Were there no other special passengers on the train that night?"

"Just me and Breslow. He went aboard before the loading began. He sent for the train commander and all the officers. He received them in the Führerwagen—actually in the Führer's sitting room: sitting in the best armchair, his hat thrown on the writing desk as if he owned the place. He had his overcoat wide open so that they could see that he was a fighting soldier. Until then the Führer's sitting room had been a sanctum which very few of us had entered; now it was crammed with curious faces. There were the marks of muddy boots on the carpet, and tobacco smoke in the air for the first time. Tobacco smoke! We all knew that the Führer would never board his train again.

"It was dark in Berlin that night. The air raids were bad enough to make the blackout regulations very strict. Even the railway men had to work with the merest glimmer of operating lights. I stayed with Breslow and we checked the manifest to be sure that the boxes were loaded safely. The Führer's personal papers were not the only freight on the train that night. The Foreign Office building had been badly hit a few nights previously, and a railway wagon of Foreign Office documents was attached to the train.

"Breslow said that we would send a signal when the train passed Halle. It was then that we would open the sealed orders. Since our message was going to be in cipher, we would have to halt. No top-secret—*Chefsache*—messages could be transmitted by radio for fear of interception by enemy monitoring services. I went and warned the communications officer that a signals mechanic must be ready to connect the teleprinters to the Reichspost landlines when we stopped the train at Halle. Then I told the senior railway official aboard of the intention to stop, and told the train's military police commander that his men must be ready to provide the normal security screen round the halted train."

"You sent the message from Halle?"

"No. There was only a single line working for ten miles north of Halle—it's a big junction and the Allied bombers had hit it again and again—the train was rerouted through Leipzig. We opened the sealed orders there."

"And?"

"Our orders were to take the Führer's personal papers to a salt mine at Merkers in the Thüringer Wald. An infantry regiment stationed at Hersfeld, not far from the mine, would provide us with help and assistance. The sealed orders specified that the papers were to be referred to as 'songs,' the military escort as 'pianoforte,' the movement of the material to the mine was a *'Lied mit Klavierbegleitung,'* song with piano accompaniment."

"Curious code names," said Stuart.

"You cannot call such words code," said Wever pedantically. "They give very little security to a message. Such words are intended only for convenience and brevity. The German word *Begleit* means 'escort' as well as 'accompany'—the FBB was the Führer Belgeit Bataillon. It would not require a team of cryptographers to guess what we were doing, always providing they had an Enigma decoder."

Wever reached into the pocket of his coat and got out a cigarette machine. He put a tin of dark tobacco on the table and then a packet of papers. "Even so, Breslow was most particular about the security of the messages to Berlin and to the army at Hersfeld." Wever pinched some tobacco and rolled it into the machine before feeding a paper into it, licking the gummed edge and rolling it some more. "You need two operators to work one of those old Enigmas, three to be really fast. It's like a typewriter, but the letters light up instead of going onto paper. Breslow helped me with it. He called out the letters as they came up." Wever continued rolling the machine as if he had forgotten what he was doing. Then suddenly he clicked it open to release the newly made cigarette. He picked it up and carefully tucked a few loose strands of tobacco back into the open ends. Then he studied it, as if pleased with the result of his handiwork.

He lit the cigarette and inhaled gratefully with that very deep breath which marks the tobacco addict. Then he blew smoke and smiled with satisfaction.

"How far did you get with the train?" Stuart asked.

"We couldn't get beyond Erfurt," said Wever. He smoked the cigarette with a furtiveness which suggested that his wife would not have approved of his weakness. "A railway bridge was damaged. The engineers said it could not bear the weight of the Führer's train which was specially constructed with tons of lead in the bogies to give an extra-smooth ride. And there was the weight of all our special equipment and the Flakwagen at front and back. It would have been too much for the buckled girders. Moving it across piecemeal would have meant several hours delay. And there were hospital trains coming back up the line as well as troop trains going westwards. Erfurt was close to the autobahn, so we called Hersfeld—which was also on the autobahn—and asked them to come and get us. What a fiasco!" Wever got up in order to tap his ash into the stove. "We couldn't reach them by teleprinter, no operators on duty. The Americans were heading directly for Hersfeld and the regiment had moved out. Next we tried telephoning them. Eventually, after a long and acrimonious conversation with a half-witted major who refused to believe that we were engaged on a special mission for the Führer, they sent us two trucks and a platoon of infantry." He inhaled and looked at the cigarette again.

"When they arrived they were more like walking wounded than infantry: old men, kids, cripples and rejects. Even the trucks the major sent us were in such poor mechanical condition that the drivers had to nurse them to keep them going.

"When we got to the mine at Merkers there was no one ready to accept the papers. It was a bleak and dirty place, the yard was muddy and littered with broken boxes and rubbish. Some of the mess was the outer packing from other treasures which had been put into the mine. There was another truck there when we arrived. It contained Reichsbank Director Dr. Frank and a Reichsbank procurist—the official who was in charge of all newly printed paper money. It was Dr. Frank who signed for our consignment, and eventually let me go.

"I wanted to get back to my parents in Berlin. The railway was still working—it was just the heavy trains, transporting big guns and tanks, that could not get through Erfurt. Breslow said he wanted to find the nearest Waffen SS outfit and get back into the fighting. It was probably true, but at the time I suspected that he was merely looking for some way of changing his SS papers and uniform for those of an ordinary army officer before surrendering himself to the Americans, who were getting closer every hour. There was a railway transport officer at Merkers who agreed to give me top-priority movement orders to rejoin my unit in Berlin. Anything less than a top-priority movement order would expose me to the risk of being given a rifle and sent into action by any military police patrol that stopped me and asked for my papers. There was a delay while I got a photo for the movement order."

"But you had top-priority papers from Hitler," said Stuart. "What could be better than that?"

"These were dangerous times, Mr. Stuart," said Wever. "The American armies were very close and the Red Army pressing nearer day by day. I would have been a fool to carry any document associating me with the Führer's immediate entourage. I wanted very ordinary military papers that showed that I was going to the Berlin signals office—no mention of the Reich Chancellery assignment—just a teleprinter specialist returning to special duty. I got hold of the army photographer but by the time the papers were all ready the American soldiers had arrived . . . that was 4 April. I was interrogated by an American military police officer but he thought I was part of a military escort provided for the gold from the Reichsbank. It was a perfunctory interrogation and after that I went to a POW cage and eventually to England."

"And more interrogations?"

"Everyone wanted to know about the gold. They kept asking me about the origin of the gold—was it from the Reichsbank, was there any gold still in Berlin, were there shipments of foreign gold? France, Holland and Norway were already asking for the return of the gold that had been taken from them. I knew nothing about any of this, and eventually the interrogators lost interest in me."

"And what happened to Hitler's papers?"

"They went down into the mine. There were only six boxes of them. I went down into the shaft with Reichsbank Director Frank. He had the keys of a vault which had been built to protect the gold and foreign currencies. It was very light; the low roof of the salt mine had been strung with hundreds of electric light bulbs. Frank warned us that the atmosphere of the salt mine was too dry to be suitable for the long-term storage of archives. He had similarly warned the museum officials who sent valuable documents there. He said that more than six months in the mine could result in permanent damage. Breslow said that he did not expect that they would remain there that long."

"I've been through the statements, interrogations and reports about the mine, Mr. Wever," Stuart told him. "But I don't recall anyone named Frank. Certainly there is no record of a Reichsbank director of that name."

Wever looked into space and nodded. "I always suspected that Frank was not his real name."

"Why?"

"Breslow was not the sort of officer who would so readily hand those secret papers to a civilian in return for a scribbled receipt. I believe Breslow had secret orders to make contact with this man who called himself Reichsbank Director Frank. I think Frank was a Sicherheitsdienst official working for Kaltenbrunner so that they could be quite sure where the documents were." Wever nodded as if to confirm this idea to himself. "And Breslow spent a lot of time with Frank—meetings from which I was excluded."

"And this man who called himself Frank had access to the gold too?"

"And also to the foreign money that was there—Swiss paper money, Swedish paper money, U.S. dollars and British pounds. All foreign money including that acquired by the SS, the army or anyone else, had to be sent to the Foreign Notes Department, Reichsbank New Building, Berlin. It was unlawful for a German to possess foreign money. The procurist was in charge of all foreign paper money, another Reichsbank director—Herr Thoms—was in charge of all the gold. Now—in 1945—virtually all the gold and foreign money was in a salt mine, and Herr Frank had the key."

"Are you trying to tell me that this gold and foreign currency was placed there to finance the escape of the Nazi leaders?"

"All I know is that, when the American soldiers arrived at Merkers, Reichsbank Director Frank was nowhere to be found, and neither was my old friend Breslow."

"You think that they had taken gold from the mine?"

"I have no theories to offer," said Wever. "I am simply telling you what happened."

"Did you look at the documents?"

"Breslow took one," said Wever. "It was a long train journey. One of the boxes was unlocked; we couldn't resist looking. Each metal filing box was divided into compartments, with thickly wadded brown manilla envelopes jammed into each. We opened one of them. Inside there were two shorthand notebooks, the pages crossed through diagonally by someone as the notes were typed up. The shorthand was hastily written but still easy enough to read. At the back of the file there were typewritten sheets which had been completed. They were the Lagebesprechungen—the Führer's military conferences, two each day normally."

"And Breslow took one?"

"As a souvenir, I suppose. It was a mad thing to do, but that final part of the war was a mad time. People did crazy things."

"Not you, Wever," said Stuart. "You never did a crazy thing in your life."

Wever stared at him. "I don't risk my life for ridiculous pieces of wastepaper, if that's what you mean. The fact that it had FUHRER-KOPIE at the top of the page meant little to me. I could never understand those fools, fighting in Russia as if they were on some wonderful crusade. What did they get out of it?"

"We know what they got out of it," said Stuart. "The lucky ones got twelve years in a Russian work camp."

The telephone rang. There was something inappropriate about the sound of it in that mean little room, smelling of mildew and farm manure. Wever rose from his chair with a crack of stiff bones, reached into the gloom for the telephone and said, "Hello?"

There was a gabble of conversation at the other end. Wever said *"Ja"* but changed it to "yes" by the time there was a need for a second affirmative. "Yes" and "yes" again.

Suddenly Wever's patience snapped. He broke into rapid German, its consonants sharp and brittle as only Berliners speak. "Damn you and damn the rest of them. For years no one cared and now suddenly. . . . You tell them I sent it almost a week ago. Negative." He nodded to himself. "The only negative. Tell them to stop their silly little games." Wever's tirade stopped and he bent his head as if trying to hear better. He stood framed against the oppressive rain clouds which pressed with a leaden weight upon the landscape through the window. He lowered the phone from his ear, and it purred for a moment before he hung up.

"Is there anything else?" said Wever.

"Not for the moment," said Stuart. "Thanks for helping me."

"There is no alternative," said Wever. "When your people arranged all my permits and permissions thirty years ago, they made it clear that they could withdraw them just as quickly."

"I wouldn't worry too much about that, Mr. Wever," said Stuart. "By now you are one of us."

Wever grunted as he bent over to retie his bootlaces.

"Can I give you a lift anywhere?"

"No," said Wever. "Go ahead. And mind the patch of mud near the shed; the baker's van got stuck in that last night. Took him half an hour to crawl out of it."

"Thanks, I will," said Stuart, and tucking his head down he hurried through the rain to his car. The motor started at the first touch of the key and he switched on all the lights so that he could negotiate the muddy lane without sharing the baker's fate.

Stuart was almost at the Red Fox when the explosion occurred. The flash lit up the grey countryside like lightning, and the force of it made his ears pop even before he heard the noise. He turned his head in time to see the column of smoke. It was not the oily black smoke that stunt crews make for war movies. This was the real thing: a wraithlike smudge which dissipated almost immediately.

Stuart heaved on the brake as a hailstorm of wood chips and metal fragments splashed into the puddles around him and nicked his car's paintwork. He opened the door and got to his feet in the pouring rain. This part of the country had long since had its hedgerows ripped away by cost-conscious farmers. The open fields gave Stuart a view of the Wever house. There was little left of it; the merest trace of smoke hung over the scattered stones and a large piece of roof was leaning upon the nearest of the chicken houses.

Stuart returned to his Aston Martin. There was no sense in going back there. Even now there would be police cars and ambulances on the way. Furthermore, the standing instructions gave a strong warning against field employees becoming involved in police inquiries of any kind. The Secret Intelligence Service got no pleasure from sending high-ranking department officials across to the Home Office, cap in hand. In spite of all this, he turned his Aston in the car park of the Red Fox and went back.

The clock, thought Stuart. Perhaps the man who had come to mend the chimes had not been installing new ones. Perhaps he had planted explosive in the long case. It was that part of the house which had suffered most. But who had phoned Wever, and was it a warning?

The kitchen was the scene of the greatest damage. Only a close scrutiny by explosives experts would reveal whether the bomb had been placed in the clock, and they would have to search a long time to piece it together. The smell was almost overwhelming. He spat the soot from his mouth.

Wever must have been standing near the stove. There were hardly any signs of damage on his face or his clothes but he was bundled up like a rag doll in a toy box, and was unmistakably dead. Stuart went through his pockets but there was nothing there that one would not expect to find on a hard-working chicken farmer who was too old to cope with the work demanded of him and had cash problems that required him to put aside the payments on a second-hand rototiller.

So that was the man who had brushed shoulders with Hitler. Well, there were worse fates than ending up on an East Anglian chicken farm. There was no sign of Wever's wife. He stepped carefully over the wreckage of wood splinters and broken glass to get to what had once been a bedroom. There was a cot in the corner. He picked up the woollen blankets. There was no sign of a baby.

The rain was still coming down steadily, soaking into the broken furniture, hissing upon the hot stove and dampening down the dust of the broken plaster. He turned back towards his car, glass cracking underfoot. It was as he stepped over the broken wall of the bedroom that he saw it. The rain had made the metal box shine and he stooped down to inspect the object more closely.

It was an expensive wall safe, built right into the brickwork of the bedroom, in a wall added to the house by the enterprising handyman, Franz Wever. The front of the safe was intact and its door firmly locked. It was the back of the safe that had sprung open with the collapse of the wall. He prised the metal back as if it had been the bent lid of a half-opened sardine can. His hand went into the gap and he found some bundles of papers.

There was an insurance policy, some letters from the local planning office giving permission for building new chicken houses. There were Wever's permits and a West German passport stamped only twice for visits to Berlin. He had lied about never going back—what other lies had he told?

With this bundle there was another one, wrapped in the black plastic from which fertilizer bags are made, held tight with two rubber bands. Stuart snapped the fastenings off and unwrapped the packet. There was Wever's old German army pay book, some souvenirs of foreign paper money dating from the war, and a medical form dated September 18, 1944, certifying him fit for infantry duties. Nothing of importance, thought Stuart, and looked at his watch. The police would surely be here any moment. There were houses and farms nearer than the Red Fox, and even there the sound had come like a thunderclap.

It was as he was about to rewrap the pay book that he saw the envelope tucked in amongst the ancient paper money. He ripped the flap open. There it was—FUHRERKOPIE, a page from one of the Lagebesprechungen, Hitler's daily military conferences, with the names of Jodl, Göring and Hitler down the left-hand side. A script of some demented screenplay which played to packed audiences for six long nightmare years. So it had not been Breslow who was so obsessed by the contents of the tin boxes that he had to steal a souvenir, but Wever himself, the arch cynic to whom Hitler meant nothing.

There were other things too: a GPO receipt for a registered letter addressed to 'General Delivery, Terminal Annex, Post Office, Los Angeles, California 90054,' dated almost one week earlier; a battered Reich Chancellery pass, stamped each month and signed up to the end of 1944. It was a good souvenir. There was a sepia, postcard-size photo, taken in some provincial studio by the look of it, the photographer's name and an Austrian address in flamboyant script on the back. A young child posed stiffly in front of a painted backdrop of snow-covered mountains. One could almost hear the anxious father calling to the child to hold still.

The other photo was unmistakably amateur: a grubby snapshot from a cheap camera, the print now cracked and dog-eared. Three men were standing self-consciously in what looked like a factory yard. Behind them posts or perhaps factory chimneys and, beyond those, low rolling hills. The reproduction was too grainy to see any detail but one jackbooted young man in leather overcoat and mountain cap looked like Max Breslow. Alongside him, Wever stood in an awkward jokey pose, his elbow resting on Breslow's shoulder, the other hand on his gun holster which was worn over a mottled camouflage jacket. The third man was in civilian clothes: a long black overcoat and, in his hand, a wide-brimmed felt hat. On the back of the photo "Max," "Franz" and "Rb. Dir. Dr Frank" were written in pencil.

Stuart put the passes, the Führerkopie of the sheet of minutes and the photographs into his pocket before putting the rest of it back into the broken safe. Then he clambered over the debris and ran back to his car. Even before he started the engine, he could hear the wail of the police and ambulance sirens. By the time his car was at the main road he could see the flashing blue lights twinkling through the haze of rain as the police cars bumped along the track that marked the end of Wever's few acres.

## 14

"And all this happened yesterday evening?" said Sir Sydney Ryden. They were in the SIS Ziggurat building. The Prime Minister's visit to Tokyo had provided him with a respite from her continual questions. The DG had hardly moved from a position alongside his desk while Boyd Stuart had been telling him about the visit to Franz Wever. It was disconcerting to talk to a man who stood with his eyes lowered to his drink and his feet planted firmly apart, scarcely moving except when he occasionally raised a hand to flick back his long hair or touch his ear.

"That's right, Sir Sydney." He glanced at the newspapers scattered on the armchair. It had been too late for the morning papers—except for some of the late London editions—to use the story, but the evening papers were giving it the front page. IRA BOMB FACTORY BLAST—MAN DIES. BOMB SQUAD ARRESTS IN LONDON FOLLOW EXPLOSION AT FARMHOUSE.

"There were no arrests by the Bomb Squad," said Sir Sydney.

"I guess it is just the newspapers' way of linking the explosion to terrorism. It sells more newspapers, I suppose."

"Don't be too hard on Fleet Street, Stuart. We have some good friends there."

Stuart looked up sharply. So that was it. It was the DG's doing; the cunning old devil had manufactured the terrorist story to put everyone off the scent.

"Better that way," said the DG. "And, with Wever being a rather taciturn German, his neighbours out there in Suffolk were only too ready to invent all kinds of evil doings."

"Norfolk actually, sir," said Stuart. "Wever said he worked for us."

The DG pursed his lips in distaste. "For *one* of the

departments in Whitehall," he said icily. The correction left Stuart in little doubt that Wever was some sort of employee of MI5, an organization for which Sir Sydney showed little admiration. "And you found a photo of this fellow Max Breslow in the ruins of his farmhouse?"

"It's been down to the archives, Sir Sydney," said Stuart reaching for his wallet to show him the photo. "There is still one German unidentified."

The DG waved him away. "No point in my looking at it, Stuart. It's not likely to turn out that he's on the committee of my golf club or anything." It was as near as the DG ever went to making a joke. The DG picked up a cactus plant and held it in the palm of his hand as if trying to estimate its weight. "So what do you make of it, Stuart?"

"At first, I thought Wever was lying about Breslow stealing the document. Later, when I'd had time to think about it, I was less sure. I think Breslow sent that sheet of Hitler's daily conference through the post to Wever, together with the photograph of Wever and himself. I think it was a way of reminding Wever who Breslow was. . . ."

"Renewing an old acquaintance, you mean?" said the DG with a trace of condescending amusement.

"Or of putting pressure upon him."

"Pressing him in what direction?" The DG was looking at the cactus, but his thoughts were entirely upon the subject discussed.

"Not to tell us the story he told us," Stuart suggested.

"Or indeed, to tell us the story he told us, rather than tell us the truth," said the DG.

"Yes, sir."

"But you believe him?"

"Wever claimed that our people were harassing him, sir. He said he'd told the same story over and over."

"Nonsense," said the DG. "No one else has talked to him on this matter."

"Shall I let you have my written report in person?" Stuart asked him.

The DG wrinkled his nose and swallowed a little of

his whisky as if it were nasty medicine. "No written reports, for the time being, Stuart. We'll keep this strictly between you and me."

"Yes, sir."

"I know it's unusual, but this one is rather touchy. The PM is taking a personal interest and I'd like to keep the paperwork to a minimum."

"I see, sir," said Stuart. It was going to be one of those operations for which all the reports were going to be written with the advantage of twenty-twenty vision—hindsight. Well, Stuart knew what happened to field men who made any sort of mistake in that situation: the desk men buried them.

"Simply for security purposes," added the DG. He looked at his watch.

"Of course, sir."

"Let me give you another drink." He took Stuart's cut-glass tumbler from him and poured a careful measure of malt whisky, as a chemistry teacher might demonstrate how to handle some dangerous compound. It was nearly 5:40 p.m.: time for BBC 1's early evening news bulletin. The DG went to the small TV set built into the antique bookcase. He switched on in time for an announcement about programme changes. Then came the news. The two men watched a short clip of film which showed the remains of the Wever cottage. Mrs. Wever had been in the milking shed when the explosion occurred, and had escaped unharmed. She told the interviewer that her husband was not interested in politics, adding that the chicken farm was said to have been sited near an old U.S. Army Air Force bomb dump. A spokesman from the local authority did not deny it, saying that an inquiry was being started. The next item concerned preparations for the Queen's visit to Africa. The DG switched the news off. "I think it will be all right," he said. "Luckily we had one of our chaps in Thetford. He hurried along to have a word with Mrs. Wever."

"Was there a wartime airfield near there?" Stuart asked.

"Bomb dumps do not necessarily have to be in close proximity to airfields," said the DG. "Anyway, it was the best story that Operations could cook up at an hour's notice. If we can sustain the doubt for another twenty-four hours, interest in the story will fade." He smiled and raised a hand to press a finger against the pink hearing aid concealed by his long hair. "What I still don't know is why you got there early, Stuart."

So that was it. "I was given no particular time to be there, sir. The written note my Los Angeles controller gave me just said that Franz Wever would be at his home from two p.m. onwards that day. In the event, it wasn't correct; Wever was a devout churchgoer. Once a week he volunteered to clean the church."

"Is that so?" said the DG, committing that departmental error to his memory. He smiled. "Well, all I can say is that you are doing a grand job, Stuart. Keep at it, and try and give me something for the PM when she returns from the economic summit conference in Tokyo. These politicians are a restless and impatient breed." The DG tipped the rest of his whisky and water down his throat and gave a grim smile. It was an unmistakable sign of dismissal. Boyd Stuart swallowed the rest of his malt and got up to leave.

"Going?" said the DG as if surprised. "Oh well, I imagine you have lots to do. Were you thinking of returning to Los Angeles immediately?"

Stuart opened the door. "Probably next week, sir."

"Well, you know best," said the DG, leaving Stuart wondering whether the DG thought his stay in London was too long or too short.

# 15

"The DG gives me the creeps."

"Come back to bed, Boyd," Kitty said. "It's two o'clock in the morning."

"I know he's a nice family man who helps old ladies across the street and takes stray dogs home, and my ex-wife adores him, but he really gives me the creeps. Wever told me that our people had talked to him over and over again. The DG won't admit it."

"Are you going to sit looking out of that window all night? What are you staring at?"

"There are two men in a car outside the butcher's on the corner. They've been sitting inside that green car ever since we came back from the restaurant."

Kitty laughed. "Are you getting paranoid? Are you starting to imagine that little men are following you?"

He did not answer.

"Boyd, I'm serious," she said. "It's just not in character. Come to bed and forget it. In the morning the men will be gone, the car will be gone and you will have slept off the effect of that Spanish burgundy."

"The DG asked me why I was early going out to see that man Wever," said Stuart. "I didn't tell him what time I got out there. I didn't tell Operations. I didn't tell my controller. I didn't tell you. I didn't tell anyone. How the hell would the DG know, unless he had someone following me from the airport?"

"If it's just hurt pride, I would forget it," said Kitty. "Internal Security run regular monitoring checks on everyone from time to time. There is no significance in your being followed from the airport. It's nothing to get hysterical about, darling."

"Then let me tell you something that is worth getting hysterical about," said Stuart softly. "Suppose I *hadn't* chanced across an old woman who happened to know that Wever was in church? Suppose I'd followed instructions to the letter: turned up a little later, gone straight to the Wever house, had a cup of tea with his wife and waited for him to come back. Then what?"

"What are you trying to say, Boyd?"

"Then it would have been *me* blown up with that bloody bomb! That's what I'm trying to say, Kitty."

"Don't get angry with me, Boyd."

"I'm all ready to get angry with someone. I narrowly missed being killed in a car in Los Angeles. And that was murder; I'm certain of it." He looked at Kitty. "The commercial attaché's assistant was killed. He was an outsider, Kitty. You know how much the department hates that."

"Yes, you told me."

"Someone phoned Wever. Someone phoned him

and checked I was there before detonating that bomb."

"You don't know what the caller told him; you said you couldn't hear."

"He had a phone call," said Stuart slowly, carefully and with mounting anger. "There were a lot of yeses, and a few minutes after that, the house was blown up by someone close enough to detonate a radio fuse."

"How can you possibly know it was a radio fuse detonated within sight of the house?"

"Because I know the department, Kitty. I know how these things are done. And when I said Wever worked for us the DG didn't bat an eyelid."

"MI5, you said."

"So the DG admits that Five is running Wever. We all know that the DG can make them leap through flaming hoops if he feels like it; and this job has all the clout of the PM behind him."

Kitty King ran a hand through her hair. She was wide awake now. "But what for, Boyd. Tell me what for?"

"Except for a minor miscalculation by the ordnance technicians, Wever would have disappeared, I would have disappeared and all that evidence you receipted tonight and put in the red safe would have disappeared too."

"Boyd!"

"And just by some remote lucky chance, the department happens to have someone in Thetford this afternoon. Someone they can contact at a moment's notice. Someone the DG can trust with the delicate task of putting a roll of pound notes into Mrs. Wever's mouth."

"Conjecture," said Kitty. "That's largely conjecture." She sat up in bed.

"Don't switch on the light," said Stuart speaking quietly and holding the curtain open so that he could see down into the street below.

Kitty forced a little nervous laugh. "Are you trying to tell me that your father-in-law arranged to have you killed? XPD, expedient demise—is that what you are saying?"

"There's no getting round the facts, Kitty."

She leaned forward towards him but he didn't turn to look at her. "The DG has no contact with any XPD orders, Boyd. You know the system; XPD orders come only on the personal authority of each individual Regional Ops. Chief, and are then countersigned by the DG's deputy. It's always been done that way. The DG has no say in it."

Stuart let the curtain move slowly back into position, then he turned to look at her. "Yes, it's always been done that way, Kitty, so that any DG can go before secret parliamentary committees and truthfully swear that he has no knowledge of expedient demise or any other authorized killings. I know how it's all done, Kitty. Believe me I do."

"No one knows about it," said Kitty. "Not even my boss knows how they assign the XPDs or even which of our agents handle them. But I'll tell you one thing, Boyd. There's no way that Sir Sydney could arrange it without the collusion of others, and I've worked there long enough to know that he wouldn't get it."

"Are you seriously telling me that in the time you've worked in Operations, you've never seen an order for expedient demise?"

"For defectors, Boyd. For traitors. For people with heads filled with secrets like the whereabouts of field agents. Then only after the department is certain that they are on the point of betraying everything to Moscow. They never XPD field people like you, pursuing an operational task to the best of your ability."

"Do you mind if I take notes," said Stuart sarcastically. "You're talking just like a field manual."

"Thanks a lot! And now I've had enough of your bad temper. I'm going home!"

"Oh, stop it, Kitty. You know I didn't mean to say that."

"Do you know what it's like for me, being in this bloody flat with you?"

"What do you mean?"

"I mean that everywhere I look there are bits and pieces belonging to your other women."

"*Woman,* not women," said Boyd Stuart. "Jennifer's things, you mean?"

Kitty's lips tightened. Even hearing the name of the

woman with whom Boyd Stuart had shared his life was enough to make her feel the pangs of jealousy, and feeling the pangs of jealousy made her angry. "Yes, your bloody Jennifer. That's right. How did *she* talk? Not like a field manual. . . . How then? Like a sex manual . . . ?" She found a handkerchief.

"Oh, my God, Kitty, don't start crying, I can't stand it."

"That's it!" she yelled. "Of course! Not 'Don't cry, Kitty, because I hate to see you unhappy'—not 'Don't cry, Kitty, what can I do for you?' It's 'Don't cry, little Kitty, because your man can't stand it.' " She was very angry now. She threw the bedclothes aside and jumped out of bed. She was still sniffing as she put on her bra and looked under the bed for her shoes.

"Your car is miles away," Stuart reminded her.

"Don't worry about me," she said tartly. "I'm not frightened of little green men in flying saucers."

"Oh, go to hell," said Stuart, and meant it. After he heard the front door close, he went down, wondering if she would be waiting there for him, but she had gone home. He undressed and went to bed but it was not easy to go to sleep. Awake in the darkness, he listened to the sound of the traffic going along Millbank. The road alongside the river was never quiet; it was one of the penalties of living here. Would Kitty King report the conversation they had just had, he wondered. How would that affect his career prospects? He chuckled to himself: what kind of career prospects does a man have when he suspects that his employer is trying to kill him? And if his employer is also his father-in-law? It was a problem still unresolved by the time he drifted into a deep sleep. When he awoke, very late the next morning, the sun was shining and the green car outside the butcher's shop and the men inside it had gone as if they had never existed.

So that, by Monday morning when he started work, the idea that someone from his own department would plot to have him killed was almost gone from his mind.

# 16

At that same time—10:30 on the morning of Monday, July 2, 1979—Sir Sydney Ryden was attending the regular weekly intelligence meeting. It is held in a small conference room on the first floor of 12 Downing Street. The room contained a long polished table, with eight chairs, four coloured telephones, some red-leather armchairs, a fireplace with highly polished fire irons, and a small oil painting by Winston Churchill placed above the hearth. The only incongruously modern item was a machine with two "letter boxes" in its top: a paper shredder.

Those present for the final part of the meeting were a deputy secretary of the Cabinet Office representing the Prime Minister, the coordinator of intelligence, Sir Sydney Ryden, and his opposite number, the DG of MI5.

The only important such person missing was the chief of GC HQ, the head of the department which obtains intelligence from orbiting satellites and radio monitoring. The reason for his absence was that nearly all his best hardware had been financed by the American government, an investment secured by the presence of American National Security Agency employees in the most sensitive posts in his department. The chief of GCHQ had departed early. He always did when the agenda included as a last item "non-electronic systems." It was a polite way of asking him to leave the room. It was better that he did not know what was discussed, rather than have to feign ignorance to his American colleagues.

"In the absence of any hard and fast evidence, we have to assume certain things," said Sydney Ryden as soon as the GCHQ chief had departed. "We must assume that a large body of documentary evidence has fallen into private hands. We have to assume that this material has not been noted, indexed, inventoried, photocopied or seen by the U.S. State Department. . . ."

"How can we be quite sure of that?" said the man from MI5.

Sir Sydney turned and, raising a hand to press his hearing aid, scowled. The MI5 man seemed ready to cower under the threat of the upraised hand. "I have people there," said Sir Sydney Ryden. "We have scoured the State Department archives."

"Even the classified ones?"

"What else would be of use?" His voice was low and resonant.

"Quite," said the MI5 chief, and was able to convey in that one syllable all his doubts that Sir Sydney Ryden had penetrated the secret archives of the U.S. State Department.

"We assume that the U.S. government have no knowledge of it," continued Sir Sydney, glowering at his opposite number. "The material in question includes messages, telegrams, cables and conversations between various representatives of His Majesty's government and the German leaders during the year 1940."

The deputy secretary from the Cabinet Office looked at his watch. He had a great deal to do before lunchtime, and that included briefing the Prime Minister on this meeting. "I think we can all dispense with the euphemisms, Sir Sydney," he said. "We're talking about the Hitler Minutes, aren't we? We're talking about the undated document headed 'Framework for a negotiated settlement' that was passed to the German Foreign Office"—he paused and wrinkled his brow—"via Stockholm, if my memory serves me correctly, in late May 1940."

It was about time, thought Sir Sydney Ryden, that his colleagues started to share some of the nightmares that he had borne for the last few weeks. It was time for them to hear his worries. "How I wish that was all we were talking about, gentlemen," he said after a long silence. "But I can assure you that that dissertation of well-intentioned gobbledegook would never cause me to lose a wink of sleep at night. There would be no great difficulty in passing that off as a clever way of playing for time during the Dunkirk evacuation."

"What then?"

"We're talking about top-level exchanges in which specific concessions were discussed. The map of Africa was to revert to its nineteenth-century colours: German East Africa, German South-West Africa, Togoland and the Cameroons would reappear. And the British government would support German demands for a return of the Caroline Islands, the Mariannes and the Marshalls." He bared his teeth. "Samoa and German New Guinea would be transferred to them of course."

"My God," said the deputy secretary. Sir Sydney looked round the room, and was not disappointed with the horrified faces of the others. There was little need to detail the cataclysmic portent of such revelations.

Relentlessly, Sir Sydney continued his grim story. "The whole of Ireland was to be placed under what was to be known as an Anglo-German administration—you know Winston's feelings about Ireland of course—and Cork and Belfast were to become permanent German naval bases for a newly created German Atlantic fleet. Some of the warships would have been ours. . . ." He hurried on through the gasps of dismay and shouts of no. "Worldwide port facilities of the Royal Navy, from Hong Kong to Gibraltar, would immediately start refuelling and revictualling any German warships as required, as well as any merchantmen flying the German flag."

The coordinator was flushed in the face by now. He clenched his fist on the table top. "If this is some sort of joke, Sir Sydney. . . ."

"No joke," said the DG. "How I wish it were."

"And the PM has been told?"

"She is particularly distressed about the Irish dimension," said Sir Sydney. "You can see how this could be manipulated by the Dublin government or by the IRA."

"Hardly any need for manipulation," said the deputy secretary with uncharacteristic bitterness. He was the youngest man there and felt that this was a legacy that his elders and betters should not have left for him.

"And credit guarantees," continued Sir Sydney. "Several hundred million pounds sterling was to be advanced for German purchases from Canada and the U.S.A. This to be backed by the British gold reserves already there. And Churchill most unwisely discussed the use that the Germans might make of elements of the French fleet."

"Oh, my God," said the MI5 man. "Every last bloody friend Britain has in the world would be enraged overnight if this sort of stuff was ever made public." He took off his spectacles and polished them with exaggerated energy. In spite of his distress, he could not help feeling some gratification that this had landed on Sir Sydney Ryden's desk rather than his own.

"Any rumours that we were prepared to hand over parts of Africa to save Britain would certainly stiffen anti-white attitudes about Zimbabwe-Rhodesia," said the deputy secretary.

Sir Sydney nodded. "It's a *political* problem of the first magnitude. It's containable if only rumours emerge—such rumours have surfaced several times over the past fifteen or twenty years—but if there was written proof. . . ." Sir Sydney let it go.

"Worse than Suez," said the deputy secretary, who was just old enough to remember that departmental upheaval. He had pencilled an elaborate maze all over his agenda sheet. Now he blocked off the beginning and end of it so that there was no way out.

"Do you realize what this would do to our delicately balanced economy?" said the coordinator. "Foreign investors would flee from sterling and the stock market would crash . . . the social consequences of that would be terrible to contemplate. The Kremlin is well provided with friends in our trade unions and on the shop floor who would welcome any opportunity for creating chaos."

"Our finest hour!" said the coordinator. "Poor old Winston would be turning in his grave."

"I'm not sure you understand me," said Sir Sydney Ryden. "I'm referring to decisions in which Sir Winston Churchill played a major role. I'm referring to overtures Sir Winston made to the German leader himself."

"Hitler?" said the coordinator, his face reflecting his incredulity. "Adolf Hitler and Churchill?"

Sir Sydney Ryden stood up and closed the locks on his document case with a loud click. "Let's not meet trouble halfway, gentlemen. Pray that my people get their hands on these wretched files before the press see them."

The MI5 director also got to his feet. "I think we'll have to point out that these documents are not authenticated." He looked at Sir Sydney meaningfully.

"I take your point," said Sir Sydney. "I think it would be as well if we talked about the preparation of a couple of items."

"Forge them, and then prove to the press that they are forgeries, to discredit the rest of the material?" The MI5 man nodded. He had a department which employed some of the most meticulous engravers, paper technicians and handwriting experts in the world. "Tomorrow lunch, eh? The Travellers' suit you?"

Sir Sydney Ryden hesitated. It would mean rearranging his morning but this was urgent. He was not an inveterate clubman and he would have preferred a private dining room in his own building, but he nodded his agreement. At least they would get a decent claret at the Travellers' Club. "One o'clock then. I dare say we'll find somewhere to hide ourselves away, after we've eaten."

The MI5 man noted the appointment in his tiny diary and replaced it into his waistcoat pocket.

"It's damnable timing," said the coordinator looking at the calendar. "Suppose it all leaked out while the Queen and Mrs. Thatcher were both in Africa. Could it possibly be a plot with exactly that in mind?"

"I don't believe so," said Sir Sydney.

The deputy secretary picked up the agenda sheets and fed them into a shredder with a hand which visibly trembled. Like all shredders for top-secret waste, it reduced the papers to narrow worms, then cross-chopped them before dropping the confetti into a large transparent plastic bag. "Churchill discredited. It would mean the end of the Tory Party," he said miserably. "That's what I can't bear thinking about."

# 17

Charles Stein was a happy man. The son of a Polish-born trade union official in the garment industry in New York City's West Side, Stein had grown up in a house where a strike meant a bare dinner table. In such times the young Steins were fed on leftovers from the table of their equally penurious next-door neighbours.

Charles had never shared the interest in books that his father had stimulated in his brother Aram, but that did not mean that he grew up illiterate. Charles—or Chuck, as he was more usually called at the garment factory where he was eventually employed as an assistant to a senior salesman—could find his way through an order book or an account sheet with the natural ease that some untutored men bring to the intricacies of horse-racing. And he was a generous boy who never begrudged the money that he paid each week into the family expenses, which in turn enabled his mother to send Aram cinnamon *khvorost* and some money to supplement his meagre scholarship at Johns Hopkins University. But Chuck was not entirely benign. From his father, Chuck Stein got an all-pervading hatred of Hitler and on Pearl Harbor day he joined the long line of men in Times Square who waited patiently to join the U.S. Army. So did his young brother.

Charles Stein's political convictions had now faded, but his natural ability to read an account book remained. It was this facility, together with the unmistakable power of his personality and the energy that even his immense bulk could not disguise, that had made Stein the leader of the men who called themselves "the Kaiseroda Raiders." In spite of the military etiquette, the nostalgia and the respect that all of them showed towards Colonel John Elroy Pitman the Third, every last man of them knew that the important decisions were made by Charles Stein. And they preferred it that way.

"You'll like the *bau,*" Charles Stein told his son. "They have shrimp inside. The chicken ones are not so tasty." he wiped his mouth on his napkin. That was the worst of eating "small chow"—one always got fingers and face covered in soy and mustard sauce and bits of food. At least, Charles Stein always did.

"I've had enough, thank you, Dad. Why don't you finish it?"

"They'll wrap it if you want to take it home."

"You have it, Dad."

"I hate to see food wasted," said Stein. He wrestled with temptation. "I've had enough to eat really, but it's a crime to see food wasted." He gulped a little of his jasmine tea and then filled the tiny cup again. "Paper-wrapped shrimp?"

"No thanks, Dad. I couldn't eat another thing."

"These little eateries in Chinatown are the only places where you find the real thing. The Breslows took me to eat in a fancy Chink joint on La Cienega last Monday. Waiters in claw-hammer coats, finger bowls with lemon slices, linen bibs to protect your necktie, and everything. But at the end of the line, what have you got?"

Stein's son shook his head to show that he didn't know.

"Chop suey. That's what you've got," Charles Stein pronounced sagely. "Not these delicate little specialties that the cooks up here on North Broadway know how to put together."

"Is Breslow going to make that movie?" said Billy.

"He's spending money on pre-production," said his father.

"I'd like to see one of the majors getting involved in it. If Paramount or Universal put their machine into action. . . ."

Charles Stein reached for two paper-wrapped fried shrimps and put them in his mouth in rapid succession. He crunched them in his teeth and wiped his hands on his napkin. "What do you do, when you are not writing your column in *Variety?*" said Stein with his mouth full.

"But I don't write any . . ."

"It's a joke, son," said his father wearily. Oh, my

god, he had heard about the generation gap but this was the San Andreas fault! "If Breslow puts together a halfway decent little film, he'll take the rough-cut round the world and get back his money four-fold, five-fold maybe, and still have a piece of the equity. He couldn't hope for anything like that if he takes this deal to the majors."

"Here, Dad," said Billy. "I didn't know you knew anything about movie financing."

"Movie financing is no different from any other kind of financing," said Stein. "Anyone who knows the difference between red ink and the black kind can understand the movie industry."

"You're seeing a lot of the Breslows lately." A girl came into the restaurant. The dining room was large and crowded with local Chinese clients. The waitress seated her in a booth on the far side of the room. Billy Stein admired her tailored suit of cream-coloured silk, its yarn slubbed to make a texture in the weave. On the lapel there was a small gold brooch. The brightly coloured silk neckerchief completed the effect. She slid her large sunglasses up onto the crown of her head in order to scrutinize the menu and then looked at the tiny gold wristwatch on her suntanned wrist.

For a moment there was a pause in the activity. Staff and customers alike watched the beautiful young woman as she produced a packet of cigarettes from her handbag. An elderly Chinese waiter hurried forward to strike a match for her. She was out of place in this run-down restaurant on the wrong side of the freeway. She belonged down in the "golden triangle" or at the Bel Air country club. But this was Los Angeles and even the sight of a radiantly beautiful woman does not halt business for more than a moment or two. The three dark-suited Chinese men in the next booth went back to discussing insurance, the two blue-shirted security men at the corner table took up again the issue of Dodger Stadium tickets, the barman finished mixing four vodka martinis and the Steins went back to the subject of Max Breslow.

"I've been seeing a lot of the Breslows," said Charles Stein, "because I want to keep an eye on what the little son of a bitch is doing."

Billy Stein took a pair of sunglasses from his pocket and put them on. The lenses were corrected for his vision and in spite of the coloured glass they gave him a better look at the young woman across the room. She was stunning, he decided. He flicked a couple of pastry fragments from the front of the faded blue denim jacket and glanced down to be sure that the large gold medallion was visible in the unbuttoned front of his shirt. He was wearing his favourite boots —light-brown suede from Italy with criss-cross laces all the way up the front to the knees. The young woman must have noticed the movement for she looked up from the menu. He caught her eye but she looked away quickly. "I thought you were getting to like him."

"I said he was a good businessman," said Charles Stein, while chewing. He waved one of the little minced pork dumplings in a horizontal movement to show that his son had got it wrong. "That doesn't mean I *like* him." He dipped the second dumpling into the dish of soy and put it into his mouth. "Means I got to watch out for what he might try to pull."

"For instance?" said Billy.

"Did it ever strike you, Billy, that if Breslow could get his hands on all the documents we got out of the mine, he wouldn't need me?"

"He wouldn't need any of us," said Billy, still giving some of his attention to the woman, who was now ordering a meal. Perhaps she was not waiting for some companion after all, thought Billy. It was unusual for a woman so stylishly dressed to take lunch over here in Chinatown; for her to have come here to lunch alone was unthinkable. Even so. . . .

"Right," said Stein. "He wouldn't need Colonel Pitman, wouldn't need me. Wouldn't need any of the 'Raiders' for anything at all. And that would suit him very well because he doesn't enjoy having me looking over his shoulder, and interfering with everything he's doing and planning."

"If he stole your papers," said Billy, "if he stole them and then didn't pay you the money you need . . ." He tugged on the gold chair round his neck, and tightened his fist in anger. "I'd take that old

Mauser pistol you brought home from Germany and blow him away."

"Now, now, Billy."

"You think I couldn't do it, Dad. You're wrong. I took that old gun out into the desert last year and spent a little time learning how to handle it. That's a wonderful pistol, that Mauser. You should see what I can do to a row of cans. . . ."

"Breslow ain't going to stand around like a row of tin cans, Billy. You forget any idea of rough stuff. I don't even like to hear you talk that way. What would Momma have said if she'd lived to hear her son talking like some cheap hoodlum?"

"OK, Dad, but what are you going to do to make sure he doesn't rip us off?"

"Well, I've been thinking of that, Billy. First, you've got to understand how much trouble we've gone to in order to prevent Breslow finding out where the files and papers and everything are hidden. It's essential that we keep the location a secret from him and from anyone associated with him. And that goes double for that Brit!"

"I forgot that you met the Brit. What was he like?"

"You missed something, Billy," said Stein. He drained the last of the tea into his cup and then waved the teapot lid at the waitress to get more. "Boyd Stuart, he calls himself. What kind of faggot name is that? But he's no faggot when it comes to weighing in; two hundred pounds at least, and I'd guess he knows how to handle himself, and never mind the fancy accent. About forty years old . . . the sort of face that makes it difficult to guess the age. Cunning! You could see it in his eyes."

"Sounds as if you like him even less than you like Breslow," said Billy Stein, who had long since grown used to his father's extreme and unpredictable passions about the people he met.

"Too Aryan for me," said Charles Stein. "I saw too many guys like him striding around in the POW cages with SS flashes on their collars."

"Did you ever stop to think, Dad, that maybe . . ."

"I'm a racist," Charles Stein completed the sentence. He took one of the hot towels that the waitress had brought along with a fresh pot of jasmine tea and, lowering his head, buried his face in it for what seemed a long time. Billy Stein looked to see if the wonderful girl was watching his father's ablutions and was relieved to see that she was giving all her attention to a plate of roast duck. "Yeah, I'm a racist," said Stein, emerging happily from the towel like a walrus surfacing for a fresh herring. "And it's too late to change me now, Billy, so we've both got to put up with it."

Billy nodded and retied the lace of his high boot.

"Ideally," said Charles Stein, "we have to get photocopies, microfilm, microfiche or whatever the hell it's called. Then we could show what we've got to any of these people, and still have the originals locked away and hidden."

"So why not?" said Billy.

"Sometimes I worry about you, Billy. Sometimes I wonder what is going to happen to all the stocks and the business investments and the nice little deal we got with that insurance broker in St. Louis. . . . Sometimes I wonder what is going to happen to all that when I finally take up my option on that small piece of turf we bought in Forest Lawn."

"Jesus, Dad, don't talk about that."

Stein was mollified by his son's horror at the prospect of losing him. "We can't get that stuff microfilmed," he said, "because it would attract too much attention. Ask yourself how we'd go about it. We can't just find some microfilm outfit in the yellow pages without a good chance they would blow the whistle on us as soon as they see what the stuff is all about."

"Buy a microfilm machine," said Billy. "What can it cost? A grand? Five grand? Not ten grand—and even that would be worth it when we are playing for the kind of telephone numbers you keep talking about. What did Breslow say—a hundred million dollars?"

"No, it was *me* who said a hundred million dollars. Breslow played it all very close." He poured more tea. Billy put his hand over his cup to show he had had enough of it. "And who'd work the machine?

Could you work it? Could I work it? No, it needs training to operate a thing like that."

Charles Stein succumbed to the temptation of the last of the chicken noodles. There was a trace of scrambled egg—a bright yellow cushion under a sliver of chicken meat and a sauce-encrusted shrimp tail, the whole ensnared in a loop of fresh noodle. Chuck Stein levered his china spoon underneath and dashed a trace of soy upon it before savouring the combination.

He closed his eyes with pleasure. Only after he had swallowed it did he speak again. "You know I'm the only person who has been through all those documents. Colonel Pitman can't read German—his French is OK but no German—and the other boys from the battalion don't give a damn."

"It's not something that interests me a great deal," said Billy, apologetically. "I read all those war books you used to bring home and tell me I ought to read, but it doesn't grab me." Billy stole another glance at the girl. "If I was to tell you the honest truth, Dad, I don't even understand who won the war, or even who was fighting it." He looked at his father hoping that an explanation would be offered.

"Yeah, well, it's easy," said Stein. "Hitler started killing the Jews, so the Jews came to America and built an atomic bomb so President Roosevelt could help them, but he dropped it on the Japanese."

"I never know when you are kidding, Dad."

"I'm never kidding," said Stein; he leant across the table. His sleeve went into the soy but he did not notice. "These documents are dynamite; you'd better understand that. If this English cat knows that I've been telling you what's in these documents—all this stuff about Churchill talking with Hitler and offering him a sweet deal for a quick peace . . . well, he might get his orders."

"What do you mean?"

Stein glanced around the room, and then whispered, even though there was no one within earshot. "What I'm trying to tell you, Billy, is that the Brits might have already decided to destroy these documents, and rub out anyone who knows about them."

"Dad, no."

"And they'd be crazy to go to that extreme and leave alive some kid whose father has told him everything that's in them. I mean, those Brits are not going to know that it just goes in one of your ears and comes out the other, Billy. They are going to think you are a bright lad who listens to what his dad tells him. Right?"

"Oh, come on, Dad." Billy smiled and waited for his father to smile too, but Charles Stein did not smile. He was serious.

"Ask yourself what you would do in their position," said Charles Stein calmly. "If you were the British Prime Minister and wanted to keep the memory of Sir Winston highly polished, what would you do?"

"I don't know," said Billy. Now his attention was no longer diverted by anything around him.

"Suppose it was Abe Lincoln," persisted Charles Stein. "Suppose a couple of lousy Brits were sitting in Liverpool with a carload of stuff that proved that Abe Lincoln was a pantywaist who sent a message of congratulation to Stonewall Jackson after the Battle of Bull Run. You think the CIA would wait two minutes before taking off after those Brits with no holds barred? You think that they would let the lives of a couple of blackmailers—that's the way they would see it, Billy, blackmailers—get in the way, if Abe Lincoln's memory was going to be sullied and the U.S.A. made into a laughing stock all over the world."

"Politics."

"With a capital P, Billy boy," said Stein. "I want you to realize that you could become a contract. From now on you watch your step; take it easy on the booze, and stay off the other stuff. Keep away from dark alleys and tell me immediately if you see anything unusual."

"I sure will, Dad. You think I should carry a gun?"

"It wouldn't be a bad idea, Billy. Just until this business is over."

"A big guy you say—about forty?"

"They won't be sending that dude to blow anyone away. They will have specialists who just arrive in town, do their thing and scram."

"Jesus, Dad. I never know when you are kidding. Do you really think these Brits would . . ."

"Why take chances, Billy? That's all I'm saying. Don't take no chances."

Billy took out a white comb and ran it quickly through his long dark hair. It was something he was prone to do in moments of stress and his father recognized this. "Maybe I'll go down to Mexico," said Billy. "Why don't you come too? That guy in Ensenada has converted the locker space into an extra cabin—all hand-crafted oak; he's a real craftsman. . . ."

"He sure crafted the bill. Did you see what it's costing us to run that damned boat?"

"Pedro's a wonderful old man," said Billy. "Long beard and that strong Mexican accent. Did you see the piece of movie I made of him rebuilding the boat? He could be a film star, or something."

"He could be a film star," said Stein bitterly, "except that he can't afford to take a cut in salary."

"Come on, Dad! It's a good investment. With the extra cabin and shower we'll be able to overnight in comfort. Drop anchor anywhere the fish are running, and stay as long as we like. No more hotel bills, see? Come down there with me this weekend."

"Just for the time being, Billy, it's best that I see to a few things here in town."

"Why do you keep looking at your watch?"

"Breslow was supposed to be joining us for lunch. He said to go ahead if we arrived before him."

"Here in this greasy spoon? Not exactly his style, is it?"

"Says he's crazy about Chinese steamed pastries. I told him this was the best place in town to eat them. He wants to talk about copyrights, he says."

"I was wondering why you sat so that you can see the door," said Billy.

He had hardly spoken the words before his father began to get to his feet. It was something not accomplished without causing considerable disarray to the plates and dishes on the table, and some spilled sauce. Billy wiped up the mess with a handful of paper napkins while his father shook hands, and listened to

Breslow apologizing for being so late. "And that is my daughter, Mary," said Breslow. He indicated the young lady who had so distracted the younger Stein. Her name was really Marie-Louise, for she was named after her mother, but here in Southern California she preferred the anglicized version.

"Mary Breslow," she said. Billy Stein thought it was the most beautiful name he had ever heard. He took her hand and lowered his head in one of those hand-kissing gestures that he had copied from an old movie.

In all the flurry of apologies and explanations Mary Breslow found a new opportunity to study Bill Stein and she liked what she saw. This tall handsome American was everything that California promised. His long dark hair was wavy and squeaky clean, his teeth white and perfect, and his suntan was the sort of dark golden brown that can never be acquired with indoor lamps. The faded denim work clothes, artfully threadbare in places, were tailored to emphasize his slim hips and muscular shoulders. Just in case anyone should mistake him for a manual worker, there was a monogrammed silk shirt, a paper-thin gold wristwatch and the suede high boots. Already she had heard her parents talk about the Steins' private plane and the big sailing boat they took down the Mexican coast. "You're such a silly girl," her father was saying. "You must have guessed that this was Mr. Stein and his son Billy. You should have looked around to find them and introduced yourself to them."

She smiled and Billy smiled too. And they all moved away from the chaos of the Steins' table to another booth. "Nothing to eat for me," said Breslow hurriedly. "But I would like a drink." He turned to the waitress. "A bloody mary, with plenty of Worcester sauce." Breslow straightened his tie and made sure that his jacket was buttoned. "May I speak with you for a moment, Charles?" he said formally.

"Why, sure." Stein recognized that Breslow's restless movements and urgent need of a drink signified unusual circumstances. It was a conclusion endorsed by the speed with which Breslow consumed his bloody mary.

"I want to show you something in my car," said Breslow.

"Well, I'm sure the kids won't mind waiting." He smiled at Breslow, for Billy Stein and Mary Breslow were already engaged in earnest conversation about discos in Acapulco.

Charles Stein followed Breslow outside into the street. The pavement was hot underfoot and, once they were out of the air-conditioned restaurant, the smog hurt Stein's eyes so that he had to wipe them with his silk handkerchief. Breslow led the way down the ramp of the underground garage across the street and said nothing until he came to where his pale blue Mercedes-Benz 450 SEL was parked. Stein looked at the car with surprise: the whole right side of the car was smashed in. The doors were both jammed tight into the warped framework of the body and the glass smashed. At the front of the car the right wing had been ripped away to expose the whole of the wheel. Inside the car, the seats were glittering with broken glass, and a bent chromium strip had tangled into the headrest so that the upholstery was ripped through to the interior padding.

"They tried to kill me, Charles," said Breslow.

Stein looked at him before answering. Breslow held his hand to his brow as if reliving the experience. The hand began to tremble.

"You'd better come back to the restaurant and sit down," said Stein. "Then we should get you to a doctor and have him check you over." Stein looked at the car again. "When did this happen?"

Breslow looked at his watch. "Not even thirty minutes ago. I took the Ventura Freeway all the way to the Golden State; the Hollywood Freeway was jammed today, I heard on the radio."

"It's Friday, the thirteenth," said Stein. He kicked the tyre to check that it had maintained its pressure.

"Surely you are not superstitious?" said Breslow.

"It can't hurt," said Stein.

Breslow looked at his wristwatch to see if it really was the thirteenth. "They nearly killed me," he said again.

"Well, it can happen to anyone, Max. Come back

and have another bloody mary and think yourself lucky you weren't killed. It must have been a truck, eh?"

Breslow took Stein's arm. "You don't understand, Charles. When I say they were trying to kill me, I mean exactly that. This wasn't any ordinary traffic accident. This fellow was working with two other drivers: one boxed me in, and the other one edged me over into the emergency lane and then tried to crush me against the median wall. Behind me, I had a big panel truck hitting my rear fender as I tried to slow."

"Max. Are you sure you're not imagining all this? Some of these guys go crazy on the freeway. It's easy enough to mistake some drunken salesman or some hyped-up kid for something else." Stein took Breslow by the arm but Breslow's gasp of pain made him release his grip.

"I hurt my arm struggling with the steering wheel," said Breslow.

Stein ran his hand over the car damage. "Look at that!"

"They weren't kids or salesmen, Charles." Breslow trembled again. "You can see the size of the truck from the way my top is damaged." He fingered the torn metal of the Mercedes' roof. "He left some red paint behind, look."

"You're a tough son of a bitch, Max," said Stein in an effort to cheer him up. "You kept behind the wheel and held on, eh? I don't know how you got this heap all the way from the Ventura intersection without a tow truck." Stein laughed and voiced his secret thoughts. "Only a German would arrive apologizing for being late for lunch after that rumble."

Max Breslow tightened his grip on Stein's arm. "Mary mustn't know, Charles my friend. She would be sure to tell her mother. You must promise me help in getting her away from the restaurant. If she comes down here to collect her mother's car," he nodded to indicate the yellow Chevette, "she'll be sure to recognize my Mercedes."

"Come and have a drink, Max." Stein sneezed as the smog got to his sinuses.

"It was the Britisher who did it, Charles. I'm certain of that."

"Why?"

"They are desperate to get the documents. They'll let nothing stand in their way. We must be clever, Charles, or they will kill the two of us, and there will be no money for anyone."

"I'll tell the kids that something important has turned up," said Stein. "Let's tell Mary that I am borrowing the Chevette. That way she'll have no reason to come in here."

"How will she get home?"

"Billy will take her home. He'll love posturing and posing in that goddamned T-bird."

"It's not parked down here?"

"It's only old dudes like us who pay for anything these days," said Stein bitterly. "Billy's left his car on the street, just the way he always does."

## 18

Max Breslow looked around the Stein home with interest. In keeping with Stein's theories about investment, his house was furnished with valuable antique furniture. Most of it had been selected for him by a dealer who had benefited from short-term loans guaranteed by Stein against the surety of the dealer's stock. Charles Stein had little or no idea of the historical background to his furniture and carpets—a discovery which distressed Max Breslow when he tried to strike up a conversation about it.

The two men settled themselves into the comfortable armchairs in the large lounge which commanded a view across the city. Breslow noted the grand piano in one corner of the room.

"Do you play the piano?" he asked politely.

"My wife insisted I get it for Billy, but that kid's got a tin ear."

Breslow nodded sympathetically and looked at the piano upon which a dozen or more framed photos vied for lebensraum. Stein's late wife was given pride of place there; framed in fine silver, she surveyed the unchanged room with a calm smile. On the rare occasions when Charles Stein and his wife had exchanged harsh words, she had told him that he would be better off and happier with a housekeeper than with a wife who slaved for her children, spent her life over the stove and was never appreciated. During his wife's lifetime, Charles Stein had always denied that possibility, but the event had proved her right. He was happier with the housekeeper, who kept to her small apartment, and did not complain when he stayed up late reading the stock prices or writing up his large collection of postage stamps. And the housekeeper did not want displays of affection from him, neither did she want to dress up and go to charity functions, nor ask why Billy had never had a bar mitzvah, nor tell Charles Stein that he would be happier if he lost fifty pounds weight.

The housekeeper brought a tray of tea and his favourite kind of fancy cakes. "Did you notice all the flowers, Mr. Stein? There was a special; I bought almost twice as many for only two dollars over what we regularly spend."

Stein grunted. He did not much like flowers but he was prepared to regard the purchasing of them within the context of the overall upkeep of the house. "Maybe you'd like a real drink?" he asked Max Breslow. The housekeeper stood, teapot in hand, waiting for the reply, but Breslow shook his head and she poured tea for both men.

"I'll tell you this, Charles," Max Breslow began after the woman had left them, "we'll have to move fast or we'll get nothing out of all this except an early death."

"You look much better now, Max," said Stein. "The colour is coming back into your face." It was a charitable remark to make about the pale visage of his guest.

Breslow smiled, "Do you mind if I smoke, Charles?" When Stein shrugged to show his agreement, Breslow reached inside his blue blazer for a leather case. Stein waved away the offer of one of the small, dark, evil-smelling cigars which Breslow lit with studied care.

"We must make all the material public," said Breslow. "I've thought about it a great deal, and consulted with a copyright specialist. . . ." He raised the hand holding the cigar, flattening the palm towards Stein. "Don't worry, Charles. The discussion was all kept on a hypothetical level: no names, no subject matter, nothing to associate it with the movie. But . . ." He paused while he took a long inhalation of the cigar and blew smoke. Stein remained impassive. "But," continued Breslow, "the fact is that we need to establish a clear claim to our rights in this material."

"It's not our copyright," said Stein. "This stuff originated from all kinds of long-dead people: Dr. Morell, Hitler's adjutants, the secretaries, translators."

"Long dead, you say?" said Breslow with a smile. "Those are the operative words. In law, as I understand it, copyright can be communicated by the transference of a document in some privileged way."

"Never mind all that legal double-talk," said Stein. "I went all through that kind of monkey business back in 1950. Get to what's on your mind."

"You have to make all your material available," said Breslow. "It's as simple as that. Until now we've continued in good faith but you've got to release the more sensitive material. At least release it to the translators, so that I can show it to publishers and film people and so on."

"Nothing doing," said Stein flatly.

Breslow leaned over until he was almost lying flat upon the sofa and, with the tips of his fingers, took hold of a brass ashtray. With difficulty, he straightened up and knocked a little ash into it before putting it at his elbow on a small side table. "We have a good script. I'm delighted with the young director I met last week and he's free to start immediately. The executive producer I've used on the last two films is lining up studio space here in the city, and we are proposing to do a few outdoor sequences at a movie ranch out in the desert. The film will soon be starting, Charles. Now comes the time for our next move."

"Let's see the way it goes for a week or two. I've never promised anything—I just said I'd think about it."

"First it was 'let's see if we can get the finance for a movie.' Then it was 'let's see if we can get a satisfactory script.' It's been 'let's see, let's see, let's see,' all down the line, Charles. Now we really have to get moving."

"There are a few ends still to be tidied up," said Stein. "I'd want to meet this director, take another look at the script and look over the contracts concerning the finance."

"Shall I tell you something, Charles? I suspect that the truth is that you don't *want* to publish these papers. You've had these documents for so long now that they have become a part of your life. You talk of them in the same way that you speak of your stamp collection. You'll never sell your stamps—you told me that last Monday—and I'm beginning to suspect that you are equally reluctant to lose possession of these papers."

"Maybe there's some truth in that," conceded Stein.

"In the ordinary way, perhaps it wouldn't matter much," said Breslow. "But we are playing for big stakes, my friend. Who knows what money can accrue from a careful and skillful utilization of this fine asset? But make no mistake about the price of failure." Breslow rubbed his arm. "Isn't it enough for you that the British tried to kill me today? How long do you think it will be before they make such an attempt upon your life too? How long before they decide to kill your Billy? Or my girl Mary? Ask yourself all this while you are demanding more time to think about the script and the director and the financing of the film."

"I'll have to get some protection for Billy," said Stein. He wiped his mouth with his flattened hand. "I'll have to get on to one of these security outfits and have them put a twenty-four-hour guard on him."

"Don't fool yourself," said Max Breslow. "If something happened to your Billy I would blame myself if I hadn't warned you that these people are professional killers. These are not muggers looking for the price of a few joints; they are killers. . . . A couple of guys from a security outfit, you say. . . . The sort of highly trained men that governments employ would kill them without a moment's thought or hesitation. No, you'll have to do better than that if you are to sleep at night without Billy on your mind."

Charles Stein did not move or even blink. Not for the first time, Max compared him with the large reptiles that he had sometimes seen out in the California deserts. But was he one of the harmless varieties, Breslow wondered, or was he dangerous? Every time he was about to make his mind up about this, he found something in Stein that made him pause. Stein stirred his tea and then sucked the spoon briefly before drinking.

"What are you going to do about Mary?" said Stein.

"Me?" said Breslow. As if suddenly remembering the traffic accident, he ran his finger along his arm until he found a place that made him flinch. "It's not worth getting killed for, Charles. And I won't let my family suffer. I shall make contact with our friend Mr. Boyd Stuart and make sure he understands that I have no access to the other papers and that I've never seen any of them. That should be enough to remove me from the firing line." Breslow leant forward and tapped Stein's arm. "It's you I'm worrying about, my friend."

"That makes two of us," said Stein. He selected one of the coconut cakes of which he was particularly fond. He chewed a piece from it and then studied the filling. "I'm too old to die a violent death," said Stein. "I've got my end all figured out. It's going to be upstairs in the best bedroom, with Billy and his grandsons listening to what I tell them about the investments."

"It's no laughing matter," complained Breslow, who felt that his own narrow escape was not being treated seriously enough.

"I'm not joking," said Stein and ate the remainder of the cake. "You should taste one of those," he advised. "I get them from a little baker in Glendale. Maybe that seems a long way to go for cakes but there's no one else who uses real coconut and makes the pastry with butter."

"Let me put a hypothetical question to you," said Breslow. "We are businessmen, are we not? And neither of us is getting any younger, my friend."

Stein's face remained expressionless. Breslow waved his cigar to indicate the expensively furnished room, the cut-glass chandeliers and the illuminated cabinet containing a collection of valuable porcelain figures at which Stein seldom glanced. "You have made for yourself the life you want. Can the world of business really offer you anything?"

"Spit it out, Max," Stein told him.

"Very well. Suppose I was able to arrange a sale of your papers? Suppose we were to include a provision that gave you a percentage of the film profits made, as well as putting a lot of money in your pocket? What would you say to getting out quickly and easily, and giving your attentions to something else?"

When Stein replied, his voice was gruff and his speech was slow. "I've told you before, Max. I am just the front man for a syndicate. I don't own these papers. I just own a very small share in them. The people I'm working with trust me and rely on my judgment. I have to stay close to this deal and make sure my syndicate gets fairly treated."

"And why not?" said Breslow. "Who's talking about selling anyone short? What I'm telling you is that a big financial backer could take over this project and make more money out of it than we ever could. I know a corporation which has diversified into movies, TV, books and paperbacks. There would be cash up front, Charles. And a company like that could never come under the sort of physical threats that the British are subjecting us to." He rubbed his arm again. "Have you got the documents here in the house?"

"Don't crowd me, Max."

"Very well," said Breslow. He placed his cigar in the ashtray in such a way that it was clear he had finished with it. Then he got up to leave.

"You mad at me?"

"My friend, how could that be possible? We are virtually partners, are we not? I'm worried about you. I wish you'd tell me something I can do that might help either or both of us in this present predicament."

"I'll phone you tonight, Max." Stein rang the spoon against his cup reflectively. "Or, failing that, first thing in the morning."

"Very well, Charles, but make sure you double-lock your doors tonight. These people mean business."

"I still got a few tricks up my sleeve," said Stein.

Max Breslow smiled condescendingly. "Of course you have, Charles. But let's hope you do not have to demonstrate what they are."

Billy had arrived and had parked his Thunderbird by the time Breslow was ready to leave. Both Steins stood by Breslow as he got into the driver's seat and nervously touched the controls of his wife's yellow Chevette. It was not a car that Max Breslow liked to drive; only in the big Mercedes did he feel really at home.

"Benedict Canyon will be better at this time of day," said Billy, who had just returned from taking Mary Breslow back home. "It will take you to the Van Nuys turnoff. The Ventura Freeway was already crowded when I was heading back. Or take Mulholland Drive."

Breslow shook his head. The hillcrest route provided dramatic views across the valley and back across Los Angeles, but it was a steep and winding road with soft edges that required an element of caution. "No, I'll stick to the freeway," said Breslow. "A determined driver would find it easy to force this little car off the road, and there are places where a car could disappear into the undergrowth for weeks."

"Whatever you say," said Stein. "But I think you're overreacting."

"We'll talk on the phone when you've had a chance to think about everything I've said."

"Sure thing," said Stein.

The Chevette backed off the ramp with a roar of engine and a puff of smoke; then, as Breslow got the feel of it, it started off down Cresta Ridge Drive, negotiating each hairpin with exaggerated care.

"What's eating him?" said Billy.

The two men went inside and Charles Stein told his son everything that Max Breslow had said. Billy walked round the large sitting room, restlessly fingering the notes of the grand piano and helping himself to one of his father's favourite coconut cakes. At the end of the long story, Charles Stein waited for his son's reaction.

"I sure wouldn't want anything to happen to Mary," said Billy Stein.

His father sighed noisily. "It's Mary now, is it? You only met her at lunchtime. What's hit you? Love at first sight?" he inquired. "Or are you writing a new musical for Streisand? Are you going to keep circling the carpet, mooing like a lovesick cow?"

Billy smiled anxiously. "I knew you were going to blow your top," he said. "I told Mary that you had this hang-up about Germans, and that you would be certain to hit the ceiling."

Billy noticed that his father was blinking very rapidly. In spite of the stillness of his father's large frame and his inscrutable face, Billy recognized this as a danger signal. "You been discussing me, eh? You cruised along in the little old T-bird, with Mantovani oozing out of the stereo, and talked about your dad's shortcomings. Tell me, Billy. Did she *exchange* confidences? I mean, did she tell you a few of good old Daddy Max's little passions and preoccupations?"

Billy was smiling with amused exasperation, waving his hands in an effort to still his father's wrath. "All I said was. . . . if you were listening to me, Dad . . . you'd know that all I said was that I wouldn't want anything to happen to her. Right? You don't have to throw some kind of one-man race riot."

"Now my kid is lecturing me on intolerance. Listen, Billy, did I ever tell you about some years of my life I gave up to fight the Nazis?"

"Did you ever tell me anything else?"

The argument had settled into its usual style, and neither of them took it too seriously. Charles Stein muttered something inaudible and ate the last of the coconut cakes.

"You didn't tell me about how lucky I was having a fancy education and the Cessna and the T-bird and the boat and everything."

"Don't press your luck, Billy," said Stein, and his son was careful enough to accept the warning.

Charles Stein went over to the red house-phone and pressed the button to connect him with the phone in his housekeeper's apartment. "I'm going out now," he told her. "Could be I'll be back very late tonight. Don't open the door for *anyone*. Make sure you double-lock the doors and check the window catches. I hear there were more break-ins up the hill last week. And it's Friday, the thirteenth, Mrs. Svenson." He hung up without waiting for his housekeeper to reply.

"Where are you going?" asked Billy.

"Visiting a pal," said Stein, and Billy knew that he would get no more from his father.

## 19

Charles Stein was not the kind of man commonly seen in the entrance lobby of the Gnu Club. His unkempt appearance and off-hand manner deceived the staff into believing that he was a tourist or a drunk looking for a small beer and some go-go dancers. The receptionist was a slim young man with rimless spectacles, who had committed to memory the faces of most of the big-spending clients and was able to recollect the names too. He exchanged a glance with a large man sitting inconspicuously behind the coatcheck hatch. Silently, the man put on his peaked cap, stepped out on to the soft carpeting and stood where the spotlight that was directed upon the long-stemmed roses illuminated his SECURITY GUARD arm badge and the big biceps muscles too. "Good evening, sir." The guard employed that veneer of exaggerated politeness which is unmistakably an intimidation.

Stein blinked at him but did not answer.

"I said 'good evening,' pal."

"I am not your pal," said Stein, "and if you will step aside, I'm going upstairs."

"Oh, that's what it's all about," said the guard wearily. "You came in to use the john?" Over Stein's shoulder he made a pained face at the young receptionist.

"No," said Stein.

"Try the Alcove Club, just a short walk down the block," advised the guard. "This is just for rich kids."

"I'm the father of a rich kid," said Stein.

"Hey, he's a joker," said the guard to the receptionist. "OK, fats, you've had your fun. Now hit the street and keep walking. You need a tuxedo to come in here. And a clean shirt." He grinned at the receptionist. The guard had moved farther into the light now. It shone on the brightly polished leather belt and cross strap and the bright chromium badge on his blue shirt.

"How would you like to move aside?" said Stein quietly.

The guard clasped one large hand in the other, and began to pull at his finger knuckles one by one, as if trying to count. "And how would you like to learn how to fly, fatso?" he said. He pushed at Stein's belly forcefully enough to halt him.

The receptionist was craning his neck to be sure that no important clients were about to enter the outer doors and so witness a would-be client being manhandled. For this reason he did not see what happened next. He expressed his regret about that many times over the ensuing weeks. He heard a grunt of pain, a strangled yell and the resounding thud of a heavy weight hitting the floor. The vase of roses toppled too and broke on the floor.

"Flying is just for the birds," Stein said softly while removing a set of brass knuckles from his fist. Delicately, with the toe of his two-toned oxford he moved the groaning security guard over until he could see his face. The long-stemmed roses were twisted round the guard's body and his uniform was wet with water from the vase.

The petrified receptionist pressed appropriate buttons on the telephone and said, "Reception. There's a guy tearing the place apart down here." A pause. "No, Mr. Delaney, I can't get the security man—he's crippled the security man already." He put down the phone. "Mr. Delaney is coming," said the receptionist, more to himself than to Stein or the guard.

Stein put his brass knuckles back into his pocket and waited for something to happen. Behind a door marked PRIVATE there was the sound of feet hurrying down stairs. Two men came through it, close together.

One was holding a short baton, while behind him a much older man had a pistol carried low and pointing to the ground. It was an old gun, its blue finish now worn shiny.

"OK!" said the man with the baton. He was a young man in an expensive silk suit and frilly blue evening shirt. His face was pinched and his hairline prematurely receding, but he had the broad shoulders and biceps that come only to the truly dedicated weightlifter. "Where is he?"

The security guard was still lying on the floor, both hands clasping his belly. He groaned. A rose was entwined in his legs.

"Who did it, Murray?" said the young man. It seemed quite wrong that this fat old man should have been able to floor the muscular young guard. The guard groaned again.

"I did it," said Stein simply.

"*You* hit him?" The young man was outraged. He said, "Murray and me work out together at the gym."

"Well, I didn't know that," said Stein apologetically.

"You're going to have to get out of here, mister," said the younger Delaney, taking care not to hold the baton in any way that might be interpreted as a threat.

"You want to be laid out cold, kid? This is Chuck Stein. He don't take no lip from anyone except me." The elder Delaney was a big man, taller than Stein, with the smooth cat-like movements that come with physical fitness. He was tanned and had that sort of naturally wavy hair that responds well to a perm every week.

By now they were all looking down at the guard who, finding he was the centre of attention, tried to sit up.

"Now I have to get myself a new guard, you son of a bitch," said Delaney to Stein. He put his foot on the guard's shoulder and pressed him roughly back to the floor. "You're fired, buddy boy," he told him. He picked up the guard's uniform cap and placed it carefully on the side table.

"This guy was no good anyway," said Stein. He shrugged. "I did you a favour."

"It's OK," Delaney senior told the receptionist.

"Get this cream puff out of my lobby. And phone the agency for a replacement. I want someone here before nine o'clock, just in case those guys from that microchip convention are still in town. I'll be in my office with Chuck. Call me if you want me." His son nodded. He knew what that meant: call me only if you're desperate.

"Still got your army Colt, I see," Stein said. "You give that heater to Parke-Bernet for auction, and you'd get a record price for it."

Delaney laughed, put an arm round Stein's shoulder and guided him upstairs. "You should have phoned, Chuck. Or are you here to sell me protection?" The two men laughed together.

Jerry Delaney's place was a topless-bottomless club which contravened the regulations of most cities in Los Angeles County, as well as violating specific rules of the Alcoholic Beverage Control Department which licences the bars. But this was Lennox, an unincorporated area on the way to Los Angeles International Airport, where anything goes. At Jerry Delaney's Gnu Club you could lay a bet or a broad; snort, smoke or mainline the stuff that Jerry brought in from Mexico and places beyond.

Jerry Delaney's share of the Kaiseroda money had all been put into this two-storey building marked by a smart yellow awning and a bedraggled palm tree. A huge oak desk dominated his large upstairs office, and around it were placed deep leather armchairs of the sort associated with exclusive men's clubs. On the desk there were three telephones in different colours, a large gold-plated pen set and a pair of baby shoes encased in a large block of transparent plastic. Soft music came from some hidden loudspeaker. Jerry Delaney pressed a switch and the music stopped. "Want to dunk that knuckle in some rubbing alcohol?" He went to a large mirrored drinks cabinet and got two glasses.

"Wine for me, Jerry, please."

Jerry Delaney poured a glass of white California wine for each of them. The evening was still young, and a nightclub owner needed a clear head in this part of town. "It's good to see you, Chuck. I got what you asked for." He put his hand against the side of the bottle to test the temperature and then, deciding it was not cold enough, tossed a couple of ice cubes into each glass.

He turned to find Stein staring at the framed photographs. They covered the wall behind his desk to the point of almost obliterating the red plush wallpaper. There were dozens of photos there, most of them of the type favoured by restauranteurs and club owners. Harsh flashlight froze Delaney and some of his more famous clients into awkward poses: leaning precariously across dining tables, holding the inevitable glass of champagne aloft and staring at the camera with a fixed and desperate smile.

But Stein was not studying any of the pictures taken in the Gnu Club. He was looking at a shiny Signals Corps glossy eight-by-ten-inch photo of a mud-spattered M-3, a half-track vehicle mounting a 75-mm artillery piece. Ranged in front of it was a group of men in woollen shirts and gaitered trousers that so suited the rainy Tunisian winter. Behind the "tank destroyer" there were some houses and a cluster of palms bent to conform to the prevailing winds. Stein, already a chubby youth, was seated on the roof of the cab, Delaney was in the driver's seat. Sitting up on the roof of the cab, both arms spread as if to embrace the world, was Stein's handsome young brother Aram. He looked very young, like a child dressed in grown-up's clothing.

"Here's to Aram," said Jerry Delaney before drinking his wine.

Stein raised his glass but did not speak. He could not take his eyes off the photo. Nowhere in his own house was there a picture of his brother; the pain was still too much to bear. But now, confronted with his brother's face, he couldn't turn away.

"You still miss him, Charlie?"

Stein nodded and gulped his drink so that it almost made him cough. "I should never have let him drive that damned jeep," said Stein.

"Jesus, Charlie. You're not still blaming yourself for that, are you? That's over thirty years ago, and it wasn't your fault, buddy."

"I should never have let him drive that jeep. He was only a kid. . . . You or I would have seen those mines."

"We hadn't seen them, coming up the track," said Delaney. "We must have passed damn close to them too." Delaney touched Stein's shoulder briefly. "Stop fretting, Charlie. Aram loved being with you. Do you think he would have wanted to miss going to war with you . . . he would have hated staying at home."

Stein nodded and turned away. The subject was closed. They both drank wine and studied each other with that impartiality all men use to observe the battle between their friends and old age. "So the bank got taken for one hundred million bucks," said Jerry Delaney.

"We got taken," Stein corrected him. "It's our bank."

"I've done all right," said Jerry.

"The colonel's upset about it."

"He'll get over it," said Delaney. "He's going to keep the bank going, is he?"

"He's going to try. But . . ." Stein raised his hand.

"I've got to like having a piece of a Swiss bank," said Delaney. "It gives me a touch of class."

"It's not all over yet," said Stein. "It's getting rough out there."

"It's not exactly Disneyland inside here," said Delaney. "Last night I had six wise guys put one of my topless waitresses into the ice-cream display. I had to call the cops, and in my kind of business it's not a good idea to start asking help from cops. Six respectable looking dudes from the microchip convention! What in hell is it all coming to, Chuck?"

Stein shook his head. Delaney did not understand what he was telling him. "Really rough," said Stein. "I'm trying to set up a deal where we patch up our losses with whatever we can raise from the odds and ends that we have left over."

"The documents and carpets and stuff?"

"But I'm tangling with some tough guys, Jerry. I took that souvenir Mauser over to the club in Roscoe. They've got a rifle range where I can try it out."

Jerry Delaney shook his head. Old fellows such as

Stein should leave guns alone; especially old war-souvenir guns. But he did not say that; instead he tried to encourage his friend. "I'd say you can still handle yourself, Chuck, judging by what I just saw you do to my security guard downstairs."

"I'm not worried about myself," said Stein. "But my kid Billy doesn't know enough to come in out of the rain. . . ."

"These kids," said Delaney, "they wouldn't know a sweat shop from a sweet shop." He sighed. He propped himself on the edge of his desk. "You see my son Joey just now? What's he going to do when I fall off my perch? Can you imagine him running this place? He couldn't handle a Girl Scout who lost her earrings. What's he going to do if he gets the mob trying to move in here, like they tried back in the sixties?"

"What did you do, Jerry?"

"You know what I did, Chuck. I took a few of my best guys and hit back."

"What's that mean?"

Delaney looked round anxiously and then leant forward before answering in a lowered voice. "I got a guy in from New York—an explosives buff. He went up to Vegas and wired a couple of ignitions for me. One of those hoods went out through the roof of his limo. They still leant on me. Then I had a hit man come in from New Jersey. He was recommended by a guy I do business with. He blew away a big man here in town, and after that they got the idea that I wasn't going to do business with them."

Stein nodded sadly. He could see no parallel for him here. "Well, this one is not going to quiet down, Jerry. I feel like I've stuck my finger into a hornet's nest. I don't see any way out of it."

"What do you mean?"

"I mean I might have to scram, Jerry. Real fast. That's why I had to ask you for those papers."

Stein left it like that and drank a little more of his wine. His friend went to the safe in the corner, swung the door open and brought out a bulging manila envelope. He gave it to Stein and watched as the contents were laid out on the desk side by side. A Brazilian passport (complete with photo of Stein) in the name of Stefan Wrzoseki.

"Polish name," explained Delaney, "so that no one will expect you to speak Portuguese." There was a birth certificate dated October 19, 1926—a copy issued by the Polish Ministry of the Interior in Warsaw in 1938. There was a driving licence issued in France. "The French licences have no expiry date," explained Delaney. There was an American Express card too. "It's a forgery. For Christ's sake, don't buy anything with it. He's taken the number from a block of unused ones, so that it can't come up on their computer. Just use it as ID, you understand?"

"This guy knows his way around," said Stein admiringly.

"The best," said Delaney. "Now you're all set up."

"No, Jerry. This stuff is to help a man who's running. But the moment he stops running, he's going to need a whole lot more than this."

"For instance?"

"He needs a history, Jerry. References, bank accounts backed up by bank managers who'll play ball . . . Social Security records, and all that stuff. He needs someone who can put him on the computers, Jerry."

Delaney pulled a face.

"I could pay," said Stein. There was a silence. Stein said, "I told you a lie just now. I told you I wasn't frightened. I am frightened, Jerry."

Jerry Delaney looked at his friend in surprise. "I'll give you the kind of help you need, Chuck. But Jesus . . ." Delaney went to the window and stared at the busy street below.

"They blew away that guy MacIver."

"That will save you a few bucks," said Delaney.

"I felt sorry for the guy," said Stein. "And that shooting in the bar on Western Avenue wasn't just some kid on angel dust. MacIver was doing business with a guy named Lustig, and the next thing I know Lustig is taken suddenly dead. Lustig's little movie company is taken over by a Kraut named Breslow, and he gets clobbered by a truck on the freeway. And what is the connecting link, Jerry? The connecting link is the stuff we brought out of the number two shaft of the Kaiseroda salt mine, Jerry."

The neon lights were on everywhere. In the street there were a few men aimlessly peering at the girlie pictures outside the peep shows, and peeking into the dark, topless bars. And cars cruised past continually, their lone occupants scanning the streets and doorways. Delaney saw none of that, neither did he see the big Caprice Classic parked near the marquee of the porno cinema across the street, or Boyd Stuart's case officer or his West Coast section head who sat well back in the shadows watching the club. The British agents had been waiting there since Stein first entered the Gnu Club.

In Delaney's office neither man spoke or moved. Delaney had never seen his friend look frightened before, let alone admit it. Finally Stein said, "And my kid, Billy. I'll have to have papers for him too." Stein drank his wine. "Whether he'll come with me, I don't know. He says I'm an ignoramus; he says I'm klutzy, and tells me I've got no manners. . . . He don't like the way I eat or the way I talk."

"These uppity kids are all the same," said Delaney, in that automatic way that people talk when their minds are concentrating upon something else. "I paid for my Joey to go to college, and he comes home with all kinds of big ideas about how we should sell the club and go into real estate . . . goddamned kids." He went to the window and pulled down the blind and then closed the heavy curtains. "You're talking about the mob, Chuck. There are no other people organized enough to give you a new identity." Delaney fiddled with the curtain cord. "They swore me to silence. I promised I'd never tell a living soul." He looked at Stein. "Petrucci," he said suddenly, like a man plunging into cold water. He turned away and fiddled with the photo of his wife and family sitting beside the pool at their holiday home at Lake Tahoe. "Bud Petrucci. Remember him? He's the one who got those things for you. He remembers you well. He sends his best wishes; he likes you." Delaney nodded towards the forged passport.

"Petrucci?"

"Sergeant Petrucci. Twitchy little guy, a survivor from the trucks that went up the valley ahead of us. Remember we saw the smoke and wondered what it was? Then we saw three bodies—one of them black—all stark naked, and you said they must be GIs because the bodies were so clean."

Stein felt suddenly cold, as cold as he had felt in that long-ago Tunisian winter. "As cold as a bookmaker's heart," his brother Aram said, and they had laughed. It was a long, slow haul for the column up the scrubby slopes of those rock-strewn hills. They were exposed to the wind here at the crest of this low ridge. Below them there was vegetation and, at the bottom of the gully where the earth was red, a glint of water. There would be cover there; cover against air attack and the eyes of enemy reconnaissance units, and against the elements too. But there would also be mud.

Stein wiped the dust from his face, as he did every minute, and resolved to obtain some goggles at any price. Everyone had them, even the desert Arabs, everyone had them except the soldiers of the army which had paid for them. Behind him he heard the movement of the machine-gun mounting as his brother Aram scoured the skies for aircraft. At least Stein had been able to get goggles for his young brother; for that at least he was thankful.

Up ahead, a smudge of smoke was marking the hill over which the supply column had gone just before radioing their calls for assistance. Delaney was driving, Stein was by his side. They were "point," and that meant the first vehicle to encounter anything that was coming. It was Stein who noticed the truck, axle-deep in soft sand, down the drift amongst the scrub. But Delaney saw the bodies.

There were three of them, sprawled at the side of the narrow track. One was black, the other two paler than any native skin. "GIs," said Stein. "Stripped by the Arabs in as many minutes as it's taken us to come up the valley. Even their dog tags are gone."

"GIs?" said Delaney. "How can you tell?" The engine stalled; it was overheating. He pressed the starter but the engine did not catch. Suddenly it was very quiet.

"Because they are so clean," said Stein. The three bodies were all youngsters, little more than children really. These were the first dead men they had ever seen.

"Maybe we should bury them," said Delaney. No sooner had he said it than Lieutenant Pitman came striding forward to see what was causing the delay. Now he too looked at the bodies, and waited to hear what Stein said.

"Let's go," said Stein. "You guys are going to see plenty more dead bodies before the day is over—leave them for the burial detail."

"Goddamn Arabs!" said Delaney. "Stripped the poor bastards bare ass."

There was a sudden noise of distant explosions—muffled like funeral drums so that the sound came more like a continuous rumble than as separate bangs. Along the crest of the ridge ahead of them patches of grey smoke appeared, moving along the horizon like a family of elephants walking trunk to tail. Then came a great ball of flame and black smoke, and a crackle of exploding small-arms ammunition.

"The Krauts have ranged in on the supply column," said Delaney in alarm. He hit the starter again; this time the engine fired and shuddered into life.

"Prepare to move out," shouted Pitman and behind them Stein could hear shouting and arguing and the scream of the engines as the men tried to manoeuvre the half-tracks on the narrow pathway. Pitman, his tie tucked into his neatly pressed, starched shirt, was holding his new binoculars to his eyes. "There's a soldier coming up the track . . . one of the guys from the column maybe—a sergeant. He's hurt . . . someone go and give him a hand." Delaney went.

Charles Stein rubbed his face. The memory ended as he intended it should. Perhaps some of the details were wrong but it did not matter.

Delaney said, "Petrucci was the sergeant—the machine gunner—who was coming towards us up the hill, just about the time Major Carson got killed. Petrucci—short guy, big black moustache, gold rings on his fingers—stayed with us all during the retreat."

"Retreat," said Stein. "Is that what we're calling it nowadays?"

"His brother is a lawyer, a mob lawyer, in New Jersey. Petrucci retired and lives in Phoenix. He'll know the people you'll have to talk to." Delaney opened a drawer in his desk and found an address book. He turned to the name Petrucci and held the book open while Stein wrote down the details. Stein noticed that Delaney did not let him look at the other pages, or even handle it.

"You're a pal," said Stein.

"Then do me a favour," said Delaney. "Don't tell him I gave you the address, huh?"

## 20

"And you've got good operatives tailing Stein's son?" asked the West Coast section head. He wanted to show that he knew what he was doing. The case officer yawned.

"Good guy; ex-LAPD cop. Not much chance Billy Stein will show him anything new." He interlocked his fingers and stretched his arms out in front of him until the joints cracked. That it was a gesture of both boredom and disdain was registered by the section head. He was not popular.

"Just one man?"

"I didn't get into this business yesterday," said the CO. "I've allocated five good men for Stein and another five for Max Breslow. They're working two turns, two guys per shift, with the fifth man for relief and emergencies. It's costing us more than we can afford. We can't keep it going forever."

"Local people?"

"Not all of them, but they all know the city well enough."

"I feel sure Stein and Breslow have those damned papers here in town. Stein was able to take that Dr.

Morell file to show Stuart at fairly short notice. I think that means they have everything close by."

"Could be anywhere," said the CO. "Stein went to Geneva last month. We don't know where he went in Switzerland. Could be that's where he has the papers. His son Billy has a plane and he spends a lot of time down in Mexico, fooling around with that twelve-metre sailing boat. The documents might be somewhere south of the border, might even be on the yacht."

The CO shifted in his seat. They had been in the car a long time by now and he was becoming uncomfortable. He watched a radio car drive slowly down the street; the cops eyed the passing crowds with careful and suspicious concentration.

"Not on the boat," said the section head after the police car had passed them. "Not unless they have split the documents into more than one lot. The boat wouldn't hold them. The report I saw describes the load as two large packing cases full."

"But maybe not all documents," said the CO. "Stein got suddenly rich after the war; I'd guess that there was also gold and stuff in the trucks that Stein helped to steal. The documents were probably a disappointment to them at the time."

"Disappointment, yes, I suppose so."

"The kind of disappointment I need once in a while," said the CO enviously.

"Who did you say he'll be talking to in this club?"

"The owner is Jerry Delaney, a smooth-talking crook who's into everything from porno movies to stolen fruit machines. Suspected of mob connections."

"In the army with Stein, you say?"

"We're not certain of that. London won't let us dip into the Washington computer, you know, not even unofficially. But they are both about the same age, so it's probable."

"I don't think we're going to get anything out of this," said the section head. "Let's tell the people in the other car to take over. I'm sure that Stein will stay in that club until midnight and then drive home and go to bed. I promised to phone London tonight with a situation report."

"I'm inclined to agree," said the case officer. "Let's call it a day." But before they did anything about it, a grey Pontiac double-parked alongside them and a young man jumped into the rear seat of their car.

"Hello, Santos," said the CO. The man grinned. He was a dark-skinned youth with an Afro hair-do and a long moustache which drooped over the ends of his mouth. He was wearing a rock-and-roll T-shirt and a football jacket.

"Santos is monitoring the tap on the Stein and Breslow phones," the controller explained to the section head.

"A call to Stein," said the youth. "A call timed at eight-thirty. A man named Bock called him from London."

"Who answered? Billy Stein?"

"Billy Stein took off for Ensenada. He phoned the Breslow girl but he got nowhere with that proposition, so he took his T-bird and headed south. We have a tail on him."

"So who answered?"

"No one. The message went on to the answering machine. I've got a transcript here." He was holding a piece of paper. "But you probably would sooner hear the essence of it."

"Yes."

"This guy Bock works for a German bank in London. Says he has life-and-death information about the documents—papers, he said on the phone, but that's got to be the documents, right?"

The case officer nodded.

"Bock wants to talk to Stein but he's acting very nervous about his contact number. We have a secretarial service number. Bock says to leave a message there."

"Could be a chance for us," said the CO. He looked at the section head quizzically. The section head nodded.

The CO said, "On an answering machine, is it? Could you wipe it clean, Santos?"

"Not without getting inside the Stein place, and his home is pretty well equipped with bolts and locks. Stein's got a lot of valuable carpets and stuff in there.

You can bet the insurance company have approved the burglarproofing."

"I smell this as being something of a break for us," said the CO.

"I think we must try to get inside the Stein home and wipe it clean," said the section head. "I've arranged a high-security phone call to Stuart on Sunday evening."

"You want us to *try* getting into the Stein place?" said the youth.

"Let's think about that for a moment. Stein might not even take the messages off the machine when he gets home tonight." The youth leant forward between the front seats. "Yeah, and he might be taking the messages off his tape right now. He has one of those musical codes that enables him to read back his own messages from any phone. Why don't we take Stein off the street while we try to clean the tape?"

"How?"

"It doesn't have to get rough," said the youth. "I could fix it so that the highway patrol pick him up for drunk driving and put him in jail all night."

"Highway patrol? What makes you think he's going out of town?"

"The CHP has jurisdiction on the freeways that criss-cross the whole of Los Angeles," explained the CO patiently to his visitor. "It would be unlikely—if not impossible—for Stein to go home without using them." The section head nodded his agreement.

"Get on to it," said the CO.

The youth got back into the Pontiac and disappeared in the direction of Inglewood.

"If anyone can fix it, Santos can," said the CO. "You can reckon on Charlie Stein being out of operation for the rest of the night. Early tomorrow morning I'll try and get a telephone repairman into the Stein home."

# 21

The phone connection that Boyd Stuart used in London to speak to Los Angeles was the highest priority "crypto-ciph B." The cryp-to-ciph network (A for America, B for Britain) is a scrambler phone. The encryption machines take the varying frequencies of the human vocal cords and, converting them first into fluctuating electrical current, use computer technology to rearrange each fraction of sound, a microsecond at a time, into new patterns. At the other end, similar machinery reconstructs the impulses and recreates a facsimile of the original sounds. Although the American National Security Agency owned and operated the network, they were so far not able to decipher intercepted conversations without knowing the day's code. Thus London advised Boyd Stuart to use the "cryp-to-ciph B" to speak to his contact clerk.

"Sorry I'm a little late. The machine was in use until a few minutes ago," said the voice from Los Angeles.

"It doesn't matter, I was only sleeping."

"Well, I said I was sorry. Anyway you'd better make sure you are fully awake. It looks like we have a breakthrough on the Stein documents."

"Speak on."

"A call to Stein from London. A man named Paul Bock wants to talk to Stein about the papers. He says he works for a German bank in London. He says it's a matter of life and death."

"Oh, he does, does he?"

"He won't give his address but he's left the phone number of a secretarial agency which will take a message for him."

"Where did this call come through to?"

"He was phoning Stein."

"All the way from London?"

"That's right. It's gone onto Stein's answering machine. Our people here have been trying to wipe the message off the tape so that Stein doesn't get it."

"What's the number he left?" Boyd Stuart wrote it down on the message pad. It was bad enough getting access to the encryption machines only at these absurd hours when the senior civil servants and the politicians were in bed and asleep, but he did not enjoy being kept waiting for nearly two hours in the Foreign Office communications room deep under the traffic of Whitehall. He thanked the machine operator who had made the connection for him and then went to follow the smell of coffee.

He came up through the basement of 10 Downing Street. The house was quiet. The upstairs apartment which provides a residence for the Prime Minister was not occupied. He could hear the policemen chatting together in the entrance hall; their voices had that special hush that night workers acquire. An elderly woman was making coffee in a small kitchen at the rear of the building. She poured him a cup almost before he had asked for one, she had mistaken him for one of the plain-clothes detectives from the ground floor, or one of the coding clerks from the basement.

Boyd Stuart looked at his watch. It was 6:40 a.m., Monday, July 16. The only sound he could hear was the press service teleprinter firing off its occasional bursts of news.

Boyd Stuart went to one of the telephones and dialled the phone number of the secretarial agency. They answered. At least they worked all round the clock. "I'm trying to contact Paul Bock," he said when the girl replied.

"Your name?"

"Stein. Charles Stein," said Boyd Stuart.

"Yes, I have the message for you. Go to Jimmy's Militaria. It's in York Way near King's Cross Station. You can't miss it, it says here."

"OK, thanks."

He hung up. He walked from 10 Downing Street through the connecting doors that gave access to the whole street of houses to emerge from the front door of No. 12. Even at this time in the morning there were three sightseers standing on the opposite side of the street hoping for a glimpse of someone important. Boyd had left his car near the foot of the steps that led down to St. James's Park. He wondered what time Jimmy's Militaria opened. He decided that it was too late to go home and catch up on his sleep. He drove through Trafalgar Square and headed north up Charing Cross Road.

You can't miss Jimmy's Militaria. Its shopfront is part of a row of Victorian houses sited between a pet shop and a launderette. It's not as busy as the launderette nor as smelly as the pet shop, but it's painted in black, red and white stripes, and the name board is surmounted with fretwork Iron Crosses. In one window there are dummies dressed in military uniforms and equipment; on the other side of the door, the smaller window is packed tightly with steel helmets, swords and daggers, buttons and badges, swastika armbands and trays filled with broken model soldiers.

The bell push was marked UPSTAIRS FLAT in red felt-pen lettering on a torn scrap of paper. Stuart pressed the button. Nothing happened, so he pushed it again, and kept on doing so until a miserable figure in a torn dressing gown made his way slowly through the life-size inanimate soldiers and draped flags to pull back the bolts of the front door.

"We're not open," he said. He was in his twenties, bespectacled, with long hair and a half-grown beard adorning his white, pimply face.

"I'm looking for Mr. Paul Bock," said Stuart.

The man took a cigarette from his mouth. "You ain't the law, are you?" He coughed and spat into the street. He had a strong south London accent.

"I'm here because he wants to see me."

"At this time of day?" said the man with disgust, but he stood back and opened the door. "You're not Stein, are you?"

"Charles Stein," said Boyd. "Yes, that's me."

"You don't have an American accent."

"I was at school in England," said Stuart.

The man looked Stuart up and down before saying, "Well, come in. Paul will be surprised to see you. He's frying himself an egg upstairs."

"The message went on my answering machine," said Stuart. "I phoned to see if there were any messages, and I have a device which makes the recording play back over the phone."

"Ain't science wonderful?" said the man. "By the way, I'm Jimmy." He led the way up a creaking staircase to a landing with cracked lino. Small plastic dishes of ancient food scraps were placed in the corner, and a black cat stretched itself and came to look at the visitor. They went up another flight of stairs before entering the kitchen. A century of ground subsidence had given the doors and windows a curious rhomboidal shape and the stained wallpaper bulged with accumulations of loose plaster. A small plastic-topped table was set with crockery of mixed patterns, and a large economy-size packet of Kellogg's Cornflakes was its centrepiece. On the wall behind the square porcelain sink there was an old Rolling Stones poster. At the ancient, cast-iron gas stove a second man was frying six eggs in a bent frying pan. He seemed fully occupied with his task, tipping the pan in each and every direction and using a spoon to baste hot fat over the yolks.

"Here's your Mr. Stein," said the bearded man.

The man at the stove put down the teaspoon and, still holding the tilted frying pan, offered his hand. Stuart shook it.

"Charles Stein," said Stuart. "I was in London."

"Phoned his home and got your message using one of those whistle gadgets," explained Jimmy.

"That's right," said Stuart.

"Jimmy is a communications engineer," explained Paul Bock, the man at the stove. "I'm just an amateur, but I've been using my little microcomputer to get into main frames by telephone for years." He had a soft German accent.

"Are you political activists?" Stuart asked.

"COMPIR," said Jimmy. "Computer pirates. We've no political ideals. Our idea of having fun is accessing password files. We're a sort of club. . . ."

"The bank where I work has got a really big computer," said Bock. "It took us months to crack the 'bug fixes' and find our way inside."

"What are 'bug fixes'?"

"Modifications that the manufacturers keep adding

to stop people like us," said Bock. "Do you want an egg? Soft or turned over?"

"Soft."

"Jimmy eats them cooked hard. They taste like plastic."

There was an open packet of cigarettes on the table. Jimmy leant across and nipped the end of one and tried to tease it out of the packet. When it did not budge he shook it more fiercely, like a terrier with a rat. Finally it came free. "Help yourself," he said and pushed the packet towards Stuart.

"No thanks," said Stuart. "It's too early for me." He watched Jimmy light the new cigarette from the stained, misshapen old one.

"Tell me everything you know about Operation Siegfried," said Bock. He turned round with the frying pan and tipped the eggs onto the plates, two at a time. He was a muscular boy with a short haircut and a carefully shaved face. Under a shabby silk dressing gown he was wearing a clean blue shirt and the trousers of a grey suit. He saw the puzzled expression on Stuart's face. "I have to go to work," he explained. "Jimmy is lucky he doesn't have to disguise himself in these absurd uniforms."

Stuart became painfully aware of the "uniform" that he himself was wearing. "Yes," he said.

"Now tell us about Operation Siegfried."

"I don't know what you're talking about."

"We can get rough, Mr. Stein," said Paul Bock. "You might find that hard to believe, but we can get very very rough."

"I believe you can get rough," said Stuart. "So why don't you believe me when I say that I've never heard of Operation Siegfried?"

Jimmy took the bread knife and roughly sliced some bread. He tossed a slice to each of the other men. Stuart dipped a piece of it into the soft yolk of his egg and ate in silence.

"If you've got something to tell me, then tell me," said Stuart.

Paul Bock cut his egg into rectangles and ate it section by section between his fingers. "I work in the bank—a big German bank—no matter its name at the moment. We got this information from the bank's computer."

"Is that difficult?" asked Stuart.

"This computer was a beauty," said Jimmy, rubbing his hand over his half-grown beard. "Could be this is one of the most complex of its sort anywhere in Europe."

"But we cracked it," said Paul Bock. "Or Jimmy did."

"Paul got the hardware keys," said Jimmy. "Until we could physically unlock the machinery, I couldn't even begin. And he completed the first codes for the terminal keyboard. Then it got trickier. The bank have performance-measuring consultants who tune the computer; they notice the access per program, and we didn't want them to get suspicious. We had to trickle the stuff out bit by bit; spread it over a few weeks." He coughed and thumped his chest with his fist still holding the cigarette.

"This material is ultra secret," said Bock. "There were many software keys, each one opening up more and more secret stuff."

"It's like a series of doors," explained Jimmy. "You've got to unlock each and every one to get into the inner sanctum. And every door has a sort of burglar alarm that will close down the terminal and store a message saying that someone has attempted an unauthorized access."

"And you managed all that?" said Stuart, not without a trace of genuine admiration.

"Jimmy's a wizard," said Paul Bock.

"So what *is* Operation Siegfried?" Stuart asked.

"We are not quite sure," admitted Jimmy. He put his cigarette into the ashtray and began to eat.

"There is a secret fund—a Trust, they call it—formed by some of the most powerful organizations of the Bundesrepublik," said Paul. "Steel companies, armaments, car-parts manufacturers, insurance companies, publishers and very big banks. We know that the senior trustee is a man named Böttger, who is president of a bank based in Hamburg. Like all the other men involved, he has never been associated with any post-war political party. That's significant."

"In what way significant?" asked Stuart.

"If you were going to resurrect the Third Reich," said Paul Bock, "would it not be a good idea to tell your agents to avoid all political activity?"

"The war was thirty or more years ago," protested Stuart. "You mean they've been asked to wait that long for Operation Siegfried?" It all seemed highly unlikely.

"They are patient and full of cunning," said Paul Bock. "The Third Reich was planned to last for one thousand years; Hitler himself said so. What is thirty or forty years to such people?" He got up to put his plate in the sink. A floorboard creaked under his weight.

"And you think these people are starting a Fourth Reich?" said Stuart. "In what way is my name involved with such plans?"

"We got your name from the computer," said Paul Bock. "We got a print-out and committed it to memory before destroying it. There were many names, each with a code word, the significance of which we have not yet decided; your name was the only one which sounded unmistakably Jewish. It seemed to us impossible that you would be a supporter of their aims. Therefore you must be an intended victim."

The two men, Jimmy and Paul Bock, looked at one another. They realized that they were not convincing their visitor. It had not been planned this way: to see Charles Stein up here in this grubby little house with the smell of yesterday's boiled cabbage coming from next door. The plan had been to meet with him in the lobby of some luxurious hotel in central London, or even take him for a meal in a restaurant. Paul Bock looked round the greasy kitchen. Why should anyone take them seriously once they had seen this dingy slum?

"It's guesswork," admitted Jimmy, "but we think they must be Nazis."

"We've done all we could," said Paul Bock, continuing the conversation with his friend as if their visitor had already departed. "We warned him."

Boyd Stuart finished his egg. "What about some

hard information?" he said. "What about more names?"

"We wondered if you could be on some sort of death list, Mr. Stein," said Paul Bock politely.

"And I'm wondering if you have been watching too much late-night TV," said Stuart.

"Get stuffed," said Jimmy. "We told you, and that's that." Stuart pushed his plate aside and stood up to get a paper towel to wipe his fingers. Through the rain-spattered windows he saw a grim industrial landscape and the Grand Union canal, its stagnant water littered with ice-cream wrappers and floating beer cans. A narrow boat, timbers rotting, had settled low enough for scummy water to lap onto its deck. Beyond the canal, the rusting tracks and ruined shed were the remains of a railway system which had once made the world gasp with envy. A diesel locomotive came into view, hooted and stopped. Stuart tossed the paper towel into the bin under the sink and said, "What about a little more evidence?"

Paul Bock said, "We'll talk about it."

He and Jimmy went out of the room and when they returned Bock was wearing the jacket of his smart grey suit. "Can you give me a lift to the tube?" He looked out of the window. "I think I'll need my raincoat."

"Certainly." Stuart turned back to Jimmy when he got as far as the landing. "But why the swastika badges and the Nazi decorations?"

Jimmy smiled. "Then I don't have to feel bad about lying and cheating my customers."

"I see," said Stuart. He followed Paul Bock down the narrow staircase into the gloomy shop and out of the front door. Summer seemed a long way away; the clouds were still grey and there was only the faintest glimmer of sunshine on the horizon. They got into the Aston, and Stuart followed the insane maze of one-way streets to the underground railway station.

"I wish you'd give me more information," said Stuart as Paul Bock got out of the car. "Give me some details of the Trust: What is its address? Do you know how it is funded?"

The German leant close to the window. "Perhaps next time," he said.

"Why not now? If my life is in danger the way you say it is, why not now?"

"Because we don't believe you are Mr. Charles Stein," said the German. "Jimmy thinks you're the police. I'm not certain who you are, but the computer print-out shows nearly one hundred million dollars against your name . . . I've worked in banks. You are not a man who's ever had use of a fortune. Men who handle such money don't come knocking on doors in King's Cross early in the morning; they send others to do it for them. You tell Mr. Stein to come in person." He smiled and was gone in the crowds hurrying into the station.

## 22

Boyd Stuart did not view every foot of the Nazi newsreel film. It would have taken five working days to look at all of it: a fact that was clearly evident from the film tins which were stacked ceiling high in the two fireproof store rooms downstairs in the basement, along the corridor from the "viewing room," as the cinema was officially called.

Two "research clerks" had begun viewing and sorting the footage as soon as the first reels arrived. It had come to the SIS Ziggurat building south of the river via a cover address in Wardour Street. Most of it came through agencies and libraries but there was privately owned footage too, and some poor-quality pirated material which had been made by reversal process from positives. All of the film submitted was in response to the news that a film company, compiling a documentary for TV, was paying top footage rates. It was wanted urgently but that was a normal requirement in the business of film and TV.

Boyd Stuart had spent all day screening the film that had been shortlisted for him. By the afternoon of Monday, July 16, he was growing dizzy with images of Adolf Hitler and his followers. He had watched the Führer staring stern-faced at maps, striding past ranks of soldiers, climbing into the Führerwagen of the train and climbing down from it, leaning out of its lowered windows to shake hands with Hitler Youths or accept flowers from flaxen-haired girls.

At 4 p.m. he first caught sight of the face he sought. He picked up the phone and told the projectionist to stop the film, mark the frame and bring it to the editing bench. Only fifteen minutes after that, he found the same man in two lengthy sequences of Hitler meeting Benito Mussolini alongside a train at Anlage Süd in August 1941. A large crowd of Hitler's immediate staff had wanted to see the two dictators together, and there were many cameras in evidence amongst the German soldiers, SS men and Italians, jostling together on the raised wooden platform made especially for the dictators to alight from the train.

Stuart put the reel of film onto the editor's flat bench. He wound it with his hand to find the frame he wanted, and held it illuminated and magnified on the small screen. He put a magnifier over the part of the image that interested him, but it enlarged the patterns of film grain and the texture of the viewing screen's Fresnel glass so that the picture became a confused blur, like some abstract painting.

Kitty King came into the room and put a cup of tea down by his elbow. "You've found something?"

"Three different sequences, and there will be more."

"And this is the photo you found after the Wever farm explosion?" She leant forward to study the big enlargement which was pinned over the bench.

"Wever said he'd never worn one of those camouflage jackets before that journey to Merkers. I've looked up the dates and times of the American advance. That photo must have been taken at the salt mine on or about April 2, 1945. That's Breslow next to him. The civilian is the one I'm trying to identify. Reichsbank Director Frank he was calling himself in 1945."

"And now you've found him?"

"I think so, but I'd like to find him enough times to get a positive identification."

"He's in uniform for this one." She pointed at the lighted screen.

"But the Germans let their security people wear any uniform and any rank they fancied when they were at work. I've got other photos that resemble him. Now I'll enlarge them to some reasonable size."

"The dark room will curse you, Boyd. They're up to their ears in work."

"I've got a triple-A priority, Kitty. There is nothing that takes precedence over whatever I need."

She looked at him. She knew about the priority but didn't understand it. She tried to find the answer in his face and, having failed, smiled at him. "It's just history as far as I can see, darling," she said. "It's only people who still remember those days who care: old fogies like the DG, and Mr. Brittain in Plans, who won the M.C. and wears it on Remembrance Day." She touched her hair to push it back from her forehead, in a manner more narcissistic than remedial. She was especially beautiful there in the half-light of the cinema. Stuart felt a keen desire for her, and he saw her arch her body as if she sensed it.

"I wish you'd move in with me," he said.

"I'll stay with you tonight, if you want me," she said softly. "But I'm not moving in; not with you, not with anyone."

"Why not?"

He expected her to raise her voice. They had had this sort of discussion before and it always had turned to the sort of jokiness that cloaked bitter recriminations. "Everything I touch. . . ." she continued in the same lowered tone, "I sit down in a chair and I wonder if it was *her* favourite chair. I go to grab a dressing gown and I stop . . . wondering if I'm going to look like *her* in it. I look in the mirror and I see other women looking back at me. That's not what I want, Boyd." There was something essentially feminine about her resentment of these inanimate objects, thought Stuart. She never seemed in any way jealous, or even curious about any women he might have met in California.

"Well, where would we find another place as good as the flat I've got now?" said Stuart. "Those people upstairs are paying more than double the rent I'm charged. And your sister is not going to want us both moving in there with her."

"It's all right for you," she said. "Men always expect women to adapt to anything they want."

Boyd Stuart put an arm round her and gave her a brief hug. It was a far cry from all those earlier declarations of sexual freedom. But, like all cries for freedom, Kitty King's had been more concerned with getting concessions than in giving them. It would always be like this, he supposed. She would tell him what made her unhappy but refuse to face any of the practical difficulties that would come from changing things. She smiled in response to his comforting arm. "Drink your tea," she said. "And I'll take the cups back. I only came down to the vault."

"For what?" said Stuart. The "vault" was the top-secret section of the archives stored in the basement strong room.

"You'd never guess," she said. "To return the DG's personal file."

"In the vault?" They both laughed. It seemed like a good example of the Alice-in-Wonderland world in which they worked that something as innocuous as a biographical file should be locked away with such elaborate care.

"He was in Switzerland for most of the war, wasn't he?"

"Except for the short time they let him serve with the army in Italy. He was deafened by the gunfire at Monte Cassino; that's why he wears that hearing aid. He went back to Switzerland in time to work with Allen Dulles. They were negotiating the surrender of some German army units in Italy. He came back to work here in 1947." She repeated it as if it were some poem she had been compelled to learn at school.

"I love you, Kitty."

"Don't be silly, Boyd. Drink your tea. I must get back to work." She flicked through the DG's file nervously, waiting for Stuart to finish his tea.

"What's that red sticker for?" Stuart asked.

"It's a 'stop mark.' The cover name must not be used at any time in the future. During the war, the

DG used the name Elliot Castelbridge. It was common to have a cover name at that time. There was a wartime order, in case high-ranking department employees were captured by the Germans. Anyone who went to Switzerland or Sweden was redocumented into a permanent cover."

"The brief and exciting career of Elliot Castelbridge: eating warm fondue with cold wine, and waiting for the German surrender. Killed by a 'stop mark.' "

"You're too hard on him, Boyd."

"He's a Byzantine bastard," said Stuart without animosity.

"Not at all. He is unmistakably Gothic."

Stuart grinned. She was absolutely right. There was nothing of the devious oriental cunning that characterized so many of the senior staff of the department. The DG was a man of brutal bluffness, and even his appearance was more like the rough weathered stone of northern Europe than the smooth silks of the schism. "Don't go."

"I must. Is your car here?" she asked.

"Yes."

"Will you be finished here in time for dinner?"

"There's a very good new restaurant in Sloane Street."

"Just as long as it's not curry." She leaned over and kissed him on the forehead. For five minutes or more he sat there thinking about her, then he went back to work. He still needed "hard reference" to the man in the film. Someone would be working all night on that one.

## 23

The following morning, Tuesday, July 17, while Boyd Stuart and Kitty King were having breakfast together in his comfortable London apartment, the man whose face he had been seeking in the old Third Reich newsreels was breakfasting in a tall building in Hamburg. His name was Willi Kleiber and the breakfast was a business meeting at which eight senior business executives met together under the chairmanship of Dr. Böttger. These were the trustees of the fund collected for the needs of Operation Siegfried, and the meeting was held in the private dining room of one of the banks which Böttger controlled.

Willi Kleiber sat on Dr. Böttger's immediate right. It was an appropriate seat for the man who had given so much of his time to the initial planning of Operation Siegfried, who not only had worked hard at the scheme but had actually introduced the idea into Dr. Böttger's head. Had Boyd Stuart seen the hatchet face of Willi Kleiber he would have called him Reichsbank Director Frank. And had Colonel Pitman's cashier seen him before he shaved off the blunt moustache he had grown over Christmas 1978 he would have called him Peter Friedman, the *beau parleur* whose letters of credit secured him the millions that had crippled the bank.

It was early and Hamburg was enjoying clear blue skies. From this glass-sided conference room, high above the city, there was a view of St. Michael's Church and the Bismarck Memorial, and the sun and the morning breeze were making the dark water of the Elbe shimmer like hammered copper.

Kleiber liked Hamburg. He liked its ever-changing weather, its bars and its restaurants, the smell of the sea and the fine clear German that its inhabitants spoke. His brief, and never-to-be-repeated, attempt at marriage had taken place in this town. That would have blighted the location for some men, but Kleiber was able to accept the pleasures of past experiences without dwelling upon the miseries; he felt the same way about his time in the war. He seldom came here without seeing his ex-wife. She was still attractive and amusing, and always wanted to hear about Willi Kleiber's latest sexual conquests. It was as if she got some perverse and vicarious enjoyment from these detailed descriptions of his lechery. More than once he fantasized about taking her back to his hotel room, undressing her and. . . . But Willi Kleiber knew that that would never happen. Not because his ex-wife would not enjoy it—but because her new husband was a senior official with the BND, West Germany's intelligence service. A man who went frequently to London for conferences with senior British intelligence officials was a contact too valuable to risk for the sake of an afternoon of grab-ass. Tomorrow he would be having lunch with both husband and wife. It was safer that way.

"Things have not gone quite as smoothly as we'd hoped," admitted Dr. Böttger. He was a scholarly-looking man, sixty years old, slightly plump, with silver hair and gold wire spectacles. His face was becoming flushed, Kleiber noticed. It was a sign of anxiety, like the way in which Böttger thrust his fist into the jacket of his expensive suit with enough force to break the stitching. "But the plan goes forward. When we took so much money from their bank in Geneva, we expected them to offer these documents to us through Herr Kleiber's man in Los Angeles. That proved to be a miscalculation on our part." Böttger twisted his head far enough to see whether Willi Kleiber showed some appreciation; actually it had been Kleiber's miscalculation. Kleiber nodded with an almost imperceptible movement, but Böttger had become accustomed to such signals in the boardroom. "It was the sensible, logical thing to do," he continued. "Perhaps if these men had been Germans, they would have reacted rationally . . . but they are Americans. . . ." Böttger smiled, hoping to draw a response from his colleagues but only Kleiber acknowledged the jest.

Dr. Böttger pressed his lips with his finger tips. "All of us have given a great part of our life to making Germany prosperous, strong and a good place to live," said Böttger. "Has anyone forgotten what we suffered under Hitler and his fellow criminals? Do I have to tell you what the Nazis did to our country and to our people; not just the physical destruction that came from the war, but the moral damage that the Nazi propaganda did to our children. Are you unaware of what our compatriots in the East suffer under a regime of Moscow-trained puppets? We live in the West, and we count our blessings; but German democracy is a delicate flower, transplanted from other climes. What we have built from the ashes of 1945 could be quickly destroyed by neo-Nazi madmen or by communist lunatics who would like to see Russian soldiers patrolling our streets."

"You're right, Dr. Böttger," said a voice from the far end of the table.

"Hitler is dead," said Böttger. "Let him remain dead. We want no revelations, no so-called Hitler Minutes, no secret plans to bring Hitler out of the grave and adorn him with the glories of newsworthy historical triumphs. Make no mistake, there are men who would snatch political power from such apotheosis." He stroked his face. "What do the British care about Churchill's reputation? They have history books full of such men. Democracy is the fabric from which their society is woven. It is our frail, newly created democracy which needs the reputations of Churchill and Roosevelt and other such leaders who have proved that a man can be warm, well-fed and happy, as well as being free to say what he likes and to vote his masters out of office. That's why we must go to any lengths to make sure that Moscow doesn't get these documents. Neither must they fall into the hands of the muck-raking journalists who think only of their careers. Nor of those men who'd tell us that Hitler was a twentieth-century Bismarck." He looked round at them. "Don't weaken now, my dear friends, don't weaken now."

Dr. Böttger sat down. There was no reaction to his speech except that each of the men now turned his attention to the German-style breakfast that had been set upon individual embroidered cloths around the long polished table.

Böttger fastidiously took a knife and cut the top from his boiled egg. The others followed his example. The formalities were finished. Now came the questions. Dr. Böttger hated questions.

"It is the violence that troubles me," admitted a frail, freckled man at the other end of the table. His name was Fritz Rau. "Several men have already been killed, you tell us. Can we be sure that that is the end of it?" He was forbidden to eat eggs, butter or cheese, and now he nibbled carefully upon the black bread.

Böttger seized the nettle. "By no means. I have no doubt that there will be other deaths, simply because the men we are up against are determined upon a collision course."

"I had not fully understood that when we began," said the frail man. "I wonder how many of us would have authorized the formation of the Trust, had we realized that money was to be paid to hired killers."

There was a shocked silence but it did not last long. Willi Kleiber stood up. He was a powerfully built man who liked to attend reunions of his infantry regiment and sing the old wartime songs over steins of dark Bavarian beer. Kleiber said, "I understood it, and everyone I spoke to understood it." He smiled. "Everyone who is not hard of hearing understood it." It was a powerful voice. Kleiber was seldom contradicted.

"My hearing is not defective," said the frail man, Rau.

"We must leave the operational side of the matter to Willi," said Dr. Böttger. For one moment he felt a wave of panic, believing that Rau must have discovered something about the British diplomat they had killed by mistake in Los Angeles. Kleiber's attempt to kill the British secret agent had been another error. Willi Kleiber was inclined to solve problems by eliminating his opponents. But Böttger had agreed to using Kleiber as "operations chief" and now they were stuck with him, so they must give him all the support he needed.

"Does 'operational side' mean killing people we don't like?" said Fritz Rau.

"Yes," said Böttger. He looked round the table anxiously before sipping some black coffee. Fritz Rau had once been one of the cleverest scientists in German industry. Even today he could sometimes be found white-coated in the laboratory of the vast chemical combine that he virtually owned, testing out some new ideas he had jotted down on the back of an envelope. Böttger knew that the silence of the other men present was largely due to the respect that Rau commanded amongst them. Böttger began to worry that Rau's doubts could undermine the whole of Operation Siegfried.

"You'd better understand this, gentlemen," said Böttger. He held a coffee cup in one hand, as if this vitally important thought had only this moment come to him. He looked slowly at all the faces. There had always been this weakness for the melodramatic style in Böttger. The truth was that he had used such mannerisms in his climb to his present exalted status. "You'd better understand that each and every one of us has already committed a crime. We are all accessories to murder. It is as simple as that. I believe that what we are doing is what every German who loves his country will approve. If we closed down Operation Siegfried tomorrow, our plans unfulfilled, what then? Can we bring those dead men back to life? No. And what if one of us decided to go to the police or to the Foreign Ministry and tell them of our plan? Shall I tell you what would happen? Everyone associated with Operation Siegfried would be ruthlessly hunted down and rigorously punished. We'd probably be sent to prison for the rest of our lives. And, quite apart from the criminal liability of what we have done, what of our colleagues? I am sure that, like me, you have secured the generous help of your business partners and colleagues in falsifying books to make the large cash appropriations available to the Trust. We have also dispersed and hidden the funds we stole from the bank in Geneva. Many people were involved in that. They didn't ask questions; they did it because they were friends. Is their repayment to be betrayal? I say no. I say that we must now hold fast, as the English held fast in 1940, and as our people held fast in 1944 while the Russians came ever closer and the Anglo-American bombers tore our cities to pieces. Hold fast, silence your doubts, my friends. Do what must be done."

Böttger smiled as he reached the end of his harangue. For a moment he feared the worst. He waited until he saw his smile reflected in the anxious faces round the table, but then he knew he had won them over. Even poor little Fritz Rau seemed temporarily reassured.

Willi Kleiber spoke next. "There will be no violence for the sake of violence, Dr. Rau," he promised. "In our lifetimes there has been enough killing and none of us wants more of that."

He paused and looked round the table. They were all men he had known for ten or fifteen years. Willi Kleiber owned and personally managed one of the finest security organizations in Europe. All these men had done business with his company. Some of them shared their darkest secrets with him; he had helped more than one of their children involved with drug peddlers, and ferreted out the secrets of two transgressing wives. Not even the tax man knew as much about these men as Willi Kleiber knew. He said, "Dr. Rau has asked if the operational side of things means killing people we don't like. Dr. Böttger said yes. With all due respect to Dr. Böttger, I must be allowed to correct him. There is no place in this delicate operation for personal animosities. The only people who will be killed are those who have knowledge which is dangerous to our cause. The list of executions will be as short as I can possibly make it. Everyone here in this room may rest assured about that. I killed men in the war. I killed them in hand-to-hand combat. It was disgusting. It was not something about which I will ever be able to tell my children. Dr. Böttger has selected me for the operations side of this plan simply because he knows that I do not relish violence. I am your sword arm, gentlemen. Be confident that I will not strike down the innocent."

"Thank you, Willi," said Fritz Rau. He was one of the oldest men in the room and thus enjoyed the privilege of addressing his younger colleagues in that informal manner.

Böttger gave a sigh of relief and hastily pressed on to the only other matter. "Money is suddenly required in London and we will need some sort of corporate structure to which to send the funds. Obviously we must not attract the attention of English government departments and I wonder if one of us can provide a way to hold half a million Deutsche marks just while we are forming a company there."

"No problem," said the expert on maritime insurance. "But you'll have to let me have the details about who will have access to the money. Specimen signatures and so on."

"Willi will provide those details. I'll let you have the money in whatever way you want it." He looked at the clock over the door. "That will do for this week, gentlemen," said Böttger. "You will all get a telex in the usual code to tell you where the next meeting will be. Kindly let me have proxies for anyone who cannot attend."

When the meeting had broken up, it was Willi Kleiber who remained for a final word with Dr. Böttger. "I wondered what old Fritz was going to say for a moment," said Kleiber. "It is the violence that troubles me," Kleiber imitated Fritz Rau's Saxon accent and the quaver which could sometimes be heard in his voice. It was a cruel parody.

"He's getting too old," said Böttger. "It will happen to all of us eventually, I suppose."

"Anyway, it all turned out all right."

"For the time being it did," said Böttger. "But you know as well as I do that it will not be one or two deaths."

"It will be messy," said Willi Kleiber. "It is hard to say how many will eventually have to be removed. I agree with you about that. I thought the explosion in England, when we had to deal with my old comrade Franz Wever, was going to become a big newspaper story."

"They were mad to do it like that," said Böttger. "Have our people there no sense?"

"The British Secret Intelligence Service already knew Wever," explained Willi Kleiber. "They were pressing him. We had to do something very quickly indeed."

"The British Secret Service. To let them get hold of the Hitler Minutes would be the very worst thing that could happen to us," said Böttger. "If the newspapers get them, we might be able to buy them off or even frighten them off. Failing that, we can put up a smoke screen. But if they get into the hands of the British Secret Service, anything could happen."

Willi Kleiber scratched his chin. "You mean the British are dangerous to us? Yes, I hadn't thought it in that light, Dr. Böttger, but I have to agree with you wholeheartedly." Böttger looked at him and nodded. He knew that Willi Kleiber had never looked at it any other way.

## 24

Sir Sydney Ryden had a lunch appointment but he was able to fit Boyd Stuart into a gap between the secretary of the estimates sub-committee on pay and a pre-lunch drink with the coordinator. Boyd Stuart waited in an empty sitting room for half an hour before the DG came in, slumped down into the armchair and ran a hand through his hair. "Everything seems to come at once, Stuart. Do you find that?"

"Yes, sir, I do. I'm awfully sorry to be making a difficult day even worse for you."

"Not at all," said the DG. "It was my own decision to keep close to your investigation. Something come up, has it?"

Boyd Stuart explained the phone call which Paul Bock had made to Stein's home in Los Angeles. And his visit to the house in north London the day before.

"Homosexuals are they?" He nodded as if in answer to his own question.

"I've no reason to think so, Director."

"They sound like two delinquents," said the DG.

"They *are* delinquents," agreed Boyd.

"Quite so, Stuart." The DG eyed the drinks cabinet but decided that his lunch was going to be a tricky one. It would be better to remain completely clear-headed. "Am I to take it that you are treating their information seriously?"

"For the time being I am, sir."

"Isn't it rather preposterous? Surely you don't believe that a syndicate of German industrialists is about to start a new Nazi movement?"

"I'm not yet at the stage where I can start enjoying the luxury of discounting anything," said Boyd.

"Well, it's your investigation," said the DG, scratching his head. "But the PM is asking for a situation report. I'm not going to relish telling her that my principal field agent thinks it's all a neo-Nazi plot."

"Paul Bock gained access to the bank computer," insisted Boyd Stuart. "The other one has worked in electronics and, according to the hasty and superficial inquiries I've made this morning, is well qualified to know about retrieving information."

"I'm not contesting any of that," said the DG testily.

"Then what could be their motive?" said Boyd Stuart. "Why would they contact Stein to warn him that his life is in danger? Obviously Stein is a stranger to them or they would have recognized me immediately as an impostor. The German boy has confessed a secret to a perfect stranger. If that stranger betrays him, he could face at best dismissal from the bank, perhaps a term of imprisonment. So what motive could they have, other than what they told me?"

"Perhaps he thinks it's fun," said the DG. "Perhaps he doesn't need to have a job of any kind; he might well have a private income. Rich young troublemakers. The Western world is full of such people."

Only with difficulty did Stuart suppress his irritation at this generalization. "I think it's safer to assume that they work for a living, sir. And I prefer to assume they're sincere."

"You don't have to read me the riot act, Stuart." Boyd Stuart did not reply. The DG looked at his watch. "Well, I can see that you want to follow this one up, so I'll not stand in your way." He got to his feet. His knee joint cracked and he massaged it briefly. "Don't mind if I make a few inquiries too, eh?"

"No, sir," said Boyd Stuart in a tone that he hoped conveyed the idea that he dreaded the thought of it.

"That's splendid then. Let's talk again tomorrow before I see the PM."

Sir Sydney Ryden did not look forward with pleasure to his meetings with the representative of West Germany's intelligence organization, the Bundesnachrichtendienst, BND. Somehow the two men seemed incompatible and what should have been an exchange of helpful information all too often developed into an exchange of complaints which sometimes came close to bickering.

The lunch they shared at Boodle's on Tuesday, July 17, was no exception. There were differences about training facilities which were not yet ready for use, a request for the return of important dossiers which Sir Sydney secretly knew had got lost somewhere in Whitehall, and an argument about a news story concerning a secret rocket, which had been leaked to a German newspaper. As an exercise in European cooperation, the lunch was a failure but, when the two men went downstairs for coffee and watched the other club members sunk deep into the ancient leather armchairs, the talk turned to gardening.

Discovering that this difficult German shared his taste for growing cactus came as a revelation to Sir Sydney Ryden, who was a well-known member of the Cactus and Succulent Society of Great Britain.

"As a general rule," Sir Sydney was saying, his coffee neglected, "it is common enough to find flowers larger than the plant, with the exception perhaps of *Mammillaria* and *Rhipsalis.* If you had seen my *Echinocactus tabularis* with three flowers—each one of them larger than the plant itself—my goodness, I think you would have been amazed." Sir Sydney slapped the arm of his leather chair hard enough to have a member across the room look up from his newspaper.

"Mealy bug is the worst," said the German. "The only thing that will kill it is paraffin, but often I have found that the plant dies too."

"I never resort to paraffin," said Sir Sydney. "As soon as you see those little grey fluffy specks, get them off with a pin. I'd rather cut away a large piece of the plant than put paraffin on it."

"That is most interesting," said the German. "I shall remember too your advice concerning seeds."

"Yes, it's not difficult at all. Wait until the flower stem has completely died before removing the seeds, of course. The *Mammillaria* seeds are in pods; keep them all until the following spring and don't sow before late April unless you can be sure the temperature won't drop below sixty-five degrees Fahrenheit."

"I shall try it," said the German.

"It's a damned pity that you can't spare the time to come down to my place in the country."

"Next time, perhaps."

"Excellent."

"I only wish that there was something I could do for you in return, Sir Sydney."

A sudden thought struck the DG. "Well, perhaps there is, my dear chap. This is a top-secret matter, but I want to check up on the likelihood of a young fellow working for the London branch of a Hamburg bank being able to get something from their central computer. As I say, it's top secret. It would have to be a very descreet inquiry."

"That's a simple matter, Sir Sydney," said the BND man. "No need to put it through my department at all. I'll handle it personally. Tomorrow I'll be in Bonn lunching with my wife and an old friend who runs one of our very best private security companies. He knows all about German banks."

"Excellent," said Sir Sydney Ryden. "I'd rather not have it made official. I'll give you the details."

The German took out his pocket diary and turned the pages to find the following day's entry: Wednesday, July 18. He wrote "mention inquiry Sir SR" under the name of his luncheon companion—Willi Kleiber.

## 25

All the efforts of British Secret Intelligence Service employees in the Los Angeles area to erase Paul Bock's message from Charles Stein's answering machine had come to nothing. The machine itself, manufactured by a small factory in San Diego, was advertised as the most reliable domestic machine on the market. One aspect of this reliability, upon which the copywriter expended much care, was the impossibility of accidental erasure of any incoming message. The "Executive Type II" even had an erase head that could be unplugged and locked away elsewhere. It was a facility that appealed to Charles Stein, who believed his son Billy only too likely to erase vital messages accidentally.

As for the attempt to get a field agent posing as a telephone repairman into the Stein residence, this too was doomed to failure. Stein's housekeeper had long since discovered that the best way to live in peace with her employer was to take his instructions literally. So when a young man, bedecked with tweezers, pliers and reels of wire, spoke to her over the voice box at the front entrance, she told him that he could not come in. He told her that her telephone was not working properly and, when she proved indifferent to this, insisted that the fault was going to affect all the phones in Cresta Ridge Drive. "You'll have to come back some other day," she told him. Charles Stein had said let no one in the house, and that is exactly what she intended to do. When the bogus telephone man persisted, she threatened to call the telephone company and complain of his behaviour. It was at that stage of the operation that all attempts to interfere with the answering machine were abandoned.

Charles Stein arrived home at 11 a.m. He was in a bad mood and his housekeeper did not ask him about anything except what he would like to eat. It was only after she served his soup that Stein confided to her that he had been arrested for drunken driving by the California Highway Patrol while moving decorously along the number two lane of the Harbor Freeway at no more than forty miles an hour.

The housekeeper nodded and remained silent except for some sympathetic noises that semanticists call "purr sounds."

"Me drunk!" said Stein indignantly.

"Did they put you on the breathalyzer?"

"And it registered nothing. I'd had only two glasses of white wine with an old pal. You know me, Mrs. Svenson, did you ever see me drunk? I practically never touch hard liquor. I don't even like the taste of it anymore."

"And they said you were speeding?"

"They said going at a careful forty miles an hour is the sure sign of a drunk, that's what they said."

The housekeeper made some more tutting sounds.

"Erratic driving, unsafe lane change . . . took me down to the county jail near Union Station . . . how do you like that?"

"It's terrible, Mr. Stein."

"I demanded a blood test. I know the law. I demanded a blood test. They said they couldn't get the damned police doctor. Maybe he's drunk too, I told them. Finally the new shift came on, and the watch commander had me released." Stein looked at his housekeeper and shook his head. "I'm mad, Mrs. Svenson. I'm telling you, I'm really sore about the way I've been treated."

"Eat your meal, Mr. Stein," she said. "Try and forget the whole thing."

Stein tore his bread roll to pieces and began to eat it with his soup.

"Those CHP guys can never admit they're wrong, you know," Stein told his housekeeper. "They held me overnight, threatening me with all kinds of driving charges. Then, this morning, they released me. Big deal. I go to jail for doing nothing and they're kind enough to release me." He finished his soup in silence. "Where's Billy?" he said as he pushed the plate away. Stein always pushed empty plates away. He needed a space on the table in front of him; he found plates and glasses—especially empty ones—constricting.

"Gone down to the boat," said the housekeeper.

"Again?"

"He's practising for the race next month. It's the championship. You know that, Mr. Stein. Billy never misses that."

Stein looked up, realizing that Billy Stein had converted another female to his cause, whatever that might be. "Time that kid got a job," said Stein.

"I'll get you the rest of your lunch," said the housekeeper.

Stein soon finished the grilled lamb chops and hashed brown potatoes which his housekeeper had calculated would provide the fastest satisfactory meal, and thus the fastest way to return her employer to his usual calm demeanour. But Stein had pushed aside the fried potatoes, choosing instead to eat the grilled tomato flavoured with some fragments of basil from the garden. But now his resolution weakened as he recalled the indignity of being handcuffed, stripped, searched, photographed and fingerprinted. He put the potatoes into his mouth with nervous rapidity. "And then tossed into the drunk tank like a common criminal."

"You should have phoned me, Mr. Stein."

"No good phoning you," growled Stein, still continuing to eat the potatoes. "They only allow you one completed phone call and I was chasing my goddamned lawyer from bar to restaurant to night club."

He finished the potatoes, took the slice of buttered toast and got to his feet. The smell of the jail was still on him. "I've got to take a bath," said Stein. "Change out of these stinking clothes."

"It must have been terrible for you, Mr. Stein."

"Goddamned fascists," said Stein. "I told them that too. I said, I fought a war to get rid of fascists like you. I told them."

"What did they say?"

"They laughed," said Stein. He shrugged. He was getting used to people laughing about the war. Billy Stein had been laughing about it for years. Why get mad because other men's kids laughed too?

Stein got to his feet, pulled off his tie and loosened his shirt collar. Restlessly, he went to the fireplace and moved some of the china ornaments on the mantel as if looking for something.

"Are you all right, Mr. Stein?" the housekeeper asked. She had never seen him like this before.

"They laughed," said Stein again. His talk with Jerry Delaney had reawakened his memories; his night in the county jail had given him too much time to brood. There was the other half of the story. He remembered telling it again and again to the untidy little captain from the judge advocate's staff who had shouted with rage and called Stein a liar.

Delaney had told the same story of course. Delaney was his buddy, a tall gangling youth with a long neck and the awkward physique of a boy who had not yet grown to manhood. Major Carson was the only old-timer with the column that day. Carson had fought in France in the First World War. He was a plump, grey-haired man, his nose and cheeks red from the cold, early-morning parade grounds and evenings of cheap booze which had made up his years in the peacetime army. "No need for binoculars," he had told Lieutenant Pitman when they saw the smoke. "The Germans are over the next hill, kicking shit out of the supply column." He parked his chewing gum on the armour plate and looked down at his map case as the next salvo sounded. Stein was watching him closely; he did not flinch. The inquiry had tried to brand Carson as a coward, but a coward would have remained with the column, not tried to take a jeep across the open country to tell the battalion what was happening. "I'll need a driver," said Major Carson.

"Take young Stein," said Lieutenant Pitman. "The kid's too young for combat."

"They all are," said Carson without looking up from the map. "And if the Germans are this far"—he stabbed at the shiny transparent map cover—"the whole damn shooting match is surrounded—CCA, regimental combat team, the whole works . . . shit! The top brass are as dumb as ass-holes, Pitman."

"Yes, sir," said Pitman, who had consistently tried to reduce such disrespect for authority amongst his men.

Carson looked at him and smiled. Pitman was ten years older than most of these kids and trained at the Point, but his experience of real soldiering was pitifully inadequate. His uniform was brand new, his tie folded neatly into his shirt, his waterproof jacket without a stain. Pitman was smaller than the rest of them, and the heavy automatic pistol and full canteen of water sagged on his belt. His fieldglasses were like a millstone round his neck. As his eyes swept quickly round the horizon—seeing only the black stony hills that had put them out of radio contact with headquarters—his steel helmet clanged against the armour plate of the M-3.

Major Carson put an arm round his shoulder in a gesture that was at once paternal and confiding. "You get these kids down into the gully, Lieutenant, and pull back parallel to the Sbeitla road." There was more smoke followed by the drumbeats of the guns. "Could be the Germans will try to push through here all the way to Kasserine."

"Kasserine?" said Pitman. It was unthinkable.

Carson was fingering the map again. His nails were worn short, his hands stained with oil and nicotine, and his fingers marked with tiny scars. They were the hands of a man who liked to take engines apart. "Don't get any ideas about winning the Medal of Honor. They'll elbow this little caravan without pausing. Go back along the gully, and get the hell out of here."

"We're tank destroyers," said Pitman. "You want us to run?"

"Get my jeep, kid," Carson shouted to Aram Stein. To Pitman he said, "Get these museum pieces out of here, Lieutenant. And that's a goddamn order. Understand?"

"Yes, sir," said Pitman giving the major an exemplary salute. Carson climbed into the jeep without even looking back.

Lieutenant Pitman took off his helmet and ran a hand round the sweaty leather of its liner before putting it back on his head and tugging the chinstrap tight. He was on his own now; commanding the whole column in the face of the enemy, just as he had so often dreamed of doing. "There's a soldier coming up the track," he said. Moments later there was another explosion, this time from down the hill. Only Stein realized what had happened, perhaps because he had spent so much time dreading it. "Aram," he shouted. He jumped out of the M-3 with uncharacteristic agility, and ran down the hill like a madman. "Don't move, Aram. I'm coming. Stay just where you are. I'm coming, Aram. Aram!"

But Aram Stein would never move again, neither would Major Carson. The jeep had hit a Teller mine half a mile down the track, its wreckage was bent and the tyres aflame. The bodies were cruelly dismembered. "Aram!"

"Can I get you anything else?" asked the housekeeper.

"I'm going to have to talk to Billy," Stein told her. He had pampered the boy too much; he must start involving him in the real problems. Stein was tired. From now on Billy would have to help, really help.

"Yes, Mr. Stein," said the housekeeper, puzzled that Stein should thus confide in her. "Don't forget that your telephone is still switched over to the answering machine."

## 26

It was almost eight years since young Billy Stein had been in London. That visit had been with his mother and father—a special vacation to celebrate his parents' wedding anniversary. They had taken him to all the usual tourist treats: the changing of the guard at Buckingham Palace, a visit to a musical show, a trip on the Thames, lunch at Simpson's in the Strand, not forgetting to tip the man who carved the roast meat. It had been pleasant enough as an interlude, but London had not attracted any of the Stein family enough to make them want to return. The chilly climate, with frequent rain showers which always seemed to catch them unprepared, made them miserable, and the hotel had been neither heated nor air-conditioned. They had all sneezed, he remembered.

Little had changed since those days. The parking problem was horrendous, the taxi service inadequate, the telephones arcane and the food not to his taste. Billy Stein had spent most of his life in Southern California and now he was rarely happy anywhere else.

These factors all militated against the young Stein in his mission to London to discover, at Stein senior's request, what Mr. Paul Bock had to tell them. Even in this luxury hotel near Park Lane, Billy Stein did not find things easy. The room-service waiter was Portuguese and could not comprehend Billy's breakfast order. The British morning newspaper was even more bewildering—devoted almost exclusively to the parochial activities of British trade union leaders, plus passionate analysis of recent British exports and some incomprehensible accounts of cricket. The headline said "Hanging: No by 119. MPs' verdict in the great debate." He laid the newspaper aside and turned his attention to breakfast. Tinned orange juice, a smear of scrambled eggs and some shrivelled fragments of bacon. He poured the coffee and sighed deeply. Why had he let his father bully him into coming to London? He could have been eating his usual sliced fresh pineapple with real cream and good coffee, in the shade of the palm trees, looking at the map, deciding where to fly for an afternoon of swimming or surfing or skiing. He switched on the TV but got only a snow storm of static and a loud hiss. He shut his eyes and swallowed the hotel coffee.

He had still not recovered from the jet lag and the misery of his transatlantic flight. The temperature of the "Japanese towels" had been little different from that of the martinis with which he had tried to expunge memories of the reheated meat and vegetables that was the first-class dinner. The oppressive mediocrity of the in-flight movie was relieved only by the banal chatter of the flight crew and the sound of a passenger snoring loudly in the row ahead. Billy Stein arrived in London exhausted, and found a helpful driver who took him to his hotel for what he later discovered was nearly four times the regular fare. Once in his comfortable hotel room, he slept for nineteen hours. And so it was that Billy had done nothing to contact Paul Bock until Friday—a week after the message had been left on his answering machine, and four days after Boyd Stuart's visit to York Way.

Even on Friday Billy Stein had to make three attempts before getting the address from the secretarial agency. After a late breakfast he put on his raincoat and hat and ventured into the chilly London summer. A taxi took him to Jimmy's Militaria and he became more and more depressed the nearer to it he came.

The squalid houses and littered streets did not fit with the polite and carefully modulated voice he had heard on the recording machine.

"Here we are, guv," said the taxi driver. A jumbo jet passed over so low that Billy Stein had difficulty hearing him. He held out a handful of change and let the driver help himself. The driver muttered a protest at this extra chore but helped himself anyway.

Billy Stein cupped his hands to peer beyond the CLOSED sign into the gloomy interior of the shop. There was an immediate incongruity in the way these slim-hipped shop window dummies, styled to look as modern as possible, capered and cavorted in the clumsy military attire of long ago. They made a weird group, these Nazis, in their dress swords and daggers, accompanying hussars and cavalry officers, dented suits of armour and a headless corporal of marines. Obviously bought secondhand, these figures bore their broken limbs, missing feet and scarred cheeks with inscrutable fortitude. It was like a morgue, thought Billy, and shivered again.

There was no answer to the bell. He looked at the lock on the shop door. It was older than most of the antiques displayed in the window. Furtively he looked up and down the street. Whether this was a hoax or not, he had no intention of coming six thousand miles without some further investigation. He used a penknife to hold the latch bolt and applied his formidable strength to the door. It creaked, strained against the woodwork and broke open with a snapping of rotten wood.

Billy Stein moved inside and closed the door, propping a large bomb against it to keep it shut. Stealthily, he picked his way between the swastika banners and the rows of breastplates, swords and guns. From upstairs he heard music: Bach played on a solo guitar. He looked inside the back room which was almost filled with cardboard boxes. Beyond them there was a cobbled yard no larger than a phone booth and on the far side of it the door of an outside WC. There was a dirty sink there, spattered with red stains.

Billy Stein went back through the shop and ascended the stairs as quietly as he could. The music seemed to be coming from the floor above. At the landing he paused. The music stopped as he listened outside the door. A man's voice said, "That was Bach's Suite for Lute, No. 2 in A minor, played by Carlos Bonell." He realized that it was a BBC announcer, coming from a radio, and turned the knob carefully to open the door.

It was a large room, looking out over the slate roof of the downstairs toilet to where a stunted little tree fought for sunshine in a yard which looked exactly the right size and shape for an execution. There was a lot of furniture in the room—several old armchairs and a large sofa with a spring visible through the torn fabric. Leaning against the fireplace were half a dozen very large, gold-painted picture frames, and a faded red sun umbrella advertising Coca-Cola. Everything smelt of cats and cooked cabbage.

He went through the room to the door of the next one. It was a heavy door, buried under layer after layer of cheap paint. Someone with yearnings for the creative arts had drawn wavy lines using a comb on the wet paint in an attempt to simulate wood graining. He leaned against the heavy panelled door. It was locked but the key was on the floor. He picked it up and fitted it in the lock. Through the door he could hear the guitar music starting again.

Whatever he expected to see in the room, it was not two men lying full length on the bed. Almost everything in the room was covered in blood, including two workmen's overalls which had been bundled up and pushed into the fireplace with the brass fire irons.

The men on the bed were dead. One was Paul Bock and the other was Jimmy. Billy Stein had no way of knowing who they were, because their killers had hindered identification by cutting off and taking away the hands and heads of both men.

Billy stood in the doorway speechless. He was not sure how long he stared at the two headless men on their blood-soaked eiderdown but he suddenly heard the radio announcer state that the next piece of guitar music was by Albéniz. He backed out of the room and closed the door more forcibly than he intended. He sat down in the ancient armchair and felt his heart beating as if his whole body was about to explode. Subduing his panic, he retreated the way he had come, closing each door behind him. He could still hear the guitar music.

Billy realized how much an investigation would be hamstrung by the absence of dentistry evidence, or the fingerprints of the victims, but there was something diabolical about men so malevolent that they could hack off heads and hands of their victims.

It was an hour afterwards, while Billy Stein still wandered aimlessly through the grubby back streets of King's Cross that he realized that his own fingerprints would be liberally distributed at the scene of the murder. But he had no intention of returning there. He asked a passerby to direct him to Park Lane. He had walked as far as Warren Street underground station in light rain before he was lucky enough to find a taxi. Once inside the cab he buried his head in his hands. It was hard to believe that yesterday he'd had no problem more pressing than whether to change the oil filter on the engine of his plane.

## 27

The duty London field controller phoned Boyd Stuart at 1423 hours on Friday, July 20. He was on an internal scrambler line so he could speak freely. "Stein went there," said the duty controller.

"And where is he now?"

"He went back to the hotel. He was as white as a sheet. He walked the streets as though he didn't know where he was going. Then he saw a taxi cruising past, hailed him and arrived back at his hotel about forty minutes ago. He's shaken."

"So would I be," said Stuart. "Still no sign of the police there?"

"The German lad told his bank that he wanted a few days off. They probably won't even report him missing until Monday. The other boy has no close friends or relatives so far as I have discovered."

"How long was Stein inside?"

"Twenty minutes, maybe less."

There was a long silence during which Boyd Stuart drew a series of boxes on his blotting pad. Then he carefully drew crosses inside each square until the design was complete. "Are you there?" said the duty controller.

"Yes, I'm here."

"This would be the time to do it, sir. Our man tailing him said Stein seemed to be in a terrible state."

"Thanks," said Stuart. "Keep me in touch."

He hung up the phone and reached for his hat. Like Billy Stein, he decided that the weather was not good enough for him to go without his raincoat.

"I'm calling on Mr. Stein," Boyd Stuart told the hotel receptionist. "I want to surprise him."

"I'm sorry, sir, but . . ."

Boyd Stuart's hand reached out and grabbed the wrist of the man at the desk before it got near to the house-phone. "I want to surprise him," said Stuart again, this time flipping open the Metropolitan Police warrant card he kept for such occasions.

The clerk stared at the identification. "I'll have to get the manager."

"Get no one," said Boyd Stuart, "or I'll have you inside on a charge of obstructing a police officer in the execution of his duty." He was speaking very quietly but he held onto the man's wrist with enough force to make him wince with pain. "I'm just going upstairs for a nice quiet chat. You understand?"

"I understand," said the man. Boyd Stuart released his grip and walked quickly across to catch the doors of the lift. By the time the reception clerk looked up from rubbing his wrist, Stuart had gone.

Room 301 was next to the lifts. Such 01 rooms were always next to the lifts, and experienced travellers tried to avoid them. Stuart wondered why Stein didn't have a suite. According to the results of the check they had run on the family's credit and level of spending, it would be well within his means. Stuart switched off the light in the corridor and then knocked at the door.

"Yes." It was Billy Stein's voice.

"Room service."

"What do you want?"

"I've got a packet for you—from somewhere abroad. It's got foreign postage."

"Put it under the door."

Stuart smiled. He remembered being caught out like that before. "It's a packet, I said. It won't go under the door." There was another long silence and then Stuart heard the lock being turned. He knew he would have to be fast, and hoped fervently that Stein didn't put the chain on the catch.

Billy Stein opened the door a fraction and Stuart lowered his shoulder and charged with all his weight. Stein was prepared, but not prepared enough. He went reeling back into the room; Stuart followed, stumbling over Stein's baggage, and saving himself from falling only by steadying himself on the bed end. By that time Stein was sitting on the floor and Stuart was facing him with a Smith & Wesson Magnum held twelve inches from his nose.

"Freeze," said Stuart and the young man froze. It was not the first time Stuart had selected from the armoury this big gun that only just fit into his shoulder holster and weighted him to one side. But he had seen the way its .357 Magnum bullets could go through the metal of car bodies, and he had also seen the way the sight of it stopped men in their tracks, as now it froze Billy Stein sprawled on the bedroom floor.

"There's no cash here," said Billy Stein, still looking at the huge pistol. "No cameras, no travellers cheques." He managed a touch of derision. "You dialled the wrong number, buddy. I'm down to my last few bucks and looking for a job."

Stuart smiled. "You disappoint me, Billy."

Stein looked up and scowled. "How the hell did you get my name?"

Stuart did not reply. He looked round the room. Stein was wearing a dressing gown and had been on the bed trying to sleep. His gold wristwatch was on the side table together with *Geographers' London Atlas* and his yellow-tinted spectacles.

"Next time you answer a knock at the door in a hotel room, put your glasses on. You might have to sign something."

"Next time, punk?" said Billy Stein. He was recovering from his surprise enough to show anger. "Next time I'll take you to pieces with my bare hands." Stein tried to get to his feet.

"Stay right where you are," said Stuart. "I know how to use this shooter, and I'll give you what you gave those poor kids up in King's Cross this morning if you provide the slightest excuse."

"Wait a minute," said Billy. "Wait a minute. What kids? What are you babbling about?"

"Don't give me all that stuff, Stein. I know what you did this morning before returning to your nice hotel for a doze. You killed those two kids and hacked their heads off. What did they do to you? Were you trying to sell them some of your dad's fancy Hitler documents, or were they behind with the rent?"

"Oh, now I get it," said Billy Stein. "You're one of the Brits talking to my dad about his papers. You know all about that stuff."

"I know about the papers," said Stuart. "What I didn't know is the lengths that you and your dad would go to hang on to them. What did you use, Billy? A hacksaw, was it, or a chopper?"

"You don't talk to me like that, you bastard," said Billy. "I didn't kill those people—kids you say they were; I don't know if they were kids or what—I was set up. . . ."

"Set up? Set up how, and by whom? You fly into London—first class with all the trimmings—and check into this flashy hotel. You leave here this morning and go directly to an address in King's Cross—not a regular call on the average tourist itinerary, you'll agree—and stay inside about twenty minutes. Is that about the time you required to do the deed, Stein? Set up? What in hell are you talking about?"

"This is your territory. I'm out of place here; I'm vulnerable. OK. But I didn't kill those people up there in that stinking little place. I swear to God I didn't."

"So who did kill them, you little creep?" Stein moved. "Keep still, or I'll blow your head off."

Stein laboriously described his father's arrest by the highway patrol, and the phone call from Paul Bock which was waiting for him when eventually he returned to his home in Cresta Ridge Drive. Stuart knew that the slow recital of events was calculated to provide Stein with a chance to collect his wits and talk his way out of his predicament, but he did nothing to hurry him or interrupt. He just waited until Stein ran out of steam and when Stein looked up at him for his reaction, Stuart was standing, gun in hand, smiling politely.

"What's so funny?" said Stein.

"Am I getting this right?" said Stuart. "You're telling me that a man phoned your father in Los Angeles, a man you've never heard of before, and on the strength of one phone call, you leapt aboard a plane and came to London? Pull the other leg, Stein, it's got bells on."

"He said it was about the documents."

"Oh, he said it was about the documents," said Stuart mockingly. "Well, that explains everything. Naturally if someone phones up and says . . ."

"The hell with you," said Stein. Now he had heard Stuart deride his explanation, he realized how improbable it would sound to the jury.

"Shall I tell you what they do with people who go into the homes of law-abiding inhabitants of north London and hack their heads and hands off? They put them into the lock-up for altogether too long. Did you ever see an English prison, Stein? Or, more pertinently, did you ever smell one? Did you ever smell one, first thing in the morning, when they are slopping out? No flushing toilets there, my friend. You won't be sitting in the lounge watching colour TV, like they do in those nice California state prisons. We're more primitive over here. This morning's headlines make it seem you'll beat the hangman, Billy. But you'll spend the rest of your natural life in some dirty, smelly, old Victorian slum that looks like an illustration to a Charles Dickens novel."

Billy Stein hammered a fist against the carpet. "I didn't kill anyone."

"What did they do? Steal some of your Nazi documents? I noticed that the shop was filled with Nazi swords and daggers and that kind of junk. Is that what they did?"

"If you are going to book me, book me."

Stuart stepped over to the dressing table and fingered quickly through Stein's U.S. passport, airline tickets, keys and coins, and a wallet containing paper money, California driving licence, Social Security card and credit cards. "Ask yourself what kind of position you're in," Stuart suggested.

Billy said nothing.

"You've left your dabs all over that house in King's Cross. The police still take fingerprints, Stein. I know that these whizz kids in the private-eye movies say it's all out of date, but the cops get a lot of convictions every year on fingerprint evidence." Stuart lifted a Samsonite two-suiter onto the bed. "Fingerprints are computerized nowadays, Stein. No more time wasted while some civilian clerk compares arches, loops and whorls—all done in a flash nowadays." He opened the catches and rummaged quickly through the clothes inside. "And even if you are innocent, who's going to believe it?"

"You won't find the Hitler documents in there, buddy."

"Won't I? Well, that's too bad, but I get an A for effort, right?" Stuart waved the pistol at him. "Keep still until I tell you to move."

"Do you know what I really think? I think *you* killed those two people. Or, if you didn't do it personally, someone employed by the goddamned British spy service did it. Then you put that phone message on my tape and staked out the house to watch me walk into your trap. It's a frame-up, as sure as I ever saw one. And one day I'll get even with you, if it takes me a million years."

"Never mind the histrionics," said Stuart. "You lean forward and put your hands behind you so that I can fit the handcuffs on you. Try to grab my gun and I'll have to hit you over the head with the butt of it—you understand?"

"OK," said Billy. "You're charging me, are you?"

"Like in the Hitchcock films, you mean?" He got one cuff on to Stein's wrist and struggled with the other until it finally clicked. It pinched Billy's skin and he gave a grunt of pain. "No, you'll be charged by a nice police inspector, in full-dress uniform. You get an inspector for a murder charge, Stein, no lesser rank may do it. It will be something to write to your dad about. I just came along to collect you. We're going out the back way. Cut up rough and you'll go out feet first. Got it?"

"Yep."

Stuart had arranged everything with great care. He used two young probationary trainees from the Foreign Office to help him with the car and pacify the hotel staff. They hustled Stein out through the baggage door, and put him into a black Rover saloon which had been passed off more than once as a police vehicle.

They put Billy Stein into a safe house in Pentonville Road. A man named Benson, dressed up as a police inspector, went through all the formalities with Stein, and certainly the cells in the basement were convincing enough. They had been built in May 1945 to hold high-ranking Nazis brought to London for interrogation. Since then they had been used to store stationery, except when charades like this one necessitated moving all the boxes of paper upstairs.

"It went all right," said one of the trainees. It was exactly the sort of task they had looked forward to when first selected for assignment to MI6.

"Let's wait until we're sure that no one took the licence number of that Rover and finds it's registered in the name of old Tom Morris in the accounting department. Did you put the fear of God into the hotel staff? We don't want anyone phoning the *Evening Standard* news desk."

"I did just what you told me, sir," said one trainee obsequiously.

"You'll go a long way, Parsons," said Stuart. "Paid his bill, and checked his room carefully?"

"Just the way they showed us to do it at the training school."

Stuart pulled a face. "No one's perfect," he said. "I'm going home now. You can give him some gentle interrogation for the next two hours. I'll take over when I return."

"What is the prime objective?" asked the first trainee.

Stuart recognized the terminology. They had been talking about primary and secondary interrogation objectives decades ago when he had first passed through the school. "Just ask him questions," said Stuart. "Any questions. Don't try to solve the murders—just keep him awake for me. I want him tired and worried by the time I take over."

"Are we certain that he didn't murder the people in King's Cross?"

Stuart looked at him. Only these young trainees asked that sort of direct question, but he let it go without complaint. "The two men were discovered dead by one of our own operatives while Billy Stein was still in the U.S.A."

"I suppose that clinches it," said the trainee.

"Let's just say that we'd need a very persuasive prosecutor," said Stuart and went home.

## 28

The top two floors of the Pentonville safe house, in a shabby part of north London, were converted into a separate apartment. Meetings were sometimes held there, although these were never the high-level "policy meetings," or the monthly so-called soviets, or even the finance meetings. All those were held in more luxurious environments: the house that overlooked the Thames at Marlow or the equally fine manor house at Abingdon. Places where, or so it was always insisted, the extensive parkland provided better security.

The Pentonville Road safe house was where men met to discuss such mundane matters as travel and petrol allowances, extra paid leave and postings—the sort of decisions that did not affect the lives of the men at the top. But Pentonville Road was comfortable enough in its bourgeois way. On the sideboard the duty officers could be sure of a bottle of Yugoslav riesling or a rather fierce claret, together with warm Schweppes and recapped bottles of Perrier water, long since gone flat. Even the key for the cupboard under the stairs, where the gin and whisky were kept, was hanging by the electric meter with the fuse wire. There was a temperamental gas stove and a seemingly endless supply of eggs and sliced Wonderloaf. The more adventurous of the department's employees had found it a convenient place to entertain young—and even not so young—ladies, when marital commitments stood in the way of more conventional social meetings.

Whether Sir Sydney Ryden knew any of this was not easy to decide, but he looked about him with a quizzical eye, and the duty officer's desperate search for a bottle of port for him had not only been successful but had also brought to light some Worcestershire sauce, half a bottle of malt whisky and a pink plastic hair comb.

At first the DG did not sit down. He strode about the large sitting room, picking up ashtrays and broken fountain pens in the restless way with which he was known to react to department bad news. He had not removed his overcoat when Stuart was shown into the room. The back of his collar was turned up and his hair was in all directions. Under the long overcoat, the director was in evening clothes, complete with old-fashioned wing-collar and pearl shirt studs. It was the small hours of Saturday, and cold enough for the duty officer to have a coal fire going in the tiny grate. The DG warmed his hands at it.

"I was celebrating," explained the DG.

"Something upon which I should congratulate you, Director?"

The DG smiled, "A dear friend was awarded a medal by the Royal Central Asian Society. It's a great honour."

"Yes, sir."

The DG turned to the sideboard. "A drink, Stuart?"

"No thank you, sir." Stuart looked at his watch. It was three o'clock in the morning.

"They have found me some port. I'm going to try some. Are you sure you won't change your mind? We have"—he picked it up, tore off its paper wrapping and read the label carefully—"a malt whisky, according to the label."

"Very well, sir. A whisky straight."

"So he sent his son, did he?"

"Apparently, sir. Billy Stein. We waited for him to make a move. He went to the house in King's Cross this morning . . . yesterday morning perhaps I should say."

"And got into it?"

"Not much difficulty there, sir. Anyone with a child's penknife would have been able to do it."

"And that's what the young Stein did, eh? That's excellent." The DG poured the drinks and brought the malt whisky to Stuart. "And then what?" He threw the wrapping paper into the fire but it did not burn.

"Thank you, sir. The man following Stein phoned in. Coordination told duty field control and I went to see Stein at his hotel."

"And what did he say?"

"He was shaken. I accused him of murdering the men. I said he'd face trial if he didn't cooperate fully."

"And will he cooperate . . . fully?"

"He *says* he will," said Stuart. "But he's still in a state of shock. A man in that condition is likely to say anything. Stein is in a foreign country, without his friends and associates. Yes, he says he will cooperate." Stuart drank some of his whisky. He smelt the harsh, smoky flavour and let it linger on his tongue. Having the DG acting as his personal controller was an unprecedented development, and not one that he in any way enjoyed. It was impossible to argue back with the DG in the way that sometimes became necessary in these operations. To make matters worse, more than one of the London permanent staff seemed to think that he was using the opportunity and his father-in-law to further his career.

"What do you propose we do?" asked the DG.

"Let young Stein speak to his father. . . ."

"Release the son if Dad gives us the Hitler Minutes," said the DG, completing what Stuart was about to say.

"Yes, sir."

The DG pulled a face, as if he had suddenly bitten into a particularly sour lemon. "Crude, isn't it, Stuart?"

"It is, sir. Very crude. Do you have a better suggestion?"

The DG looked up quickly and studied Stuart's face closely for any sign of intended rudeness. Having failed to discover any, he said, "No, Stuart. At the present time, I do not."

"Father and son are very close, sir."

"Never been on a tiger shoot, have you, Stuart?" The DG rested a hand on the mantelpiece and stared at the fire as a fortune teller might gaze at a crystal ball.

"No, sir."

"You put out a line of beaters in the early morning, and they walk forward kicking up the very devil of a din. The guns are moving towards them, well strung out . . . on elephants, of course."

"Of course."

The DG turned to face him. "Good beaters can get the creatures moving at just the right pace. You don't want your tigers galloping past." The DG drank some of the port they had found him down under the stairs. It was Marks & Spencer's own label and not the sort of vintage the DG favoured, but he sipped it without complaint. "There's usually some bloody fool who fires too soon. He fires towards the beaters, you see. That's not the idea at all. You've got to let your tiger come past; shoot him as he passes, or even after he's passed. But never while he's still coming towards you."

"Yes, sir."

"Or Timmy Tiger goes back and mauls one of your beaters, Stuart. You see what I mean, don't you?"

"You mean Stein."

"Indeed I do, Stuart. I mean Mr. Stein, our Timmy Tiger." The DG sat down on the big sofa, stretched his feet out and ran a hand back through his ruffled hair. "You'd better tell me what's on your mind, my boy. I can see something is troubling you."

Stuart sat down carefully in the armchair and balanced his drink on the armrest. "I'd like to be transferred to some other operation, sir."

"Transferred?" There could be no doubt that the DG was surprised. "This is the most important operation we have going at the present moment. Don't you realize that the reason I keep looking at that damned clock on the mantelpiece is because the PM will be expecting me in the ante-room of the Cabinet Office, tomorrow at eight-thirty a.m., ready to tell her the latest news. She'll be off to Africa on the thirtieth. She insists we clear up this business before she goes. I'm under pressure, Stuart."

"Yes, I understand that, sir. But I think you could find someone more suited to the job. I'm at a disadvantage; Stein and Breslow both know that I'm working for this department."

"You're not being entirely frank with me, Stuart. Is this something to do with you and Jennifer? You know I never interfere. I've never taken sides. I think I can safely claim that."

Stuart did not reply. His father-in-law had interfered with his marriage right from the very beginning, and as for his claim never to have taken sides . . . Stuart was simply at a loss for words. "It's nothing to do with me and Jennifer, sir."

"You treated my daughter badly, Stuart. I'm speaking man to man now, of course. Your behaviour was unforgivable and I'll never forget what Jennifer told us the night we took her back home. You've knocked about the world, Stuart, and I dare say a man's no worse for that. But you married a child and made her suffer. The sooner the divorce comes through the better."

"It's nothing to do with Jennifer or our marriage," said Stuart. "It's this operation. This afternoon Stein was in a state of near collapse. He'd been to that house and seen two decapitated men. From what I understand, they had their hands cut off too."

"Perfectly correct, Stuart."

"From the last report I got, the police have still not been informed of the crime. Our people have been in and out, and even taken photos. Stein accused me of arranging the murders. I'm no longer so sure we didn't do so, and I don't like that."

The DG nodded and sipped some of his drink. "You've been in some scrapes, Stuart. I looked through your dossier when Jennifer first met you. There was the time when we had to get you out of Turin in the very devil of a hurry. And your file has an embargo slip for two or three countries where you are still facing charges, I understand?"

"I didn't hack any heads off, if that's what you are implying, Director."

"I'm implying nothing, Stuart," said the DG calmly, "I'm stating facts. If you want to contest what is on your dossier, this would be an excellent opportunity to do so."

"I'm not disputing it."

"We didn't choose you to captain a junior school tennis team, Stuart. You knew this might be rough. I told you so myself, if I remember rightly."

"You did, sir."

There was a long silence. Then the DG said, "When did you first hear about the killing of the two men?"

"Wednesday evening, July 18, that is, about eleven o'clock in the evening. I was at home. A courier came with a verbal message."

"About the same time that I was informed," said the DG and scratched his ear. "I was at a dinner party in Hampstead. I came back here to the office. I thought of sending for you but I wasn't sure it was necessary."

Stuart did nothing, waiting while the DG fidgeted about, trying to decide how much secret information he should be given. "You believe the department had those men killed?"

"It wouldn't be the first time such a thing has happened."

"No, it wouldn't be the first time," agreed the DG. He wrapped his overcoat across his legs, as if he were suddenly feeling the cold.

"I saw them alive," said Stuart. "Last Monday. They were little more than kids . . . I liked them."

"You reported to me that they were delinquents."

"Just talk," said Stuart. "They were full of talk. They weren't dangerous."

"One of them was taking high-grade information out of an important German computer. Not exactly harmless, would you say?" The DC maintained an unruffled and almost jovial manner. Stuart felt he was being lured into some sort of verbal trap but could not see what it was likely to be.

"Taking information out of a computer isn't yet a capital crime," said Stuart evenly.

"Depends where you are," said the DG. He sniffed loudly, and sipped his port. "I wouldn't give much for the chances of anyone who tried that sort of antic in Russia. I'd think it probably *is* a capital crime there."

"In any case, sir, I'd like to be assigned to something different."

"Request refused," said the DG without hesitation. It was as if he'd prepared himself for this demand.

"Refused, sir?"

"We can't have field operatives changing their assignments just because they begin to imagine that the department is not handling matters with the sort of deference and decorum that they think necessary. Drink up, Stuart, and have another. Then I must rush. No, we can't start changing round like that. In next to no time we'd have chaps complaining that they didn't like the climate in Darwin, or wanted to evade an irate husband in Rio." The DG smiled, and touched his bow tie to be sure it was not crooked.

"Did you order those men killed, sir?"

"Certainly not, Stuart. It's not my style. I would have thought you'd have known that by now. How long have you been working here with me—nearly ten years, as I recall?"

"Eleven, sir."

"One of these days I must try that stuff you are so fond of; pure malt, isn't it? It always smells so much like medicine to me." The DG brought the bottle over and poured a new measure into Stuart's glass. "Eleven years, is it? Time flies past. I can remember you coming over here. You had a bit of trouble over at MI5 as I recall . . . an argument with a constable, was it?"

"I knocked a police superintendent unconscious," said Stuart.

The DG gave him a cold smile. "Yes," he said. "That was it. I knew it was some silly difficulty like that. They had a lot of ex-policemen running desks at the Home Office at that time. I could never understand why the DG over there didn't just straighten it out between you."

"I refused to apologize," said Stuart. They both knew that Sir Sydney had been through his dossier with meticulous care, not just the abstract but the whole thing: bank accounts, medical and dental charts, confidential assessments, psychiatrist's and school reports. Sir Sydney probably knew more about that punch Stuart had thrown at the police superintendent than the superintendent who had suffered it.

"Refused to apologize." He nodded. "Yes, of course. A matter of principle, was it? I've always said that matters of principle are the very last things that should provoke a man to seeking recourse in the law courts. The same might well be said of the recourse to violence." A milk truck passed, its engine roaring and the bottles rattling as it changed gear at the traffic lights.

"It was a long time ago."

"And men change," said the DG. "We all did silly things when we were young. Did I ever tell you about the time when I dismantled all the bicycles at Winchester?" He looked at his watch. "Anyway, I mustn't bore you."

Stuart had not pursued his demand for a change of assignment. His dislike of this sort of bullying made his mind turn to thoughts of resigning altogether.

The DG seemed to read his mind. "Don't think of resigning, Stuart. There would be all the continuation money to pay back."

Stuart remembered the lump sum he had received two years ago when he decided to sign the contract for a further ten years' engagement. It had seemed an enormous amount of money at the time, but so much of it just drained away. It would be extremely difficult to repay it. "Yes, sir."

"You'd have to sell off your little weekend cottage and so on. Don't do it, my boy. My wife sold off some fields near where we live in the country. She was sorry afterwards. The way the market is now, it's better to hold on to property." The DG smiled again. He wanted Stuart to know that he had sifted through every available piece of information about his financial affairs. He wanted Stuart to realize right now that there was no alternative to keeping at this job. The last thing he wanted to tell the Prime Minister was that he had just lost his best—or at least his most suitable—field operative. "And there could be liabilities arising from the divorce." The silence seemed to last forever.

"I'll keep at it," said Stuart.

"Good man," said the DG. Now that he had won he could afford to be generous. "You'd put us in a devil of a pickle if you wanted to get out now. The PM's meetings in Lusaka with the Commonwealth Heads of Government will give her a chance to achieve something that every previous PM has failed to do."

"You mean a settlement . . . changes in the Zimbabwe-Rhodesia constitution?"

"Exactly, Stuart." The DG seemed surprised that Stuart knew about the story which was being told interminably in all the papers and news magazines. "And I think she'll do it, Stuart."

"She's had some amazing successes already, sir."

"She has. And between you and me, old chap, it's making her the very devil to work with. A new broom sweeps clean and all that. I have a feeling that if we don't whitewash old Winnie in just the way that Mrs. Thatcher and the Conservative Party have always liked him to be . . . I think we might be in for the new broom business here. You see what I mean?" The fire flared as the ball of paper was heated to combustion point. Then the ball of ash lifted gently from the coals and toppled into the hearth.

"I'm an admirer of Sir Winston myself, sir." Stuart drained his glass.

"Of course you are. We all are! He was a great man. That's the essence of the matter. We must do a good job on this one because it's something we all believe in. Luckily, I can assure you that the Hitler Minutes are forgeries. We have to make sure everyone knows it."

Stuart said nothing. He knew the papers were not forgeries. There would not be such a fuss about forgeries. Perhaps the DG read Stuart's thoughts for he touched Stuart's arm and turned him towards the door, as a torpedo might be aimed at an enemy cruiser. Stuart walked to the door and turned for a moment before opening it. The DG looked up and raised his eyebrows. They were big bushy eyebrows surmounting a large craggy face. "Yes, Stuart?"

"If, in the line of duty, you had to give orders for the expedient demise of two men, you'd not necessarily feel you had to tell me about that, would you?"

The house was still, and there was no sound of traffic. The DG stood for a moment and pondered the question, as if a profound philosophical principle were at stake. He rolled on his toes like a dancing master about to demonstrate a particularly tricky step. "I would use my judgement, Stuart."

## 29

By Monday, July 23, it was becoming increasingly easy for Sir Sydney Ryden to believe that fate was working against him. He dined that evening at the Beefsteak, an old-established gentleman's club consisting of little more than a small ante-room, an office, a few armchairs—providing a view of some public lavatories and a war memorial—and a narrow room in which members and their guests dined, all at the same long table.

Fortune placed Sir Sydney next to a bearded TV scriptwriter with decided views upon the government's promised cuts in the civil service. "Take the Home Office," said the scriptwriter, reaching for a silver-plated cow which had been emptied of milk. "Half the people there are making tea whenever I have been inside the building. You are not at the Home Office, are you?"

"No, I'm not," said Sir Sydney gravely.

The scriptwriter tilted the silver cow so that he could use its nose to draw patterns on the table cloth. "I did a documentary there last year. Disgusting waste. . . . We said that in the programme, of course."

"Most interesting," said Sir Sydney. He glanced round to see if his host had yet escaped from the man who had button-holed him with a request about joining the club committee.

"What part of the civil service are you with?" the scriptwriter asked, having failed to discover this by means of indirect remarks.

"The Foreign Office," said Sir Sydney Ryden.

"They are helping us with a programme we'll air next April," said the scriptwriter. He confidently assumed that everyone was fascinated by a behind-the-scenes glimpse of television. Sir Sydney sipped his port and hoped the young man would talk to his host and leave him alone. He would have made his escape, except that there was still a small matter of paying his share of the cost of the cigars.

". . . and the Germans had put all their gold down into this salt mine . . ." he suddenly heard the scriptwriter saying. "The greater proportion of the entire German gold reserves and God knows what documents and stuff. . . ." Sir Sydney's stomach tightened and the port suddenly became vinegar in his mouth. He turned to the bearded man and nodded.

"Really. And this was your idea?" said Sir Sydney encouragingly.

"Some looney historian from one of those dud universities in the Midlands. A professor he was. . . ." The bearded man laughed. "You should have seen him. I wouldn't have given him a job as a cleaner. But he had the stuff all right. Unusuable, mind you. Scriptwriting for TV is a very specialized technique. The Beeb gave him a few quid and sent him packing. The poor old fool was furious but there was nothing he could do about it. 'Sue the BBC,' I told him, 'and see where that gets you.' One of my people took over the project and started it rolling so that we can air it on the anniversary of the end of the war. That's when the Yanks got to the mine and found the loot there."

Sir Sydney relit his cigar, noting with some satisfaction that the flaming match did not tremble. "Tell me how your script begins," he said, this being the simplest way to have the story retold while he gave his full attention to it.

By now the scriptwriter was steering the silver cow round the salt and pepper so that it left tracks in the table cloth. "It's not my script," he said. "I'm what they call a script editor. I phone up any writers I think might be able to handle it. We've had a four-page outline. The actual script won't be ready until next month, as I remember."

"It must be an awfully interesting job," said Sir Sydney and gallantly sat through another half-hour of finer points of script editing until the subject of the salt mine was quite, quite cold.

The next morning Sid Sydney arranged an urgent meeting with the assistant director at the office of the Director of Public Prosecutions. The DPP is the official department which advises law-enforcement agencies about the legal aspects of serious criminal proceedings. The assistant director promised Sir Sydney that they would support an action against the BBC or any of its employees, and any other person concerned, should they not cooperate with MI6 in its endeavours to suppress the publication of material which was protected by the Official Secrets Act, as clearly this was.

On that same day Sir Sydney Ryden arranged a meeting with the chairman of the BBC board of governors. Without going into any detail, he explained that the revelation of certain aspects of the recovery of the treasure in the salt mine would not be in the public interest.

In the absence of the BBC's Director General, who was indisposed, the chairman got Sir Sydney Ryden's permission to bring the head of external services (who was the ranking executive) into the meeting.

Sir Sydney produced a map that one of the MI6

cartographers had prepared overnight. It showed the city of Frankfurt, and the autobahn north which led through Alsfeld and Bad Hersfeld, and the convoy route on the small side road off the autobahn. It showed too the present-day border, with its barbed wire, man traps, minefields, searchlights and machine-gun posts.

"Director Janecke and Director Thoms of the Reichsbank were the two men who handled all the gold in Nazi Germany," said Sir Sydney Ryden. "I have here some of the documents which show the shipments made to the Kaiseroda mineshaft at Merkers during those final weeks of the war. You see the signatures."

The two BBC men looked at the map and the border of East Germany which encompassed the tiny town of Merkers.

"This is the document from the Reichswirtschaftsministerium which assigned space in certain selected mines for the protection of such treasures as they considered most valuable," said Sir Sydney, passing it across the desk.

**SECRET**

**List of Money, Gold, Bullion, Found in Salt-Mine Cave, Merkers (H-6850) Germany, 8 April 1945**

Gold Reichsmarks, bags 446
Austrian crowns, bags 271
Turkish pounds, bags 73
Dutch gold, bags 514
Italian gold, bags 62
Austrian coins (miscellaneous), bags 3 (nos. 2, 15, 96)
British coins (miscellaneous), bags 3 (nos. 12, 17, 15)
Gold bars, bullion 8198
American 20 gold pieces, bags 711 (25,000 dollars per bag)
Miscellaneous coins, bags 37
Gold francs, bags 80 (10,000 francs per bag)
Miscellaneous money and coin, bag no. 1C

Italian gold coins, bags 5 (20,000 per bag)
British gold pounds, bags 280
Foreign notes, miscellaneous, bags 80

Reichsmarks

| | |
|---|---|
| 1000 Mark notes, bags 130 | 650,000,000 Marks |
| 100 Mark notes, bags 1650 | 1,650,000,000 Marks |
| 50 Mark notes, bags 600 | 300,000 Marks |
| 20 Mark notes, bags 500 | 100,000 Marks |
| 5 Mark notes, boxes 800 | 60,000 Marks |
| | 2,300,460,000 Marks |

Gold bar, 1
Silver bars, 20
Silver plate, boxes 63 and bags 55
Gold, 138 pieces in bags 49
Gold, miscellaneous pieces, bag 1
Gold, French francs, bags 635
Swiss gold, bags 55
Crated gold bullion, boxes 53
Crated gold bullion, long boxes 2
Valuable coins, bags 9
Coins (not marked), bags 5
Turkish gold coins, bag 1
Mixed gold coins, bag 1
American dollars, bag 1 (12,470 dollars)
Austrian gold (marked GA "V"), bags 13
Miscellaneous gold of various countries, bags 6
Danish gold coins, bags 32
Platinum bars, bag 1 containing 6 bars
Roubles, bags 4
Silver bars, bags 40
Gold bullion, bags 11
British pounds, bag 1
Documents (metal boxes marked FHQu) 82

The two BBC officials studied the documents and looked at the map. Soon they exchanged significant glances and one of them asked, "You'd not want the full list of gold and valuables made public, Sir Sydney?"

The DG gave one of his cheerless smiles. "I wouldn't like to define exactly our priorities."

This evasive reply was enough to convince them that the Russians had been deprived of their rightful share of the treasure from a mine which became part of the Russian zone. Now, believing that they understood the full implications of Sir Sydney's mission, they were fully ready to help. The producer of the documentary would be informed that there was litigations threatened by an unspecified complainant. Photocopies of all relevant material made ostensibly for the legal department would actually be sent to Sir Sydney Ryden's home address within twenty-four hours.

The DG expressed his gratitude and was pleased he had not had to mention his visit to the DPP's office. It was always better to handle these things at the very top, where the people concerned knew where their duty lay.

By eleven a.m. the following day, Sir Sydney had personally read all the material the BBC delivered to his office.

"Just a lot of bilge," said Sir Sydney. Fatigue muted the relief and delight he might otherwise have shown. "A boring little script about the U.S. finding the bullion in the mine; the documents and archives are scarcely mentioned. Interviews with some high-ranking officers who were nowhere near the mine, and some U.S. Army Signal Corps photographs of the sacks of gold." He looked up at Boyd Stuart. "I had a sleepless night for nothing, Stuart."

"Yes, sir," said Stuart. "In fact, the research office is collecting all references to the Merkers mine—worldwide in all languages."

"Are you trying to tell me that we have this damned TV programme material already on record?"

"Not quite all of it, sir. Research picked it up from their routine scrutiny of police permission for filming. The BBC wants to send a camera crew to get footage on the Foreign Office exterior and interior, for the beginning of their documentary. We asked the FO to request a copy of the treatment before giving permission. They would have got a copy of the script too, as soon as it was completed. That was to be a condition of giving the BBC the permits."

"Oh, well," said Sir Sydney philosophically. "I suppose it's better that we catch it twice, and find it harmless, than miss it altogether and have a disaster on our hands."

"Precisely, sir. Perhaps you underestimate the organization you have yourself created."

"Don't butter me up, Stuart. I can't abide it."

"Very good, sir."

"How is the interrogation of young Stein going?"

"He doesn't seem to know very much, sir. His father probably doesn't confide in him a great deal."

The DG nodded. Such paternal secretiveness came as no surprise. He hadn't discovered the names of his father's clubs until the old man was almost on his deathbed. What man did confide in his son, he wondered. "Nothing at all, eh?"

"Inference, sir. I think we can rule out this house in which Colonel Pitman lives. Stein says his father told him he'd moved the documents out of there some time ago, and I believe that. Stein senior has a protective atttiude towards Colonel Pitman. I think he'd remove such documents simply to make it safer for the colonel."

"It sounds extraordinary to me," admitted the DG, who could not imagine any of the young men in his department adopting such a protective attitude towards him.

"I believe it, sir," said Stuart. "Wherever the documents are, I think that the Pitman house can be eliminated.'"

He looked Stuart up and down. "Has something happened?"

"We have a positive identification on the photo, Director."

"Start at the beginning," said the DG. He sat down on the sofa, stifling a sigh, to convey to Stuart the complexities of his job.

"The photograph of three men that was found in the safe belonging to Franz Wever," said Stuart. "It was taken in wartime. One of the men was Franz Wever himself, the second man was Max Breslow. Now we have identified the third person in the photo."

"And . . ."

"His name is Wilhelm Hans Kleiber. He made

quite a name for himself during the war. We have references to him from the Berlin documents centre. He's also on RFSS microfilm series T-175 in the Washington National Archives, and we found him in the Hoover Institution document collection at Stanford University. He was born in a village near Königsberg, East Prussia. Kleiber joined the army in 1938, became an Abwehr officer and then the SS took him into the RSHA as they took over all the intelligence services. He was taken into the Gehlen organization when it got going again after the war."

"A dedicated fellow," said the DG bitterly, but there was a trace of respect in the irony.

"A cynic perhaps," said Stuart. "A mercenary."

"Consistently anti-Communist, isn't he?" said the DG. Before Stuart could answer, he asked, "Still alive then?"

"Very much alive," said Stuart. "Resident in Munich, at least that seems to be where he pays his tax. He is the senior partner of a security company. They own a small fleet of armoured cars used to transport bullion and bank notes . . . for bank and factory payrolls."

"What else?" It was impossible to guess how much the DG really knew.

"That's all we have officially, sir."

The DG smiled. "And unofficially, Stuart? Am I to be taken into your confidence about what you've learnt unofficially?" The DG was able to imbue even the friendliest words with a tone of biting sarcasm.

"He might be a Moscow Centre operative," said Stuart.

"And who has provided us with this alarming scenario?"

"The collator, sir."

The DG was taken aback. He had been expecting Stuart to name some junior clerk in the Identity Department, or some long-retired field agent to whom Stuart had indiscreetly mentioned his quest. "So the collator says he's Moscow Centre," said the DG thoughtfully. He pulled his nose. "Not such an anti-Communist as I thought, eh Stuart?"

"If there is some sort of war-crimes guilt hanging

over Kleiber's head, the Russians might have used it to blackmail him into working for them."

"You read my mind, Stuart. We've seen that one before, haven't we?"

"We have indeed, sir. Many times."

"It's a tricky one," admitted the DG.

"We are still 'red-flagged,' " said Stuart. "No computer readouts, no police files, no foreigns."

"Are you complaining, Stuart?" He said it mildly.

"Such a decision was obviously necessary, sir. But we are being overtaken by events. Unless we have a chance to use the normal channels and procedures, there is a danger that these people will do what they plan to before we have a chance to frustrate them."

"You put your case most judiciously," said the DG, but he gave no sign that he was swayed by it.

"Shouldn't we tell Washington about Kleiber, sir? They could help us such a lot on the German end."

"How would you go about it?"

"A request for information exchange. Give them details of the King's Cross murders, the explosion at Wever's farmhouse and the photo of Kleiber. Ask them if they can link any of it with Max Breslow and so on."

"Very well, Stuart. Assemble a telex and let me have a look at it after lunch. I don't like the idea of Moscow Centre getting involved."

"No, sir."

"I don't like the sound of that at all, Stuart. Think what the Kremlin could do with the Hitler Minutes if the stuff was turned over to their propaganda machine."

"Exactly, sir."

Boyd Stuart's meeting with his opposite number in the CIA's London station was unofficial.

"And the old man agreed?" said the CIA man.

Stuart swallowed some gin and tonic before answering. "He'll make it official this afternoon."

"You told him what we think about Kleiber?"

"I said our own collator thought Kleiber was a Moscow Centre agent," said Stuart.

"Suppose he checks?"

"That's OK. I talked with the collator. The collator will hum and haw and say maybe. You know what Leslie is like. He's been there too long to make the mistake of giving anyone a definite opinion."

The CIA man laughed. "Especially when that opinion might explode in his face and dribble all down his Eton tie."

"Harrow," said Stuart. "Leslie went to Harrow, and his tie is Guards Armoured Division."

The CIA man punched Stuart playfully. "You're a goddamned kidder, Boyd."

"It's true," said Stuart. "I'm simply stating facts."

"And I like the way you tell 'em," said the CIA man. He waved a hand and ordered more drinks from the barman. They were in the Salisbury, an old pub in St. Martin's Lane, glittering with cut-glass mirrors, shiny brass fittings and shiny brass show-biz people, getting into the swing of the midweek matinee performances which they would soon take on stage at the nearby theatres. A lady with pink hair and stage make-up blundered backwards into Stuart and spilt his drink. "Don't worry about it, dear," she said, "no harm done."

Stuart patted the whisky drops from his sleeve.

"Even my station chief couldn't beat that one," said the CIA man admiringly. "She blunders into you, and tells you there's no need to apologize."

Stuart moved backwards into a corner and took his companion with him. "What I need to know," Stuart said, "is whether Max Breslow is a part of the Moscow Centre network. And I need to know fast."

"I've promised you the print-out," said the CIA man. "And you'll have it as soon as it comes off the terminal. But I'll have to retype it. I can't risk the original going outside the building." There was a cheer from the other side of the bar as one of the regulars arrived, a pretty blonde girl in a white trouser suit. "For you alone, Boyd. That's the deal, remember? No one you work with is to be told where this information is coming from."

"Was *that* the deal?" said Stuart, as though trying to remember.

"OK, Boyd, I apologize. We both got to live with

our own people. I know you're OK. You're going to need the follow-throughs. I'll be in Washington on Friday but I'll check with you at home late Sunday night. Don't try to reach me at the office, just in case."

"Kleiber's security company," said Stuart. "Fill me in on that."

"You're trying to measure him up for the killings, are you? No problem there, pal. He's a rough asshole. That organization of his takes on some tough jobs; debt collection from clubs, bars and brothels where I wouldn't go without I was inside a Tiger tank. Credit investigation, anti-terrorist stuff and anti-bomb assignments. That decapitation is something he'd be able to handle, Boyd. He's got to be a number one suspect as far as we're concerned. Did I tell you that we've got a similar decapitation killing in Los Angeles?"

"You told me."

"You think it connects up?"

Stuart looked at the CIA man, wondering how much he knew and how much he might have guessed. "Could be," he said finally. What the CIA man did not reveal to Stuart was that the preliminary scan was already done, and that it showed Kleiber was a one-time employee of the CIA.

## 30

"If any of you people want Cokes or Seven-Ups, get them now," said the project chairman. "We don't want a lot of getting up and walking around, the way it was last week. OK?" He looked over his spectacles, which he wore well down his nose. He was a red-faced man with a shirt pocket full of pens. He had once worked the White House assignment and liked to mention it whenever the opportunity came; now he worked for the Domestic Operations Division of the CIA. This was one of the most demanding assignments in the entire agency, handling as it did covert operations in mainland U.S.A. where it so often came into acrimonious conflict with the FBI.

There was the sudden hiss of an opened drink, and in response to a raised eyebrow a cold can was sent sliding down the polished table to a graceful catch at the far end. It was a hot day. Even through the tinted glass the landscape of Virginia shone with a fierce glare. The air-conditioning made the temperature almost chilly but the CIA men were all in short-sleeved white shirts with unbuttoned collars.

"The deputy director, DOD, has instructed us to open a new file on this one. You've got the agenda on the table in front of you. The Brits family came through with something useful. It's a 'hottie' and I think it will take us right inside the Soviet embassy for a few PNGs." The project chairman picked up the pink data card, tilted his head well back and looked at it carefully through his spectacles. No one spoke. "OK, Sam. Why don't you give us the linkage, the way it is so far?" He looked at the electric calendar clock: it was 10:48 a.m., Friday, July 27, 1979.

Sam Seymour was a small, grey-haired man with rimless spectacles and stubble moustache. His voice was low and soft, better suited to telling the long shaggy-dog jokes for which he was famous than to addressing this group of men who all had pressing business waiting in the locked boxes on their desks. Seymour was the "file editor," his job was to assemble the facts and figures and evaluate them for the men who made the decisions. "OK, guys." He tapped the edges of his papers on the polished conference table and waited until they were all looking at him. "You've got to remember that in the early part of this current year we did not—repeat did not—have any evidence that Yuriy Grechko was anything but an assistant military attaché assigned to the Washington embassy."

"We figured him for KGB," interrupted the project chairman. As he leant back, his head almost touched the Currier and Ives lithograph of a trotting race: pneumatic-looking horses with spindly legs raced past cheering top-hatted spectators. There was other such nineteenth-century popular art on the floors below, but up here, on the executive floor of the CIA building, the lithographs were originals. "We figured him for KGB the day he got off the plane," said the project chairman. He turned his head so that he could see the clerk who would be using the tape recording to prepare the minutes of the meeting. The clerk nodded: he would make sure that it was established that Grechko had been identified as a member of the KGB. The project chairman nodded to Sam Seymour to continue.

"Our big break came in April when Grechko lunched a man we'd never seen before. This man is named Parker, and we triple-digited him into the police computer and passed his name to the FBI Identification Department. Then in June Grechko has got a walk-on part at the Soviet embassy in Mexico City. Starring that day we've got none other than General Shumuk—the famous, fabulous, and we were beginning to think mythical, General Stanislav Shumuk—the First Directorate's Operational Division deputy. And if that isn't already a protein-enriched diet, who comes to the embassy and stays approximately the same time as the other two? None other than our mysterious pal, Edward Parker of Chicago."

"And the Los Angeles killing?" prompted the project chairman, who liked to have the events in strict chronological order.

"Meanwhile, back at the ranch," said Sam Seymour, "we've had a guy butchered in Los Angeles, and the L.A. cops are asking Chicago about Parker's car and what it was doing parked near the victim's office at the time of the murder."

"Hold it, Sam," said Melvin Kalkhoven, a tall, thin thirty-five-year-old. He was prematurely balding, and his straw-coloured hair and pale bony face made his dark, active eyes seem unnaturally large. "We've had a guy butchered, you say. You mean this was one of our people?" Melvin Kalkhoven was a field agent, and he took the deaths of his colleagues very personally. In such moments of stress as this, it was possible to detect his Texan accent.

"His name was . . . ," Sam Seymour looked at his papers, ". . . his name was Bernard Lustig. He was some kind of movie executive. Nothing to do with the 'pickle factory': we put him through the computer every which way. No agency connection whatsoever." He looked up. "No, sincerely; no connection with CIA or FBI or any other government agency." He nodded to the FBI representative. "Right, Ben?"

"Yes, sir."

"So why was he killed?' said Kalkhoven.

"Well, let's not get into that one for a moment," said the project chairman. "Sam is the file editor; he can only tell you what we know. Don't ask him to make guesses. If you want me to make a really far-out guess, I'm going to say that Lustig might have been a KGB operative who went sour on them. But, let's keep to what happened. . . . Sam!"

Sam Seymour continued, "The Brits have had a double slaying in London—just nine days ago—with all the same *modus operandi* as the Lustig killing. They've asked us to scan the computer for a man named Wilhelm Kleiber. Well, gentlemen, Kleiber has been on the computer for nearly three years. He came onto old Office of Strategic Services files back in 1945. He strolled up to the OSS desk of Third Army HQ and offered to show us where the Nazis had hidden foreign currency and suchlike, in exchange for a job with us. We already had the currency but we gave Kleiber an undercover job. He did OK. He went on to work for the Gehlen set-up back in the good old days, when it was the South German Industries Utilization Company. . . ."

There was a responsive laugh. It seemed unlikely that the cover which Gehlen had used for mounting intelligence operations against Russia was ever very convincing; by today's standard, it was nothing less than childish. "When Gehlen set up his cover organizations—and made money—in everything from wholesaling wine to public relations, Kleiber set up a security company for them. In 1958, Kleiber was pensioned off and allowed to buy the security company at a bargain price."

"Poor old U.S. taxpayer," said Kalkhoven.

"Right," said Sam Seymour. "It was that kind of deal. The security company was his 'pension' from Gehlen, but the bottom line was that we picked up the tab. He was, in effect, working for us." He took off his spectacles. "But it still wasn't good enough for Kleiber. He got into financial difficulties two or three times in the middle sixties. But he always seemed to survive."

"Moscow got to him?" said Kalkhoven, who hated Seymour's sort of double-talk. "Is that what you are implying?"

"It's what I'm trying to avoid saying," said Seymour, raising his hands in surrender to Kalkhoven's critical tone. "It's taken us a long time to get the message. But let's not go jumping to conclusions until we've got the evidence. And let me make it clear, Kleiber was taken off the agency payroll in 1969."

"Don't push, Melvin," the project chairman told Kalkhoven. "Sam here is a very cautious individual, you know that. But let me be the fool who rushes in where Seymours fear to tread. Sure, Kleiber was turned for money; it's as clear as daylight. No evidence anywhere, but I'm telling you, that's what happened. Kleiber is a Moscow Centre agent, and a damned dangerous one. There's good indication that Kleiber was the hit man who helped Parker knock off Lustig in Los Angeles last May. It's likely the Brits are right in thinking that Kleiber did the double killing in London last week."

He nodded to Sam Seymour, who took up the story again. "We have something on him for the Los Angeles murder. We know he went through Los Angeles International two days before the killing and left on an intercontinental flight a mere three days after. A ground hostess and a flight purser recognized him as a passenger on the Frankfurt flight. He left his reading spectacles in the first-class lounge. A pretty dumb thing to do it you're a KGB hit man, but people are like that, as we well know."

"And thank the Lord," said the project chairman.

"Yes, indeed," said Sam Seymour. He looked again at his papers. "We've only had this material since Wednesday, so we've got a long way to go. TWA is checking the tickets for that flight, so we might get lucky. But what we have so far is enough to link

Grechko, through the mysterious Mr. Parker, with Kleiber and three killings." He rustled his papers on the table. "We've pink-starred Kleiber with customs and immigration. If he continues travelling on the same passport, we could nail him." He looked round the room to see the reaction. "He seems to travel everywhere alone."

" 'Woe unto him who is alone when he falleth, for he hath not another to help him up,' " said Kalkhoven, whose father had been a lay preacher.

"We think Parker might be the illegal," said the project chairman. "The resident illegal," he added in case there was any misunderstanding.

There were murmurs of surprise and congratulation round the table. The chairman smiled. "But we want something better out of this than swapping Parker for some American kid who got caught buying black-market bubble gum on Red Square. And I want something better than Grechko going PNG and winging his way home with a medal. Persona non grata means nothing anymore. I want Grechko caught with his pants down. I want solid evidence to show that these decapitation killings were planned here in the god-damned Russian embassy. I want to see it spread good and big across the headlines. The Brits have given us Kleiber but the important targets are Grechko and Parker. Now don't forget it."

"What do the Brits want out of it?" asked Ben Krupnic, the FBI representative at the far end of the table.

"Their SIS people are interested in a guy on the coast named Stein and a German-born U.S. citizen named Max Breslow. We've had to give them a hands-off undertaking for both. They've given us a hands-off undertaking on Kleiber."

"Sounds like a fair deal," said Krupnic.

"Yeah," said the project chairman. "Sounds like a fair bargain. Let's see if anyone sticks to it."

The FBI man smiled. He wondered whether that caustic aside was directed at his own bureau.

# 31

Westlake Village was a habitat that exactly suited Max Breslow. It was far enough from the smog and noise of Los Angeles, and yet not so far that he could not be in Beverly Hills inside the hour. There was the lake and its sailing dinghies and the heated swimming pool which he shared with a few of his immediate neighbours. And if there was also a measure of pretension and pettiness, then it was no worse than he had known in such small towns in other parts of the world. And here there was the sunshine to compensate for everything.

Max Breslow sat by the pool, watching his daughter swim twenty lengths. She had the same sort of determination that he had found in himself at her age. Sometimes it frightened him to recognize that fixed expression on her face; he could see it now as she touched the edge of the pool and twisted back through the water with hardly a splash or a ripple to mark the place. She swam underwater for a long time. Max could do that when he was young; he remembered the discipline at Bad Tölz. The big new SS training establishment had only been open a few months. He remembered still the sour smell of damp cement mingled with that of the new paint. Day after day of boxing, rowing, running, jumping and swimming. Long days too; awake at 4 a.m. and falling into bed exhausted. It had been all right for the others—farm boys for the most part, who hardly dared believe that at the end of all this they were going to be able to return to their families and friends wearing the uniform of a German officer. Max sometimes wondered what had happened to them all; dead long since, he supposed. He remembered reading in one of the old comrades' magazines that *none* of the men commissioned at the Junkerschule Bad Tölz in 1934 survived through 1942. Did anyone, Max wondered, really and truly regret the passing of the Third Reich? As much as he deplored the stupid self-indulgence of the young, he would not want to expose any of them to what he had gone through. Not even Billy Stein. Max Breslow paused for a moment—perhaps it was going too far to say "not even Billy Stein"; a few weeks at Bad Tölz might work wonders for that fellow.

"Wake up, Papa!"

Breslow flinched as the cold water dropped on him, and he felt his daughter's wet face and wet hair as she bent close and kissed him. "The water's wonderful. How can you not swim?"

Breslow smiled and shook his head. He had left some toes behind in the snowy wastes outside Kharkov. It was ridiculous, but he was self-conscious about the deformity even in front of his own daughter. "They are building the sets in the workshops. I'm going downtown to inspect them at three p.m."

" 'I'm going to inspect them at three p.m.,' " she repeated in a funny nasal voice. "That all sounds very Teutonic, Papa."

"I have to maintain a schedule," he said, trying not to sound irritated, although in fact he was. "The cost of the workshop space is nothing compared with what we will be paying for studio time once the sets are erected there. I have to make sure they are exactly right."

"I read the script, you know." She rubbed her hair with a thick towel. "Have you found an actor to play the role of Hitler?" She was very beautiful. Even allowing for his natural paternal pride, there was no denying that.

"We have about three hundred to choose from," said Breslow. "Every agent in town seems to have someone he fancies for that part."

"It's not much of a part, is it?"

"It's what the industry calls a cameo. Whoever plays Hitler will get press attention out of proportion to the importance of his role. All actors thrive on publicity; it could lead to something bigger."

"It's all hokum, the Hitler sequence, isn't it, Papa?"

"We have to have some quick way to explain to the audience why all the treasures were taken and hidden in the Kaiseroda mine. The Hitler sequences were the quickest way to achieve this."

"And it will get a lot of press coverage," said Mary Breslow.

"And it will get a lot of press coverage." They smiled at each other conspiratorially.

"I'm going into the sauna now. Can I come with you to the workshops?"

"I thought you weren't interested in movies."

She leant down and kissed his cheek. "I'm only interested in *your* movies, Papa," she said.

He smiled. He wanted to tell her not to bring Billy Stein, but it would only precipitate an exchange of feelings on a subject which, for the time being, he preferred to avoid. "I'd like to leave immediately after lunch."

"Yes, Papa," she said. In the Breslow house, lunch was always served on the dot of one o'clock, and Max Breslow rose from the table at two whether he had finished his coffee or not. The Breslow women had got used to this by now. "At two p.m. precisely."

The set was bigger than Max Breslow expected. He knew that art directors always sketch the human figures out of scale, when they prepare glamorized pastel renderings of their ideas. But this time the reality was even more overwhelming than the perspective drawings had suggested.

Max Breslow stood for a long time without speaking. The workshop was very high; in spite of the big lamps, its ceiling was lost in the darkness. There was a smell of freshly sawn wood, an aroma which took Breslow back to his family's holiday home in the Eifel. As a small boy he had gone out to watch the foresters felling the huge trees and cutting them into segments. Now he smelt it once more. And here in the studio there was also that acrid smell of fast-drying paint and plastic glues. "Can you put the fans on?" Breslow called. There was a distant rumbling and then the air-conditioning began to clatter. Max Breslow tilted back his head and tried to see to where the top of the newly built sets disappeared in the darkness. "They are big," said Breslow. "Very big."

"You've got a lot of height in that studio," the art director explained. "I talked to the director and he wants to use a big crane and start with a shot that majors on one of those Nazi eagles up there, and then pans round to Hitler's desk."

"The conference shot," said Max Breslow.

"Yes, the conference shot," said the art director. "Hitler and all his generals crowded round his desk looking at maps. We have built the set with four walls like this so that he can shoot the reverses in any way he wants. The two end walls float, of course."

"Of course," said Max Breslow, although he was not quite sure whether floating a wall was to move it, open it for a camera trolley or dismantle it quickly.

"It's quite a place," said Breslow's daughter from the other end of the set. Her voice echoed in the rafters.

"You'll have more space than this in the studio," said the art director. "They're a bit close together here in the workshop for ease of building."

"Was Hitler's Chancellery really like this?" called Mary Breslow.

Max Breslow did not answer. Eventually the art director said, "We are working from photos of the real thing, Miss Breslow." He turned back to her father. "There's all the set dressing to be done yet. This is just the bare essentials, but I think it works OK." The art director couldn't conceal his pride.

Max Breslow walked across to the wall and rapped his knuckles against the marble. It made the unmistakable sound of hollow plastic. The art director smiled. "It's good, isn't it? You wait until you see the polystyrene bust of Hitler, and the plastic floor. When we put the sound track on the film, so that you hear metal studs striking marble as the actors march about, no one will guess this wasn't the real place."

"The real place was destroyed by Red Army artillery in 1945," said Max Breslow dryly.

"You'd never know it," said the art director.

Max Breslow walked across to where his daughter was examining the doors and looked back to get the effect of the whole gigantic room.

"This must have cost the earth, Papa."

"Only a fool tries to spread his spending over the whole production," said Max Breslow. "I looked at that script and I realized at once that the scenes inside the Kaiseroda mine could be filmed for practically nothing. It's little more than a dark tunnel. I'm negotiating to go out and shoot some outdoor locations in Solvang village near Santa Barbara."

"Papa, that's Danish."

"I've been up there to look at it, Mary. The director and I believe that with careful shooting we can make Solvang look like the village of Merkers in Thuringia. And of course we'll get permission to take down the television antennae and remove the billboards and so on. And we'll put up authentic-looking street signs and posters, and paint Nazi slogans on the walls. We can fit a couple of bomb-damaged buildings —just the fronts, of course—between the houses. These American villages are far more spread out than the German ones ever were. And those fronts we add will be complete with damage and so on."

"You're so clever, Papa."

"My Hitler scenes will take place on this set, and we'll see him outdoors in a small convoy of vehicles, using some big three-axle Mercedes that I'm arranging to rent."

"So this set we're on is the only big one?"

"No. If all goes well, I'll have an even bigger one than this. I want to re-create Hitler's private train for the sequence in which Hitler argues with Göring about whether the fighting should continue. If I can persuade this museum in Chicago to rent me the two Pullman cars they have, I will convert them into the Führersonderzug. Then I will woo the railroad company into letting me shoot five days in Union Station, right here in the city."

"In Union Station?"

"It's a wonderful building, Mary. Did you ever take a proper look at it? Can you imagine what that would look like draped with fifty-foot-tall red swastika banners, lined with German soldiers of the Führer Begleit Bataillon and packed with extras shouting and screaming the old Nazi slogans, while Hitler walks slowly past them to his train? Can you imagine what a great sequence that would be?"

"I can imagine how many column inches you'd pick up in the local papers and TV news."

Max Breslow permitted himself a thin smile. "There would be that too, Mary, of course." He went out through the main workshop into the smaller rooms. All of them were putting together hastily constructed furniture for the Hitler Chancellery scene. His immense desk was receiving the plastic spray that would make it look, to the camera's eye, like a masterpiece of French polishing. Only two chairs were so far constructed from the pile of ornate legs and seats.

"Everything's so oversize, Papa. Is that the way it was?"

"They are working from photos," said Max Breslow. "All the original furnishings were deliberately made too large. They say it was intended to overawe the visitor, and make him feel insignificant in the presence of the Führer."

Mary Breslow walked over to the part of the workshop where the working drawings were pinned to the walls, along with dozens of large glossy photo prints of the Reich Chancellery in its days of glory. "What a place," she said. "You can smell the megalomania." She turned to her father. "Were you ever there, Papa? Tell me truly. I want to know."

"I saw it," admitted Max Breslow. "More than once. And I saw the monster too."

"Was he a monster, Papa?"

"Let history be the judge," said Breslow. "It is too early to rake over the reputations of those so recently dead."

"It's thirty-five years ago, Papa," said Mary. She watched him closely and he knew he was being observed although he did not turn round, nor even move his head.

"It's only yesterday for some of us," said Breslow. How did he ever get into this absurd situation? The money was welcome of course, but this wretched film about Hitler, which he had never wanted to have anything to do with, might be the very thing to get him into trouble with the Americans. If the newspapers discovered that he had served with the Waffen

SS, that might be enough to have him deported. Damn Kleiber. Damn him, damn him, damn him.

"Cheer up, Papa," said Mary.

## 32

Since the beginning of July, Max Breslow had rented a temporary office on the block where the sets were made. It was shabbier than his previous office on Melrose, and certainly not the sort of place where he would want to bring clients, but it was clean and convenient enough until they actually started shooting. Then he would move into a proper suite of offices which would house all the production staff in one building. He reached into his pocket for the well-worn key; goodness only knows how many other producers had used it—big hits, big flops, mostly men like himself, he supposed, small-time producers shrewd enough to plan towards a modest profit, rather than to risk everything in the hope of a bonanza. But surely no other producer had been blackmailed into making a picture.

Max Breslow went outside, across the lot, and up a single flight of wooden stairs. He walked along an open balcony to a door marked "Number Fourteen" in elaborate, painted script lettering. He went inside and one of the phones rang. The receptionist doubled as telephone operator in this block. She must have seen him come up.

"Breslow."

"There is a message in your clip, Mr. Breslow. A visitor is waiting for you downtown."

Breslow sighed. "Where downtown?"

"A pizza parlour on La Cienega between Pico and Venice Boulevards intersection. Buster's, it's called. It's one of those eateries which screen old movies all day." She had a shrill New York accent that fascinated Breslow. He wondered whether she had at one time been an actress.

"Who?" said Breslow. "Not the press, is it, Lucy?"

"Did you ever hear of a press reporter lunching in

Buster's? Those guys are all in the Polo Lounge. No, this was a message from someone called Kleiber. Do you want me to spell that for you?"

"No, I don't want you to spell it, Lucy. What time did he call?"

"About half an hour ago. He said he'd just arrived on the airplane. That's why he wants to meet you near the airport, I suppose."

"Anything else?"

"Your wife says, will you pick up her shoes if you are back in Westlake before six? She said you'd know where, and they'll let you have them without a ticket."

"Thanks, Lucy. Get my daughter a car, tell her I'll see her for dinner at Tony Roma's Rib Place in Beverly Hills and I'll drive her home. Explain that I had an unexpected meeting, will you, Lucy?"

"Sure will, Mr. Breslow."

Max Breslow never had any trouble spotting his friend. Willi Kleiber never changed very much. Apart from a little weight around the hips and some grey hair, he had changed little since the days when he had been with Max in the war. He had always favoured very close-cropped hair, and his teeth still flashed when he smiled. Even the colour of the expensive suits he wore never varied much from the drab hues of wartime feldgrau, and he liked to wear old-fashioned high boots, so like the ones the army had given him.

He was sitting at the back of the pizza parlour. It was typical of Willi to choose such a place for a meeting, a *"Treff"* he would have called it; he had never really stopped fighting the war. Max Breslow looked round him with a shudder. The plain wooden tables and uncomfortable benches, littered with paper plates, the remains of a pizza and salad and some Coke cups. It was not the sort of place that Max Breslow would have chosen for a meeting. At the sides of the eating room there were a dozen coin-in-the-slot amusements, most of them with video screens and warlike themes. "U-boat-commander," "Blitzkrieg," "Dive Bomber" or "Panzer Clash," from each of the machines in use there came the electronic bleeps of ricochetting bullets and the continual rat-a-tat of simulated machine-gun fire. This was the war we won, thought Max Breslow, this war that came after the war.

"Max, it's good to see you again." Willi Kleiber was sitting behind a pile of plates and had obviously enjoyed his meal. It was the nearest thing he could get to dining in a foxhole, thought Max Breslow.

"Hello, Willi. You're looking well." On a big screen in the corner there was an old scratchy silent film being shown. A fat man in a black suit and top hat sat at a table, while an obsequious waiter set a vast meal before him. Max Breslow looked away. He hated silent comedies.

"I came straight from the airport. I don't sleep very well on these long-distance flights."

There was a roar of childish laughter. As his eyes became accustomed to the gloom, Max Breslow realized that the other side of the restaurant was crowded with small children.

"Get some coffee," said Willi.

Max got a paper cup from the counter and the youthful assistant poured weak black coffee into it. Breslow returned to the table and sat down, carefully avoiding the shredded lettuce and spilt ketchup. Willi Kleiber reached into his back pocket and produced a silver hip flask. With a furtiveness that he clearly relished, Willi Kleiber poured a measure of brandy into Max Breslow's coffee. It was always like this. And every time they met they went through the same ritual. It was like meeting a stranger, thought Breslow, rather than someone he had seen only a few weeks ago. Perhaps that was what they were: not friends or old comrades, simply two strangers who met often.

"Your family is well?" Kleiber asked.

"Marie-Louise loves California," said Breslow with automatic politeness. "And so does my daughter Mary."

"And you, Max?"

"There are things I miss, Willi, but the sunshine works wonders for my old joints. And what about your family? Still well?"

"My father is very old, Max. He is tired and in pain."

"I'm sorry," said Breslow. "I remember your father well. He was a fine old man."

"My father's life ended in 1945, Max. The war is the only thing he ever wants to talk about. Now he is forgetting even that."

Max Breslow could see the movie screen out of the corner of his eye. In spite of all his resolution about old films, he shifted his position slightly to see it better. The camera position had just changed to show that the man sitting down to dinner in the top hat was on a railroad track which stretched to the horizon. Breslow said, "But your mother is quite well?" It cut to a locomotive in mid-shot, undercranked to make it seem as if the train was speeding at two hundred miles an hour.

"Thank God," said Willi. He had his back to the screen. He always sat facing the door, Max remembered that now. They said he had been wounded in a restaurant in Athens during the war. Some passerby had thrown a grenade.

"We have a lot to be thankful for," said Breslow.

Kleiber put some more brandy into both cups of coffee. It was like a ceremony. Only after these preliminaries would it be possible to have the real conversation.

"A lot of things have happened," explained Kleiber. "I thought it was best to come myself."

"I'm surprised you found me at the workshops," said Breslow. "You have lost none of the old skills, Willi."

Kleiber had been an Abwehr officer. He had made his name infiltrating a French underground network in 1942. Later the Abwehr had been taken over by the SS intelligence service and Willi's subsequent career included many incidents of which he never spoke. "There has been a bad failure of security," said Kleiber. "Some youngster gained access to the big new FRÜHLING computer that Dr. Böttger's bank have installed in Hanover. He went right through all the security checks and was retrieving data from the *zweiter Fall,* something the experts said was impossible."

"Experts!" said Breslow. "A couple of years in the movie business and you'd no longer listen to the experts."

"They say it would have been impossible from anywhere in Germany," said Kleiber, "but some bloody fool asked the programmes to insert a simplified series of 'keys' for retrieval from overseas. It was to save the bank money, Max! How do you like that? Forty million Deutsche marks that damned computer cost the bank, and some idiot simplifies the security in order to save a few pfennigs in telephone charges."

"What did they discover?"

"It was a German—a clerk in the London office—who decided to try his hand at getting as far as he could into the secrets."

"What did he get?"

Kleiber nodded to acknowledge the repetition of the question. "He found his way right into Operation Siegfried."

"Good God, Willi!"

"I told them not to use that code name."

"Operation Siegfried," said Breslow. "It was a foolish choice. The name smells of the Third Reich."

"They are old men," said Kleiber. "Old men become romantic. They do not readily face up to the realities we face."

Intuitively, Max Breslow began to realize what Kleiber was about to tell him. "You had this boy killed?"

"What alternative was there, Max? He had all the names and addresses. He knew the way in which all the banks and our companies were working together. He had the details of the trust fund from which we are financing the work."

"Sometimes a man can read such material without understanding its import."

Willi Kleiber studied the bottom of his coffee cup and then, without replying, went across to the machine at the counter and took the coffee pot off the hot plate. He poured more for himself as he planned his reply. "It's easy to be critical afterwards, Max.

But that boy had already placed a long-distance call from London to the Stein house here in Los Angeles. He couldn't get a person-to-person, so finally he left a brief message on Stein's answering machine."

"I know all about that," said Breslow. "I used the musical tone to intercept the stored calls. I know all about that."

"Do you?" said Kleiber with mock surprise. "You were behaving as if you had forgotten it." Kleiber turned round so that he could see the movie. There was too much light in the room, and the images on the screen were muddy and blurred. A locomotive roared through the picture, scooping up the man in the top hat, but in the subsequent close-up he was still eating. The camera shot widened to show that he was seated astride the cow-catcher, the table and table cloth still in position and his elaborate meal undisturbed.

"You said the killing of the Britisher from Washington would be the end of it," said Breslow. "You tried to kill the Englishman Stuart, and wiped out the wrong man. It was a bad business, Willi. And killing Stuart would have solved nothing. I hope you realize that."

"It's easy to be clever afterwards," said Kleiber. "Don't tell me you are losing your nerve, Max. I knew that the others would squeal like stuck pigs the moment the business started, but I depended upon you for support."

"Then our old comrade Franz Wever. Why did he have to be killed?"

"Our old comrade Franz," said Kleiber bitterly, "only wanted to discover what we were doing. Had he found out, he would have reported everything to the British intelligence. He was *their* man. Franz Wever would have betrayed us."

Breslow said nothing. Franz Wever had always been envious of him and had gladly admitted it. Franz was permanently posted to the communications job while Breslow had seen front-line service at the war. Perhaps it was this frustration that had caused Franz Wever to jump into the Danube so promptly that cold evening at Linz, where they had spent their leave together. The drowning child would never have survived the current. For a moment he had thought both Wever and the child would be swept away. They had spent a miserable evening in the local police station, waiting for Franz's uniform to dry. Only months later did Franz receive the letter from the boy's father: "Carry this photo to remind you of the life you saved; may my son grow up to be worthy of your gallant act," and there was a snapshot of the child standing in front of a ghastly painted backdrop of mountain landscape. Franz had carried it everywhere.

Kleiber pursed his lips to indicate that he disapproved of Breslow's silence. What had happened to his friend, he wondered. Was this something to do with living in California? "People are going to get hurt, Max." He tapped the table silently with a fingertip. "Stein will have to be disposed of—you realize that, don't you? He knows too much to remain alive. Anyone who reads the material will have to be dealt with in the same way. It is regrettable . . . I don't enjoy it . . . but it is a fact."

"Where is Stein now?"

"Are my people here in Los Angeles not keeping you informed?"

"The last I heard he sent his son Billy to London."

"Yes. Billy Stein went to London. The English secret service sent their man along to see him. There wasn't time to put a microphone in the room so we don't know what was said. Personally, I think they found the bodies before the police did. I think they found them even before young Stein did. They are cunning, Max, we have to be most cautious."

"Bodies? There was more than one?"

"An Englishman, a friend. We think he was the one who told him how to get into the computer memory. It was better to get rid of both. He was sure to have told his English friend how well he'd succeeded."

"How did you discover the leak?"

"It was the only stroke of luck we have so far had on this business. A very close friend of mine in the BND got it over lunch from the director general of the British secret service. The inquiry came to me soon after you took the message off Stein's answering machine. It was clever of you to do that, Max."

"There was nothing clever about it," said Breslow. "I have the same model of answering machine. Stein got it for me wholesale. I was able to get a whistle with the same musical tone as Stein's machine."

"Well done," said Kleiber.

Breslow did not reply. He did not have Kleiber's long experience of intelligence work; the business with the answering machine had left him feeling defiled and ashamed.

Perhaps Kleiber realized this. He said, "It was of immense help to us. Knowing what the message was, meant I could get on the plane to London immediately. I didn't have to wait to hear what this fellow Paul Bock wanted to tell Stein—we knew already." He smiled and patted Breslow's arm in a congratulatory manner. Breslow flinched. He could never get used to such physical contacts. Masculine embraces might be *de rigueur* for restauranteurs, footballers and film stars, but not for old comrades.

"Don't underestimate Stein," Breslow warned him. "He may look like a slob, but under that gross and unattractive exterior there is a man of great physical strength and considerable intellectual resource."

Kleiber waved his hand as if to waft away these praises of Stein. "By this time, Stein should be on his knees, begging for money."

"Well, he isn't," said Breslow. He lifted the paper cup and drained the last dregs. The coffee was thin and tepid but the taste of the good German brandy was welcome. "He's being very evasive."

"It was a good plan," said Kleiber. "We calculated that the failure of the bank would make them part with the documents within a few days. You'd think they'd want to get some money as soon as they could. You'd think their bank would be the first priority. . . ." Kleiber rubbed his face wearily. "Do you think Stein believed that story about the British trying to kill you on the freeway?"

"I improvised it at short notice, Willi, and I was rather shaken by the accident. . . . But, yes. I believe he did. My Mercedes was very badly damaged. It was only too easy to persuade him that it was deliberately done."

"It was lucky. It put Stein off the scent, and probably made him think the British were trying to kill you."

"Yes, I told him so."

"You did well, Max. When did you last see him?"

"Charles Stein? The day before yesterday. Why?"

"The truth is . . ." began Kleiber. He yawned. It was a sign of anxiety as much as of loss of sleep. "The truth is that we've gone a little wrong in London. We've lost contact with the younger Stein."

"I'm certain he hasn't returned here to Los Angeles."

"How can you be certain?"

"Because he would be with my daughter Mary."

"Your daughter . . . Mary and the Stein boy?"

"Better him," said Breslow, "than the Mexican gas station attendant who chased her everywhere last year. Finally I sent her to Europe for a month."

"The Stein boy has vanished," said Kleiber. "I had one of my very best men in charge of the London end. I can't understand it; Stein left the hotel, paid his bill and took his baggage. And my people saw nothing of it."

"You think the British intelligence service is holding him?"

"Yes, I do. I think they waited for Stein to go to the house, arrested him and are now interrogating him."

"What a mess," said Max Breslow. If anything happened to Billy Stein, his father might hold him responsible. Max Breslow was not of a nervous disposition, as his war record proved, but he knew that the wrath of Charles Stein would be terrible to behold. What if Stein took revenge upon Breslow's daughter. He suppressed this terrifying idea. "What now?"

Kleiber stretched his arms and looked very smug. "We have had an amazing stroke of luck, Max." This, Breslow suspected, was the moment that Kleiber had been looking forward to. He was right. Kleiber said, "As I have just told you, we have a contact with the very top level of the British intelligence service—MI6 they call it—a good friend of mine is the liaison between London and our own BND in Bonn. They lunch together and talk of horticulture. . . ." Kleiber smiled at Max Breslow's puzzled espression. "It is their mutual passion: cactus plants. This passion has proved a most wonderful advantage for us, Max."

"And yet you don't know if the British are holding Stein?"

Kleiber did not miss the note of sarcasm in his friend's question. He smiled. "I think we can safely assume that they have Billy Stein in custody, and that they have interrogated him very successfully." There was something in Kleiber's face that told Breslow that this was his most important item of news. "What is our grestest problem, Max? Surely it is finding the whereabouts of the Hitler Minutes. Well, now we *do* know where they are. The British have discovered that the Hitler Minutes and all the rest of the documents are in the house of Colonel Pitman in Switzerland. We even know what sort of strong room protects them."

"It all fits together neatly," said Breslow. "They *must* have got this information from young Billy."

"The Englishman was carrying catalogues from Schiff, the well-known Swiss locksmiths, and he actually asked my old friend for some assistance in translating the German language. We know the make, the model and the year."

"You are not thinking of raiding the house?" Breslow asked.

"A burglar will not have enough time, or the sort of equipment, to open the door of a strong room such as this," replied Kleiber.

"I beg you to reconsider, Willi," said Breslow. "A burglary is one thing, an armed raid is going too far. You can cut anything open with an oxyacetylene flame, or one of the new thermic lances. Get a really good safe-cracker and let him do the job in the way that professional thieves do it."

"Is this what you have learned from your movie scriptwriters?" Willi Kleiber made a noise of disparagement. "You are years out of date, my friend. The oxyacetylene flames and the thermic lances generate too much heat. Thieves find cinders and ashes inside a safe they've cut open by those methods. I fit such safes for my clients, Max. I know what can be done to make a door impregnable. There is an inner cube of glass; heat it and a complex of bolts are sprung, and the door locks so solid that even the makers take two or three days to cut it open." Willi Kleiber chuckled and rubbed his hands. "I don't even know where I could find a thermic lance expert. These days they're all in retirement in the Italian sunshine. Safecrackers are extinct, Max. They've been replaced by men who carry shotguns and automatic weapons and take a bank by assault."

"How terrible," said Max Breslow.

"Terrible?" said Kleiber. "Wonderful, you mean. How do you think I could have got my security company to its present turnover without the dedicated gunmen? The improvement in safes, which gave the armed bandits their chance, gave me my chance too, Max." He laughed.

"Aren't you worried in case Colonel Pitman's safe is wired to alarm the local police station?"

"Yes, I am, Max. That's why I must not plan this project in the style of a thief. We have to get into the house and talk to Pitman. We have to convince him that it's in his interest to open the safe."

Max Breslow picked up his empty coffee cup in an automatic gesture of alarm and dismay. He knew exactly what methods Willi Kleiber would use to "convince" Colonel Pitman to open the safe. He shuddered.

"What's the matter with you, Max?"

"It was filthy coffee," said Breslow.

"Come along, Max. It will be wonderful. It will be just like old times."

"You're mad, Willi," said Breslow, but his voice lacked conviction. "You'll get yourself killed."

No comment could have been more encouraging to Kleiber. He swelled with pride. "I'm not afraid to die," he said. "We lost some good comrades in the war. It would not be so terrible to join them once again."

Max Breslow was saddened by the answer but he

smiled. It was as much a nervous reaction as anything.

"Why are you smiling, Max? Have I said something funny?"

"No, my friend. I am smiling because only last week I heard Stein express the same idea, in virtually the same words."

"You'll have to be in Switzerland too, Max."

"There is so much to do here."

"This is more important than your film," said Kleiber. "I want you with me." From his pocket he got a recent newspaper cutting. It was a Washington newspaper, the headline said U.S. GOVERNMENT ALLOCATES $2.3 MILLION FOR NAZI-HUNTERS. The piece continued, "After six years of lobbying, Congresswoman Elizabeth Holtzman of New York saw U.S. Justice Department set up an Office of Special Investigation on Nazi war crimes." Breslow read it through and returned it folded to Kleiber.

"You should have changed your name, Max," said Kleiber.

Max Breslow shook his head. "I didn't want to meet old friends in Germany and have to explain why my U.S. passport bore a different name." He sighed. "Surely someone else could go?"

"Be ready to go early next week, Max. That's an order from the Trust."

"Very well, Willi. I'll be ready to go."

"The Trust has money, Max, and lawyers. The denaturalization and deportation proceedings take place in a civil court. Good lawyers and good advice—and a good word in the right place—can work wonders in this country."

"I said I'd go," said Max Breslow. He was angry and a little afraid.

## 33

Willi Kleiber's "amazing stroke of luck" had its origins on the afternoon of Friday, July 27, following Sir Sydney Ryden's difficult meeting with the Prime Minister. The DG went back to his office, poured himself a large gin and tonic and looked again at the tiny black notebook filled with cryptic initials and hieroglyphics which were meaningless to anyone but himself. Sometimes he needed this when answering the Prime Minister's questions. Never had he needed it more than this afternoon when she had subjected him and his department to some particularly telling criticisms. When he'd finished his drink he went to the window to look at his cactus collection, prodding the dry earth and using his tweezers to manicure the plants. For a moment his hands were still. He stared out of the window to Westminster Bridge, over which came streams of men and women, hurrying through the rain to Waterloo Station and the suburban train services. Soon the streams would become torrents and finally, as the rush hour reached its peak, hordes of these dark-suited figures would be filling the pavements and spilling over into the roadways and clogging the motor traffic.

Suddenly the DG's hands moved once more, touching the plants with brisk deftness—the sort of displacement activity that often marked the end of a difficult working day. The Prime Minister was right, Sir Sydney regretfully concluded: his department had produced no tangible results since his last report to her. It was no use reminding her that nothing disastrous had occurred, that Stein and Co. had not published the Hitler Minutes and created an international scandal. While Secret Intelligence Services thought that staving off disaster was a considerable feat, politicians always wanted tangible results. Politicians were not interested in the status quo—they wanted results: files closed, fears eliminated and accounts rendered. She had virtually said as much, and Sir Sydney knew that she was right to do so. He touched the most fragile of his new plants. It was tempting to give it just a trace of water but he resisted the temptation—better that it was forced to adjust to its new environment. Too much care and attention could ruin it—it was a characteristic that cacti shared with agents in the field.

"There has obviously been a leak, Sir Sydney," the PM had told him. His first reaction was one of anger, but he had learnt to hide his emotions. He had learnt that during his first few weeks at prep school. The bullies had soon taught him to cry inside without permitting any sign of it to show. Stick it out, his father had written in those letters from Simla in the Indian hills, and Sydney had stuck it out. For years his only visitor at school had been his dear old nanny. It was not her fault that one year she had let him down by weeping when she said goodbye. How cruel children were to each other; the other boys had never permitted him to forget the old woman with the working-class accent who had shamed him with her tears. His only consolation then, as now, was hard work.

"A leak, obviously." The PM's shrewd deduction could not have been based upon the scanty facts he had provided, so was it that famous intuition of hers? Or was it no more than the natural hostility that all politicians show to the civil service, in order to keep them on the defensive?

The DG picked up another plant. It was not in good condition. For weeks he had been trying to persuade himself that it would recover its strength, but there was little chance that it would. A pity, for it had been a fine specimen once, one of his favourites. Actually, he knew exactly how the PM had concluded that there was a leak from his department, and that it had led to the King's Cross murders. The truth was that the PM had stated what she saw clearly reflected in Sir Sydney Ryden's own troubled face. If he searched deeply into his innermost thoughts, he would have to admit to some unease about that lunch he had given to the chap from the BND. Now, every time he fussed and fiddled with the potted plants, he recalled the conversation. Had it been one of his subordinates, Sir Sydney would have described it as indiscreet, if not insecure.

He looked at the clock. It was almost time to go downstairs. His car had been ordered and the driver was always a little early. He was dining with the German BND official tonight. He had carefully rehearsed exactly what he intended to say, but now, at the last moment, he was having second thoughts. Sydney Ryden had never worked as a field agent. There was nothing unusual about this, hardly any of the senior officials of the department had ever spied upon anything more secret than their colleagues' expense accounts. Like them, Sydney Ryden was a desk man, skilled in administration but ignorant of all the rigmarole of spying. He was well aware of his limitations, and it was quite obvious that good men's lives were at stake if he handled this evening badly. If, on the other hand, he could get this German to believe that the Hitler Minutes were at the Pitman house in Geneva, he might be able to make up for some of the harm already done. And given a little additional luck he might be able to put this man Kleiber into the bag, despite the "hands-off" assurance he had given the Americans. He picked up the phone and dialled Operations. "Hello. Director here. Anything new on the Stein business?"

There was a delay while the duty officer checked not only the locked CURRENT filing cabinet but also the pigeonholes and the message pad. "Nothing since the dossier went to your office at five o'clock, Director."

"Thank you." He put the phone down. That was it then. It was worth a go. He picked up the heavy, illustrated catalogue of Schiff locks, bolts and strong rooms. On the cover there was a burglar with a black mask and a bag of swag over his shoulder. He folded it and slipped it into his pocket.

## 34

From the East River to the Hudson, 10th Street cuts right across Manhattan at its widest place. Property speculators tried to call the east side of it "the East Village" but there were not many takers among the Russian emigrés, Italian waiters or Puerto Rican delinquents who lived there. Still less interest was shown by the drunk sprawled near the Russian Baths not far from the intersection with First Avenue. It was the morning of Monday, July 30, and the hot summer had made the city into a stone oven which, even at night, did not cool. Two old men had put a table on the pavement to continue the chess game they started inside the old brownstone house. Kids were working to get the fire hydrant opened, cheered on by some teenage girls who were sunbathing on the rusty fire escape above.

Three men emerged onto the flat roof of the property next to the all-night grocery. They vaulted effortlessly over the low wall that separated this roof from the one next door, dodging between washing hung on the roof clotheslines to dry. Their sweat shirts were dirty and stained, their jeans worn white at the knees and frayed at the pockets. The first man was dark complexioned with an Afro haircut and Zapata moustache. The other two men were white. One, a slim youth with tattooed arms, laboured under the weight of a blue metal tool-box. The third man of the trio was Melvin Kalkhoven, whose clean face and short haircut ill suited his grubby clothes. He detoured to peer into the street below.

The three men stopped at the dilapidated little shed which gave access to the building's interior staircase. Once they were inside, the stale heat of this old building hit them like a hot towel. The black man—Pete—put on a set of Con Edison coveralls which he had been carrying under his arm. The other two waited for him and listened to the sounds of the street and watched for any movement inside the building. A fire engine could be heard somewhere over on the west side, and below them the janitor was arguing with a drunken tenant; their raucous voices echoed in the stair well.

"These old houses smell bad," said Pete.

They moved quickly to the top landing. Pete went to the window and with difficulty got it open. He looked down into the street. The other two men donned white cotton gloves.

Melvin Kalkhoven looked at his watch, "Ready to go, Pete?"

Pete nodded. The tattooed youngster put down the tool-box and began working on the door lock of apartment No. 8. The lock had already been examined by a CIA team the day before. The skelton keys they had been provided with were the correct choice. It was only thirty seconds before the door swung open.

"All clear," said Pete. He too looked at his watch.

Kalkhoven and his assistant moved quickly inside the apartment and closed the door behind them. "What a lousy little lock," said the youth. "Are you sure this is the right place?"

"Expensive locks in a district like this could draw just the sort of attention these people are trying to avoid," said Kalkhoven. "This is a safe house . . . nothing secret, nothing valuable here . . . just a place to meet." He looked quickly into the tiny rooms. There were two telephones: one in the bedroom and a wall phone in the sitting room. No, not the telephones, he decided, the electricity supply sockets would be more suitable. It was very hot and airless inside the apartment—the windows had not been opened for weeks; they were secured by screw locks. The two single beds in the smaller room were neatly made up, bedclothes and matching green nylon overlays folded in envelope-corner style, as beds are made in hospitals.

"They haven't been slept in in months," said Melvin Kalkhoven. "It's just a meeting place." Already he was at work removing the cream-coloured plastic cover from the electricity outlet by the bed. His assistant began work on the one behind the refrigerator. His name was Todd Wynn, a thin, wiry twenty-five-year-old—he looked no more than eighteen.

"Watch that screwdriver," said Kalkhoven. "We don't want scratch marks on the plastic covers."

"Why are we using such old-fashioned equipment, Melvin?"

" 'Be not curious in unnecessary matters,' it says in the good book. 'For more things are showed unto thee than men understand.' "

"Don't kid around, Melvin. Why aren't we fitting voice-activated bugs, or something more sophisticated?"

Kalkhoven said, "Because the guys who use this place are pros. Like I tell you, don't mark the plastic.

These are the kind of people who will check the place."

"You didn't answer the question."

"OK," said Kalkhoven. Working quickly he removed the screws holding the wall plate and pulled the cover off. From his pocket he took a tiny carrier transmitter, no larger than a packet of razor blades. He fitted it into position, squeezed it to bend the wires and replaced the plastic cover. "Because if we put voice activated sets into this room anyone could locate them using a vest-pocket detector. Blast off any powerful sound and the voice activator will sing for you. Easier than hell to find them."

The youth was slower in putting his carrier transmitter into position. "So someone's got to sit outside and monitor this baby?"

"Right," said Kalkhoven. "But at least they won't be transmitting until we switch them on. These are good sets. They're small because they take their power off the mains supply and use the wiring as far as the junction box as an antenna. They're old but they're good. I've got no time for some of this space-wars junk that the Technical Services Division has developed; it goes on the blink too often. You done that one? Now do the other room. And don't get jumpy. We got all the time in the world. We get anyone showing up here and Pete outside will hold them off. Pete's a good guy."

From the landing outside, Pete was watching the street where a uniformed police sergeant walked as far as the grocery, helped himself to an apple and stood eating it while watching the traffic pass. He was not one of the regular precinct cops, he was a nursemaid sent from police HQ to watch over such capers.

The kids had abandoned their efforts to get the fire hydrant going. The cop studied the chess game for a moment. "He's going to take that bishop," he advised.

The old man who was the subject of this good advice gave the officer no word of appreciation. "Why don't you go find Dillinger?" he asked.

"Come on, pop," said the police sergeant good-naturedly. "The FBI got Dillinger back in the thirties. You're smart enough to know that."

"So why wouldn't I know how to play my bishop?" said the old man.

The decline of the U.S. dollar in world money markets during 1979 played havoc with Edward Parker's budgets and plans. Suppliers in Taiwan and South Korea had contracts expressing their payments in Japanese yen, but virtually all the companies buying Parker's radio components were in the United States and Canada. Now Parker was being squeezed by the movements of the world's economy. His profit margin was getting thinner day by day and he knew that, unless some miracle happened within a year, he would have to start laying off workers at his assembly plant. If he was eventually going to be forced to a closure, he knew it would be better to face that fact sooner rather than later. He had seen what happened to other businesses where the management had refused to face the facts; the results had been total tragedy for everyone concerned. One man he knew, until recently a senior partner in a small but profitable radiophone company in Michigan, was working as a gas station manager in Ohio and, let's face it, gas stations were not a growth industry. Poor man.

"He complains all the time. He was always like that. In the army he was the same way," said Kleiber.

Parker wrenched his mind away from the capitalist problems that faced him in his business affairs. Truth to tell, he had become obsessed with the technical tasks of capitalism. He had to remind himself that he was the U.S.S.R.'s illegal resident and, whatever happened to his radio components company, Moscow Centre would demand that his espionage work be exemplary. He concentrated his mind upon the man sitting opposite him in this seedy New York apartment. He was a plump, cocksure man with a cropped head and ready smile. Willi Kleiber was not someone Edward Parker would choose as a dinner companion but he was one of his best agents, and they were on the brink of a success that might well enable Parker to go back to Moscow in a haze of vodka fumes and accompanied by the sound of clinking medals.

"Who complains all the time?" said Parker.

The light was orange. It was evening and the dying sun was huge and pincered between the tall buildings. Outside in the street some boys were playing softball on a diamond marked in chalk. They could hear their shouts.

"Max Breslow complains all the time," said Kleiber, looking at Parker with narrowed eyes and wondering why his boss was so slow to comprehend him. "The joke of it is that Böttger's people have encouraged him to continue making this film. Once they had seen the script, and decided it was harmless, they told him to actually go ahead and *make* this damned film." Kleiber laughed. He wrinkled his nose as he did it. The sound was more like a snigger than the sort of belly-laugh one would expect from this jackbooted German rowdy, thought Parker, but he allowed himself a smile.

"There is no chance that Breslow guesses you are working for the Soviet Union?" Parker looked at his watch. It was 6:10 p.m. He must catch a plane back to Chicago in time to do some paperwork before going to bed. At one time the illegal resident had always lived in Canada, but Parker had pressed Moscow Centre to let him be in the U.S.A. Because he travelled so much of the time, they had reluctantly agreed.

Kleiber laughed. "My old comrade Max would challenge you to a duel if you suggested such a thing." They were speaking English. Kleiber's English was heavily accented compared with Parker's, but Kleiber prided himself on his command of languages and Parker was wise enough to indulge his agent's ego.

"And what of Böttger and these other madmen? Are you sure they have no suspicions that you are working for the Soviet Union?" His lungs gurgled on the humid air. Parker removed his jacket and loosened his tie. He detested these New York City summers. The buildings trapped the damp, stale air and made the ugly sounds of the street unnaturally loud.

Kleiber grinned. "Eddie, Eddie, Eddie," he called in a lilting tone that mocked Parker's caution. "Böttger, Rau and the others are senile, my friend. Crazy! . . . *Meschugge!* . . . Nuts! . . . *Loco rematado!* . . . I tell you this over and over again, but still you don't believe me. Listen, Eddie, these old fools are going through their second childhoods. They are liberals, they think I am a liberal, they don't suspect me of anything. Now quit worrying, will you?"

But Parker did not quit worrying. He was a worrier by nature and he had mixed feelings about Kleiber. Kleiber's loyalty to Moscow Centre was never in doubt, but then he would have given equal loyalty to any organization that gave him a realistic opportunity to relive something of his wartime life. He was as hard and fit as many men half his age, and as dispassionate as a machine. He was intelligent and, judging from what Parker knew of Kleiber's security organization, a shrewd businessman. But for his weaknesses—women and gambling—he would by now have been wealthy. But Kleiber did not want to be wealthy. Kleiber was in love with hardship.

"And Breslow will make money from the film," said Kleiber. He laughed again. He seemed to think it was genuinely funny. Obviously he had no resentment about the money that Breslow would make. Parker noted that; it was unusual in a man.

Parker said, "General Zhadov has ordered that the Stein documents are top priority. Nothing must stand in the way of our getting them." Parker had always used the name Zhadov—his old commander in the Fifth Army—to personify the whole bureaucratic empire of Moscow Centre and any orders or instructions emanating from it. But this time Parker had General Shumuk in his mind when he said it. "And General Zhadov," Parker added, "is a very tough cookie who doesn't get his priorities wrong."

Kleiber smiled. "You tell your General Zhadov to get stuffed," he said."I'll get the Stein documents, and I'll get them my way. And it won't be because some senile old fart in Moscow Centre tells me it's a top priority." The air was heavy and unmoving. Somewhere on the other side of the city they heard a police siren wailing.

Parker said nothing, although for a moment he relished the vision of Kleiber confronting General Shumuk. Parker knew that Shumuk had accounted for tens of thousands of Kleibers in his time. He would be trampled underfoot without pause.

"You'll end up a general there someday, Willi," said Parker, "then you'll change your tune." It was the standard Moscow line for outstanding agents. You gave them medals and military ranks. Once, Parker had gone to all the trouble of getting a Russian colonel's uniform, complete with orders, medals and all the trimmings, just to show it to a nasty little computer programmer in Kansas City who was stalling with material that Moscow Centre kept demanding. The uniform did the trick; the programmer paraded in front of a mirror with it. The following year Parker promoted him again and the little jerk responded by wanting to go to Moscow for a visit. What a fiasco that would have been. Luckily the little fellow's employer lost his War Department contract, so that he was no longer handling material that Moscow wanted; sudden reduction in rank! Parker smiled at the thought of it.

"Me, a general?" said Kleiber. "No thanks. You'll never get me to Moscow, Eddie. Forget that idea, right now."

"They all say that at first, Willi," said Parker. It was fun to encourage this man's egomania, to see how far he would go.

"You know they are in Geneva," said Willi Kleiber. "You know Stein's documents are in this big house on the lake front." He had already told Parker his important news but he wanted to enjoy it again.

"Yes," said Parker. "It's a small package. Bring it. There should be no trouble."

"Fly stateside from Geneva?" said Kleiber. He wrinkled his nose, as if detecting a foul smell. "Geneva has more Moscow Centre people living there than you'll find in Moscow itself. It's the espionage capital of Europe, you know that, Eddie. Why bring the documents back here, when I can hand them over in Geneva for the diplomatic bag, and have them in Moscow the same night?"

Parker realized that he should not have baited Kleiber, who was an intelligent man. This was his retaliation. Kleiber knew that if the documents were handed over to a Russian agent in Geneva, Parker would share little of the credit for the coup. Perhaps he guessed too how badly Parker needed some credibility with Moscow Centre.

"I'd prefer you to bring the documents back here," said Parker. His voice was cold and pitched a little higher than previously. His nerves had tightened the muscles of his throat. Kleiber had a quick eye for other men's weaknesses; he smiled. Parker added, "How do we know who we might be dealing with in Geneva, Willi? You might be handing the result of all this effort and hazard to some dumb clerk who'll file it, or lose it, or some damned thing. These things happen, you know."

"Is it an order, Eddie?"

In fact, Edward Parker had no authority to make the carriage of the documents back to the U.S.A. a direct order. Not only was it in contravention of standing instructions about briefing agents for missions overseas but it exceeded his territorial authority. The rulebook said Kleiber should be provided with a "drop" and "letter box," if not a proper structure and "cut-out." This was especially true of Task Pogoni, the very high priority mission for which the Centre had sent General Shumuk all the way to Mexico City.

But this was a chance for Edward Parker to redeem his reputation with his Russian superiors. It would perhaps provide a chance for him to see once more the wife and grown-up son whom sometimes he missed with a yearning which bordered on physical pain and was all the more agonizing because he could speak of it to no one. "Bring them back here, Willi. It's an order." He looked at his watch again and began calculating how long it would take to get to the airport. Before going to bed tonight he must go through his factory accounts.

The FBI sound engineer and his assistant were pleased that the meeting was at an end. Boxed inside a poorly ventilated panel truck together with a photographer, driver and clerk, they were all shiny with perspiration. They had long since emptied the tiny refrigerator of its cold drinks. The sound engineer removed his headphones. "That's it," he said. In the street outside someone started shouting at the children playing softball. A transistor radio was playing "Hello, Dolly!" and whoever was carrying it banged on the panel truck as he passed. It was a normal extrovert action in that locality, but the men knew it was their signal to move.

"Son of a bitch," said the sound engineer. "He wants him to bring the papers back to the U.S.A. That's good. The boys will snatch him when he reenters the country. The poor bastard is going to get a hundred years in the pen."

Todd Wynn, Klakhoven's young assistant, checked his shorthand notes, then took the spool of tape off the machine and pocketed it before signing a receipt for the driver.

"What gets into these guys?" said the driver bitterly. "They have no loyalty to their friends or the people they work with. Do they get a kick out of betraying people?"

"They should get the chair," said Melvin Kalkhoven. "These two hoodlums are the ones who snuffed that movie producer in L.A. and hacked his head off. And Scotland Yard are looking for them on account of the same kind of job they did in London."

"Let's get out of here," said the driver, as he climbed carefully over the recording equipment. "I've got a lovely wife waiting in bed for me."

The other men laughed. They knew he meant some other man's wife.

Todd Wynn glanced at Kalkhoven, who, if he had a biblical quotation apt for such hypocrisy, kept it to himself.

## 35

While Kleiber and Parker suffered the humid languor of that Manhattan evening, Boyd Stuart in London watched the hands of the clock move to midnight and on into the first day of August. His windowless basement room in the Ziggurat was bleak and far too deep underground for him to hear the chimes of Big Ben, or the traffic which moved unceasingly over Westminster Bridge. The shiny brickwork interior was finished in the same acid green that Whitehall had been specifying for official habitation, from post offices to prisons, since Queen Victoria's reign, and perhaps before. Two wooden trestle tables had been moved close to the wall, in an attempt to steady precarious piles of books and documents which now reached almost to the low ceiling, the sprinklers and the blue fluorescent light which hummed.

Stuart shifted in discomfort on the hard wooden chair. It had been repaired by the Department of the Environment and was now relegated to this "Secure Room No. 4" because it rocked on its uneven legs. There was little else in the room, except for a red fire extinguisher and a framed, fly-spotted notice which went into considerable detail about the Official Secrets Act's references to official papers. It was dated 1962, but little had changed.

The hours had passed quickly as Stuart went through these references to the events of the summer of 1940. All the published accounts were here: the memoirs of the victors and of the conquered. There were unpublished accounts too: dusty typewritten bundles of reports, diaries and memoirs, detailing the days of men long dead and half forgotten.

Stuart had been sceptical at first. Had Winston Churchill actually become so depressed and demoralized, as the German Panzer divisions swept through France so effortlessly, that he had himself gone to see Adolf Hitler, the man he so abhorred? Had he really gone to the German Führer, cap in hand, and offered to trade away his allies to the men he called "gangsters"? Boyd Stuart had prepared a large sheet of paper and noted down the movements of both men through the days of May and June.

It was the clock striking midnight that made Stuart realize how long he had spent with his history books. There could no longer be any doubt about it. The diaries clearly showed when it was that Churchill had made his secret trip to meet Hitler. It would be obvious to anyone once the facts were assembled.

Churchill's visit to Paris on May 16 was far too early, the German advance had only been going six days and the Allies entertained hopes of a complete recovery. The visit to Château de Vincennes—HQ of the French supreme command—on May 22 was equally impossible. It involved all the complications of another visit to Paris, and all the witnesses to the Prime Minister's movements.

On May 31 Churchill flew to Paris for the third time. With him went General Dill, General Ismay and Clement Attlee. This time, instead of visiting the Quai d'Orsay, Churchill went to see Paul Reynaud, the French Premier. They met in a room at the War Office in the Rue St. Dominique. As on all his visits to France in May, Churchill slept in the British embassy and returned to England the following morning.

None of Churchill's visits in May provided any chance for him to confer with German plenipotentiaries, let alone with Hitler himself. But Churchill's next visit to France on June 11 and 12 was curious in every way. Even though German spearheads were at the gates of Paris, and were to occupy the city three dates later, Churchill's private aircraft flew beyond the German columns, to land at a very small airfield near the little country town of Briare. In Volume 2 of his memoirs, Churchill admitted that the rendezvous was not fixed until the day of departure. This was because he was waiting for a message from Adolf Hitler, sent to London through the Spanish embassy.

The clue to Winston Churchill's secret onward flight was contained in the fact that the British Prime Minister did not remain with the others of the British contingent. General Dill, General Ismay, Anthony Eden, the Foreign Minister, and even Churchill's translator were all accommodated in a nearby military train. As soon as the aircraft landed, Churchill departed again unaccompanied.

Boyd Stuart turned again to the memoirs of Sir Edward Spears*—no one had been closer to Churchill during those terrible days. Of the morning of June 12, 1940, which followed that night spent in France,

* Sir Edward Spears, *Assignment to Catastrophe*. Vol. 2. *The Fall of France* (Heinemann, London, 1954) page 159.

with the German armies racing ever closer, Spears wrote, "I did not look up for a while, and when I did I was astonished to see the Prime Minister's detective, Thompson." Thompson was a permanent feature of the Churchill household and had been for many years. It was amazing that he should be separated from the man he protected. Spears continues, "Surprised into tactlessness I said, 'Why, Thompson, what are you doing here? Why aren't you with the Prime Minster? Surely he will need you?'

" 'I had to sleep here, and the French failed to realize I needed a car.' "

So that was it. Not even Winston Churchill's own bodyguard had stayed with him. Was that a condition that Adolf Hitler had imposed, or had Churchill decided that his secret flight must put no one to hazard but himself?

For by that time, on June 14, 1940, Winston Churchill was alone, far away from his staff, his interpretor, his bodyguard and his advisers. He had already had two long sessions with Adolf Hitler.

If Churchill's movements were significant, then Hitler's were even more so. On June 6, 1940, after frantic construction work carried out at short notice, a secret meeting place had been improvised in Belgium at the tiny frontier zone village of Brûly de Pesche. The air-raid shelter there was still damp from freshly poured concrete and Hitler refused to go inside it. Here the airstrip was no more than a meadow big enough to land a small communications aircraft, so Churchill's twin-engined de Havilland Flamingo had landed near to Hitler's Junkers at Rocroi, just across the border in France. The Fieseler Storch that was to take him on the final stage of his mission was already warmed-up when Churchill landed, and by the time the little plane was airborne, Churchill's Flamingo was shrouded in camouflage nets on the far side of the airfield.

Significant too was the fact that the Brûly de Pesche headquarters was used once only, for this meeting with Winston Churchill. The whole elaborate place was constructed solely for this secret summit meeting and after its few days of importance was left to rot.

On June 17, his hopes of a British request for a ceasefire faded, Adolf Hitler travelled to Munich where, in the Prince Carl Palace, Benito Mussolini was hoping to hear that the British would no longer resist his armies in Africa. By June 21 the fighting in France was all but finished. Hitler was motoring through the Forest of Compiègne in his open Mercedes, arranging that the German army engineers bring out of its museum the railway coach in which the Germans had signed a peace with France after the First World War. On the June 22 the French armistice was signed in that same Pullman car. The brief chance of early peace between Britain and Germany had gone forever.

Stuart went through the papers again and again. He looked at the Waffen SS and army unit war diaries that the War Office had provided from their archives. He looked at the tall stack of biographies that described Adolf Hitler's life in such minute detail. He looked at Xerox copies from the Berlin document centre and the West German archives. He looked once more at the published memoirs. Once the truth was known, so many other mysteries were solved. For instance, why had the twelve Hawker Hurricanes that escorted Churchill's aircraft out of Briare on June 11 not been sent out to escort him for the return flight the next day?* It was especially puzzling in the light of the RAF's order of battle, which showed that six Hurricane squadrons were based *in France* until June 17. The fighters would not even have had to cross the channel to get to Briare.

The real answer was obvious now, but the official reason had been given as bad weather. (It hardly fitted with the fact that on this same day RAF aircraft had found the weather and visibility good enough to make low-level bombing attacks on bridges over the Albert Canal in nearby Belgium, to say nothing of long-range bombers flying from England to Turin.) The fact was that the Hawker Hurricane pi-

* Spears, Vol. 2, page 172.

lots might, by some error or disruption of the schedule, have glimpsed the unthinkable.

They would have seen a Staffel of Messerschmitt Bf 109Es flying close escort on Churchill's unarmed Flamingo. The aircraft, from Jagdgeschwader 51, had been ordered to this task by direct order to Luftflotte 2 headquarters from the Führerhauptquartier. These German fighters circled the airfield until Churchill's aircraft was in the air, and then protected him across the German lines into French airspace.

Significantly, it was the Luftwaffe high command in Berlin (Ob.d.L.) which had issued the special instructions for this small tactical mission. Stuart turned the teleprinter message over in his hands. The cryptic language of the signals unit at Luftflotte 2, which passed the secret message to IX Fliegerdivision HQ, did little to hide the nature of the instruction. No routing was mentioned in the message but HQ insisted that all pilots must be specially briefed that the Sonderflug must be kept safe at all costs. No fighter pilot must leave the escort formation to attack enemy targets no matter how tempting. The Geschwaderkommmodore, the message continued, was to lead the mission in person. Failure to carry out the terms of this commander-in-chief's order would mean court-martial for all concerned.

Adolf Hitler had done everything in his power to ensure that no ghastly calamity mar this chance of the British Commonwealth's giving up the struggle so then he could become the undisputed master of Europe.

Boyd Stuart closed the file, and pressed the buzzer to summon the duty archive clerk. Suddenly he felt tired and rather old.

## 36

There were plenty of larger boats to be seen on Lake Geneva that summer but *Die Zitrone* was a fifty-foot motor yacht with factory-fresh diesels, modern radar and a powerful launch swinging from the stern davits. *Die Zitrone* cruised very slowly along the south side of the lake, keeping close to the shore, but not dangerously so. On the afterdeck two men were seated at a table, each with a Campari in one hand and Zeiss binoculars in the other. From time to time they would raise their binoculars to look at the shoreline.

It was a warm day, the first Saturday of August. One of the men was dressed in dark trousers and a white shirt with a neat monogram on the pocket flap—as used to mark expensive made-to-measure garments. A blue yachting cap completed the sort of informal outfit favoured by owners who chartered and sailed their own yachts for their clients and was calculated to indicate superior skills while maintaining social equality.

The second man wore a striped shirt and grey shorts. It was hot and he was sweating. From time to time he ran his hand through his closely cropped hair. On the table in front of him there was a tape recorder. From it came a thin black cord which ended at his shirt collar where a tiny microphone was clipped close to his mouth. "The first boatload of men must stay at the lake shore until all the boats are secured," Willi Kleiber said into the microphone. "The Pitman house is one hundred and fifty metres from the landing stage. Any boats found at the landing stage must be totally disabled by the landing party from boat one. No one will move from their position until all boats are secured and contact has been made with the party arriving by road. The two advance men of the road party will use red flashlights to identify themselves. The two advance men of boat one will use only green flashlights." He switched the tape recorder off and took one last look at the big lakeside house of Colonel John Elroy Pitman the Third before *Die Zitrone* steered away northwards to cross the lake.

It was a hot, cloudless day. The mountains were crisply drawn against the blue sky and very close, or so it seemed. The two men put down their binoculars and put on their sunglasses. They sat for a moment, still dazzled by the harsh reflection of the sun off the flat water.

"It will be easy," said Willi Kleiber.

"I don't like it," said Max Breslow. "We still don't

know what the documents are like. If they are all contained in those metal filing cases, it will take all night to get them out of the house and loaded onto the trucks."

"Of course it will," said Kleiber. "At least it would . . . if that's what I intended to do."

"When then?"

"We'll take possession of the house, I've told you so. Do you think I've changed my mind?" said Klieber. "We'll hold it for two or three days"—Kleiber saw that Max was about to argue—"a week, if it takes a week. We'll stay there as long as we have to."

"My God, Willi. You don't know what you are saying."

"I'm a gambler, Max. I always have been."

"Stay there? Holding those Americans captive?"

"You saw what it's like, Max. There will be no difficulty in embarking our people from the lakeside. It will be quiet and discreet. They have only to come from Coppet on the far side of the lake. One carload of our best people will arrive at the Pitman house by road. No one in the village will hear shooting, there will be no lights."

"I've heard of such plans before," said Max Breslow dryly. "Have you told the Americans that there will be no shooting, no shouting and . . . what was the other thing you've forbidden?"

"You should know me better than that, my friend," said Kleiber. "In the boats we are wearing party clothes. If the Americans get rough and the neighbours get nosy, we'll be there in fancy dress to explain the commotion and apologize for the disturbance."

"How many?"

"Fifteen men should be sufficient," said Kleiber. "They are all well-trained people from my own security company. These are fellows I use only on the most dangerous assignments: kidnap threats, murder threats and so on. They know what to do."

"Can they keep their mouths shut?"

Willi rubbed a finger on the side of his nose. "These are all men who depend upon *me* to keep *my* mouth shut," he said, and smiled. "These are good men, Max. These are all men like us."

When *Die Zitrone* reached Coppet on the Swiss side, it followed the coast until it reached a curious-looking mansion with a well-kept lawn which came down to an ornate wooden boat house.

The main building was fifty yards away. Finished in a hideous shade of yellow, its stucco was stained and peeling, and the wooden balconies were warped and weatherbeaten. But the inside of the house had been cleaned up and redecorated in plain colours. Most of the lights were unshaded bulbs and the seats were new and of a folding type more commonly found in schools and lecture halls. Max Breslow shuddered. There could be no doubt that this was all done to Willi Kleiber's taste. Kleiber took a great personal pride in choosing things that he described as practical and without frills.

"There is everything we are ever likely to need in here," said Kleiber, his voice echoing slightly against the bare walls. "Guns, machine-guns even, handcuffs, other types of restraints, cutting tools and a thermic lance that will carve through solid steel." He looked at Breslow and smiled. "You mentioned such devices. Downstairs we have extra inflatable boats and enough food to feed a company of soldiers for a month."

Max Breslow did not answer. He followed Kleiber through the first room and downstairs. A man was sitting on a hard chair in the hallway. Kleiber motioned to him and he unlocked a wine-cellar door to show them inside. Kleiber waved his arm. "Look!"

Inside there was an array of guns. Fitted into wall racks were a couple of dozen HK 54 machine pistols, of the sort issued to the German border police. There were also some Swedish Carl Gustaf 9-mm machine guns, and two sniper's rifles with infra-red sights and lights. Glass-fronted cases contained hand guns and there was a wooden box of concussion grenades.

"MACE," said Kleiber tapping another box. "Still the best disabling weapon I know. And it contains no toxic apart from the tear gas." His low voice was resonant in the tiny windowless strong room.

"You *are* crazy, Willi."

"Where have you been living for the last few years? Venus? Saturn? Mars?" said Kleiber. "I'm the virtual owner of the best damned security company in West Germany, even if we are not yet the biggest. All of this material is legitimately owned and operated by our Swiss associate, of which I am a vice-president. The company is licensed to have the weapons you are looking at, Max. Our only undertaking to the government is to have them under proper safekeeping, so that they are not stolen by terrorists."

"It's all legal for you to have this stuff?"

"The police turn a blind eye to me. My company undertakes some dangerous work, Max. I have contracts to provide protection to many members of the government, as well as to very wealthy businessmen. I've helped to plan the security of some international conferences. We're hoping to get the job of protecting the next OPEC meeting in Europe."

Willi Kleiber stepped back into the corridor again, and Max Breslow was relieved to follow him. As they left, Kleiber watched the guard double-lock the armoury, and then took down a clipboard and signed the day sheet with a flourish.

"We've got to hit them suddenly and hard," said Kleiber. "That's one thing I learned in the war, Max. We've got to get into the Pitman house and let them see a lot of men and a lot of firepower. That's the way to save lives, and save ourselves a lot of trouble."

"I suppose so," said Max.

"I wish you would shake off this negative attitude, Max. I wish you'd tell me that you are committed."

"I read in the Los Angeles papers about more Germans being deported," said Breslow.

"I read it too," said Kleiber. It was not something he wished to discuss.

"Did you know that the Americans deport men back to the place where the supposed war crime was committed?"

"Are you worrying about that old woman in Boston again?" said Kleiber.

"I was at Lyubomi, Willi. I wasn't there when the massacre took place, but I did go there. I wonder if that is where she saw me; I've stayed awake night after night thinking about it."

"Poland?"

"That town is now inside the U.S.S.R. borders, Willi. I'd be deported to Russia. You know what *they* do with anyone who was in the SS."

Kleiber drew a map using his stubby finger on the plastic table top.

"Would you go in the gate with the road party, Max?"

"Yes," said Max almost as if he had been waiting for the question.

Kleiber was caught off balance for a moment; he had been preparing all kinds of arguments to persuade Breslow. "That's excellent. I need someone who knows the true situation that side. I will be with the boats, of course. If something went badly wrong, I want someone who can talk himself out of trouble and extricate the truck and the road party. For us in the boats it will be easier to disappear."

"Are you arming the road party?"

"I can't decide. There's every reason to hope we'll go right into the house and need nothing more lethal than a finger in a coat pocket. But we have to remember that the *Amis* are ex-soldiers, just as we are. They might be the sort of men who conduct their affairs in a proper military style. They might have sentries posted. They might be armed to the teeth, Max."

"I doubt it," said Max Breslow. He couldn't think of anyone less military than Charles Stein.

"And so do I. I doubt it very much. Let's go upstairs. I want to take a shower and change my clothes."

"When we get the documents, what then, Willi? Do we take them to Dr. Böttger?"

"I will handle it," said Kleiber. "It is all arranged."

"Suppose you are hurt, Willi, or even killed?"

Kleiber stopped suddenly and turned to face his friend. Like all brave soldiers, he had never truly faced that prospect. What a catastrophe it would be if Max gave the Minutes to Böttger. Kleiber had no doubt that in such a case Moscow would keep to the threat of sending all Kleiber's war crimes evidence to the West. That would kill his mother with shame, and certainly mean the end of his father.

"No, Max," said Kleiber. "If anything happens to

me, you must telephone Chicago, a man named Edward Parker." Kleiber scribbled the phone number on a page of his notebook and passed it to Max Breslow.

"Does he know about Charles Stein?"

"He knows about everything, Max. He knows about everything."

"I feel sorry for Stein," Max confided. "He's not so bad as I once thought him."

"You've changed your attitude," Kleiber chuckled. "I remember you telling me you couldn't abide him." They went upstairs, Kleiber leading and taking the steps two at a time to demonstrate how fit he was. "What sort of man is he, this Stein?" Kleiber was not even short of breath. "We've more or less finished his bank. They'll lose a hundred million dollars. . . . Böttger's plan was faultless."

"Or they will run," said Breslow.

"But why didn't he offer you the papers for whatever he could get for them? Do you think he understood the offer?"

"He understood all right," said Breslow. "I told him I'd arrange to sell the documents to a big corporation which would give him cash up front and a percentage too."

"So why does he turn down the chance to salvage his business affairs? Doesn't he realize his life is in danger?"

"The other way round," said Breslow. "I told you not to underestimate him. He knows that nothing will happen to him until we get our hands on the Hitler Minutes. After that, as you've already told me, his life will be forfeit. He's no fool, Willi. He's frightened, but he's not so frightened that he will hand over those damned papers."

"Well, now we *do* know where the papers are," said Kleiber. "He's missed his chance."

"Poor Stein," said Max Breslow, but if Kleiber heard him, he gave no sign of it.

# 37

On that same Saturday of August the director general arrived in his office at 9:25 a.m. He sent for Stuart. He had done that for the previous three mornings, so Stuart was ready for the call. The DG was seated at his desk reading the *Daily Telegraph*'s account of the PM's speech to the conference in Lusaka. He put down the newspaper when Stuart entered and got to his feet.

"Nothing fresh, Stuart?" The DG was not wearing his usual black jacket and pinstripe trousers but a hound's-tooth check suit. It was a startling tramsformation which made the director look like a prosperous bookie, Stuart thought.

"Geneva just made contact," said Stuart.

"Is he a good man?"

"Yes, sir. Excellent."

"Koch, isn't it?"

"Yes, sir." The old man never lost the capacity to surprise.

"I spent a lot of time in Switzerland," said the DG. "As you probably know from Jennifer, my wife and I go there every year . . . although nowadays I'm a little too old for climbing. I had a fall when a half a dozen of us tried our luck on the Zmutt ridge of the Matterhorn. That was ten years ago. I said, Ryden old chap, you're too old for this sort of thing. Never mind all these modern contraptions—pitons, snap links and stirrups—the fact is that sleeping one night at that sort of altitude could kill an old man."

"You fell, sir?"

"Damn near fifty feet, Stuart. Into soft snow, thank God. But it was a lesson. A man ignores such signs at his peril." The DG moved across the room with a restlessness that Stuart found distracting.

"Yes, sir," said Stuart wondering if the DG was trying to tell him something. The director was rather fond of imparting suggestions by means of such parables.

"I go there regularly and smell the air, Stuart.

Know what I mean?" The DG didn't wait to hear if Stuart knew. "Good people, the Swiss. God-fearing, industrious and logical. I like them, and they have helped the department a lot from time to time. Yet what do you ever hear about the Swiss intelligence service—nothing! That's what I like about them, Stuart."

Stuart noted it. He inferred that fear of God, industry and logic were probably the virtues the DG would have claimed for himself, had he not been saddled with that old-world reticence of which he made so much. "They seem to have taken your bait, sir," said Stuart. "Geneva reports a lot of activity at the lakeside house, opposite the one owned by the American colonel. One neighbour says that security company cars arrived with boxes of guns. . . ."

"Boxes of guns?" The DG was amused. "You mean boxes with the word GUNS stencilled on the outside?"

Stuart did not rise to this provocation. "It's one unconfirmed report, sir. From a neighbour . . . and we know how unreliable neighbours can be."

"Guns, you say?" The DG smacked some invisible speck of dust from his fine new trousers.

"Security company cars—armoured cars by the sound of it, wire netting on the windows and so on. It's not the sort of van that delivers groceries, sir. It was driven to the back of the house to unload . . . heavy crates. . . ."

"Very well, Stuart. You make your point. No need to labour it. Yes, it sounds like guns. And Stein knows about his son? We'll have to release him soon. I'm coming under considerable pressure from the Home Office."

"The Los Angeles controller put it all to Stein senior yesterday morning—they are eight hours behind us, of course."

"Yes, eight hours behind us, Stuart. I'm not quite senile."

"No, sir. Well, Stein drove down to Sunset Boulevard and bought an airline ticket, we don't know where to yet."

"Why don't we?"

Stuart suppressed a sigh. "We'll have to get it off

the airline computer, and that means several different airlines. A direct approach to the travel agency is very likely to get back to Stein."

"And do we care if it gets back to him?"

"The field agents have to live in that town," said Stuart. "It's all very well to sit in London critical of everything the field men do, and impatient to close the dossier, but our man who goes to the travel agent might be storing up trouble for himself, dangerous trouble."

"This is vitally important, Stuart."

"It's all important," said Stuart angrily. "When was the last time a field agent was briefed to take his time? All the dockets in the traffic room are red ones. Where are the stickers that say 'Take your time' or 'Watch out for your back—this is just something to buy promotion for some London desk man'? Where are they?"

The DG seemed amused by Stuart's outburst, or was his fixed grin just a nervous and angry reaction to it? "There are no stickers like that, Stuart. Perhaps we should ask the stationery office to let us have some."

"Perhaps we should, sir."

The DG stopped his pacing. For a moment he seemed about to rebuke Stuart but he swallowed his annoyance. He put both his hands into his trouser pockets and rattled his change. "Suppose we are wrong, Stuart? Suppose Stein *has* got the Hitler Minutes in the house on Lake Geneva?"

Stuart said nothing. The two men looked at each other.

The DG continued with his gloomy scenario. "In that case we will have sent Kleiber and his thugs to the very spot that we don't want them to be. They will get those damned documents, Stuart. And we will have given them every assistance. How will I explain that to the PM?" *En passant* he smacked the newspaper's account of Mrs. Thatcher's speech with the back of his hand.

"I'm very busy downstairs, sir, without the added task of compiling explanations for mistakes that we've not yet made."

The DG wet his lips and stared out of the window.

He knew that his son-in-law was having some sort of affair—a liaison was perhaps a better word—with the blonde secretary who worked for the deputy chief of Operations (Region Three). He had mentioned it to his daughter Jennifer but she insisted that she didn't mind. The marriage is all over and finished with, she had said, and Sir Sydney had been pleased by her determination. Young people were different today, more's the pity, but that would not prevent him from posting the blonde secretary away. He felt uneasy about the relationship: Boyd Stuart was "agent in charge" of one of the most delicate operations they had mounted, and the girl was secretary to one of his key officials. It was bad security; he should have done something before this. He remembered that she had brought his own personal file up from the vault. That was something he did not like being handled by anyone but himself. He did not want even senior SIS staff to know that he had once been Elliot Castelbridge. "Don't meet trouble halfway, you mean?" the DG said, and nodded still looking out of the window. "Quite right, quite right." Then he turned to face Stuart.

Stuart waited, knowing that the DG was about to say something more. The old man had this disconcerting habit of pausing before he spoke. Probably he was rehearsing the exact words he would use, to ensure that he was revealing nothing more than was absolutely necessary. "Don't worry about this chap Kleiber and his house full of guns, Stuart. Our Swiss friends will take care of that."

Stuart waited for more information, but none was forthcoming. So that was it. The DG had given the Americans a "hands-off" undertaking on Kleiber. Now he was arranging that the Swiss security people pick Kleiber up. How very convneient; the Swiss computer was not available to the Americans and the DG knew that all too well. It would be interesting to hear the DG protesting his innocent surprise when the CIA liaison man came over here with news of Kleiber's arrest in Switzerland.

The DG watched Stuart carefully. It was always instructive to see how long it took one of his departmental employees to work out what was happening when provided with sufficient facts. He smoothed his hair and touched in passing the hearing aid. "Think it's going to rain, Stuart?"

"When the wind drops."

"Well, let's hope you're right. Not about the rain, of course." He gave his deadpan grin. "About Stein and Pitman not having those documents in the lakeside house in Geneva."

## 38

Charles Stein also arrived in Geneva on that first Saturday of August. He was worried. His telegram to Colonel Pitman had said they would meet at the "nut house." He wondered if Pitman might have forgotten that when the bank had been at its original premises near the cathedral—a chaos of muddle and excitement—they had always called it the "nut house," and when Madame Mauring took over, filling the new shop window with almond cakes, the name seemed newly appropriate.

"I need something from the safe." The cathedral clock chimed and Stein looked at his watch.

"Here's the key, Mr. Stein. You'll find everything in good order. There's not much petty cash, I'm afraid."

"I don't want to touch anything of yours, Madame Mauring," Stein told her. "I want that packet I left here."

"It's all as you left it, Mr. Stein. You help yourself."

The safe was an absurdity—a single key operating a set of four spring bolts. It would impress no one, except perhaps some proud owner. On the other hand, who would be looking for anything very valuable in the safe of a small tea room? And there was more to it than that. Stein leaned to direct the green-shaded desk light into the safe's shallow interior. Using both hands he inserted the stubby index fingers of both hands into small recesses. It was awkward and Stein breathed heavily with the exertion of it, until with a soft metallic click the whole back wall of the safe's interior hinged forward, to reveal the dials of a far more modern safe.

Stein had committed the combination to memory and now he quickly twirled the dials, before opening the inside door. From it he got an envelope. It was no larger that a medium-sized book, perhaps a centimetre thick. Stein opened it to check the contents. These were Hoffman-La Roche bearer shares. Each sheet had a nominal value of 3.3 Swiss francs and an actual value of about twenty-five thousand pounds. The contents of this packet were worth some two and a quarter million dollars to anyone who pushed them across a bank counter anywhere in the world. Then, reverently, he took from the safe another package even more valuable: the Hitler Minutes. It was not impressive looking: a cheap office folder, as thick as a packet of cigarettes.

Stein had brought with him the small brown canvas bag which he usually carried on trips. Now he emptied it on the table to make room inside it for the packet of bearer bonds. The outer pocket contained a toothbrush, shaving tackle, Bufferin tablets, nail clippers and an unopened plastic box containing one tablet of Roger & Gallet soap. Charles Stein was most particular about soap and he had used this particular brand—sandalwood perfumed—for over twenty years. In the bag's larger pocket there were shirts, underwear, socks and handkerchiefs. He felt inside the plastic wrapping of the shirts to be sure that the identity papers he had got from Delaney were still there. He looked again at the Brazilian passport. Stein's photo was not a recent one but it would do.

"The colonel has arrived," said Madame Mauring looking round the door. "More coffee and cake?" She seemed to sense that something terrible was about to happen.

"Yes, please, Madame Mauring."

"The colonel said coffee doesn't agree with him."

"Maybe today he won't care," said Stein.

She smiled and opened the door so that Colonel Pitman could enter the room. "I say, today maybe you'll have coffee," said Stein, speaking slightly more loudly so that Pitman would hear.

"Yes, please, Madame Mauring." He waited until she had gone. "So this is where you had the Hitler Minutes."

"They're right here," he said. "You want to see?"

Colonel Pitman nodded. Stein indicated the package on the table and then Madame Mauring brought the coffee tray. She pushed the Hitler Minutes aside to make room for the cups and saucers. Pitman picked them up. The cardboard folder had been blue originally but now the colour had faded to almost light grey. A long time had passed since some clerk of the U.S. Army's Government Affairs Group, G-5 Section, had hurriedly typed the inventory tag: "Merkers H-6750. Typewritten documents, German language, approx. 300 pages." American metal seals, and earlier German wax ones, were still in place but the tapes and strings had been cut. The initials of the archive specialist from the MFA&A were still faintly legible on the box-shaped, rubber-stamp mark. Pittman riffled the corners of the documents, like a card sharp preparing for a good evening.

Madame Mauring fussed with the coffee things, looked at the two men and then left without speaking. "She's all right," said Stein in reply to Pitman's unasked question. "She's always been grateful to us for letting her have the lease."

"What shall we do, Charles?" Sometimes it was Corporal," but now it was "Charles."

"Get out of this store, then get out of this town, then get out of this country."

"I would hate leaving my house," the colonel said. It was easy for Stein, he was comparatively young and fit and still had everything he would need to settle down in some new environment and start a new life. But Colonel Pitman did not want to leave this place. He liked to be near the doctor he trusted, with the servants he liked and in a house he had grown to love. "Must I go too, Charles?"

"I think you should, Colonel."

"What about your son Billy?" said Pitman. He fidgeted with the papers as he looked at them. It was damnable when a man needed a good cigar and a large brandy and could not have them.

"I told that *shmendrick* the British sent to see me in L.A.," said Stein. "Them holding Billy don't cut any ice with me. If I give them these papers, we've got nothing to bargain with. I told them I'll get lawyers and fight for Billy through the State Department. That's the only language these government bastards understand. I told him that if they didn't release Billy, I'd give Xeroxes of all this junk to *Stern* magazine and the *Washington Post,* making it a condition that they campaign for Billy's release."

"My God, but you're a hard man," said Pitman.

"It's logical," said Stein.

Pitman nodded. It was logical, but how many men would be able to make such a decision about their son? Perhaps that's what leadership was. Perhaps leadership was asking people to do things the hard way, simply because that was the way you were prepared to act yourself. Pitman chided himself that he had never been prepared to do anything the hard way.

"There was a man tailing me," said Stein. "The Brits I guess. How do you like that; the sons of bitches had a man tailing me. He was on the plane too."

"Did he follow you here?" said Pitman nervously.

"Nah! I changed planes in Paris. I got rid of him at the airport. You stay in the toilet long enough, the guy following you will eventually come in, to check up. Some tough kid I used to know in New York City told me that. I waited for him, and beat him senseless."

"You did what?"

"I slugged him. I put him inside the toilet and set the latch to show it was in use. The cleaners will find him."

Pitman shuddered. "I'll drive you to the airport, Chuck." Then Pitman said, "How do you know he was somone the British sent?"

"Who else would have sent him?"

Pitman nodded. "I'll drive you to the airport, Charles. Then I'll take the car across the border into France. There is a hotel on Lake Annecy where I go sometimes. I could stay there for a few days until it's blown over."

"It's not going to blow over, Colonel. We're fighting City Hall, don't you see that? The Brits and the Krauts both want the Hitler Minutes. If we don't let them have them, they'll blow us away. But if we *do* let them have them, they'll also blow us away."

"I'm too old to run, Charles," said the colonel. "Too old and too exhausted. When you get to my age, nothing matters anymore; the whole damned world becomes boring, like a movie you sat through too many times."

"Where's your car?" said Stein. "We've got to get going."

## 39

By the time Kleiber had shown his friend the house, the guns and equipment Breslow was hungry. The men had not eaten lunch. Breslow sniffed the air, hoping that a meal was being prepared for them but there was no sign of it. Kleiber seemed to be able to miss meals without noticing, but Max Breslow liked good food served punctually, as it was at home. He decided that he must go and eat, preferably without his friend Kleiber.

Breslow respected Willi Klebier. He had been a tough, honest soldier who could hold his drink, go days on end without sleep and who was never heard to complain. And yet Breslow's respect for Kleiber fell far short of admiration. Kleiber's avowed enjoyment of army life had in peacetime been replaced by his pleasure in hunting and camping trips, always in the hardest and bleakest of environments. Kleiber *liked* shaving in cold water by the light of a gas lamp at four o'clock in the morning inside some icy-cold tent in some god-forsaken part of the world, with the prospect of wading for hours in a cold swamp to shoot a few wretched ducks. Such strenuous pursuit of discomfort seemed childish to Breslow, and he made sure that he did not join such expeditions.

For all these reasons, Breslow was determined not to accept the spartan accommodation that Kleiber had prepared at the house on the lake shore. Breslow had been taken to inspect the bleak little uncarpeted room at the top of the house. The folding bed covered with two thin blankets and a threadbare cushion to be used as a pillow was not to Breslow's taste, niether was the chilly bathroom which was one flight of stairs and a long draughty corridor away.

Kleiber was disappointed when Breslow told him that he had already booked a suite at a luxurious downtown hotel. He had keenly looked forward to an evening of cigar smoke and schnapps, as they swapped stories about life at the Führerhauptquartier or discussed intimate details about Kleiber's latest mistress. He had even put a bottle on ice and brought a box of hand-rolled Havanas from the duty-free shop at the airport.

Mac Breslow relented a little. "I'll have a bath and some dinner and come back for a drink," he finally offered his friend.

"That's good," said Kleiber, his disappointment changing suddenly to manifest pleasure. "I'll drink you under the table, Max. Be warned."

Breslow managed a brave smile, although he dreaded the prospect of such an evening. "I mustn't be too late to bed," he mumbled.

"Nonsense," said Kleiber, patting his friend on the back. "A Saturday evening in August with the whole town waiting for us—how can you talk of going to bed early? We'll probably end up in that new striptease club I was telling you about, or we could go across the border to Evian and try our luck at the casino. Or, if it's girls you are in the mood for . . ."

It was difficult to counter Kleiber's persuasive ebullience. "I don't know how you do it, Willi. I really do not."

Kleiber straightened himself to his full height and smiled to show his pleasure. It was easy to compliment him, thought Max Breslow—one had only to imply that he was a libertine or a rogue to earn his eternal approval.

"Meet me here at eight-thirty," suggested Kleiber.

"It will give you time for your preening, and give me time to win a new client. If the new job is what I think it is, Max, the evening is on me."

"Something good?"

"When a man calls long distance every thirty minutes and says he needs to speak to me concerning a matter of great importance, it usually turns out that his wife is jumping into bed with his chauffeur."

"Does it, Willi?"

"Or that his mistress is jumping into bed with his chauffeur," said Kleiber. "The more they make it sound like it's a matter of international diplomacy, the more certain I become that it's a little domestic drama."

"I didn't know your company took on such domestic dramas nowadays."

Willi smiled again. "My staff are very highly paid. They don't mind if they are guarding the President or recording the whispers of an insatiable wife, and why should they mind? I tell these clients that using my organization will cost them ten times what a small company specializing in divorce would charge. They don't care, Max. They want to pay more. The elemental fury of vengeance motivates these people; they want to hurt, they want to humble, they want to assault the one who has caused them pain. Lacking the physique or the skills or the temperament to do it directly, they use the only weapon they have—money! They pay, Max, because they want to pay." He smacked a fist into an open hand to illustrate the similarity between the act of violence and of payment. "Yes, I'll take on a domestic drama."

Max Breslow smiled, but the smile was a fixed one. He remembered the terrible arguments between his parents that had woken him as a child. Unable to hear the words, he had understood the hatred in the cadences of their voices. Those duets had climaxed in a harmonic hysteria and the bang of the front door, as one or the other of his parents stormed out of the house.

"I'll give this fellow thirty minutes," said Willi Keliber. "He's a wealthy man, he's come all the way from Dortmund to see me. It will save me seeing him tomorrow morning."

"If it develops into something important," said Max Breslow, "phone me at the hotel and let me know." He tried to hide from his voice any suggestion that he would infinitely prefer an evening on his own.

"Thirty minutes is all he gets," said Kleiber. "I'll see you here at eight-thirty tonight, and that's a promise."

Max Breslow took his leave. He sighed. With a person such as Willi Kleiber one had to be grateful for even a couple of hours off duty. Once back in the hotel, he made phone calls to California. It was Saturday morning in Los Angeles and his production manager was just beginning a day's work.

The Chancellery set was completed and they were about to take it from the workshops and store it ready to erect in the studio. The Kaiseroda mine-entrance set was being built, the plasterers would begin work on Tuesday morning and it would be ready for Friday. The location manager was excited by an office building near the Music Center. He said it would be suitable for the scene in which General Patton tells Eisenhower about the discovery of the treasures in the mine. Breslow listened to all the details of the production and found little to criticize or change.

Reassured by all that, Breslow took a bath and then ordered a small bottle of burgundy and a grilled steak from room service. He phoned his wife and told her that everything was all right. His wife was nervous about flying, and Breslow had got into the habit of phoning her after every flight, and phoning her every day he was away. It was an extravagance but it all went onto the film production account. They talked about the weather, the price of gasoline, the enormous estimate for repairing the Mercedes. Max listened dutifully. He had never told his wife much about the freeway accident, and certainly not told her that he'd pretended that it was an attempt on his life. Mrs. Breslow also made passing mention of Billy Stein. He was still out of town, she said. Mary had become moody and difficult because she had not heard from him.

Billy's father said merely that his son was in Europe on business; Mary had sobbed.

By now, Max Breslow had hoped that his daughter's infatuation would be waning but his wife said nothing to confirm this hope. On the contrary, Mrs. Breslow spoke rather warmly of the Stein boy. So even his own wife was not immune to the Stein kid's smooth charm and good looks. Perhaps that motivated Breslow to abandon the potato salad, bread, butter and cream untouched on his tray. It influenced him too when later he chose his favourite dark-blue worsted suit and knitted tie. Damn it, thought Breslow, perhaps he *would* go with Kleiber across to the casino at Evin. He could afford a small wager at the gaming tables, and who was to say he would not win?

Geneva was not a town that Breslow knew well. He kept to the most obvious route, going to the centre of town and looking for the *autoroute* signs. The lake was beautiful at this time of evening. Tourists crowded the promenade. He stopped his car at a pedestrian crossing where three young girls waited to cross.

One of them, in a see-through top, smiled at him. She had long hair and a round baby face with large eyes, and he was suddenly reminded of a girl he had once known in Dresden, before the war. It was strange how such memories surfaced without warning after being so long forgotten. Were those two pretty girls waiting for a ride to Lausanne . . . to dinner . . . to bed? As he pulled away again, the car spluttered. These damned rented cars were all alike—shiny and clean interiors but mechanically always second rate.

Once on the *autoroute* the car's blocked fuel line cleared and seemed to be all right again. He drove carefully, enjoying the darkening sky and the mountains which looked like the backdrop for grand opera.

He came into the little streets of Coppet very slowly and was looking for the high gates of the house when he noticed two grey Mercedes panel trucks. Two uniformed policemen came out of the gate as he got there. One staggered under the weight of some H & K machine pistols and the second man, an officer, carried a box of smoke grenades. Two of Kleiber's employees were handcuffed and waiting to get inside the second truck.

Breslow decided to carry on straight past the house. The policemen looked at him with interest and paused for a moment to see which way he would go. Breslow decided it would be better to seem equally surprised. He slowed almost to a stop, turned in his seat and stared at the policemen before continuing slowly down the street.

Without hurrying, Breslow turned up towards the main road. It was not the first time that he had come so near to disaster, he'd known many such close scrapes during the war, and learnt to restrain all temptation to run. It was a wise precaution. At the intersection with the main road, there was another police car waiting. Breslow decided to turn right and continue along the lakeside towards Lausanne. He went to Nyon before turning off to get to the *autoroute* and coming all the way back to Geneva again. It was only when he was back in the busy anonymity of the town centre that he was able to think properly. He decided against phoning either Dr. Böttger or his contact in Geneva. Who knew to what extent Operation Siegfried had been penetrated if the Swiss were taking Willi Kleiber's men into custody? He'd phone only Edward Parker, as Kleiber had requested.

When Max Breslow saw the signs for Geneva airport he moved into the exit lane. He had decided to go home to California.

## 40

Colonel Pitman drove the car after he left Madame Mauring's cake shop with Stein. Colonel Pitman no longer enjoyed driving, which was why he employed a chauffeur. Driving made him tense, and long journeys affected his bad back. A young man in a red Audi came weaving through the fast traffic carelessly enough to make Pitman brake sharply. He felt the bile rise to his throat, and winced with the pain of indigestion. The anxieties of the last few days had played havoc with his regulated working hours and disrupted his mealtimes. Now there was nothing he would like better than an Alka-Seltzer and a long doze in his favourite armchair. He rubbed his chest, hoping to alleviate the discomfort. He saw Stein looking at him; he smiled, but he couldn't help wondering why he was chauffeuring his ex-corporal. He should have told Stein to drive the car. Instead, Stein had got into the passenger seat and told him to get going. It had always been like this: Stein giving the orders and Pitman being carried along by his energy and determination. It had been like that the first day he had met Stein, the day Pitman had arrived at the battalion headquarters—a bone-rattling, dusty truck ride from Casablanca. Lieutenant Pitman was straight from the U.S.A., newly assigned to the tank-destroyer units that everyone was promising would knock hell out of the panzers of the Deutsche Afrika Korps.

Pitman was greeted by a snappy salute from the sentry at the gate. He felt important as he carried his kit up the hill to the tent marked REPORT HERE. It was a warm day. The tent smelt of new canvas and the waxy resin used to preserve it. The sun made the light inside the tent bright yellow, and there was the loud buzzing of flies. A middle-aged master sergeant sat at a table with a field telephone and a stateside newspaper. He was reading the sports results aloud, very slowly. Private Stein—plump, red-faced and perspiring—sat on an upturned box and punctuated the sports results with sneers, jeers and snorts. Lieutenant Pitman gave them a moment or two to acknowledge his presence but when they did not do so he said, "Sergeant, I'm Lieutenant Pitman. I'm looking for the battalion commander."

Master Sergeant Vanelli looked up and nodded. He folded his stateside newspaper and laid it on the table with the sort of reverence that such rare documents were given at that time, but he did not get to his feet. Stein, without moving from his position on the upended box, looked the officer up and down from the factory-fresh steel helmet and the pale skin unused to African sunshine to the newly issued brown boots. "Take my advice, Lieutenant," said Stein. "You get your leggings and your pistol strapped on and paint your bar on the front of your helmet *before* you see the CO."

"Is that your advice?" said Pitman coldly.

"This is General Patton's command: twenty-five-dollar fine for officers without their pistols; and officers without leggings pay fifteen bucks." Stein smiled and aimed a smack at a fly which had settled on his arm, but it flew away unharmed.

"Which is the colonel's tent?" Pitman asked, pointedly addressing the sergeant instead of Stein.

"The one with the rolled tent-sides," said Stein. "The colonel likes a draught, and don't mind the sand."

"Is this man your mouthpiece, Sergeant?" Pitman asked him.

"I guess he is," said the sergeant, as though he hadn't considered it before. "Charlie Stein kind of runs things for us up here."

Lieutenant Pitman looked at the two men, wondering whether to complain about their unsoldierly manner, but decided that it would be an unwise move for a newly assigned officer. He ducked his head to go out of the tent just as Stein called, "And ten bucks if you are not wearing a tie."

Pitman ignored him.

"Cut the speed a little," said Stein. "This is no time to get a ticket for speeding." Pitman glanced at the fat., balding man sitting beside him. Who would have guessed that their lives and fortunes could have become so interdependent? Stein was twisted round awkwardly as he pushed his brown shoulder bag on to the rear seat. The documents he placed on the floor behind him, and from time to time he reached back to touch them and reassure himself that they were still there.

"Sounds like it's all over for the bank," said Stein, hoping to be contradicted. But Colonel Pitman didn't argue the matter. "Sounds like they want us to be skinned alive," Stein added despondently. "You don't want to spend the next ten years arguing your way through law courts, do you?" He pressed the lighter button in the dashboard, just to check if it worked.

"It's a good car this," said Stein, approvingly stroking the leather.

"I tried to get inter-bank loans," said Pitman. "But none of the big banks are willing to cover us. Maybe they are scared of Creditanstalt. Maybe they are sore because we didn't syndicate the deal with them."

"And maybe they've been warned off by that bastard who set us up. Or Friedman or Dr. Böttger or one of those other people in on the swindle."

"Going away will not help me," said Pitman sadly. He stopped at the intersection from which a road led to the French border and the south side of the lake. Instead he turned the other way.

"Remember Petrucci? A little Sicilian kid . . . a machine gunner from one of the B-column vehicles which was knocked out ahead of us?"

Colonel Pitman rubbed his face reflectively. He could not remember.

"Delaney still sees him. He fixed me up with fake papers: Brazilian passport, driving licence, the whole works. He'd do the same for you, and we've got enough money here for both of us, Colonel. We'll split it down the middle, you and me."

"It's your savings, Charles. No, I couldn't."

"What do I want with savings?" said Stein. "How long have I got ahead of me? Ten years. . . . Or, if I lose fifty pounds and stick with the nuts and natural yoghurt—twenty. So how much do we need? I got over two million bucks here, Colonel. Stop thinking about the dog faces from the battalion. They're all OK, and they'd want you to say yes." But Pitman was lost in his own memories.

"I'm not sorry," answered the colonel at last. "If I could go back to that night round the stove when we first talked about it . . . I'd do the same thing all over again."

"Germany? You mean 1945? The night you came back from that blonde who worked in the mayor's office?"

Pitman nodded. "Remember the rain? I thought it would never stop. I had the worst jeep in the battalion that night and I had to nurse it halfway across Germany."

"You said you were in her apartment," said Stein. "That was only three blocks from the town hall. What are you talking about, halfway across Germany?"

Pitman continued to drive in silence as he remembered that night in the final days of the war in Europe. There was no blonde; there was just the general. He would never tell Stein the truth; he would never tell anyone.

"I know it's a big disappointment for you, Pitman," the general had said, "but it's the way the goddamn war is." The one-star general had modelled his appearance and behaviour upon General Patton, his commander. He did not have a pair of pearl-handled pistols at his waist—that would have been too obviously an imitation of his mentor—but he did keep his Colt .45 strapped on tight at all times and even here, miles away from the fighting, he kept his helmet on his head and a grenade clipped to his shoulder strap.

Outside it was raining, the sky streaked with pink and mauve, the last daylight almost gone. The endless convoys of supply trucks splashed through the mud in the dark pock-marked streets and crawled round piles of bricks and rubble, the result of a twenty-four-hour bombardment that had entombed half the German inhabitants in their cellars. "The war's nearly over," said Pitman. "Ever since the Rhine you've been promising me a chance to fight."

"See those trucks out there?" said the general, pointing with his cigar. "I'm trying to push half a million tons of material into position with quartermaster units that are nearly asleep on their feet. Some of those truck drivers have had no shut-eye for fifty-six hours, Pitman." Urgently, the general pushed some papers across his desk. "I've got medical officers yelling down the phone at me, I'm cannibalizing trucks so fast that I'm losing whole companies. My clerks are trying to sort 'Dangerous Cargo' from 'Valuable Cargo' and 'Immediately Vital Cargo' from 'Essential Cargo' . . . will you look at all this crap! Now you're telling me I've got to let you go play soldiers in the front line. Well, I'm telling you no, Pitman. Have you got that?"

"I'm a career officer, General. I need battle experience if I'm going to get any kind of promotion in the post-war army. We discussed it and you promised to help."

"You did all right, Pitman," said the general puffing on his cigar. "I made you a colonel and now you've got a battalion. That's not bad."

"I want to fight, General. You said you'd make sure I had my chance."

The general looked at him and blew smoke. Quietly he said, "You had your chance, Colonel. You had your chance at Kasserine, long before I was lucky enough to get over here. It was a big snafu, the way I read it; your guys took a powder and the Krauts just came rolling over our support areas. It's not the kind of lousy performance that makes me want to send you forward."

The bulbs in the desk lights flickered and went yellow and dim as the army engineers nursed the wrecked German power utilities. In the gloom the general's cigar glowed very bright before he added, "Do you know, I still have to take a ribbing from some of these crummy Brits? 'Remember Kasserine?' some Limey major says to me the other day, 'they put us into the line when you Yanks folded.' He says it like it was a joke, of course. That's the way the Brits always let you have the poison. It's a joke . . . so I have to laugh with that bastard. But I don't like it, Pitman, and when I hear about Kasserine I don't like you."

Pitman said nothing. There was nothing to say.

"Now you get back to your battalion HQ and keep your trucks moving. I'm due at army for a conference in two hours' time, and by then I'm going to have every last lousy truck in this man's army loaded and rolling."

Colonel Pitman got back to his battalion HQ at midnight. The heavy rain found its way through the canvas roof and ill-fitting side-flaps of his jeep, so that his short overcoat was soaking wet as he leant over the pot-bellied stove and warmed himself. "Am I supposed to be the commanding officer of this lousy battalion?" he complained rhetorically to his orderly room corporal. "So why do I get the worst jeep in the battalion?"

"You have trouble, Colonel?" Stein asked.

"That's one of the jeeps from that detached company we took over," said Pitman. "All those vehicles are unreliable. Make sure you don't give me one of those again. Got it?"

"You been with the general, sir?"

"I've been in bed with the blonde chick we saw this morning in the mayor's office. Why do you think I asked you for a bottle of scotch?"

"For the general maybe," said Stein. He was pouring boiling water onto coffee grounds and the aroma emerged suddenly. "You took a bottle for the general last week when you went to see him. I thought maybe you were trying to get detached for a spell with those armoured division guys we fixed up with extra gas and rations."

"Do you read all my private correspondence. Corporal Stein?"

"I sure do, Colonel. I figure that's what you need me for. You want some of this coffee?"

"Yes, I do . . . with sugar and cream."

Stein put the steaming coffee before his colonel. It was in an antique porcelain cup discovered in the wreckage. Colonel Pitman sniffed at the coffee and drank some.

Stein watched him with close interest. "So you weren't with the general tonight?"

"I was laying that little blonde number in a top back room in one of those apartment houses near the delousing centre."

"It's not like you, Colonel," said Stein with polite interest.

"Well, from now on it's going to be like me," said Colonel Pitman. "From now on I'm going to keep the army in perspective, and I'm going to start counting off the days, like you do, Corporal."

"You show me a way to get out of the army tonight, Corporal, and I'd take it."

"I might be able to do something like that," said Stein. "And I might be able to show you how to take enough dough to retire with."

"What are you talking about, Stein?"

"Not Uncle Sam's money, Colonel; Nazi gold stashed not far from here. Looks like we are going to get the job of hauling it to Frankfurt."

"Gold?"

"Millions and millions of bucks, Colonel. This lousy war is just about over. I was sitting here on my own tonight, and I was thinking about Aram and the old days back in North Africa . . . and I began to wonder about something. Could I just run over this idea with you, Colonel? In strictest confidence . . ."

Colonel Pitman sat down on a packing case near the stove. His coat was steaming as the heat penetrated his damp uniform. "You sure could, Corporal. I've never been in a better mood to listen to any proposition that comes my way."

"The boys always trusted you, Colonel," said Stein.

Pitman's memories faded as he reminded himself that this was 1979 and half a lifetime had passed since the day they made that fateful decision. "No one ever wanted to vote you out of office."

"I'm proud of that," admitted Pitman. "1952 was the toughest year . . . three of the boys died in as many months."

"Tricky Richards, Corporal Arbenz who had the car accident and Moose Menzies. Yes, I remember," said Stein. "Yeah, that was a real bad year."

"I paid out the families without having any proper authority from the syndicate," said Colonel Pitman. "It was complicated. We were deeply committed to fixed-interest investments."

"You did wonders, Colonel."

"I've always tried to be fair," said Pitman. He stopped at a traffic light. "I was never a great financial brain, or very good at administration. You know that I was never much of a soldier. . . ."

"Come on, Colonel! You . . ."

"No. We're getting too old to go on deceiving ourselves. I was not much of an officer. It was you and Master Sergeant Vanelli who kept us going. Did I tell you that Vanelli died?"

"Yes, Colonel, you did."

"You kept us going. You understood the men better than I ever did."

"We were all too gung-ho," said Stein.

"I was a hot-head trying to get the Congressional Medal of Honor in my first hour of combat. Major Carson realized that—he warned me against myself."

"You nearly made it, Colonel."

Pitman allowed himself a faint smile. "Yep, I nearly did, Chuck. The trouble was, I wiped out half the company in the attempt."

"It's time you forgot all that, Colonel. You did what seemed best at the time."

"Some fine men died that day, Corporal." Colonel Pitman's eyes half closed as he relived the worst and the best moments of his life. "Your brother and Major Carson. Arias who tried to get back to the machine gun. Kaplan and Klein—next-door neighbours who signed on together and stayed together right until the end. Sergeant Scott, who didn't know how to drive that damned truck but wouldn't get out of the driver's seat. Sergeant Packer who said he'd shoot the last man to go forward . . ."

"And then trod on the S mine," said Stein.

"Heroes," said Pitman.

"Not heroes," said Stein calmly. "Not cowards, Colonel. Not cowards the way that the newspapers and the Limeys and the brass wanted to pretend they were. But not heroes either. It's time to face up to that, Colonel."

"We were raw troops. Even during our combat training we didn't have more than half a dozen men on the training staff who'd ever heard a shot fired in anger. What chance did we stand against those German veterans?"

"We ran," said Stein softly. "We ran, Colonel."

"It was politics. Washington wanted Americans in action and wanted them commanded by Eisenhower. It was all part of the political plan to put Eisenhower into the job of Supreme Commander Europe in time for D-day. Without some American blood spilt, the Limeys would have got Montgomery into that Supreme Commander slot."

"Ike did a good job," said Stein. He could not

share the colonel's bitterness. "With that son of a bitch Monty in command we'd still be there, waiting to start the invasion."

"Why did they wait so long before bringing Georgie Patton in to command the corps?" said the Colonel. "The same of that damned week still remains with me. I remember it every day. Can you understand that, Corporal?" It was "Corporal" now, and Pitman's voice had that shrill ring to it that Stein had not heard for nearly four decades.

"The top brass were right," said Colonel Pitman. "I cursed them every day for years, but they were right. We would never have had the guts to go into battle again. We were write-offs. . . ."

"Retreads," Stein corrected him. "OK, so we were humiliated—tankers dumped into a redeployment depot, then relegated to the quartermaster corps—but we did what had to be done. We gave a few years of our life, and fought the war that put the Nazis out of business."

"It was all I ever wanted," said Pitman softly. "That commission in a first-class unit with men I liked and respected. It broke my heart to see them driving those damned trucks."

"And what about the war?" Stein said consolingly. "We wouldn't have got a few million bucks in bullion if we'd stayed with those tank destroyers."

"I had nothing to lose, that's why," said Pitman, as if an explanation was being forced from him. "Could I have gone to lunch at the University Club and returned those stares I would have got after my friends read about Kasserine?"

"I feel no guilt," said Stein stoically. "We faced the best the Krauts could throw at us, and we ran. But we slowed them up a little, Colonel, don't ever forget that."

"Don't fool yourself, Charles. They brushed us aside like bed bugs in a whore house." Pitman reached up to adjust the driving mirror.

For a while the two men sat in silence, Pitman driving with exaggerated care, while Stein stared out at the suburbs of Geneva with unseeing eyes. On that warm Saturday evening in August everyone who could afford it was spending the weekend in the countryside or along the lake. These suburban streets were silent and empty.

"You heard Major Carson order me to turn back," said Pitman suddenly. "You heard him, didn't you?"

"You were obsolved, Colonel. I gave evidence to the little curly-haired captain from the judge advocate's staff who flew down from Algiers. Delaney told him the same. You remember."

"Goddamn it, Corporal," said Pitman in an uncharacteristic display of bad temper. "I'm not asking you whether you got me off the hook. Answer my question: did you *hear* Major Carson or didn't you? I need to know." He was shouting by now.

Stein looked out of the window. It was all a long time ago. What the hell difference did it make? In Stein's world, trouble arrived was dealt with and then forgotten as soon as possible. Why travel back into the past to rake over old worries, when there were so many right here and now, just screaming for attention?

Stein looked at his colonel—his bald head made ridiculous by the curly hair around his ears—and then looked back at the wide, graceless streets of the city. By now, Stein no longer really remembered how much he had heard, and he no longer cared. He said, "Sure I heard him, Colonel. You didn't want to pull back but he insisted."

"That's right," said Pitman triumphantly. "That's exactly what happened. I was obeying orders."

Stein nodded. He had other more pressing things on his mind than the colonel's battle with his conscience. "Maybe we both should scram," said Stein. "We'll both go to Mexico or Canada. You wait there while I go to New Jersey using my Brazilian passport. I'll take passport photos of you with me, see Petrucci and bring passport and paper for you."

"Shall I keep on the airport road?" said Pitman. He bit his lip. Why did he always ask Stein what to do?"

Stein took his time in replying. Every damned road out of Geneva, except the north lakeside road and the *autoroute* alongside it, led into France. Stein wondered whether the French Compagnies Républicaines de Sécurité men who policed the border crossings would have received orders to detain them. Did the French work that closely with the British? And what would they charge them with? Perhaps the French would simply confiscate the Hitler Minutes as contraband and then deport them; he had heard of such things happening to people time and time again. The Compagnies Républicianes de Sécurité were a law unto themselves. "The *autoroute,*" said Stein.

"I think we are being followed," said Colonel Pitman, eyeing the mirror. "The same car has been behind us ever since we left Rollins. It's a white Mini."

"Put your foot down. It's fast, this Jaguar, isn't it?"

"I doubt we could pull far away from him," said Pitman. "I'm not any kind of ace driver. I suppose he must have seen us." He flicked the right indicator and watched anxiously until the indicator of the car behind them was also flashing. "He's following us," said Pitman. "There's no doubt now." He felt another twinge of pain and rubbed his chest. If only he could belch as readily as Stein could.

"Stop on the *autoroute,*" said Stein. "I'll take care of him. Then we'll come back to the airport afterwards."

"We'll see if we can pull away a little," said Pitman. He slowed for the Lausanne *autoroute* turn-off and swung the wheel over. There was a soft squeal of brakes and the car behind followed closely. Once on the big highway, Pitman put his foot down; all thoughts of indigestion pains vanished. His Jaguar was a new and powerful model with only three thousand miles on the clock. Kept in perfect mechanical order, the car responded to the open throttle and leapt forward like a racehorse. The car following them was equally new but it had been ill used by nearly one hundred drivers with little in common except a careless indifference about things borrowed. The Mini spluttered and objected as the driver brought the speedometer needle past sixty. Only with difficulty could he keep behind the Jaguar.

The cars were touching eighty miles an hour when Colonel John Elroy Pitman the Third suffered his third, and terminal, heart attack.

# 41

Willi Kleiber hated to be alone. After his friend Max Breslow had gone back to his hotel. Kleiber went upstairs to the little room which he used as an office and called the phone number that his new client had left with him.

In spite of Willi Kleiber's off-hand remarks to Breslow, he was in fact extremely pleased at the prospect of working for Helmut Krebs, who was one of the richest men in West Germany. He owned the greater part of a chain of supermarkets that were to be found all over Europe. In the last few years, he had begun manufacturing and packaging many of the goods sold there. His own brands of instant coffee, yoghurt and soft drinks were as good as any of the better-known labels and always just a few pfennigs cheaper.

It was the Krebs family background that attracted Kleiber to the idea of having him as a client. Kreb's brother was an ambassador, and his wife and sister were both well-known patrons of the theatre. Some member of the Krebs family was usually represented at any chic international social gathering. Such a client—who mingled in a world where widespread concern about kidnapping, murder and blackmail was on everyone's mind—could open unlimited business opportunities to a company which traded on its capacity to reassure potential victims.

Kleiber was not surprised therefore to find that Krebs's confidential secretary was guarded in his response to Kleiber's suggestion that he should see Mr. Krebs at once, rather than wait until the appointment they had made for the next morning.

"Mr. Krebs has a dinner engagement," said the secretary.

"So do I," said Kleiber. "I must leave by eight o'clock."

"Mr. Krebs is having dinner in Venice," said the secretary coldly. "Venice, Italy," he added in case there should be any doubt. "He will be using his private jet." Nothing could have been better calculated to sharpen Kleiber's interest.

He told Kleiber to hold the line and it was several minutes before he returned to say, "Very well. Mr. Krebs will see you this evening. Be at Geneva airport at six o'clock sharp. You can speak with Mr. Krebs on the aircraft, which will bring you back to Geneva again at seven-thirty. I'll arrange a car to take you to your appointment if you wish."

"No need," said Kleiber. "I'll use my own car."

"I'll ask the pilot to send someone to collect you. Wait by the bar on the departures level and one of the staff will take you through the formalties. Be sure you bring your passport. You'll have to clear customs and immigration of course."

"I understand," said Kleiber, although the self-importance of the man at the other end was intolerable to him. It was always secretaries and clerks and doormen who were so rude, thought Kleiber; it was likely that Mr. Krebs himself would prove to be gracious and charming.

"One more thing, Mr. Kleiber," said the voice at the other end. "I am responsible for Mr. Kreb's personal safety and security. You will make quite sure that you are not carrying anything that could possibly be used as a weapon. I include even small penknives or boxes of snuff in that category. You might be asked to submit to a body search. You are a professional, I believe? I'm sure you'll understand the reasons for such precautions." His voice made it clear that he did not care at all whether Kleiber understood.

"I do," said Kleiber. He kept his temper under a tight rein. He guessed that Krebs had been threatened by one of the lunatic left-wing student groups. Perhaps it was not going to be a divorce case. Perhaps it was going to be something more important than that.

"Six o'clock sharp at the bar on the departures level, Geneva airport. The crew member will be wearing a plain uniform with peaked cap."

"I'll be there," said Kleiber, and tried to hang up before the secretary did, but lost the race. He smiled to himself. It would be amusing to be able to tell Max that he had been to Venice, Italy, since seeing him this afternoon. He consulted his watch. There would be enough time for a game of tennis before he showered and got ready for the meeting. He wondered which of his staff he would be able to beat soundly. Willi Kleiber only enjoyed tennis when he won a resounding victory.

Promptly at six, Kleiber arrived at the rendezvous. He was wearing a grey, lightweight, wool-and-polyester suit, white shirt, English club tie and polished side-zip ankle boots. The uniformed man who met him nodded deferentially and escorted him through the special customs and immigration room provided for private aircraft movements. A blue Ford Escort was waiting to take them out to the far side of the airport.

Kleiber looked at his watch and nodded in admiration at such efficiency. It was only fifteen minutes past six when he stepped into the Jet Commander. This eight-seater was one of the older types of twin-jet executive aircraft, but the sleek design and its blue and grey livery made Kleiber decide that it was one of the most beautiful aircraft he had ever seen. Inside, the leatherwork was blue, with grey carpeting to match the exterior colouring. There was that fugitive smell of real hide, metal polish and warm oil and some other undefinable aroma which distinguishes expensive sports cars from the mass-produced imitations, and there was the sound of ice cubes rattling gently in Waterford glass.

"Would you take a seat at the very front, Mr. Kleiber," said the man who had escorted him through the immigration and formalities. "Mr. Krebs is already aboard. He'll come forward to join you in a few minutes."

Kleiber touched the leatherwork with sensuous appreciation. The aircraft had been designed to provide the passengers with a clear view; the leading edges of the wings were to the rear of the rearmost windows. From here he would have a fine view of the landscape.

"Champagne cocktail, sir?" A steward appeared with some glasses on a silver tray. Kleiber nodded, and a large cut-glass goblet was placed on his armrest, together with a linen napkin and a platter of thin water biscuits. Kleiber twisted in his seat to look for Mr. Krebs but the rear of the passenger cabin was curtained off. "Please fasten your seat belt, sir. We're about to take off."

Kleiber nodded and settled back into his seat again. This was the life he wanted. He closed his eyes; for a moment this was his private jet and beside him there was some big-breasted girl accompanying him on a weekend of hot sun, cool ocean and crisply laundered bedding. Without opening his eyes he sipped more of his champagne cocktail.

The motors of the aircraft rose in pitch to an ear-splitting scream and then, brakes released, the jet ran forward and onto the perimeter track. Kleiber sat back and drank his champagne. He could see the pilot talking into his microphone to clear the take-off with flying control. At the end of the runway, the plane rocked on its wheel brakes for a moment. Then, with engines at full revolutions, it started down the runway, gathering speed until it hurled itself into the air.

Kleiber looked round. The cabin attendant, and the man who had greeted him by name, were strapped into their seats two rows behind him. There was no one else in sight. He rested his head back on the seat and looked out of the window. The landscape tilted away more and more as the jet pulled its nose back into a steep climb, to gain altitude for the flight over the Alps.

The sun painted the peaks bright yellow as the sheer-sided valleys sank into limpid pools of blue shadow. There was nothing comforting about such beauty, thought Kleiber; it was daunting. For countless years the slowly moving glaciers had chiselled at the mountains; now only the very hardest crystalline substructure remained. It was just one more example of the way that nature favoured the strongest—or the most adaptable. The cocktail contained too much brandy and not enough bitters for his taste, but no matter. He looked at the spectacle below them. A direct route to Venice would take them right over the highest peaks of the Alps. He spotted the Matterhorn, its gaunt, angular shape like some hungry beggar among its plump, snowy brethren.

Kleiber passed a hand over his eyes and felt a feverish sweat upon his forehead. Even the champagne glass pressed there did not cool his brain. He felt giddy and tried to hold his drink more tightly, but in spite of his grip the glass fell from his twitching fingers and smashed against the metal bulkhead. He saw the bubbling champagne splash across the toes of his boots and felt the nausea and the curious sensation of endlessly falling that he had known before only after reckless drinking. He pushed a hand over his mouth as he felt the vomit; he could not undo the buckle. His tie seemed to be choking him and he felt the sweat dripping down his face. He reached forward to . . . he reached forward . . . and then there was only falling and blackness, and eventually only blackness.

"He's gone, Melvin. Where in hell did you get those Mickey Finns?"

"New York. A bartender on Third Avenue. Used to be a singles joint but lately it's turned really rough."

"Remind me not to go there."

"They wouldn't let you in, Todd. You got to be eighteen." Kalkhoven's assistant grinned. The pilot was looking round. Melvin Kalkhoven gave him a thumbs up and the pilot began talking to the ground, asking for a change of route to Frankfurt am Main.

Todd Wynn began to pick up the broken pieces of glass from the smashed champagne goblet. Kalkhoven went back to get the U.S. Army blankets and the stretcher. By the time they got to Frankfurt, the unconscious Wilhelm Kleiber would have to be ready for transfer to a U.S. Air Force medical transport aircraft. The documentation was all ready. Kleiber had become Captain Martin Moore, an infantry officer stationed in Berlin, now suffering from an unidentified virus disease and being returned to a specialist hospital in the U.S.A. for tests.

The decision to abduct Wilhelm Kleiber had been taken at the highest level of American intelligence. On Wednesday, August 1, the deputy director of Central Intelligence had taken what by now was being called "the Parker File" to the director's seventh-floor office in the CIA building in suburban Langley, Virginia.

The transcript of Kleiber's conversation with Parker, recorded the previous evening, was an important factor in the decision.

The deputy director asked for freedom to handle this case in the way that the project chairman proposed, but the involvement of Yuriy Grechko—a Soviet embassy official—in Edward Parker's espionage activities meant that the decision would have to be agreed to by the President's closest advisers. The director discussed the file with his deputy for ninety minutes. At the end of what was actually a briefing, the director left, using his private key-operated elevator and chauffeur-driven black Lincoln for a pre-lunch meeting with the Secretary of Defense and the President's national security adviser. Eventually it was decided that President Carter's well-publicized successes with the Soviet leaders at the SALT talks in June were not a good reason for modifying in any way the CIA's actions to limit Russian espionage against the U.S. The CIA was given permission to act against the spies "with maximum vigour."

The new importance that the project had now been given, and the need to tackle it on a worldwide basis, meant moving it out of the Domestic Operations Division and giving it a new file number. However, the project chairman and Sam Seymour, the file editor, retained their roles. So did Melvin Kalkhoven, the field agent.

It was Kalkhoven who planned the seizure of Wilhelm Hans Kleiber. Kalkhoven flew from Washington to Frankfurt on the night of Wednesday, August 1, in order to obtain the full cooperation of the German security service. The BND's officer in Hamburg (who was responsible for direct contact with London and liaison with the British Secret Intelligence Service) was not told of this development. Neither was the British SIS informed. As with all such high-priority matters, it was dealt with on a strict "need-to-know" basis.

Melvin Kalkhoven made urgent contact with a well-known German business man—Helmut Krebs—and asked him if his name might be used in connection with a security operation. Krebs, a man of impeccable credentials, well known in Washington, readily gave his consent. Together Krebs and Kalkhoven arranged how phone calls should be placed to discover the whereabouts of Wilhelm Kleiber. Repeated urgent messages left with Kleiber's office and at his home finally produced results.

There are thirty-six telephone links between Germany and Switzerland. Each link has five hundred telephone lines. Thus it was necessary to tap—or at least monitor calls on—some eighteen thousand separate phone lines during the period when Kleiber's office staff or family would be expected to pass on to him the fictitious message from Krebs.

The telephone call that Kleiber received from his Munich office enabled the telephone monitoring department—Amt 3—of the federal intelligence service of West Germany to give CIA field agent Kalkhoven a transcript of Kleiber's conversation and the address of the lakeside house near Geneva where he took the call. It confirmed that Kleiber had swallowed the story about Krebs. The CIA office in Frankfurt, having already secured a luxuriously fitted Jet Commander, now had it flown to Geneva and put a CIA crew on standby there.

Kalkhoven's brief included a strict instruction that the final phase of the operation must have top-level approval. So, at 5 a.m., Friday, August 3, the duty officer on the Operations floor at Langley received Kalkhoven's coded telex marked NIACT (to get action before the following morning). Decoded, the message read, "He whom thou blessest is blessed, and he whom thou cursest is cursed."

The seriousness of abducting a German national from Switzerland, and the repercussions it could bring, meant another long meeting with the deputy director and the project chairman. The reply did not reach Geneva until the following day. It was 2:25 p.m. on Saturday, not much more than two hours before Kleiber phoned asking for an immediate meeting, when Washington's reply got to Kalkhoven. The text of the cable from Langley approved of the Kleiber kidnap plan and revealed a new dimension of the project chairman. "Whosoever shall compell thee to go a mile, go with him twain." But, as Kalkhoven pointed out, that is New Testament.

By the time the prostrate body of Wilhelm Kleiber was loaded into the Military Air Transport Service Boeing C-135 at Frankfurt, Melvin Kalkhoven was holding a handful of messages and instructions. The CIA knew about the raid that the Swiss police had made upon Kleiber's lakeside house, and their contact inside the Swiss intelligence service office in Berne believed that the tipoff had come from London.

Kalkhoven sat at the purser's desk at the rear of the big Boeing transport. The cabin ahead of him was dark, except for the dim red safety bulbs and a crack of yellow light round the crew-compartment door at the very front. He had a small reading light by which to read the documentation. His assistant came back from checking that Kleiber was still unconscious. They had administered an anaesthetic that would have to be renewed before they got to Andrews Air Force Base in Maryland.

"What will they do with this guy, Melvin?"

"Looks like there'll be enough evidence to hang that California murder on him."

"Don't kid me, Melvin. We didn't snatch this guy in order to deliver him to the Justice Department. And, if he goes into court on a murder rap, he's going to complain mightily about the travel arrangements we made for him. The agency would end up with a lot of egg on its face, Melvin, so why not level with me?"

"I don't run the company," said Kalkhoven. "I just work for it. This operation has become very high powered. I have to get written permission from Langley every time I defecate."

"You think they're going to turn him round?"

"Give him a job with us, you mean? I sure as hell hope not, Todd. I don't want to be working next to a murderous bastard like that guy out there."

"New policies mean new allies, new allies mean new friends. That's the name of the game, Melvin, you only have to read your newspapers to see that." Todd looked round to see Melvin Kalkhoven's face. It was underlit by the low-voltage desk light; hunched over the sloping desk, he looked more than ever like some nineteenth-century Bible-puncher, thought Wynn.

" 'Forsake not an old friend, for the new is not comparable to him; a new friend is as new wine; when it is old, thou shalt drink it with pleasure.' "

Todd Wynn smiled nervously and wondered if Melvin Kalkhoven knew that people called him "the Bible-basher." Probably he did; he always seemed to know more than he revealed.

## 42

London's man in Geneva was a desiccated-looking ex-policeman named Hugo Koch. He had made a name for himself in the Zurich police force until, in 1965, a scandal involved him with the seventeen-year-old daughter of a senior police official. Koch resigned from the force. Now, aged forty-nine, he lived and worked in a small apartment in suburban Geneva, collecting debts, serving legal papers on reluctant defendants and following errant wives. It was not work that Hugo Koch enjoyed very much, but then he had never enjoyed any work very much; Koch was by nature gloomy. He did not drink, he did not smoke and, since that ignominious affair in Zurich, his relationships with women had been dispassionate.

Koch had been pleased when, in 1969, a man describing himself as an agent of the CIA offered him a retainer. Koch agreed and served his masters well. They had never called upon him to do more than collect or deliver packets, observe and report on selected individuals, or provide postal addresses. No task had given him the slightest moral qualm or compromised his allegiance to Switzerland, which he loved with a constancy that many of the women in his life had yearned for and failed to get. Sometimes he wondered whether he earned his keep for his foreign masters, but payments went regularly into his bank account and there were no complaints. Over the years, Koch had come to realize that he was employed not by the Americans but by the British Secret Intelligence

Service; but that was the sort of discretion that Koch's Swiss soul found easy to understand.

Once told to follow and report the movements of Colonel Pitman, Hugo Koch was worth every penny of his payments from London. Whatever shortcomings he might have shown in scientific criminal investigation were more than compensated for by his skill on the streets. He was an instinctive cop who could shake a stolen purse out of a football crowd, or guess his way to a confession by looking at the suspects. But he had never enjoyed being a police driver and the Mini he had rented for this surveillance was not to his liking. Koch saw Colonel Pitman indicate a right turn and moved his own car into the filter lane. The two cars turned the corner at the Rue de Monthoux in close succession, and turned again at the quay to follow the lake.

It was a good run Pitman gave him and he almost enjoyed it. The rented Mini was surprisingly fast and the burst of speed improved its performance. Too much town driving had coked up the valves and dirtied the plugs. Now, with his foot well down, Koch was keeping pace with the Jaguar while leaving plenty of space between them.

When Colonel John Elroy Pitman suffered his heart attack his hands loosened from the steering wheel and the car mounted the curb of the central divide, jolting both men in the Jaguar up against its roof. The car hit the fence and tore its way through the white stakes like a band-saw through matchsticks, tossing them high into the air and sprinkling them across the oncoming traffic.

The Jaguar lurched further across the grassy median until, still travelling at over seventy miles an hour, it hit the steel girders which are the standard safety fitting on all Swiss *autoroutes*. There was a deafening crash as the Jaguar struck a shower of white-hot sparks from the barrier and bounced back onto the highway again. The glass began to break as the car's frame distorted. As it crashed back on to the highway, the jolt of the high curb was enough to demolish the front nearside tyre and the car tipped down a second time to begin a roll. Askew in the centre of the highway, still travelling very fast, it went over onto its side and then, with another spray of sparks and a terrible scream, it slid along on its roof, scattering door handles, wipers and hub caps in its wake. Like some huge missile, the wrecked Jaguar hit the verge. Still it kept going, throwing into the air a cannonade of ploughed turf and chopped grass until it came to a final halt in a cloud of steam as the radiator boiled and the horn jammed screaming like a tortured baboon.

Behind the Jaguar, Hugo Koch was fighting the wheel as pieces of debris came flying towards him. A hub cap clanged down on to the front of the car and hit the windscreen with a resonant clang. Koch threw an arm across his face but by a miracle the glass did not break and the silver hub cap flashed in the light and skidded off over his roof with a noise like a pealing of church bells.

Ahead of him, the Jaguar came careering back across the highway only inches ahead of his front wheels. As its windscreen shattered, a shower of broken glass rattled over him like a snow flurry. The cars banged together. He hit the brake.

Koch glanced in his mirror to see the chaos of the littered highway. As he watched, an articulated truck hit a Ford Cortina. It went sliding cross the road out of control, its tyres exploding. As the metal wheels engaged the road surface it began a violent spin. The articulated truck began to jack-knife.

Koch almost stood up as he applied his whole weight to the brake pedal. Wtih a scream of brakes and a smell of scorched rubber he brought his Mini to a halt at the roadside. Behind him the articulated truck hit the barrier with a clang that deafened him and then came past him out of control like some huge building roaring down the highway as loud as a low-flying jet.

Koch ran to the Jaguar. Pitman was strapped in but his legs and arms were twisted and lifeless and his face was bloodied. Stein's weight and bulk had jammed him down against the floor. This saved him from anything worse than a blow to the head which had caused him to lose consciousness. Koch opened the doors and dragged the two limp figures on to the roadway. He looked at Pitman; the old fellow was dead, but Stein's pulse was firm enough and although his respiration was quick and shallow, it was regular. Stein groaned; he seemed to be regaining consciousness. Koch turned him on his side so there was no danger of his swallowing his tongue and choking on it, then he went back to the wreckage of the Jaguar to see what was inside it. He had only a few moments with the car before it caught fire.

On that evening of Saturday, August 4, the Geneva to Lausanne side of the *autoroute* was closed for four hours while the police cleared up the mess. Hugo Koch helped as much as he could. He recognized two of the policemen and contributed an excellent eyewitness description of the collision, although he omitted to mention that he was in any way connected with the occupants of the wrecked car. Neither did he mention the brown canvas bag or the packet he had taken from Pitman's Jaguar before it caught fire.

Hugo Koch opened the packet he'd taken from the Pitman car and then telephoned London from a call-box. He had been told that was the best way in an emergency. The SIS exchange called Boyd Stuart's home and connected the caller to him. Koch explained briefly what he had seen.

"My orders concerned only Colonel Pitman," said Koch. "Well, he is dead. His white Jaguar is a complete wreck. It burst into flames, but I managed to get Pitman out before that happened. There was a passenger with him, a fat man—it sounds like Charles Stein from your description."

"What happened to Stein?"

Koch shed a little of his stolid Swiss composure. "I've just been in a bad traffic pile-up, mister. There were bodies everywhere—I saw a whole family laid out by the roadside—I didn't go round doing a body count, and there was not much time for careful detective work. . . . I don't know what happened to Stein. He'd gone when I went back to search him."

"OK. OK. But you searched Pitman?"

"Credit cards, some money, passports. Nothing unusual. I put it all back."

"You did a great job, Hugo. Go home and get some sleep. . . ."

"Very well," said Koch unenthusiastically. "And I have a packet here. The car was on fire and the trunk was locked, so I didn't get inside that, you understand."

"Packet?"

"It was under Colonel Pitman's seat in the white Jaguar. I thought it might be something you were interested in. A sealed plastic bag containing an old wartime dossier. There are U.S. Army inventory tags on it. One label reads, 'Merkers H-6750. Typewritten documents, German language, approx. 300 pages.' It's very old. The car burnt afterwards so no one is going to miss it. I hope I did right."

"You got it out of Pitman's white Jaguar?"

"You get an instinct about the things that are worthwhile. It was within reach but out of sight—that's usually a sign of something people value. If it had been on the rear shelf I wouldn't have burnt my arm getting to it." Koch yawned. "Do you want me to send it? I haven't opened it."

"Leave it sealed, and don't let it out of your sight, Koch. I'll get the first flight tomorrow and come straight to your home. Meanwhile don't go out, not even to get cigarettes, you understand?"

"I don't smoke," said Koch.

Boyd Stuart timed the call, reported the message in somewhat cryptic terms, to the duty officer and told him to alert the SIS section in Los Angeles to the fact that the department had lost contact with Stein. There was always the chance that he'd sooner or later go through Los Angeles International Airport. He also asked the duty officer to arrange a seat on the early flight to Geneva. After that he reset the alarm and climbed back into bed with Kitty King.

"Who was it?" she asked. She reached for him sleepily.

"Wrong number."

"You rotten liar," she said.

"It was the girl upstairs needing help with her zipper."

"You bastard," she giggled as they embraced. "Stop it! Your hands are too cold!"

Even travelling by the first morning flight out of London, it was almost mid-morning on Sunday, August 5, by the time Stuart got to Hugo Koch's apartment in Geneva. It was on the second floor of a block which mostly housed dentists and lawyers. They were large apartments, designed so that the occupants could live and work from the same premises. The street was empty apart from a few churchgoers.

The outer door, bearing Hugo Koch's name on a neat black plastic rectangle, was unlocked. As Stuart pushed it open, a buzzer sounded down the hall, and Hugo Koch emerged wiping his hands on a kitchen towel.

"My name is Stuart . . . from London."

"Koch. Hugo Koch. I got the message. There is coffee ready. Will you have some?"

In the room that Koch used as an office, there was a tray already prepared with big flower-patterned cups and saucers, linen napkins and a jug of cream, with chocolate biscuits arranged geometrically on a side plate with a doily. It was as if all Koch's efforts had gone into the elaborate preparation of this snack, for the rest of the room was austere, not to say shabby. The tubular office chairs needed repairs to their upholstery, and the wallpaper was old and faded. On the wall there was a framed watercolour painting of the Alps and a calendar advertising a watch company. On top of the metal filing cabinets that lined one side of the large office room there were piles of documents and old newspapers. An antique pendulum clock on the wall was silent, its hands set to twelve o'clock. Koch returned from the kitchen with a blue china jug of coffee.

"You weren't hurt in the accident?" said Stuart politely as he accepted the coffee and poured himself a little cream.

"I spent a year driving a police car," said Koch. "I keep a stretch of road between me and the cars ahead."

"Can I look at the documents? Umm, good coffee."

"They have already gone to London."

"Gone?"

"He was here before seven. Luckily I'm an early riser. I was having breakfast."

"I was on the earliest flight."

Koch shrugged. "There are other ways . . . private planes, military planes. . . ."

"Who?" said Stuart.

"An old man, very tall, long hair over his ears. Ryden, he said his name was, although that never means much in this business." Koch smiled to show that he suspected that Boyd Stuart was also a false name. "I checked back with London and they confirmed he was O.K. He signed my receipt. It was all in order, I assure you."

"Ryden?"

"Hearing aid in his right ear. Doesn't fit properly, he's always having to push it back into his ear again. Too old for this sort of work, if you ask me, but I suppose an old fellow like that can do a messenger job."

"Yes," said Stuart, registering the fact that Koch regarded him as no more than a messenger too. Nearby church bells pealed loudly across the quiet trafficless city.

"So there's nothing else?"

"Nothing else," said Koch. "I'm sorry about that. By the time this old fellow arrived, I knew you would have left. Have a chocolate biscuit."

"Thanks," said Stuart. So his father-in-law had got the transcript of the departmental phone call to him and acted upon it immediately. He was a cunning old bastard who revelled in the lies and deceptions of his craft. Koch had no idea that his "messenger" was "super-spook"—the Director General—in person.

Stuart looked round the room. He knew the sort of life that resident operatives enjoyed and he did not envy Koch. Behind Koch's desk the kitchen door had swung open and Stuart could see inside. There was a sink filled with dirty saucepans and dishes. He could see the flower-patterned cups from which the DG had no doubt had his early-morning coffee. On the kitchen table a packet of Bircher Muesli and a large economy-size tin of Nescafé had been pushed aside to make room for a brown canvas shoulder bag and what had been its contents. There were two factory-wrapped shirts and men's underclothes, a pair of sunglasses and a packet of Roger & Gallet soap, sandalwood perfumed. Stuart wondered if Koch was preparing for an overnight trip; he found it strange that he should have only new linen and that he should be so extravagant in his choice of soap, but Stuart had long since found that even the most ordinary mortals display surprising foibles.

There was of course no way for Stuart to know that this inscrutable man had just come into possession of well over two million dollars' worth of Hoffmann-La Roche bearer shares, to say nothing of a serviceable Brazilian passport which would, after a little work by a man he knew, be good enough to provide him with a new identity.

"A little more coffee?" said Hugo Koch solicitously. "I sometimes think I'm getting too old for this sort of work. Do you ever have that feeling?"

"Almost every day," said Boyd Stuart.

## 43

Although Stein's injuries from the motor accident seemed no more than superficial, he never fully recovered from the concussion caused by the blow to his head. His eyes saw the continuing world of 1979 but his mind recognized only the memories, fears and dreams of long ago.

He began to regain consciousness just as Koch was leaving. He looked at the burning wreckage of Colonel Pitman's Jaguar and at the corpse of the colonel, but he saw the blazing jeep under the African sky.

"Aram," called Stein. "Major Carson is dead. Stay where you are, I'm coming, Aram." Very slowly he got to his feet. The police were on the scene by now, but they were all busy coning off the wreckage and trying to slow down the traffic. They had no time to attend to Stein.

Concussed and confused, Stein made his way along the *autoroute,* staring uncomprehending at the passing traffic and sometimes calling for his brother. A motorist, having passed the scene of the accident, slowed and backed up for Stein. "Airport," said Stein, not once but half a dozen times. The Geneva-Lausanne *autoroute* passes Geneva airport and this good Samaritan took Stein all the way there and up to the departures level. Stein stumbled out of the car mumbling, "Thanks, Colonel."

It was a measure of Stein's stamina—and of the apathetic indifference with which airlines treat their passengers—that he was able to go through the procedures of buying a first-class ticket to Los Angeles. Perhaps he would have attracted more attention in the economy section of the jumbo, but airline staff have by now become used to encountering dirty and dishevelled travellers at the luxury end of airplanes.

That Saturday evening Geneva airport was crowded with tour groups and Stein's appearance was not remarked upon by the airport staff. But he was noticed by Max Breslow, who was waiting in a line at the bank counter. He immediately telephoned Chicago.

"Are you Edward Parker?" Breslow asked the man on the phone. He brushed aside Parker's question of who was calling. If it was one of Kleiber's friends or colleagues, the less he knew about Breslow the better. "My name does not matter but I am telephoning from Geneva, Switzerland, on behalf of a mutual friend named Wilhelm. Do you understand?"

"I understand," said Parker.

"It has all gone wrong here. It is a catastrophe! I doubt if you will see our friend Wilhelm for a long time; he's in trouble with the police. I have just seen Mr. Stein going through the immigration and security to the transit lounge. He is almost certainly going to board the Los Angeles direct flight. Perhaps he has the documents with him, but I didn't see him carrying a bag. Do you understand all that, Mr. Parker?"

It was Saturday afternoon in Chicago. Parker was sitting at his desk eating what remained of a toasted ham-and-cheese sandwich long since gone cold. He guessed immediately that the caller was Breslow and fingered his desk clock as he calculated the flight times between Chicago and Los Angeles, as well as the flying time between California and Switzerland. "Yes, I understand," he said. "Go through and make sure Stein boards, would you? I'll arrange that someone meets him at the other end. Call me again only if he does *not* board that flight. Will you do that for me?" Parker had acquired the North American habit of making his demands sound like polite inquiries.

"Yes," said Breslow reluctantly.

Edward Parker was also uncomfortable. He drank more of his coffee without tasting it, his eyes still on the gold-plated desk clock. He would need help in Los Angeles. The only man he could use there was Rocky Ramon Paz, an overgrown ex-wrestler who had—with some financial aid from Parker—made money in the used-car business. Parker could always find local muscle at short notice. But Rocky Paz was not very bright, and Parker knew that direct flights into L.A. got the attention of customs and immigration, which inevitably meant the presence of the FBI, and often the CIA too.

Parker finished his coffee and then dialled Paz. Suddenly, before getting through, he hung up. He remembered that his latest reports said that the British were in evidence at Los Angeles International. Damn! It was risky but if Stein was walking about with the Hitler Minutes under his arm, getting hold of him was worth almost any risk. And there was the new safe house in Beverly Hills. That would be a perfect place to hold Stein while Paz and his boys worked him over. Parker looked at the clock for the hundreth time and then dialled Paz again.

In summer Los Angeles becomes as dry and as dusty as the little desert towns farther inland. And yet, like an oasis in this gray urban sprawl, Beverly Hills is half hidden under a jungle of greenery—its trees so robust and leafy, its lawns so bright and green, that to go there is like entering the sharp-edged world of the hyper-realist painters.

Bronwyn is a large mansion with a fifteen-foot-wall surrounding its half-acre of garden. Its heated pool is bright blue, with springboards, ladders and tiled surround so clean and new that it looks like some piece of surgical equipment. However new the pool and Jacuzzi, Bronwyn was built in the early thirties, which makes it one of the oldest houses in the neighbourhood. Following the anglophilia that was then rife, it was modelled on photos of a timber-framed Elizabethan mansion in Essex. Unfortunately, the architect had not visited England and there were no photographs of the sides or back of the original, so the part of Bronwyn that faced the pool was Hollywood Spanish. The stucco cloisters had been decorated with bright-red, patterned tiles. Huge chinaware pots overflowed with pink camellias in flower and there were blood-red, double-flowering bougainvillea and golden chrysanthemums.

All of this was reflected in the still water of the pool and there was an uncanny silence until, from the far side of the house, there was the bark of a guard dog and a curse in rapid Spanish as a man tried to quiet the restless creature. Boyd Stuart's feeling of confidence changed to one of unease. He was watching the back of the house through a thin gap between the wall and the warped wood of the service door, which bore a neatly painted notice stating that deliveries were only accepted between eight and eleven Monday through Friday. Stuart was dressed in the same blue coveralls that the contract gardeners wore, and he had moved along the garden wall of Bronwyn snipping at the already perfectly trimmed hedge with a large pair of shears. Close inspection would have revealed that the pair of shears was not of the type normally used for topiary but was an instrument of heavier weight and finer steel which combat engineers use to dismantle wiring defences. Bending down as if to inspect the roots of the hedge, Boyd Stuart applied the jaws of the tool to the chain-link fence. He cut through it with a satisfying snick. Quickly, he continued the process until he had cut a door in the fence.

There was a shout from inside the house and a girl in a small two-piece swimsuit came out of the kitchen door. She was a short, active girl with black, shiny hair and bronze-coloured skin, for which her yellow swimsuit was a perfect foil. She turned on the controls for the steaming hot Jacuzzi and it began to boil and bubble like a witch's cauldron. There was another call from the man inside the house, asking about the Jacuzzi. The girl did not answer. The man emerged from the house and stood almost hidden in the flowery cloisters. He was a huge, barrel-chested man; even at this distance it was easy to see that he was well over six feet tall, with hairy arms and chest and oily black hair that was long enough to grow into ringlets. "Someone must be upstairs always," said Rocky Paz angrily.

"Then you go," said the girl. "You are always in the pool. We are not your servants."

"Whore," shouted the man.

"Cuckold," shouted the girl, but she reached for a towelling coat and put it on. "For just one hour," said the girl. "Then I must go to Rodeo Drive; I have a hair appointment."

"Hair appointment," said the man, rubbing his hand on his chest and tossing back his head in a gesture of contempt. "Do you think this is a goddamn garden party?"

The girl pushed her way past him and flounced into the house. The man sighed and went after her. "Now don't get into one of your moods," Stuart heard him say as he disappeared inside. Stuart pushed at the wire fence to bend it open and make a gap large enough for him to get through. Then, with a quick look over his shoulder at the empty streets of Beverly Hills, and a quick scan of the upper windows of Bronwyn, he was through the fence and racing—head down—for the shrubbery.

Boyd Stuart got behind a wooden alcove built as an outdoor dining space. There was a large, glass-topped table there and a dozen metal dining chairs, their bright plastic seat pads piled in the corner. He removed his blue coveralls and pushed them out of sight. He could hear only his own breathing; the house was quiet. The dining alcove was conveniently near to the main structure of the house. Stuart stepped inside. The air-conditioning was on and the air was cool, and the house shuttered and dark. The oak staircase was wide and elaborate with large carved roses at each landing.

Stuart hurried upstairs to where he could see a light burning, but as he got to the top of the stairs a man's voice said quietly, "Hold it, pal, or I'll blow you apart."

Stuart turned to see someone he had not seen before. He was as big as the man he had seen at the pool but ten years older—a muscular man with high cheekbones and wavy grey hair. He was fully dressed in a single-breasted grey flannel suit. In his hand he held a .38 revolver very steady. It was Boyd Stuart's first confrontation with Edward Parker, the U.S.S.R. illegal.

"Who are you?" Parker said.

"I'll tell you who I am," said Stuart feigning anger. "I'm your bloody landlord, that's who I am." It was a reckless improvisation but it seemed to work. He saw it in Parker's face. "So you can put away that damned gun or I'll have you thrown out." It was Stuart's British accent that helped the deception—that and Stuart's confidence and obvious lack of fear.

"Landlord?"

It was absurd, thought Stuart, that he could be so calm and calculating when men were waving guns at him. It had been like this in the shoot-out in the bus depot in Turin, and when the Hungarians spotlit him climbing through their border wire, to say nothing of going through the police lines in Rostock. "Yes, *landlord,*" said Stuart. "I haven't signed the agreement, you know. Perhaps your lawyer hasn't told you that. . . ."

Parker frowned and tried to remember whom he had asked to arrange for the use of this safe house and what the details had been.

Stuart gesticulated angrily, waving his hands and shaking his head. It was all a matter of timing, of course. Stuart was watching the gun out of the corner of his eye. It scarcely wavered but Stuart had moved closer. The closer a man is to such a weapon the safer he is, providing he is adroit and well trained, until, with a gun that actually touches the body, even a first-month trainee should be able to knock it aside more quickly than the trigger can be pulled.

"Are you listening to me?" said Stuart keeping up the pressure and moving ever closer. "I'm the landlord, not a burglar. Now put that damned gun away." That was probably as much as he would get out of that one, Stuart decided. Any moment now, Parker would stiffen, become more suspicious and he would have lost the momentary advantage.

Stuart chose his moment well. A gesture with the right hand, slightly more frenetic than the previous ones, became a hand chop that landed on Parker's wrist, while Stuart's left hand grasped the gun barrel and twisted hard. Parker's fingers were trapped in the trigger guard and the wrist turned back hard enough to inflict severe pain and torn muscle. Parker screamed. By now Stuart had the pistol in his left hand. While Parker was still gulping air to fuel his screams, Stuart brought the pistol butt down upon his head. It skidded across Parker's skull and took a small piece of flesh from his ear. This glancing blow would have felled most men, but Parker had exceptional strength. In spite of his pain, he continued to fight. His hand injured, he lowered his head and butted Stuart in the chest. It was like meeting the shovel of a bulldozer. It was Stuart's turn to grunt with pain but he kept hold of the gun, and still held it in his hand as Parker locked his arms round him in a bear hug that squeezed the air from his lungs.

The two men blundered round the landing like some broken mechanical toy. Stuart felt his strength going and struggled to breathe. He kicked viciously. Now he had lost his cold calm, and his actions were generated by a growing panic as he swung his weight backward and forward, trying to break free from the terrible bear hug that seemed to black out his brain. His strength was almost spent when Parker's foot missed the edge of the landing and the two of them, still locked in the embrace, crashed down the stairs, rolling over and over, arms and legs thrashing the air, elbows, knees and head rattling upon the uprights, and bodies bumping down the carpeted steps.

It was Stuart's good fortune that Parker's head hit

one of the carved roses with enough force to chip the wooden petals from it and render Parker unconscious. Stuart took a moment or two to recover himself and then, with leaden footsteps, he dragged himself back up to the upper landing.

"Who is it?" It was Stein's voice. He had heard the commotion.

"It's Stuart—the Brit," called Stuart. "Stand away from the door." He put his foot up and, bracing his hand flat against the wall behind him, kicked at the lock. The door splintered and left the remains of the lock dangling from the frame.

Charles Stein was inside. He was in his underclothes and bound to a chair with a nylon clothes line, but he had managed to loosen the sticky tape from his face and spit out the gag. A low-wattage bulb provided meagre light.

Stuart reached into his pocket for the Swiss Army knife that was a part of his normal attire. He sawed at the nylon until it parted. Stein remained in the chair and began rubbing his ankles where the bindings had constricted him.

"Who are these bastards?" said Stein.

"They work for the Russians," said Stuart. "Can you walk? We've got to get out here, there are more of them."

Stein was still rubbing his wrists and ankles as the blood gradually resumed its circulation. He looked at the pistol that Stuart was holding. "You didn't shoot any of them?"

"Not yet," said Stuart, helping the fat man to his feet.

"I can make it," said Stein.

"You go ahead. There's a car at the front." Stuart looked at his watch. "At least, it will be there two minutes from now; a light green Cadillac. Get inside and wait for me."

Stein hobbled down the stairs clinging to the baluster rail and flinching with the pain. When he got to the unconscious form of Parker at the foot of the stairs, he stepped over him gingerly.

"Go ahead," called Stuart. One by one he looked into the rooms to check them. They were all empty, until he got to the main hall and opened the door that led to the drawing room and to the kitchen beyond it. Inside the drawing room he found his case officer and the girl in the beachrobe. She was standing disconsolately in the middle of the room, while the case officer pointed a pistol at her.

"All clear upstairs?" the case officer asked Stuart.

"Seems to be OK," said Stuart. "Stein is groggy but he's able to walk. The big grey-haired fellow is out for the count."

"I heard you come down the stairs with him."

"Thanks for your help," said Stuart bitterly.

"You were doing all right."

Stuart rubbed his grazed and battered face. "Let's get out of here."

The girl pulled her beachrobe tighter round her body and tugged at its knotted belt. "Where's the other one?" Stuart asked.

"One of my boys is taking care of him in the kitchen," said the case officer.

"A neat job," said Stuart. It had been a perfect snatch-squad operation. From the twenty-four-hour watch at the airport to seeing Rocky Paz kidnap Stein as he came out into the street from the baggage hall, it had been exemplary. But perhaps Stuart was tempting providence to say so, for no sooner were the words out of his mouth than there was the sound of two shots and a cry of pain. As if on cue, the girl dashed for the door. The case officer fired but the bullet went high and ricochetted off the oak ceiling of the hallway beyond.

Stuart ran towards the front door to make sure that Stein was in the car, but he was nowhere to be seen and Parker was no longer stretched out on the floor; two more bullets whined past Stuart's head. He turned and, using Parker's gun, fired at the upper landing where the gun flashes had come from.

Someone had extinguished the fluorescent lights in the kitchen. The inside of this shuttered house was dark. There were two more shots and the sound of feet coming down the stairs very fast. The big man with ringlets came past, pumping a shell into a shotgun. He kicked the inner door open so that it swung round and banged against the wall. The daylight from the doorway lit the hall like a photo flash. There, in the rectangle of the doorway, Stuart saw the whole scene. There was the unnaturally blue water of the pool, a great transparent cube against the dark greenery, and framing it a fringe of bright flowers. The case officer had gone through the kitchen and now was running along the poolside as the man raised the shotgun.

There was no time to think. Stuart aimed and fired automatically. The ringleted man in the doorway was too close to miss. The bullet shattered his shoulder blade, as Stuart intended that it should, and the shotgun went off and covered the surface of the pool with a thousand tiny splashes. The man was yelling, and kept yelling even after he too had tumbled forward into the hot bubbling water of the Jacuzzi.

Stuart ran forward and onto the patio. The case officer had turned towards the sound of the shotgun. "Take the car," he yelled to Stuart, and already he was kicking open the decorative tea house at the end of the garden to be sure that Stein was not there.

From the front of the house Stuart heard the Cadillac engine as the getaway car arrived. He ran round the side of the house and jumped into it. The driver was tickling the gas pedal nervously. Stuart pushed him aside and climbed behind the wheel. "Jesus, what a mess," said the driver. "Of all places . . . Beverly Hills, where the cops are thickest. They'll be all over us."

Even as the car began rolling forward the double gates were closing. Stuart had studied them closely from the outside during his half-hour of gardening. They were electrically controlled, reinforced with steel cross-braces and topped with a tangle of barbed wire. "Hold tight!" shouted Stuart above the noise of the engine. "We're going to have to get a good run up to it." He put the car into reverse and touched the accelator. The Cadillac shot backwards. Before he could apply the brake, the back of the car had crashed through the conservatory. There was a sound like heavy surf hammering on to the beach as the glass shattered and potted plants and shelving crashed down upon them. A flower pot broke upon the windscreen. Stuart revved the engine as the rear bumper locked into the bent ironwork. It broke free with a bang and the car sped forward faster and faster until it hit the gates with a clang like a peal of bells. It ripped the hinges and tangled up the barbed wire. With a terrible scream of tyres it broke loose and Stuart brought the steering wheel round as the car skidded across the grass and onto the road. Something caught in the car's underside, rattled loudly, then broke free. They were away.

"We lost your dad," Stuart told Billy Stein.

"What in hell does that mean; you lost him?"

The three men were in the sitting room of the Stein's home. The case officer was in an armchair near the window, pretending to be fully occupied by the view across the city of Los Angeles. Without turning round he said, "Your dad was in his underclothes—bright blue shorts and singlet—he came out of the house holding onto a towel round his neck. We thought he was jogging."

"You thought he was jogging!" said Billy Stein. "I hear you talking about guns going off, and girls screaming. You wreck the car, ramming the gates. You thought my dad was jogging! You told me you were going to rescue him."

"We did rescue him," said the case officer. "But he scrambled over the fence and came out through the front lawn of the house next door."

"Jesus," said Billy Stein. "You've got to hand it to the old man. Concussed in a car accident, kidnapped by the Russians, held prisoner until you rescue him and then he takes off up the road in his underpants . . ."

"We're laying it all on the line for you," said Stuart "because we need to know where he's likely to go."

Billy Stein smiled. "He won't come here. He's not so dumb that he'll come home where you are waiting for him."

"Does he have an apartment anywhere?"

"What the tabloids call a love-nest—is that what you mean? No, that's not him at all. My dad was never that subtle, or extravagant. If he had some kind of affair going, he'd have brought the girl right back here to the house. You can forget that one."

"Clubs?"

Billy Stein shook his head. "Only his regular poker game."

"We're going to leave one of our people here in the house," said Stuart.

"That's OK," said Billy Stein. "There's lots of food and stuff." He looked at Stuart for a moment before continuing. "You're not kidding about the Russians? Did they really kidnap the old man?"

"Your dad will tell you all about it, once we find him," said Stuart.

Encouraged by the friendly tone in Stuart's voice, Billy Stein said, "It was a frame-up in London, wasn't it, Mr. Stuart? Your people know I didn't kill anyone?"

The case officer turned his head to see how Stuart handled this question.

"It was a frame-up," Stuart replied. "But they could make it stick if you don't cooperate with us."

"I'll cooperate," said Billy, "but I wanted to get it clear between you and me." He looked at his watch. "Is it OK for me to phone Mary Breslow?"

"You phoned her this morning," the case officer said over his shoulder.

Stuart nodded his approval. "But Billy . . . nothing about your dad, or about the murder charge in London. Just sweet nothings, OK?"

"Sure thing," said Billy.

"You know Max Breslow was a Nazi?" said the case officer.

"You sound like my dad," Billy told him. "Are you another one of these guys who can't stop fighting the war?"

"Go and make your call," Stuart said. "But remember that the guy in the hall will be listening on the extension."

"You're too damned soft with that kid," the case officer said after Billy's departure.

"I think he's a good sort," said Stuart. "No grudges, no tantrums, no smart-ass remarks. Hell, even when I admit that he was framed in London he practically thanks me."

"Rich kids," said the case officer. "They're all like that."

"Are they," said Stuart. "Then let's hope I meet more of them."

The case officer got up from Charles Stein's favourite armchair, and took out his cigarettes so that he could light a fresh one from the stub in his fingers. "Chain-smoking," he said after it was alight. "Does that disgust you?" Stuart didn't reply. "Because it disgusts me." He stubbed the old cigarette out with unnecessary vigour. "OK, so I'm hard on the kid. You're right; he's OK."

The case officer sat down again and watched the sun put on its act of dying. Finally, when the room had darkened, he said, "You were the one who got those two agents out of Rostock two years or so back?"

It was a breach of regulations to talk of such things but the two men had got to know each other by now.

"What a cock-up," said Stuart. He could remember only arriving back in London to discover Jennifer's bed companion.

"The way I heard it you should have got a medal," said the case officer.

"I didn't even get paid leave," said Stuart.

"I knew one of them," said the case officer. "A little Berliner with a high-pitched laugh . . . liked to wear a blade in his hat. He escaped from a prison in Leipzig back in the fifties when they broke up one of our networks."

"I remember him," said Stuart. Both the men he had rescued were old-timers, men who had worked for London for many years. If they had been younger and stronger he might have left them to save themselves, but for these two he had gone back through the road blocks and brought them out again with him. Looking back he wondered at the madness of it.

"You were the big hero of the department at the time," said the case officer. "There were guys in East Germany who would have had you canonized."

Stuart laughed. "You have to be dead to be canonized."

"I didn't know before," said the case officer apologetically. "I wouldn't have kidded around with you if I'd known you were the agent who brought those two guys out of Rostock—that was really something!"

The two men sat in silence for a while. Then the case officer said, "I heard a rumour that these Hitler Documents—or whatever they are—have been destroyed."

"I heard the same thing," said Stuart.

"But the department will keep the file open?"

"The department will keep the file open," said Stuart. "That's one thing you can be sure about. My orders are unchanged; I've got to locate Stein and Kleiber, then ask London for instructions. Kleiber is now the centre of all London's queries."

"We'll find Stein," said the case officer, as if reading Stuart's mind. "I've put every last man I can spare onto it. I'll locate him, I promise you. It wasn't such a fiasco tonight. At least it will make the Russians run for cover and maybe think again before kidnapping anyone else at the airport. When Stein does show up, we'll have a free hand to work on him."

"I like Stein," said Stuart.

"He's a crook," said the case officer. "And from what I hear the concussion has made him a little crazy."

"But I like him," said Stuart. "And this is not the sort of business where one can be too choosy about the crazies."

## 44

To the casual observer, Charles Stein might have appeared a little drunk, but the uniformed studio policeman scarcely gave him a glance. The suit he wore was an old one; it had been in his locker at the club in Roscoe ever since he'd played squash there many years ago. They had had all shapes and sizes going through the studio gates that morning. Goodness knows how many actors must have attended those earlier downtown auditions, he wondered, when so many had been selected for these screen tests with make-up and costume.

Charles Stein's concussion had produced many of the symptoms of drunkenness and yet, like those people who gain a reputation for being able to hold their drink, Stein learnt how to disguise and hide those symptoms. But he could not shake off the belief that Aram was still alive and well, and events following his accident on the *autoroute* were confused and somewhat hazy in his mind.

Find Max Breslow. It was as if this was the one coherent, rational, all-consuming motive for everything that Charles Stein did. It had been in his mind when he fought his way back to consciousness after the car crash. It had troubled the dreams he had had in the upstairs lounge of the jumbo and screamed in the voice of its engines. Now his lips moved as he gave himself that same instruction and clasped it to his mind as fiercely and as lovingly as he cradled the gun in his arms.

"Breslow?" The corridor stretched to infinity and the doors were set close together. Puny doors on flimsy hinges which, with a little extra effort, Charles Stein could have ripped away.

"No." Adolf Hitler, dressed in a well-cut grey jacket and plain black trousers, shook his head. "No," he said again.

The next room was little different. Adolf Hitler was admiring himself in a full-length mirror. He waved Stein away with an imperious hand. "Breslow!" shouted Stein, his voice echoing in the narrow corridor. In the next room, a third Adolf Hitler was tying a shoelace. Charles Stein slammed the door very hard. A voice complained loudly from somewhere at the other end of the building.

The fourth Adolf Hitler was sitting slumped in his chair. He did not respond to Breslow's name. The fifth was crouched over a table, staring closely at a mirror as he combed his hair over his forehead and positioned it with a long squirt of hair spray. The sixth Adolf Hitler was applying make-up, touching his cheeks with greasepaint and rubbing it carefully into the surrounding colouring. Dozens of bare yellow bulbs outlined his reflection, so that another Führer touched foreheads with this one. And the images—reflected from one mirror to another—made a long golden tunnel peopled with Adolf Hitlers, their balletic gestures synchronized to perfection.

"Breslow!"

A thousand Hitlers stood up and glared at Stein, raising their hands mockingly in mute salute to him.

"Breslow!" Stein's voice was so loud that it made the thin hardboard walls of the dressing room rattle as they echoed back the sound of it. "Breslow!" It was more like a cry for help than a threat. "Breslow!" shouted Stein again. He was beginning to realize that Max Breslow controlled a thousand Führers. It was Breslow he would have to finish off. Breslow had become the focal point of all Stein's anger, sadness and frustration. Through the painful haze of his concussion, he blamed Breslow for everything, from Aram's death to that of Colonel Pitman.

"I'm coming to get you, Breslow!" Stein shouted again.

"Close that door!" called the make-up assistant. "Every kook in town is auditioning for this Hitler role," he muttered. "And that fat guy toting the old gun has got to be the noisiest ham in the building."

"The moustache is coming off again," Hitler told him quietly. "Will you give me a little more of that gum?"

Max Breslow had counted the days to when he would first enter the studio and see the Reich Chancellery set. First and foremost came his anxieties about the film itself. This was the most expensive set and it was important that, in the jargon of the trade, its "production value" got to the screen. He ran his hands across the twenty-foot-high doorway of simulated green marble. Over the entrance Adolf Hitler's initials were carved into a gigantic shield. Max Breslow pushed open the mahogany doors to the Führer's, study, remembering the two black-uniformed SS guards with their white gloves and impeccable jack-boots who used to stand there.

Yes, this was it. Nearly a hundred feet wide and fifty feet across, with dark red marble walls nearly forty feet high. Max Breslow had often been in the Führer's study. He remembered the great cofferwork ceiling of rosewood and Lenbach's full-length portrait of Bismarck over the marble fireplace. Facing him there were the windows that gave onto the colonnade and the Chancellery garden. Once the big lights were illuminating the trees and shrubs and the painted background, it would all come to life. All the batteries of photographic lighting were dark and idle, for the time being there was only the feeble studio lighting that enabled the technicians to see their way round the set. And yet this too helped to bring the place alive for Breslow, for there was an artificiality to film lighting, a whitewash effect which even the best-designed set could never survive. This shadowy place was more like the one he had once known. Breslow reached out to the silk-shaded light on the Führer's desk and switched it on. It was "practical," and its light shone across the Gobelin tapestry on the wall. Breslow had never lost his admiration for the technicians who were able to produce such convincing imitations of woods and metals. He looked at the Führer's desk inlaid with leather. The set dresser had carefully prepared everything for the first day of shooting. The green blotter, the telephone, some reference books and the pen set had all been faithfully copied from old photographs taken by the propaganda service soon after the new Chancellery was built. Breslow went round the desk and sat down to survey the set from Hitler's high-backed, brown-leather chair. Often, when bringing messages to the Führer, back in those exciting days of the war, he had wondered what it would be like to sit here, seeing the world from the point of view of the man who had changed it out of all recognition. Well, now he knew. From Hitler's point of view, the world consisted largely of that huge painting of Bismarck at the far end of the room. Was it the daily sight of Otto von Bismarck which had provoked Hitler into ever greater excesses? Had it driven this mad fool to the final smash-up?

Max Breslow sat for a long time, lost in contemplation of the events which had taken him from the Reich Chancellery and brought him in a complete circle back to it again. Staring into the gloom of his imposing set, Breslow's eyes moved down from the Bismarck portrait to the armchairs grouped round the fireplace below it. He leant forward to stare into the darkness.

"It's me," said the voice of Charles Stein. "It's me, Breslow. I knew you'd come."

Breslow stood up. He felt his heart beating at abnormally high speed. "What the devil do you want? I thought you were dead."

"I'm going to kill you, Max. I've been waiting here a long time. I've been waiting to kill you. That's what kept me alive, Max."

Breslow reached for the carved wooden armrest to steady himself. He was frightened by the tone of Stein's voice. There was some quality in the voice that persuaded Breslow immediately that he was in earnest. Breslow held tight to the arm of the chair and felt the palm of his hand sweaty under his grip. There was not much light here. He could only just see the gross shape of Stein slumped in the big armchair, his crumpled white suit visible against the dark-red marble wall behind him. Breslow had mistaken the white shape for a dust sheet thrown over some genuine piece of antique furniture.

"No," said Breslow. "What kept you alive were the papers, and all the power you've enjoyed by manipulating them."

"All gone," said Stein. "All the papers. All the money. I lost every penny I had in that auto . . . bearer bonds . . . two million dollars' worth."

Breslow inched along the edge of the Führer's desk. He had always thought that desk absurdly out of proportion to the human scale and now, as he moved along it, it seemed as long as a football field.

"Just stay exactly where you are," Stein called. Now that Breslow's eyes had become more accustomed to the darkness, he could see that Stein was not sprawled back in the armchair; he was crouching forward. Breslow continued to move sideways only a fraction at a time. He knew that the left side of the desk was in line with the double doors behind it. He had remembered that from the real thing, and from the photographs he had given the set dresser. Now he prayed to God that the technicians had placed everything exactly the way the research indicated that it had been. At last he could get his left hand to the chamfered corner that surmounted the massive leg.

"You're moving," called Stein loudly. It was a good-natured complaint of the sort that children might use when playing the game of "statues." Breslow strained his ears and fancied he heard the distant sound of a police-car siren. It was no more than a stifled whine, but then sometimes they only used the siren just before crossing the intersections and cut it off until they got to the next one.

"I've got a gun," said Stein. He still had not moved from the armchair. "And I know how to use it." Breslow remained very still. There was no point in getting killed if the police were already on their way. He was comforted by the fact that he could not now hear the siren. The police dispatchers only authorized one police car at a time to use the siren: that was how you could differentiate police sirens from those of the fire department, which let all vehicles use them.

"Stand still, damn you!"

Suddenly Breslow remembered that this was a sound stage. Those vast padded doors he had passed through would not permit even the roar of low-flying aircraft on the approach to Los Angeles International Airport to mar the recordings. There was no chance that he could have heard a siren of any kind. No sound could get into here, and none—not even a pistol shot—could get out. That's why Stein had chosen this place. He could play with him like a cat with a mouse.

Breslow felt himself sweating and knew his face must be flushed and shiny. He wondered whether Stein could see from that distance. Perhaps he had even planned it carefully enough to bring night glasses. He must run; once Stein got closer to him he would have no chance. He whirled round and ran for the doors. Crack! There was a flash as Stein fired but the bullet whined over his head, chipped a piece of wood from the "marble" and threw a handful of splinters at him. By now Breslow had reached the big mahogany doors and was struggling to get through them and away. His panic seemed to give him the agility and the strength of two men, but no matter how hard he tugged at the doorknobs the doors didn't budge or even rattle.

"Oh, my God!" These were not practical; these were dummy doors, as solid and immovable as the remainder of the wall. Breslow turned the other way and ran, as another shot flashed and whined through the darkness. Breslow was suddenly punched in the abdomen and felt a blow to the knees. He nearly cried out aloud but enough of the old discipline remained to repress his emotions to a grunt. He had blundered straight into the mahogany cabinet that was placed under the seventeenth-century Gobelin tapestry. His splayed arms encountered the ornaments on the cabinet top. There was a crash as some statuettes and a beautiful George II bracket clock hit the floor with an agonizing crash of breaking movement and jangled chimes. He heard Stein chuckle.

By now Breslow was at the next set of doors. He wrestled with them and waited all the while for the sound of the next shot and inevitable blow that would crack his spine and tear out his belly. At first he thought that these must also be dummy doors but then he felt them move under his weight. His shoulder was against the carved mahogany, and he pressed so hard that he thought he must fracture his bones. But the doors were twelve feet high, and even the version that the studio carpenters had fashioned seemed as heavy as lead. He squeezed through them as soon as they were partly open. Behind him he heard another shot. It sounded closer and the flash of the gun seemed nearer too. Stein was behind him.

Breslow looked right and left. On one side of him there were the gigantic studio doors through which large pieces of scenery were moved. That was out of the question. On his right—down the dark corridor marked only with blue safety lights—there was the door usually used by the sound technicians going into their glass-fronted room. Breslow dodged to one side and swung under a microphone boom and behind one of the big searchlights that the industry calls "brutes." It was dark here and he waited a moment in the hope that Stein might hurry off down the corridor and give him a chance to recross the studio and escape through the vegetation of the "gardens" outside the Chancellery windows.

But Stein halted at the sign RECORDING IN PROGRESS marked with the red warning light that was now dark. He seemed to realize that Breslow had not gone that way and he turned back and carefully surveyed the space behind the high walls of the Chancellery set. The great Nazi eagle threw a huge shadow across the complex patterns of the simulated marble floor. There was a clang and a muffled curse as Stein's pistol struck a lamp stand and his foot caught against a cable. But Stein did not stumble; he was moving slowly towards Breslow as he scanned and eliminated each part of the studio.

"I can see you, Max. Come on out, I can see you."

Breslow did not move. He held his breath. He could see Stein's ungainly form as he ambled very slowly forward, crumpled and dishevelled like some disturbed gorilla.

"I can see you, you bastard," Stein called loudly when he was only a few feet away, but Breslow remained motionless and felt his heart beating so loudly that he thought he was going to faint from the exertion. Just as Breslow was going to speak, Stein turned away from him and went towards the camera crane that was parked against the wall. "I can see you," he repeated.

Breslow cursed his foolishness at not having brought his little pocket pistol with him. He eased slowly backwards toward the padded wall of the studio. His foot caught in one of the electrical cables but he untangled it carefully and stepped out of the loop. Stein was inside the Führer's study now and Breslow was able to get back to the doorway which, with clever use of some trick photography, would look like a part of the long hall of the Chancellery. He stepped over some elaborate bronze wall-candelabra that were placed on the studio floor ready to be positioned after the camera dolly had moved back this way.

"Breslow!"

Stein's shout told him that the fat man was now on the far side of the set. Breslow grasped the foot of the fixed metal ladder and, moving quickly for a man of his age, he climbed up it towards the lighting rail, a gallery which ran all round the studio. He heard Stein call again. From up here on the gantry, Breslow could see Stein as he stepped cautiously into the potted plants and imitation branches which were suspended outside the windows. They never look up, thought Breslow—he remembered the instructor telling him that when he went on the assault course at Bad Tölz. Only children look up, adults never do.

"Breslow!"

Stein's voice was almost imperceptibly higher now, as he thought that Breslow must have escaped from the studio by some exit that he did not know about. Breslow crouched behind the rail. It would be difficult to see him here, for the whole gantry was crammed with photographic lights of every shape and size. He felt safe now and had the almost hysterical desire to laugh aloud, to shriek and shout at Stein and call him names. Stein moved again. He was under one of the little lights and Breslow could see him clearly. He was carrying a First World War Mauser pistol of the sort for which the wooden carrying case could be converted into a shoulder stock. It was a museum piece; only in California would such a bizarre contraption still be seen. And yet it was a superb old gun and, in the hands of a man who could use it, deadly. Perhaps it was a deliberate choice of weapon. Certainly, in any of the film studios it would be dismissed as a prop for some old film rather than a murder weapon. He watched Stein bring the weapon up to his shoulder and swing it round experimentally.

"Breslow. I can see you, Breslow." He was aiming at the dark space where the "garden" gave way to a corner of the studio. Spare furniture was piled there. They were going to film a corner of this set a second time, with specially antiqued chairs to emphasize the passage of time.

"Breslow!" Stein's voice was distorted by the way that his face was pressed close to the wooden stock as he squinted along the sights of the gun. He fired. Crack! Up on the gantry the sound echoed against the metal. "Got you!" he shouted, but there was no cry of pain and Stein realized that there was nothing there. "I got all night, Breslow. You ain't never going to get through those doors quick enough to get out alive. I said I'm going to kill you, Breslow, and I'm going to do it. You'd just better believe me."

Breslow leant over the rail to watch as Stein moved under him. To his horror, he saw the glint of gold as his pen fell from his pocket. It glinted as it fell and clattered to the floor at Stein's feet.

"Ahhh!" roared Stein. "You cunning little creep. You're up there on that gantry, are you?" He pumped three shots into the air. They came uncomfortably close and Breslow shrank away and fell against the wall as the bullets hit the metal racks and richochetted back across the studio.

Breslow ran along the lighting balcony while Stein reloaded his gun. The gantry swayed and groaned with the violent movement. Breslow wondered if he would be able to climb over the rail and jump down onto the camera crane. It was a distance of about six feet. In the old days it would have been nothing to him but now it was daunting. He looked over the rail. There was only one metal ladder up to the gantry and now, to Breslow's horror, Stein began to climb it. Breslow was on the far side of the set, over the Führer's desk. There in the leather inlay he could see the pattern of the famous half-sheathed sword that the Führer himself thought so appropriate for his desk top.

"I'm coming, Breslow."

Stein was halfway up the ladder now and already the exertion was making him puff. Once Stein was up here he would have a clear view all round the balcony. There would be nowhere to hide then. If Stein truly intended to murder him, then there would be no escape.

"Stein," shouted Breslow. "Let me talk to you. It is madness for us to fight."

"You killed the colonel, my best friend! You cheated my buddies!" It was as much as he could do to get the words out and still have breath enough for climbing. It was slow work.

"I killed no one."

"You goddamn Nazi! You killed my brother."

Stein was at the top of the ladder now. He struggled to get over the top of it and onto the lighting gallery. He was holding the huge Mauser in one hand and supporting himself with the other.

"Look out, Stein!" Perhaps it was madness to shout a warning of danger to a man who was trying to kill you, but Breslow's cry was spontaneous. Stein had put all his weight on the spotlight bracket, a clamp that was not designed to hold such weight. Normally only the electricians ever came up here on the balcony, and they knew every frailty of the metalwork and every uncertainty of the guard rail. Stein did not. Perhaps if Stein had released his hold on the Mauser, he might still have regained his balance and steadied himself against the rail, but he would not relinquish his gun.

"Awww!!" Stein felt himself beginning to topple as the lighting bracket bent outwards and down. He was arched backwards now, his broad-brimmed white hat fell and drifted down into the studio. His mouth was open and his gun flailing the air as he made a frantic effort to swim upwards into the darkness. "Help!" But he was already falling. The huge, untidy bundle of white clothes somersaulted very slowly off the ladder top, his arms spreadeagled and the gun outstretched. Head downwards, he gathered speed as he dropped past the expanses of red marble and the eagles and insignia and, with a terrible crash, hit the studio floor.

"Stein!"

Breslow ran back along the gallery and clambered down the metal steps as fast as he could. "Stein," he said again as he bent low over the crumpled shape. He had fallen head-first, his skull was cracked and his face bloody. There was little chance of mistake. Breslow had seen enough dead men to recognize one.

"Why?" Breslow asked him leaning close. "Why did you want to kill me? It's too late for that."

Boyd Stuart swung into the forecourt of the Big O Do-nut Shop, where the Santa Monica Freeway passes over La Brea. The tyres of the car squealed loudly enough to make the police officers drinking coffee there crane forward to look out of the window.

Billy Stein and Mary Breslow were in the car with him. He had contacted them as soon as news came that Stein had been seen. Boyd watched while Billy Stein ran into the coffee shop to talk to the policemen. It was better that there was a relative present; the policemen would be more understanding about a relative. Whatever it was that Billy said to the two policemen, it was enough to make them abandon their coffee, pick up their doughnuts and hurry out to their car. It swung round and up the ramp to the freeway with Boyd Stuart in hot pursuit.

"They won't be in time," said Mary—more because she wanted to hear Stuart contradict her than because she was calculating her father's peril. She did not dare do that. If Billy's father really wanted to carry out his threat, he had surely had time enough to do it by now.

"It will be all right, Miss Breslow," said Stuart. He put his foot down. It was not easy to keep up with the police car. The black-and-white swung over to the number one lane and had its lights flashing. An old Buick accelerated past and cut steeply into the space between them. Stuart cursed. People did that sometimes, following police cars for no other reason than to join in the excitement.

By the time the police got to the studio entrance their radio had sent the news ahead. A studio guard in a smart black-leather zipper jacket was standing at the open gates.

"Studio number four," he shouted. "The chief will meet you at the main door," he told the driver.

The car moved off again, grunting and groaning in the dips and potholes of the badly maintained studio road. Stuart's car pulled through the gate behind the police car. The gateman decided they must be some sort of undercover detail and let them go.

They parked alongside the black-and-white and scrambled out. The officer, name-tagged Cooper, reached for his pistol.

"It's my father," Billy added hurriedly.

The cop turned round to look at them both. "Take it easy, folks, he said. "And stay outside." The passenger officer had unlocked the shotgun from its rack under the front seats. Now he pumped it to put a shell in the chamber.

The chief security guard for the studio let them inside through the massive soundproof doors. There was an oppressive silence. Silently, Officer Cooper put his hand on the chest of the security man to indicate that he should remain here at the door. The passenger officer, still holding the shotgun in the high-port position prescribed by regulations, moved silently over to the vegetation, keeping away from the windows. From this side of the set, he could see what a fake the whole thing was: the heavy window openings and marble surrounds were plasterboard and laths, with the rumpled ends of patterned paper poking out of the clamps.

"This is the police." The voice sounded unnaturally loud. There was no reply. The policeman stepped into the set, keeping well behind the half-open door. "Jesus!" he said softly as he caught sight of the opulent room and the huge Nazi eagle over the door.

Breslow released his hold on Stein's pulse. It had been nothing more than a formality: Stein was dead. From somewhere a long way away, Breslow could hear voices but his mind was too absorbed to hear them properly. He picked up the ridiculous Mauser that Stein had been carrying and stood up. Poor old Stein.

Officer Cooper saw the sudden movement, shouted "Freeze!" brought his pistol up high and double-gripped it to shoot.

"Papa!" It was a scream rather than a call. Mary Breslow came running into the line of fire and grabbed her father. "Papa, Papa, Papa," She kissed him and held him tight, seeing nothing and caring for nothing, even when her foot accidentally touched Stein's body.

Breslow seemed to see the policemen and Billy Stein for the first time. He blinked.

"He fell, Billy. He fell from the gantry up there."

Billy Stein looked down at the body and twisted his hands. He did not want to touch this bloody figure which bore such slight resemblance to his father. He looked round at the others. They expected something from him, so Billy knelt and, suppressing a shudder, put one hand upon his dead father's shoulder. Perhaps they expected him to cry or to wail, but all that would come later. It would be something only between him and his father; Billy Stein was not given to public display of emotion.

"My father couldn't climb up there, Mr. Breslow."

"He could and he did, Billy. He had this gun; he was trying to kill me. He said I'd killed his brother."

Officer Cooper turned to the chief security guard. "Where's the phone?" And to his partner he said, "We'll tell them he's badly hurt, OK?"

The detective nodded. It was always better to say the body might still be showing signs of life. That way they would not have to wait for the coroner's office to send someone down here. Better that he went to the receiving hospital and was pronounced "dead on arrival"—that way they could get back on the job.

"I'm going to take you for treatment, then to headquarters, Mr. Breslow. We'll soon get it sorted out downtown." Officer Cooper had spent nine years on radio cars. He had long ago learnt that it was easier to take a prisoner into custody who thought it would all be sorted out quickly and conveniently.

"No need for the handcuffs," said Mary Breslow.

"Regulations, I'm afraid, miss. Felony suspects have to be cuffed." He flicked the cuffs onto Breslow's wrists with practised agility. The last time Mary saw her father on that terrible day he was in the back seat of the black-and-white, leaning well forward with his hands stretched behind him, and the passenger officer was reading to him the Miranda rights.

"Well, you're happy now, I suppose?" Billy Stein asked Stuart.

"What are you talking about?"

"You chased him and harassed him. You threatened me and locked me up. Now he's gone and you'll get your medal."

"Don't, Billy!" Mary Breslow told him. "Don't talk that way."

"They killed him," Billy insisted. "Your father didn't kill mine. These bastards did it."

"Get in the car, Billy," said Boyd Stuart. I'll take you home."

"What am I going to do?" said Billy. "Me and dad . . . we've always been together. He's always done everything for me."

Stuart took Mary Breslow's arm and guided her close to Billy Stein, who was leaning on the car roof with his face buried in his folded arms.

## 45

Willi Kleiber had regained consciousness in a wooden hut in South Carolina. The lush green marshlands, through which the rains from the Appalachian Mountains flow in a thousand rivers to the Atlantic, provided an ideal hiding place. Rutted, potholed tracks meandered through the trees to a dilapidated pier. From there they had taken him to one of the little islands which hang along the coastline like iron filings on a magnet.

There was no electricity and the only communication with the mainland was by short-wave radio. The men with Kleiber wore cotton trousers and sweat shirts, with lace-up boots to protect their ankles against the snakes. It was hot and almost unbearably humid. The only sounds came from the insects and the ocean, and the only movement was that of the shrimp boats far out to sea.

There was a physician there—a young man, his skin as black and shiny as a newly polished limousine. He had come from Charleston on a motorcycle and now, as twilight came, he was fretting to get away. He pronounced Kleiber fit and signed accordingly, before they heard the sound of his bike clattering down to where the motorboat was waiting to ferry him back to the mainland.

Melvin Kalkhoven did the primary interrogation but it was the project chairman who, later that evening, got down to what was expected of Kleiber. Kleiber listened, as he had listened to Kalkhoven, without saying very much. He stared at the fly screen, which throbbed and vibrated under the weight of moths which desired nothing more than the chance to dash themselves into the flames of the kerosene lamp hissing on the table in front of him.

"But why would I make direct contact with the Soviet embassy in Washington?" Kleiber said finally. "No experienced agent would do that. It's damned dangerous, and it goes against everything that Moscow Centre teaches."

The project chairman leant back so that his rocking chair creaked. He rested his elbows on the arms of it and put his fingertips together. Intended as the mannerism of a scholar or philosopher, it looked more like the attention-seeking gesture of a man who liked to listen to himself.

"You'll scare him," he promised. "You'll scare Yuriy Grechko half to death. When he hears you tell him what is happening to his network—that Parker is going into the bag and the rest of them are being rolled up—he'll be terrified. Moscow Centre hates that kind of foul-up. They'll recall him; he'll be scared—really scared."

The project chairman broke off as another aspect of the case came to mind. "Is Parker a Russian?"

"He's never admitted it," said Kleiber. "But yes, he is."

"How do you know?"

"I was born in a house that looks out over the Baltic. I can recognize a Russian when I see one."

The project chairman nodded contentedly and tapped his fingertips together. "So Grechko will be worrying if we'll dig that out too. You'll tell him it's going to hit the fan, Willi. Grechko won't be reading the instruction book to tell you you shouldn't have called him; he's going to be worried sick."

Kleiber said, "Grechko will ask me where those Hitler Minutes are."

The project chairman turned away to get his coffee cup. There had been several mentions of something called the Hitler Minutes but that was of no concern to him or to the CIA. He was determined not to have any red herrings drawn across the very satisfactory path of this investigation.

"You tell him the papers were taken off you by the customs officials at Kennedy. We'll fake you the kind of receipt that the customs use. Give it to Grechko. Let him worry about that."

"He'll be furious," said Kleiber. "He'll be furious with Parker for ordering me to bring the stuff back to the U.S.A."

"Exactly," said the project chairman, wiping coffee from his lips with a paper handkerchief. "Now you see what I'm driving at, Willi. We're going to create a problem for Grechko . . . and the only way out of it will be to make you the illegal resident."

"Illegal resident!" said Kleiber. "Now look. . . ."

The project chairman stared at him, blank faced. Kleiber ran a finger round inside his collar, and there were beads of perspiration on his forehead and in a line along his upper lip.

"Well, you don't think we went to all that trouble in there unless it was going to yield something real big, do you, Willi?" The project chairman scarcely moved his head to indicate the room next to where they were sitting. Displayed in there had been all the accumulated evidence of the murders that Willi Kleiber had committed. There were colour photos of the corpses of Bernard Lustig and MacIver and some black-and-white shots of the two men killed in London. There was other evidence too: the damaged wristwatch that provided an estimated time of death, the parking ticket and teleprinter messages and other police paperwork. There were even fingerprints; Kleiber had thrown his cotton gloves into the car trunk with Lustig's body and then closed the lid with his bare hands. There was also a signed statement from someone who had witnessed the MacIver shooting that took place that same evening. The murderer's description fitted Kleiber exactly. Kleiber had spent fifteen minutes studying the material and then had declared that there was not enough evidence to get a conviction. The project chairman had shrugged. Tell me what else we need and we'll get it manufactured, he had said. Kleiber believed him.

"Illegal resident for the Russians? Controlled all the time by the CIA?"

"Keep the Ruskies happy, and then they won't release your war-crimes file, Willi." He smiled and slapped a fly on his arm. It was a sudden movement and it made Kleiber start in surprise. "We've got a common interest, Willi old pal, we want to keep those Ruskies smiling."

"They'll suspect me." Willi had begun to waver as both men knew he would.

"We'll give you some real good breaks, Willi. Don't worry about that. We'll keep Moscow happy. We know the sort of thing they so desperately need: undersea warfare technology, computer advances, cruise missiles data. We won't keep you short of stuff to feed them. We'll make you a big man, Willi."

Kleiber shook his head. "We were talking about my feeding Parker, not replacing him. . . ."

"Maybe that's what *you* were talking about," said the project chairman. "But I'm talking about the big one."

"It's something I'd have to think about," said Willi Kleiber.

"Yes. You think about it, Willi," said the project chairman in a fruity, avuncular voice which was all the more worrying because of the quiet confidence that it showed.

"Where the hell are we?" said Kleiber for what must have been at least the hundredth time. It was the sound of an airliner passing over which made his mind go back to that question. It unsettled him not to know where he was—just as it was intended to do.

The project chairman ignored the question, as he had ignored it all the previous times. He stepped across to where a white plastic fascia panel disguised a stove. The wormy floor of the shack moved slightly under his weight. He scooped some instant coffee and milk powder into a thick white mug he got from the cupboard. "Quit worrying, Kleiber. I tell you it will be all right."

"What do you know about what will be all right?" Keliber grumbled. "Were you ever a field agent?"

"It will be all right, compared to the alternative," said the project chairman ominously. He lifted the lid of the vacuum flask and, deciding that the water was still hot enough, poured some into the mug. "Coffee?"

"Why can't I have a proper drink?"

"The doc says no." The project chairman had no great liking for this arrogant hoodlum. "You'd better know this, Kleiber, old sport. There are quite a few people working on this project who'd like to see you arraigned on a murder indictment."

"The Bible man for one," said Kleiber. "Yes, he told me that."

The project chairman nodded. Melvin Kalkhoven had been vociferously opposed to any deal that allowed Kleiber to escape punishment. Kalkhoven had told the project chairman, "I called thee to curse mine enemies, and behold, thou hast altogether blessed them these three times." His indignation was fired by the knowledge that Kleiber would be paid at a higher grade than Kalkhoven himself.

"But not me," added the project chairman. "I'd XPD you if I had my way."

## 46

In the last two decades the KGB have been less paranoid about their huge Moscow office block with its infamous Lubyanka prison and rooftop exercise yard. Fewer Russians have been arrested for loitering in Dzerzhinsky Square, and it has been a long time since a tourist has had his camera confiscated in this vicinity.

This is not due to any change of policy by the upper echelons of the world's largest and most powerful political police force. The large, grey, stone building which before the revolution belonged to the All-

Russia Insurance Company now houses only less important echelons of the secret police. A large computer and a specially built telex network have made it possible to spread KGB offices throughout the city. The First Main Directorate's Section 13, together with the personnel office, now occupies six floors of the thirty-one-storey SEV building. This well-designed modern block is at the Tchaikovsky Street end of one of Moscow's widest and most modern boulevards, Kalinina Prospekt, not far from the Ministries of Foreign Affairs and Foreign Trade.

The SEV building is sited at a place where the slow-moving Moskva River loops towards the city and back again. From its higher floors there are magnificent views across the city, and away to the south where the gigantic—and hideously ugly—university sprawls across the Lenin Hills. But not many of General Shumuk's staff of nearly four hundred spent much time admiring the view. These floors, occupied by specially selected KBG employees, are noted for cleanliness, industry and silence. Even the telephones are specially muted.

General Shumuk's office was large, its size emphasized by the lack of furniture. There was only a metal desk, swivel chair and a high-back wooden visitor's chair with uneven feet which, rumour said, Shumuk himself had designed to cause concern and discomfort to any sitting in it. The new linoleum had already cracked around the places where the hot water radiators were let into the floor. On the desk there were two trays, three telephones and a concealed button for calling his secretary. The only picture on the wall was a cheap lithograph of Peter the Great. Shumuk had always been careful not to identify himself with any of the more modern residents of the Kremlin; it was too dangerous. Behind the picture there was the standard steel safe provided for all senior KGB officials. Each evening it was ceremoniously sealed with red wax.

There was a knock at the door and the duty cipher clerk entered. Without a word the clerk put a red folder on General Shumuk's desk and passed to him the timed receipt. Shumuk initialled it without looking up, and started reading the telex decodes. It was the one from the Soviet embassy in Washington which spoiled his even temper. It was a long message: four pages of text largely concerned with low-grade trivia which should not have been sent on the signature of Yuriy Grechko, the senior KGB man in the embassy. It should have been consigned to the weekly summary. Shumuk read on hurriedly. He had once been an embassy legal himself; he too had learnt how to wrap up bad news.

When he came to the paragraph in which Grechko reported that Wilhelm Kleiber had phoned the embassy asking for an urgent meeting, Shumuk put down the telex sheets. He took off his steel-rimmed spectacles and laid them on his desk while he placed the palms of both hands over his face. Long, long ago such mannerisms had been mistaken for grief, alarm anxiety, but by now everyone knew that it was just a way in which Shumuk was able to concentrate his thoughts. If there was a way in which he manifested grief, alarm or anxiety—or any strong emotion other than anger—no one working with him had yet discovered it.

Kleiber had failed to obtain the Hitler Minutes, that much was obvious. An agent did not make contact in this reckless, unprofessional manner to report success. If Kleiber had secured the Hitler Minutes in the way that the popinjay Grechko and his sleepy-eyed friend Parker had promised, then by now they would be here on Shumuk's desk instead of this long telex cluttered with nothing better than gossip culled from *Aviation Week*. He read the paragraph again.

> PARA EIGHT TASK POGONI 922 [Grechko's submission numeral] SUGGEST MEETING KLEIBER ROUSILLON BEACH MOTEL VERNON FAIRFAX COUNTY 2200 HOURS TUESDAY TWENTY FIRST AUGUST STOP CONSENT REQUEST TWO END PARA

General Stanislav Shumuk could not think about Task Pogoni without seeing in his mind's eye the two men upon whom he had relied for its success. Shumuk had no confidence in either Parker or Grechko. He had been a member of the promotions board that had selected Grechko for his present KGB appointment in the Washington embassy. Needless to say, Shumuk had strenuously argued against giving Grechko such responsibility, but he went unheeded. Shumuk was over six feet tall and he could never reconcile himself to the fact that Grechko habitually wore elevator shoes which gave this overconfident little man a sorely needed increase in height. Stanislav Shumuk believed that the elevator shoes revealed the fundamental flaw in Grechko's personality; his desire for elevation—literally and figuratively—characterized his attitude to his job, to his family and to the women with whom he wasted so much time. Several times Shumuk had made formal complaints about Grechko's womanizing, but on every occasion Grechko had been able to "prove" that the ladies in question—who included the wives of foreign diplomats—were a valuable source of intelligence material.

Shumuk put on his spectacles, got up and looked out of the window. Across the street the COMECON annex building was in the course of construction; work continued all round the clock—when darkness came, the construction workers toiled under floodlights. Many of the labourers were women. A line of people waiting for a bus were watching a brawny peasant woman mixing cement. There were long bus lines. A militiaman and some Young Pioneers in their green uniforms were waiting for the special bus that would take them down the Minsk Highway to the battlefield of Borodino. It was a necessary pilgrimage for all the party faithful. Here they would see the place where the might of Napoleon was broken, and where in a later war the Soviet Guards halted the Nazis and stood outnumbered for five long days and nights. Borodino never failed to inspire new faith in the onlookers. Perhaps Shumuk now needed such an infusion of fervour to help him endure the machinations of his colleagues in the Political Bureau. There was little doubt that they had prepared their enthusiastic report about the propaganda value of the Hitler Minutes as a way of putting Shumuk on the spot. Now there were memos, reports and inquiries coming every day, some of them from the Central Secretariat. All could be summarized as "How much longer?" Shumuk sighed. It was time, he reluctantly decided, for drastic action.

Essentially, Parker must be brought out of danger—that was the code of Moscow Centre. None of its professional Russian-born agents were ever abandoned to their fate. It was imbecilic of Parker to involve himself with the man who had committed the murders in Los Angeles and London, but that did not change matters. On the contrary, it made it even more vital to get Parker home, for, if he was taken into custody by the Americans, he would be facing charges of first-degree murder.

And yet to pull Parker out would mean that Grechko would come back to Moscow with his reputation unimpaired. Grechko would be able to blame the collapse of Task Pogoni on Moscow's decision to move Parker. Knowing the way that Grechko could always muster support and sympathy from certain highly placed enemies of Shumuk's, one could easily envisage Shumuk himself being blamed for the failure of Task Pogoni. That was something he was determined to avoid.

Shumuk always kept a pair of high-powered binoculars on his windowsill. He found it interesting and instructive to study the people in the streets below. The Red Square bus arrived, and the line of passengers began to board. There was not enough room for everyone. One woman stepped out to hail a passing taxi and a man in a bright-blue woollen hat shouted angrily at the bus driver as the bus pulled away. It was unseemly and un-Russian, and the others, although equally angry, turned away to pretend it had not happened. But after the bus had gone, the anger of those left behind abated. Shoulders hunched, they turned their backs against the wind and watched the big blonde girl mixing cement. Shumuk put his binoculars down. The bus for Borodino still had not arrived.

Shumuk touched the Washington telex decode with the tips of his bony fingers. He could almost feel it: a lifetime of intelligence work—devious tricks and complex lies, half-truths and betrayals—had given him an instinct that seldom faltered. The Kleiber business was all part of some CIA trick and he would have no part of it. He sat down at his desk and scribbled a message for his Washington KGB office on the special encoding pad, laboriously writing one block capital letter in each grey, printed square so that the cipher clerk could insert the coded message into the empty spaces below each line.

> PARA ONE CONFIRMATION MOSCOW CENTRE PERMISSION GRANTED FOR 982 MEETING STOP LOCATION YOUR PARA EIGHT MESSAGE NUMBER 907372-KLT TIMING 2200 HOURS TWENTY FIRST AUGUST STOP PROCEED CAUTIOUSLY STOP COMMUNICATE RESULT IMMEDIATE STOP CEASE ALL CONTACT WITH 907 [Parker's submission numeral] REPEAT CEASE ALL CONTACT 907 WITH EFFECT IMMEDIATE STOP END PARA END MESSAGE MOSCOW CENTRE.

Shumuk finished pencilling the message and smoothed it on his desk to read it through again. Perhaps this development was a blessing in disguise. This go-ahead for Grechko might provide a chance to end Grechko's blundering career. Shumuk read the message again. PROCEED CAUTIOUSLY—that got him off the hook but forced Grechko to attend the clandestine meeting. If that meeting was a CIA trap, then Grechko would be totally compromised by the Western intelligence agencies. That would certainly mean the end of Grechko's chances of a seat on any of the directorate committees.

There was another aspect of the present situation which gave Shumuk comfort. If the Kleiber-Grechko meeting on August 21 was a CIA trap, the Americans would be most careful not to alert the KGB to impending danger. They would certainly not move against Parker until their trap closed. That would provide Shumuk with time to get Parker home to Moscow. He pursed his lips and nodded to himself. Such a scenario would give him a triumph with Parker at the very moment when Grechko fell prey to the CIA. He smiled. After all, Parker was the most important factor; Grechko—whatever mess he made of things—could rely upon his diplomatic immunity. Shumuk imagined himself explaining this modestly to a committee of inquiry, shortly before they commended him for his brilliance.

As Shumuk pressed the button to call the cipher clerk, another thought came to him. Why not make certain that the Grechko meeting with Kleiber was a fiasco? It was no great secret that the British intelligence service were looking for Kleiber, so why not tell them where he was going to be on August 21? He could give details of the meeting to London providing they would make Kleiber XPD. It was safer that way; Kleiber's indiscretions would embarrass both London and Moscow.

At first the notion was no more than something to toy with, like a pain that can be activated by the careful movement of a loose tooth. But within half an hour Shumuk had learnt to live with such a notion. Rationalization being man's only natural genius, it was not long before he was able to convince himself that revealing Kleiber's expected whereabouts to the British was the method whereby he could embarrass the CIA.

He picked up his binoculars and nodded to himself. The bus for Borodino had arrived; it was mud-spattered and dented. As he watched, the doors hissed open and the uniformed young men filed into it. One boy used his hat to clean a patch of window.

## 47

Jennifer Ryden's priorities were hard to comprehend, thought Boyd Stuart. She had insisted that she must see him urgently but now, in a couturier's in Sloane Street, she seemed to be little interested in anything but the dress she needed for a weekend party.

"Thank God you weren't in California." Her voice came through the red-velvet curtain of the changing booth.

"Why?" said Boyd Stuart. He was sitting on a small gilded chair, watching himself reflected in the full-length mirrors.

"Darling!" said Jennifer Ryden, who was able to imbue this word with any one of a thousand meanings. "Dar-ling!" It was the mother speaking to the small child, or the film star assailed by fan-club secretaries. Her head came out of the curtains, while her hands grasped the cloth tight against her neck in decorous precision. "Because you finally found all my treasures."

"They were in the steamer trunk."

"Thank goodness." Her head went back inside the booth. "Let me have the pink dress again," she called to the salesgirl.

"You put them there, Jennifer. You said leave it in the box room and don't touch it," said Boyd Stuart to the curtain.

"But you opened it." The salesgirl passed the long pink dress through the curtains.

"And found all the things you've been asking for," said Stuart.

"You might at least have let me open it myself. Did you force the lock?"

"It was unlocked," said Stuart. "You complain about losing the things, and you complain about my finding them. What the hell does make you happy?"

She swept out of the changing booth and brushed past him, flaring her skirt with the side of her hand and striding up and down in front of the mirrors while turning her head as if to catch her reflection unawares.

"Not you, my darling. You are far too clever for me." She looked to see if the salesgirl had heard her but she gave no sign of having done so. She was standing, arms folded, head tilted, eyes unseeing: the sort of pose that only women who work in dress shops adopt. Jennifer turned on her heel to swirl the thin silk of the dress, then she posed with arms akimbo. Her arms and legs were long and slim, her hands so elegant that she flaunted them, holding them against her cheek and splaying them on her hips.

"I'll try the green one again," she called loudly to the salesgirl, who gathered an armful of dresses from the chair and went downstairs.

Jennifer looked at herself carefully, smiling distantly as if at some joke that she would never reveal. "Did you tell Daddy?" she asked quietly, now that they were alone.

"Tell him what?" So that was it. She simply wanted to be sure that Boyd had not told her father of the night when he came home unexpectedly from Rostock in East Germany. He had found her in his bed with the husband of a girl she had been at school with. "Tell him what?"

"That silly business with Johnny." She went back inside the booth, pulled the dress off and dropped it to the floor.

"What silly business?"

"Would madam like to try the striped one?" The salesgirl had reappeared. She was still standing with folded arms, but now half a dozen long dresses were draped over them.

"Just the green silk," said Jennifer. But the girl reached inside the booth and hung all the dresses on the hook and then went back to the store room.

"Me and Johnny . . . that night," said Jennifer in a loud whisper. "Did you talk to Daddy about that? He's been in a filthy temper the last few days," she said, flicking at her hair with the ends of her fingers.

"I didn't tell your father that I returned unexpectedly early from a departmental fiasco in Germany and found you testing the mattress with our dear old friend Johnny," said Boyd Stuart. "I'm saving it up for the day I resign from the service."

She smiled. It was the same mirthless smile that her father used to punctuate his dialogue. "That's good," she said, looking at herself in the mirror, and holding the belt tight so that it emphasized her hips. "But Daddy has been frightfully short-tempered lately. And it can't be simply because I lost his beastly pocket-watch, can it?" She looked at him in the mirror, caught his eye and smiled archly, moving her hips slightly, as if to remind him of what he had forsaken. Then she returned to the changing booth and put on her own woollen dress.

"The watch inscribed 'to Elliot'?"

"I thought it *must* be something you'd said." To the girl somewhere in the store room she called, "I'll have my hair done, and come back again. I simply can't decide on a dress when I'm not looking my best."

The salesgirl said, "Yes, madam," in a voice like an answering machine. She came upstairs and began picking up the dresses.

Jennifer Ryden came out of the booth with two Harrods carrier bags and some other packages wrapped in the coloured papers of Knightsbridge stores. She gave everything to Boyd Stuart, who could carry them only with some difficulty. Together they went out of the shop and stood for a moment on the pavement while Jennifer adjusted the Liberty silk scarf she wore on her head.

"There was a message for you, Boyd," she said. She watched him dispassionately as he waved at passing taxi-cabs.

Boyd Stuart said, "What sort of message? A bill, you mean?" A cab passed them with its FOR HIRE sign lighted; the cabbie did not see them because he was busy shouting at the driver of a double-decker bus. "If those people at Barclaycard say the computer went wrong just one more time. . . ."

"It was a phone message about your work." She had grown up in a household where the comings and goings of shadowy visitors were commonplace. She was used to finding pistols in the wardrobe and bags of golden sovereigns on the mantelpiece, and hearing soft foreign voices and the slam of car doors in the middle of the night. This aspect of Boyd Stuart's life she found easy to accept. "A man calling himself Shumuk wants to meet you at Widewater, Sollerod, near Copenhagen, on Sunday. I told Daddy about it."

"And what did Daddy say?"

She looked at him calmly and chose to ignore the

sarcasm in his tone. "Daddy said pass the message on to you."

Boyd Stuart nodded. The Shumuks and Rydens of this world were careful not to commit themselves to any action that might go wrong. Careful, too, not to have anything in writing.

"Mr. Shumuk seemed certain that Daddy would want you to go. And Boyd! How the devil did this fellow guess that I would be seeing you today?"

"Shumuk is a KGB general. I imagine he knows a great deal about all of us. His job in Moscow corresponds to your father's position here."

"You sound as if you admire him."

"I hate the evil old bastard," said Boyd Stuart.

Jennifer shivered and moved away; she had forgotten such frightening glimpses of the cold violence within him.

"You mustn't go, Boyd. It sounds dangerous." She said it too quickly, too automatically, for it to have been a measure of her love.

"Daddy wants me to go, Jennifer. And what Daddy wants, Daddy gets."

"That's loutish, Boyd." She waved her hand and a taxi, turning the corner at Point Street, immediately flashed its headlights to acknowledge her summons.

Sollerod is a village on the Danish island of Sjaelland. The old coast road runs close to the large house that is called Widewater. Here the Baltic Sea narrows to emerge into the Kattegat and from the garden of the large house there is a view of the Swedish coastline.

General Shumuk's attempt to appear inconspicuous had resulted in a slightly absurd mixture of Western garments. A bright green shirt hung limply on his thin frame, and from its short sleeves his arms emerged like sticks. His trousers were of corduroy and his shoes had gilt buckles. The effect was of a man rescued from a disaster at sea and clothed by an overworked charity.

The house was large and of modern design, with floor-to-ceiling glass and interior walls of white-painted, rough brickwork. The furniture was light-coloured teak of that sort of uncomfortable Scandinavian design that aspires to being art. And the walls were hung with large abstract paintings in primary colours and spotlit by polished-steel lamps. To alleviate the bleak interior, there were oriental carpets strewn across the polished wood-block floors. From the window there was a clear view of the water and of clouds combed thinly across the blue scalp of the sky.

"The Americans abducted Kleiber," said General Shumuk, his voice not revealing his attitude to this event. His hand waved impatiently in front of his face to disperse the strong-smelling Russian tobacco. "But London has designated Kleiber XPD. Did you know that?"

"So where is Kleiber now?" said Stuart. He was amazed that news of something so secret could have reached Shumuk already. The XPD directive for Kleiber had only been signed a day ago. He wondered if Shumuk's phone call had actually been to Sir Sydney Ryden.

Shumuk stretched out his legs so that his bones creaked. His head was propped on the hand-woven cushion, his long hand caged the cigarette so that its smoke emerged between his bony fingers.

Was Brezhnev dying? wondered Boyd Stuart. Was there some new crisis with the army or trouble with the harvest? Was this a new step in the Kremlin's endless game of musical chairs? Or was he going to bargain for Kleiber's life? A maid brought coffee for them and the conversation stopped while she arranged the cups and saucers and a plate of biscuits.

There were sailing boats in view through the huge window. Sunday yachtsmen, four boats, one with an orange spinnaker, racing before the wind. Beyond them, blurred by the haze on the water, there was the grey shape of a patrolling warship. Boyd Stuart remembered the day he had sailed across from Rostock in East Germany. The warning had come that morning—a mumbled sentence muffled by a handkerchief. The accent was Polish, a girl's voice: someone's daughter, girlfriend or wife asked to take a terrible risk for the Englishman. The police cars passed him on his way to the harbour. My God, but that had been a close one. And it had been a damned long sail to the Danish coast. Never since had he ever heard Danish without offering up a prayer of thanks.

"I have no need to tell you that my participation is unofficial," said Shumuk.

Forget any hopes of blackmail or bribery, thought Boyd Stuart. Such a reptile does not move before his lair is fully protected.

"Of course," said Stuart. He returned the stare of this evil old man; skinny and wrinkled, with a constant sneer, like the Uncle Sams depicted in the political cartoons in *Krokodil*.

"Kleiber will be meeting one of our embassy people at a hotel at Mount Vernon, just across the state line from Washington, on the evening of Tuesday, August 21."

"That soon."

"You'll have to move fast, Mr. Stuart. But it gives you more than a week."

"Are you asking that your embassy man be protected?"

"As far as possible," said General Shumuk.

"And Kleiber not protected at all?"

Boyd Stuart looked at the old man. There was nothing to be read in his eyes or his impassive features. He wanted Kleiber XPD and his embassy official arrested, and Shumuk's rank in the upper echelons of the KGB was secure enough for him not to care what accusations came his way afterwards. This was the only safe way to arrange such treachery of course. No couriers, no messengers, no confidences; just Shumuk talking to an enemy agent with no record of what was said.

"You're throwing your man to the wolves, are you, General?"

Behind General Shumuk a huge abstract painting filled the white brick wall between the polished-steel light fittings. Its design was like a silver blade upon which some winged shape was impaled, and the general was seated at the hilt of it.

"The Americans will have no alternative to letting you be there," said the general. "Now that you know about it, they'll have to cooperate." He placed his cigarette in his mouth and inhaled with great care.

"What has he done, this man in Washington?" Stuart persisted. "And why must Kleiber die?"

"Don't cry for him, Mr. Stuart," said Shumuk. He flicked his ash into the plant pot at his side. "No one will cry for *us*." He moved his hand across his face like a small child waving goodbye from a railway-carriage window, but it was just a way of dispersing the smoke.

# 48

It was surprising, wrote Boyd Stuart in his report afterwards, that the CIA resisted the temptation to riddle the Rousillon Beach Motel with the customary electronics. It was the project chairman who held out against the adviser from the Technical Services Division, who had come to his office loaded with an extraordinary array of equipment from low-light cameras and parabolic microphones to a miniaturized video recorder which, although small enough to be concealed inside a light fixture, defied all the demonstrator's attempts to make it function.

The CIA sent Kleiber to the meeting "naked," apart from Kalkhoven sitting in the back office of the motel manager's unit along with Boyd Stuart. There was no way of preventing the Brit participating: there was in fact some enthusiasm for letting him witness what no one doubted was going to be a memorable coup.

Yuriy Grechko came directly from the U.S.S.R Washington embassy. He was in a green, rented Ford Fairlane at 7:30 that evening, having booked a double unit, with sitting room fronting the poolside, water bed and colour TV, using the name Lewis. He paid for the room on arrival and asked if there were any messages for him; there were none. At five minutes before eight, Grechko called the office and complained that there was no ice in his refrigerator and he would be needing more cans of Seven-Up. The coffee-shop waitress who delivered this order reported that he was drinking heavily, from a bottle he'd brought with him.

Willi Kleiber arrived exactly on the dot of his appointment at ten o'clock. Kalkhoven was behind the desk. He gave him the key to unit No. 12 and told him that "Mr. Lewis" was already there. Kleiber phoned Kalkhoven three minutes later and was laughing so much that he could hardly speak.

"You'd better get over here, Mr. Muller," he said. ("Muller" was the cover name by which Kalkhoven was known to him.) "You'd better get over here." He was laughing hysterically. "You're going to need another scenario, Mr. Muller, sir. But don't hurry yourself, there's no hurry at all. Did you know that Yuriy Grechko calls himself 'Yu-yu'?" He howled with laughter at the thought of it.

General Stanislav Shumuk had organized his scheme with commendable skill, but his failure was at the human level. His dislike of Yuriy Grechko, and Grechko's weakness for pretty women, had convinced Shumuk that Grechko was a notorious libertine. In fact, Grechko was foolishly, sadly and forlornly in love. He was in love with that desperation which only the unfortunate do not know. It was Grechko's fate to fall in love with Fusako Parker, the "wife" of his most important agent. For her, he regularly proclaimed, he would give his life. Now he had done just that.

It was Shumuk's formal message—passed by an agent of Moscow's Communications Division—telling Parker to leave his house in Chicago immediately together with his "wife" that brought Grechko to his final frantic act. Parker and his "wife," Fusako, were immediately moved to a safe house in Toronto. On Thursday, August 16, the Parkers flew to Moscow. In the six days leading up to his suicide Grechko exhausted every method of communicating with Fusako Parker: all failed. On the night of Sunday, August 19, having finally discovered that the Parkers had gone to Toronto, he had even sent a team to break into the house. It was a desperate course of action; the act was poorly planned, the men untrained and hastily briefed. They had been arrested by local police.

After arriving at the motel with slurred speech and whisky on his breath, Grechko drank a whole bottle of Cutty Sark and swallowed an unknown amount of barbiturates. (The man from the Soviet embassy who claimed the body would not permit an autopsy.) In his hand when he died Grechko held tightly to a sheet of Rousillon Beach Motel notepaper bearing the message, "Darling Fusako, I cannot go on without you. I love you, my beloved. I will always be your darling Yu-yu."

"Can I talk to Mr. Kleiber, Melvin?" Boyd Stuart asked.

"Talk to him!" said Kalkhoven, with his eyes still on Kleiber. "You can take him away and feed him to the alligators as far as I'm concerned. XPD the bastard!"

"You listen to me," said Kleiber. He was on his feet and his eyes were bright. "We have a deal. . . ."

"Sit down, Kleiber," said Kalkhoven. He took a box of matches from his pocket. "You've run out of stock to trade, the shelves are empty, man. Grechko was your dinner ticket. You talk with this nice man here, or else. . . ." Impassively Kalkhoven took Grechko's suicide note by the corner and set light to it. London and Washington had agreed that all such evidence would be destroyed on the spot, and that had been the order.

"Go to hell," said Kleiber, but there was no conviction in his words.

" 'I have set before you life and death,' " said Kalkhoven, " 'blessing and cursing; therefore choose life, that both thou and thy seed may live.' "

Kleiber looked at Boyd Stuart. "Can you find a bottle of scotch?"

"Probably," said Boyd Stuart. "Let's go and find somewhere quiet to sit down. This place will be a madhouse when the heavy mob from Langley arrive to show us that the training manual way is the only way."

## 49

Someone had parked a large truck so that it obscured the view from the windows that faced away from the courtyard. Kleiber did not think that the truck had been parked like that by chance. All he could see of it from the kitchen window was the bottom of a gigantic K for Kleenex, or perhaps it was Kellogg's—he could not see enough of the truck to decide; it was so close to the wall.

From the front window there was a view of the pool, artificially blue, lit by underwater floodlights, and the other units which made up the motel. Behind the low, sloping roofs there were a few dusty palm trees and a high chimney which at night was lighted by a red warning light. Kleiber wondered whether that meant they were near an airfield, but there was little sound of aircraft. He knew they must be near Washington.

It had been like this ever since leaving Geneva. The Americans hauled him round the country like freight, never divulging where they were, where they had been or where they were going. They did not trust him; he could hardly blame them. Would they eventually kill him? he wondered. Was this process just a way of ensuring that there was no paperwork, no trace, no witnesses to his having arrived in the U.S.A.?

"You say the Hitler Minutes never existed?" he asked the Englishman. He did not wait for him to reply. "Well, I know they did exist."

"Really," said Stuart, without displaying too much interest. "How could you know?"

"I was at the Merkers mine when Wever and Breslow delivered them there."

"So you were the mysterious Reichsbank Director Frank?" Kleiber nodded and smiled. "Is that why Dr. Böttger and the others selected you to get them back?"

"Can I have a drink?" said Kleiber. Stuart broke

the sealed cap of the whisky bottle and poured some into the clear plastic beakers the motel provided. He had watched Kleiber fidgeting, but now, with the drink in his possession, he was calm and made no haste to consume it. "No, it was the other way round. I selected *them.*" He put the whisky to his mouth and drank some. "I selected *them.* I went to them and told them that someone named Lustig was collecting material to make a film. I told them he was digging deeply into the story of the Kaiseroda mine. I told them he'd already found an officer named MacIver who was spilling his guts out and that the story of the Hitler Minutes was sure to surface. I'd had money from Böttger before for such missions; I knew he'd buy this project."

"Well, you won't get any more cash from him, Kleiber. He knows now that you were working for Moscow."

Kleiber's mouth tightened but he managed to force a strained smile. "What did he say?"

"I wasn't there," said Stuart. "But they're returning a hundred million dollars to the bank in Geneva. Their official explanation is that there was a computer error. The name of Friedman is not mentioned."

"Young Stein will benefit," said Kleiber. "He'll take the money and get married to Mary Breslow . . . that's the final joke, eh?"

"A lot of people will benefit," said Stuart, who knew that the final horrible joke was yet to come. "There's Delaney, the night-club owner, an ex-gangster named Petrucci, Pitman's nephew in Arkanas. . . . They'll all benefit, but the real beneficiaries are the clients of the bank—they're the people you swindled, Kleiber."

"Put away your violin," said Kleiber.

"How did you hear that Lustig was making a film?"

"I was having dinner with Max Breslow one evening in Frankfurt. He mentioned the film quite casually. He asked me if I thought it could prove dangerous to us. I told him it wouldn't be dangerous if the production was in our hands. I told him I might be able to raise enough money to buy Lustig out."

"Did Breslow know the money came from Böttger?"

Kleiber settled back in his chair and sat in silence for a moment before replying. "Max Breslow was a war casualty. When he was a young soldier he had guts. Once, long ago, he was tough, Mr. Stuart, in the way that you and I are tough."

"Do we have something in common?"

"You don't fool me with your soft voice and your fancy accent, your old school tie and your vague smiles and deferential manner; I recognize the killer in you, Mr. Stuart. I've had too many like you on my payroll to make a mistake."

"And Max Breslow?"

"He believed that propaganda shit that the Nazis fed us all. He couldn't see that the penpushers writing all that stuff about Aryans, the historical destiny of the Fatherland and *Ein Volk, ein Reich, ein Führer,* were writing it because it paid better than doing translations of Karl Marx."

"But there came a time when doing translations of Karl Marx paid better?"

"You play the music; I'll sing the words, Mr. Stuart. But poor old Max wasn't so adaptable. When he realized that the Nazis were just another set of crooked politicians, it broke his spirit. He was never the same again. Now what is he—a nothing!"

"But he took over the Lustig film when you asked him."

Kleiber laughed. "You think he might have turned me down, eh? Max is finished; nearly bankrupt. Who'd invest money in one of Breslow's shoddy little films? His house is mortgaged to the very limit, he's got no money saved, and only put his daughter though college by selling off his wife's jewellery piece by piece. Sure, he jumped at the chance of taking over the Lustig film with the finance guaranteed and a standard producer's fee. He couldn't afford to do otherwise."

"And all the time you were reporting to Moscow?"

"The Russians were threatening to release some phoney evidence about me being implicated in war crimes."

Stuart allowed the word "phoney" to go unremarked. "And the KGB approved of your idea to involve Böttger and his Trust?"

"The Trust provided perfect cover, and through them I got help from people who would never have helped the Russians. And what expertise! I could never have arranged that hundred-million-dollar coup against Pitman's bank without having all the resources of the Trust behind me."

"What exactly did you tell Dr. Böttger?"

"They didn't need much persuasion. Those fat businessmen could see the economic consequences of rewriting the history books to make Hitler into a hero. They didn't want anyone saying that he'd been clever enough to make Winston Churchill come cringing."

"But Churchill changed his mind; Churchill turned down the peace terms."

"So Churchill becomes the warmonger who continued with the war that caused twenty million deaths. Any way you present the facts, Hitler comes out best."

"And that would have hurt the West German economy?"

"Publicity and controversy leading on to speeches and demonstrations. Neo-Nazis fighting left-wingers in the streets. Once it started there is no telling where it might have ended."

"Especially with General Shumuk pulling the strings," said Stuart, but Kleiber had never heard of Shumuk and did not respond to this remark.

"We Germans are like that," said Kleiber. "We're always too anxious to please the people who conquer us. We flatter them and imitate them. Split down the centre, we now have two halves each trying slavishly to adopt the system, myth and methodology of our masters. But Böttger knew that West Germany needs the untarnished memory of Churchill and Roosevelt in a way that the Western countries don't need them. Moscow Centre thought Böttger might be right and, judging from the effort your people put into it, London did too." He smiled, and drank more whisky.

Stuart said, "They thought it might be a blow to the value of sterling on the international exchanges. It doesn't need much to start a run. They worried about the psychological effect the idea of Churchill's asking for peace would have on American public opinion. Here in the U.S. most anglophilia depends on Churchill's wartime reputation as a man who never considered giving up the struggle. My people worried too about public opinion in those countries which Churchill was prepared to consign to the Nazi empire. Some of those countries now sell Britain oil and vital raw materials. There was plenty to worry about."

At the sound of conversation outside, Kleiber got to his feet and went to the window. He looked across the pool to the units where two men in white coats were going to examine Grechko's body. He watched them enter the door and then turned back to Stuart. "I was there," he said suddenly. "You know that, don't you?"

"I guessed," said Stuart. "I got your army service record. You were attached to the Führerhauptquartier for roughly the period of the Churchill visit. You were an intelligence officer; I guessed it was an attachment for security purposes, for the summit meeting."

Kleiber looked at him. The British were like that. He never knew quite where he was with them, but they didn't frighten him in the way the CIA men did.

"I went out to the site with Dr. Todt and the survey team. Before they even started on it."

"It was built especially for the Churchill meetings?"

"Sure. It wasn't much of a place. It's still there. A couple of years ago I stopped off and had coffee at the hotel there. It's not much changed: a church, a hotel and a few houses . . . a concrete bunker, plus a few wooden huts. 'Wolfschlucht' Hitler named it."

"So you were there before Churchill arrived?"

"I helped arrange the new passes and the perimeter and so forth. It was a small party that arrived. No military attachés or war correspondents, no one in civilian clothing at all. It was obviously something very unusual. We were told only that it was to be a conference, and thought Mussolini was coming north. I suppose that's what we were intended to think."

"But it was Churchill."

"He was the only one in civilian clothes. He wore a misshapen, grey roll-brim hat, a spotted bow-tie and a lumpy-looking overcoat. His plane had no markings as I recall. We saw ten Messerschmitt fighters in loose formation above Churchill's de Havilland when it arrived. They continued to circle while he landed at Le Gros Caillou, near Rocroi in France, about ten kilometres from us. They brought him up to Brûly in a Fiesler Storch communications aircraft. There was just room to land in the field behind the hotel."

"Churchill was alone?"

"There was one person with him, a British colonel in civilian clothes. The Führer had a small guard of honour made up from the SS Begleit Kommando and the army's FBB. Churchill was invited to inspect them but he waved the guard commander away. The two leaders went directly to the wooden hut where the secretaries and translators were waiting. The Führer greeted Churchill at the door of it; the two men did not shake hands. I got the idea that Churchill was making sure that there were no photographers there. He had stipulated that beforehand. We had special instructions to confiscate all cameras from everyone, and there were notices in the barrack huts threatening the death sentence for anyone not handing his camera over to the security service."

"So who was present at the meeting?"

"Hitler, Churchill, Churchill's colonel, our translator from the Foreign Office. . . ." Kleiber scratched his head. "That's all, I think. Nearby there were secretaries and two more translators waiting in case they were needed."

"So who wrote up the Hitler Minutes?"

Kleiber smiled. "Reichsführer Himmler had a bureaucratic turn of mind. He persuaded the Führer that some proper record of the proceedings must be made. The Führer was nervous about compromising the talks and eventually Himmler took it upon himself to rig an underground line and a hidden microphone so that one of the army's shorthand writers could keep a record of what was said."

"Who was that?"

"You've guessed already, haven't you?" said Kleiber. "It was Franz Wever. The Führer used him many times for keeping shorthand notes of important meetings. He was one of the best shorthand writers they had."

"Franz Wever." So Wever had known who Reichsbank Director Frank really was.

"He even denied it to me. That's funny, isn't it? He denied it to me: the man who helped to rig the cable to the hut where he was sitting. Franz was terrified that someone would find out about it. He was frightened that he'd be murdered on account of his secret."

"And eventually he *was* murdered because of it."

Kleiber pulled a face and seemed about to argue the facts but decided against it. Franz Wever's death was not a subject he wished to discuss with a member of the British Secret Intelligence Service.

"Hitler was clever," he said. "He knew how to be modest and magnanimous. Instead of adopting the manner of the conqueror he was quiet spoken and polite to Churchill. He was a wonderful judge of character, you see. He knew he'd get far more out of Churchill if he behaved like an English gentleman in the presence of another such 'lord.' "

"But Hitler's terms were tough. You must have read the transcript."

"Considering the situation, no. He admired the British Empire but he envied it too. His first concern was to make the German war machine entirely independent in terms of raw materials—rubber, oil, tungsten, chrome and so on. He was obviously planning to attack the U.S.S.R. once the West was resolved."

"You mean he would have taken over British colonies?"

"He said the Union Jack would continue to fly everywhere from Vancouver to Calcutta to Hong Kong but he wanted his trading links secured. A large proportion of the British merchant fleet would have come under German control. Hitler had drafted some ideas about that. Then of course there was the Royal Navy. Germany could not have permitted Britain to retain control of the Atlantic sea routes; it would have been like offering Churchill a chance to have his hands round our throat."

"Occupation of Britain?"

"No. Just a few Germans in sensitive posts. Himmler to vet all senior police appointments. It would have given us enough control, or at least warning in time to counteract trouble."

"There was no shouting?"

"No shouting at all. The summit went off remarkably well. The second meeting was very late—after midnight—and then there was the final meeting on the morning of Wednesday, June 12. That was even more promising. Churchill and the Führer even shook hands. There were some muttered cheers. Churchill was smoking a cigar and smiling. . . . To be allowed to smoke a cigar in the presence of the Führer—this was something unprecedented. We were all sure that the peace had been arranged. At least until the following Sunday."

"What happend on Sunday?"

"It began very warm. I went past the church and saw four army officers kneeling in prayer. They were offering prayers for peace, they said. Hitler's driver brought the big black three-axle Mercedes tourer up through the trees. Its roof was folded back, as it was for the big parades. The Führer drove to Schloss Acoz, near Charleroi, Belgium. I was one of the security detail that accompanied him."

"Schloss Acoz?"

"To meet the young colonel who'd been with Churchill. He'd come to withdraw Churchill's offer. He was a tall fellow, much taller than the Spanish staff officer who was with him. Spain was neutral of course. The Spanish officer came along to guarantee the safety of the Englishman. They were both in civilian clothes. The meeting took place in the open. There were just three of them standing under the trees, the sun dappling the ground and making patches on the men as they shifted positions. Hitler was stiff. We saw his face tighten. We all knew that was a danger sign. The English colonel spoke first. He went on talking for two or three minutes. He had no notes to refer to but it was obviously a prepared message that he had committed to memory. Then Hitler asked some questions and there was a general conversation. The Spanish general said very little; he was there just to conduct the Englishman and be responsible for his safety."

"No one made a record of that conversation?"

"We were all out of earshot."

"So what went wrong?"

"Within forty-eight hours of the Churchill-Hitler conference our army had occupied Paris. By that Friday lunchtime, Hitler was drafting tougher terms. And Churchill had talked with Roosevelt on the trans-Atlantic telephone. Roosevelt told him that if he was re-elected in November the U.S.A. would come into the war."

"How do you know that?"

"The Research Bureau of the Reichpost monitored the trans-Atlantic telephone; it was a radio link with a very simple scrambling device. Roosevelt promised aid and that was enough to change Churchill's mind. Hitler had the transcript within three hours. He knew what the answer was going to be." Kleiber scratched his nose "Churchill phoned the French premier the night before he dispatched his courier. The French reacted immediately. On that same Sunday that the Führer went to Schloss Acoz, the French government resigned. Marshal Pétain took over and asked for peace. Churchill went on the BBC that Monday night and made a speech saying that, ". . . we shall fight on unconquerable, until the curse of Hitler is removed from the brows of men.' By Friday, Hitler was sitting in Foch's chair in the railway coach and hearing the peace terms that the French would have to accept."

"What about the Englishman who brought the message to Hitler?"

"He returned with the Spanish general," said Kleiber.

"I mean in respect of Operation Siegfried. Surely he's another one who knows the secrets?"

"He's dead," said Kleiber. "He was one of the first people we had to check out. He must have been completely in Churchill's confidence. He probably knew more about those secret meetings than any other man, except for Hitler and Churchill. We ran a check on him some years ago. His name was Elliot Castelbridge, from the Coldstream Guards. He was awarded the D.S.O. fighting in Italy, partially deafened by a shell burst at Cassino. He got another medal in northern Europe in 1944. I can't remember the rest of it. We got the whole dossier through the British War Office. We know everything about Elliot Castelbridge."

"You say he's dead?"

"Long since dead," said Kleiber. "Died on the operating table after a motor-car accident in 1959. Your people are thorough, I must say that for them. They had every last detail of that man's life on paper. Death certificate, report by the operating surgeon, statements by the hospital registrar, blood transfusions, X-rays. Everything you could ever wish for in an investigation."

"Yes, they are thorough," said Stuart. That was truly an XPD, he thought. He heard the first of the cars arriving from Langley.

Stuart reached out suddenly to grab the front of Kleiber's jacket. "Where is it, Kleiber?" He banged him back against the wall with enough force to make the thin partition wall shake. "You came here to give it to Grechko. Grechko is dead; give it to me." The sound echoed. "Give it to me!" Stuart slapped him. Kleiber's head hit the plasterboard wall again, and a large table lamp fell to the floor and broke. Kleiber shook his head slowly and blinked; his eyes watered with pain and surprise. Boyd Stuart said softly. "Give me the photo Franz Wever sent to you General Delivery in Los Angeles."

Slowly Kleiber unbuckled his belt and slid it through the loops of his trousers. He unzipped the inside of the belt to open the money compartment and took out a very tattered snapshot and a single-frame 35-mm negative.

"How did you know?"

"You collected the cameras; you just told me so. You were in a unique position to get a photo of Hitler and Churchill shaking hands." Stuart smoothed the photo to look at it. "And you could hide in a good spot to get the picture, concealment would be expected of a security guard."

Kleiber nodded.

It was a blurred photo; Hitler squinting into the light, Churchill—cigar in mouth—frowning as if perplexed. But the two men had grasped hands firmly in an unmistakable gesture of solidarity.

"Now what?" Kleiber asked. He wiped his face with his handkerchief, watching Stuart warily and still surprised that his guess about the Scotsman's violent nature was so soon confirmed.

Stuart had discovered everything he wanted to know. Already he had begun to decide how much of it should go into his report to Sir Sydney Ryden. He looked at his watch and wondered if the cashier would complain if he went by Concorde. "Now what? Now nothing, Kleiber." The man was a repugnant creature but that made his job only marginally more bearable.

Stuart patted his pockets as if searching for cigarettes. He felt the box inside which the hypodermic was wrapped in cotton gauze, with a spare phial inside his silver cigarette case where it was not likely to be broken. He hated these XPD jobs that the laboratory experts arranged. It was horrible enough to dispose of men with gun, blade or explosive, but these toxic chemicals were loathsome.

"I'm sorry, Kleiber," he said. "But it's the end of the story."

"I'm a soldier," said Kleiber. It was almost as if he welcomed the chance to die like a hero.